❧DARKNESSES❧

L. E. MODESITT, JR.

DARKNESSES

The Second Book of the Corean Chronicles

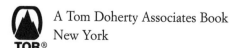

A Tom Doherty Associates Book
New York

DARKNESSES: THE SECOND BOOK OF THE COREAN CHRONICLES

Copyright © 2003 by L. E. Modesitt, Jr.

This book is printed on acid-free paper.

Edited by David G. Hartwell

Map by Ellisa Mitchell

A Tor Book
Published by Tom Doherty Associates, LLC
175 Fifth Avenue
New York, NY 10010

www.tor.com

Tor® is a registered trademark of Tom Doherty Associates, LLC.

Library of Congress Cataloging-in-Publication Data

Modesitt, L. E.
     Darknesses / L.E. Modesitt, Jr.—1st ed.
       p. cm.—(The second book of the Corean chronicles)
     ISBN 0-765-30704-9
     I. Title.

     PS3563.O264D367 2003
     813'.54—dc21   2003040195

First Edition: August 2003

Printed in the United States of America

0 9 8 7 6 5 4 3 2 1

For Lara and Van

I.

DARKNESS OVER THE MILITIA

1

Tempre, Lanachrona

Five men sat around a circular table. The tabletop was of rose marble, the carved and elaborate pedestal legs of oiled and carved lorken so dark that it could have passed for ebony. Three of the men wore the blue-and-cream uniforms of the Southern Guard. The fourth wore the silver vestments of the Recorder of Deeds. The last was the Lord-Protector, who wore a tunic of violet blue, trimmed in cream, similar in cut and style to those of the officers.

The cold silver light of a winter sun flowed through the tall and narrow windows on the south side of the room, windows whose lorken casements were framed by rose marble columns. Under a white-plastered vaulted ceiling, rose damask covered the walls between the pillars framing the windows, but failed to impart warmth to the conference room.

"You have all heard and understood what the Recorder of Deeds has said, have you not? You know the limitations of the Table?" asked the Lord-Protector.

"It cannot show what will happen, and it can display only what is happening or what has occurred recently. Is that not so?" Marshal Wyerl paused and cleared his throat, then brushed back a short lock of light brown hair. Despite the lines radiating from his eyes, his clean-shaven face conveyed boyish charm. As almost an afterthought, he asked, "How recently?"

"Two or three days past are most clear," replied the older man in the silver vestments. "Most happenings can be recalled for a week. If an event has great impact on what will be, then it can be discerned for perhaps a month, even a year, but it is impossible to predict what events the Table will regard as having great impacts." The Recorder added, "It will usually not show anyone possessing great Talent, and even the results of their actions will show in silver shadows only for a few glasses or a day at most. Of course, by what is not shown, one can at times deduce the use of Talent by one's enemies."

The younger blond man, also wearing the uniform and insignia of a marshal in the Southern Guard, asked, frowning slightly, "Why does it not show those with Talent?"

"The Tables were designed and created at the height of the Duarchy by those with Talent. I would rather imagine that they did not wish it used against themselves." A dryness infused the Recorder's words.

"Do we face anyone with such Talent?" Marshal Wyerl inquired.

The Recorder of Deeds smiled faintly. "There are always those with Talent in Corus, but they are few indeed. The Matrial was the only one that the Table could not focus upon directly. Others may arise, but for the moment, all those with some vestige of Talent who oppose us can be discerned in the Table."

"Such as Aellyan Edyss?"

"The nomad warleader appears clearly in the Table," the Recorder affirmed.

The Lord-Protector cleared his throat and looked pointedly at Wyerl. "You were about to report, Marshal?"

"Yes, Lord-Protector." Wyerl squared his shoulders. "The Regent of the Matrial has fortified Dimor as well as the high road approaches on the south side of the South Branch of the River Lud and placed at least ten regular horse companies there. There are five foot companies, and possibly as many as another ten Auxiliary companies. They retain the terrible crystal spear-thrower." The marshal inclined his head toward the younger marshal. "Marshal Alyniat can provide more detail on the situation in Zalt and Southgate."

The Lord-Protector—the youngest man at the table by at least a decade—nodded.

"Lord-Protector," began Alyniat, "in one respect, we were most fortunate. Because the Recorder of Deeds discovered the crystal spear-thrower, we could alter our tactics. The siege of the fort at Zalt was effective in forcing the Matrites to retreat, but the Matrites were careful to use the spear-thrower to cover that withdrawal. We now hold Zalt, and it is largely intact, as is the fort there, which we have enlarged and reinforced. However . . . all those in Zalt have settled in Dimor and put their energies to strengthening it. With those forces, and the crystal spear-thrower remaining there, it is most unlikely we will be able to take Dimor in the next several years without an extraordinary commitment of troopers and supplies, and . . ." Alyniat paused, as if he knew his next words would not be well received. "I would strongly recommend against any such effort."

The Lord-Protector laughed. "You have delivered Zalt and Southgate when those before you failed. I accept your recommendation." His next words were slow and deliberate. "So long as we continue to hold Southgate." A brief smile followed. "Now, what of the seltyrs there? The ones who remained?"

"Seltyr Benjir vanished in the final attack on Southgate. None have seen him or his sons in the year since. The new advisory council to the Lord-Protector remains under the control of Seltyr Sinyen. They have accepted the rule of Lanachrona, and the change in tariffs. As you know, we had to execute several of the seltyrs and some of their families before they grasped the concept that bribing tariff collectors was no longer acceptable. Those who have accepted the rule of law, as opposed to the rule of coin, are prospering, and they will soon control most of the commerce of Southgate. We have been most careful to spare the women and to insist that they receive the same treatment as women do in Lanachrona." The blond Alyniat shrugged. "That also required some executions, but the women are most kind to our troopers and merchants, and, over time, we will have a most loyal province."

"My lady, and indeed, most of the women in Lanachrona, will find that pleasing," the Lord-Protector replied, before turning to the sole submarshal, a thin-faced older man with graying hair. "What of the shipyards and commerce?"

"We captured the shipyards without great damage, and to date we have completed three deep-ocean trading vessels. Two were already under construction. The first warship will be ready within the season, and we can build five more in the next year, if the coins are available."

"How many will be required to take Dramur?" asked the Lord-Protector.

"More than we can build in ten years," replied Submarshal Frynkel. "We will also have to develop a school or a system for training officers and crews for sea war."

The Lord-Protector frowned. "The problem of Dramur will not vanish, but we must also consider the growing strength of Aellyan Edyss. Already, we are receiving protests about the tariffs he is levying on trade along the Lost Highway. He is also beginning to take over sections of Ongelya with his new Myrmidons."

"That will take years," Frynkel pointed out. "Ongelya stretches over a thousand vingts from the northwest to its southeast border. His Myrmidons can only travel so fast on horseback."

"He has conquered all of Illegea in but a handful of years," replied the Lord-Protector.

"He now holds the northern third of Ongelya, and I would not doubt he will hold all of it within a year, if he so desires. There is little of worth in the south, not compared to, say, Deforya."

"Yet we hear of his depredations in the south," offered Frynkel.

"He may be spreading such reports to lull us into believing that, while he moves elsewhere," suggested Marshal Wyerl. "Most likely into Deforya. Why else would the Landarch have consented to sell his note from the Iron Valleys Council to the Lord-Protector?"

The Lord-Protector frowned.

Ignoring the expression, Wyerl continued. "Edyss already controls the Lost Highway. If he moves into Deforya and takes Dereka, he will gain control of the Northern Pass high road—"

"And all land trade with Lustrea." The Lord-Protector nodded. "By tariffing both high roads, he can expand his coffers and purchase arms . . . But who would sell him arms? Certainly not the Praetor of Lustrea. We would not."

"Ah . . . Lord-Protector," interjected the Recorder of Deeds, "like the Iron Valleys, the Landarch of Deforya has iron mines. Unlike the Iron

Valleys, the Landarchs have always maintained a foundry and an arms manufactory. Their weapons are excellent."

"But the Deforyans do not fight so well as the Iron Valleys Militia," added Marshal Alyniat.

"What would you four suggest, then?" The Lord-Protector's voice contained equal measures of amusement and exasperation.

"Just a message of support to the Landarch," replied Wyerl, "one perhaps hinting that the Lord-Protector stands by his friends, and that is why you relieved him of a nonproducing note with hard golds. But wait for Aellyan Edyss to act first. All view us with suspicion. If we act or press ourselves upon the Landarch, he may turn to Edyss as the lesser of evils. Also, his forces and the mountains that surround Deforya may defeat the nomad warrior. If so, then you are free to address whatever enemy is the most pressing. If not, and the Landarch requires support, send enough forces to be meaningful, but not so many as to look as if you plan to turn them against him."

"What of the Iron Valleys?"

"All the traders of Dekhron wish is the freedom to trade and gather golds. All the herders of their north wish is to herd and to be left in peace," said Wyerl slowly. "Surely, there must be a way in which those needs could be met honestly and fairly. Since you hold their note for, what, six thousand golds plus interest, you might even forgive most of it if they agreed to become a Lanachronan province."

"You think our Traders' Guild would accept them as equals?"

"One trader is like another. Our lands speak close to the same tongue, and neither their traders nor ours wish higher tariffs to support a war." Wyerl smiled. "You might even suggest that an additional tariff of but one part in twenty—or fifty—is a small price for both sets of traders to pay for avoiding a war, and that you will pledge that the same laws that apply in Tempre and Borlan will apply in Dekhron, and, further, that no Southern Guards will be placed anywhere in the Iron Valleys, save upon the request of the Traders' Council of Dekhron."

"And what do we gain by such?"

"More tariffs, Lord-Protector, and the ability to move many of the Southern Guard companies to the eastern borders. You also avoid the cost of a war with the Iron Valleys, and that cost could be most high, as the late Matrial discovered."

"And what if they reject such?"

Wyerl smiled. "Then perhaps someone else should attack them, and you will offer condolences . . . and wait. You might also suggest that few will want to trade with them if they do not honor their debts."

The Lord-Protector laughed—explosively. "Bring me a plan, Marshal, and we shall see."

"As you request, Lord Protector."

The faintest trace of a sad smile played around the mouth of the Recorder of Deeds as the Lord-Protector stood to end the meeting.

2

Two men rode on each side of the nightsheep flock as they guided the animals back to the eastern side of Westridge, toward the stead that lay beyond the western edge of the ridge that was too long and too gentle to be a hill, and too high not to be. The winter sun had already set, and the silver-green sky had rapidly begun to fade into a deep purple-green. To the east, the quartz outcroppings on the edge of the Aerlal Plateau—looming over the rolling rises of the stead— shimmered in the last light of the sun. The light snow of two days earlier still dusted the red sandy ground and the quarasote bushes that dotted the rises.

The lead ram tossed his head, if slightly, and his razor-sharp horns glinted in the fading light, his black wool and face standing out against the snow where he paused before continuing to follow the ancient trail across the lower section of Westridge, the flock behind him.

The younger man was Alucius. Riding in the black nightsilk and leathers of a herder felt strange to him after the years of wearing first a trooper's uniform, then, for the last year, a militia captain's uniform. A gust of wind, acrid and bitter, blew out of the northeast, ruffling the hair that was a dark, dark gray—not the gray of age, but of a shade that was close to black, but was not. His silver-gray eyes, flecked slightly with green, continued to study the flock and the quarasote bushes, which were all that grew in the red sandy soil of the stead.

With the force of experience and habit, Alucius guided his mount—Wildebeast—around a dying quarasote bush that had already seeded. He didn't see any seedlings, but those would not appear until spring. In the meantime, Alucius avoided the bush, as he would any quarasote, since all had spikes able to rip deep into the flesh of almost any animal, except the nightsheep, who foraged on the newer shoots. The nightsilk—for all its smoothness, apparent softness, and flexibility—stiffened into a mail-like hardness under pressure—one reason why Alucius wore nightsilk undergarments, especially when on duty in the Iron Valleys Militia.

The older man, Alucius's grandsire Royalt, eased his mount around the laggards and toward his grown grandson. "You've seen most of the stead while you've been on furlough. What do you think?"

"It was dry last year. Not so many new shoots, except near the plateau. Was there more rain there—or more snow last winter?" Alucius tilted his head, taking in what his Talent revealed. He could sense the gray-violet of sandwolves somewhere to the north, along with the faintest hint of the red-violet of sanders, but the sense of the sanders was so faint that he could not discern where they might be—except that they were not close to the nightsheep.

"More snow, mostly. I've kept them closer to the plateau than I would have liked, but their wool is coming in strong. Despite everything, be a good year."

Alucius glanced toward the lead ram—young for the role—but wise beyond his years. Absently, with his Talent-sense, he studied the nightram, noting that even the ram's lifethread linked him to the land close to the stead, a thread, like all lifethreads, that, if severed, would result in death.

"He even looks like Lamb," offered Royalt.

"He does. I miss Lamb, though. I'd hoped to see him once more."

"He was close to twenty—long life for a nightram."

"I had still hoped," Alucius said.

"The young one takes to you like his sire. I can see that."

"I wish I were here, rather than at Emal." Alucius remained uncomfortable whenever his grandsire even hinted that Alucius would be the herder before long.

"You have but ten months before your obligation's met."

"We'll see then." Alucius was all too aware of what could happen in ten months. In less than three, once, he'd been a scout for the militia, captured by the Matrites, collar-slaved, and retrained. In another two-month period, he'd broken the collar torques of the Matrial, formed his own company from escaped captive troopers, traveled six hundred vingts, and returned to service in the militia as a captain—and managed to keep anyone from knowing the extent of his Talent. In some ways, he reflected, the last had been the hardest task of all, but the silence about Talent was one of the strongest herder traditions, because, on it, in a fashion, rested the fate of all herders in the Iron Valleys.

"It's been quiet. Even Kustyl says so," Royalt offered.

"Sometimes, that's the time to worry." Alucius laughed, ruefully. "Someone once told me that."

"Use my own words against me, would you?"

"Not against you. I just worry." Alucius shifted his weight in the saddle as Wildebeast reached the crest of Westridge. The stead buildings lay a good vingt—two thousand solid yards—due west and perhaps fifty yards lower than the ridge crest.

"You worry more now that you're married."

"Wouldn't you?" Alucius quickly added, "Didn't you? You didn't stay in the militia long after you and Grandma'am were married. Not from what Mother said."

Royalt chuckled. "Let's just say that being a herder suited me better, especially after the traders started begrudging every gold spent on the militia."

"Like now?" questioned Alucius.

"Worse, then. Right now, they still fret a bit about what happened. Been less than two years since the Matrites were in Soulend, and they'd still be there if the Lord-Protector hadn't wanted Southgate."

"That may be, but there's been no real fighting in more than a year, and the Council's cut the militia to twenty-one companies, from close to thirty."

"Be only twenty, weren't for you." Royalt gestured toward the out-buildings of the stead, now less than half a vingt ahead of them. "Let's get them in the shed. We can talk more at supper."

Alucius nodded, and eased Wildebeast back to the east and south to make sure that the stragglers followed the lead ram into the nightsheep shed. One of the older ewes lagged, as if she wanted to remain in the open air. Alucius projected a sense of sandwolf, and the ewe closed the gap with the rest of the flock.

Once all the nightsheep were in the shed, Alucius dismounted and tied Wildebeast to one of the posts of the lambing corral. Then he checked the shed a last time.

Wendra appeared at the shed door as Alucius slid the last flange bolt into place. She was wearing a herder's jacket that Alucius's mother Lucenda had tailored for her and given to her on her birthday. Both her generous mouth and her golden-flecked green eyes smiled as Alucius turned. She was wearing the green scarf he had brought from Zalt—the only thing of value he had brought back from Madrien.

They just looked at each other for a long moment, then embraced. After a time, they separated, but Alucius could sense how their life-threads entwined whenever they were close.

"Why . . . how . . . ?" Alucius wasn't quite sure how to phrase the question. He untied Wildebeast.

Wendra laughed. "Your mother practically ordered me out of the kitchen when we saw you coming down Westridge." The laugh died away. "She said you were leaving tomorrow, and she wouldn't allow me to make the mistakes she did."

Alucius nodded soberly. His father had been a militia captain who had ridden out when Alucius was less than three and never returned. "I still have to take care of Wildebeast."

"I'll come with you. Your grandfather's already finished with his mount—while you took care of the flock."

"He deserves that. He'll have to go back to doing everything tomor-row."

"I know," Wendra said quietly.

The herder who was also a militia captain could sense that his wife was upset and trying to hide it. "What happened?"

"It's nothing." Wendra's breath was a white fog in the winter twilight.

Alucius looked hard at Wendra. "I don't think so."

"It really is. It shouldn't bother me at all. Father sent out a half barrel of good weak ale. Korcler and Mother brought it. We asked them to stay for supper, but Mother said they had to get back. They'd been delivering barrels to Gortal at the dustcat works." Wendra paused. "Father wishes he didn't have to sell to Gortal, but without his orders . . ."

"He couldn't keep the cooperage going," Alucius finished her sentence as he led Wildebeast into the stable, then into the third stall.

Wendra nodded, pausing at the end of the stall. "It seems so . . . unfair . . . so wrong. Father's a good cooper, and he wasn't lucky enough to have the Talent to be a herder. He works hard."

"He does." Alucius began to unsaddle Wildebeast, then to groom him. "You have to wonder, if there is the One Who Is, why there is so much evil and unfairness in the world." Thinking of the torques of the Matrial, he added, "And so often, it seems like the efforts people make to redress one evil just create another."

"You're thinking about Madrien, aren't you?"

"Yes."

"You look at things differently, now."

"Is that bad?" Alucius offered a laugh.

"No." Wendra shook her head. "It's still hard to believe that one person controlled the collars of every man in Madrien." She looked at Alucius. "And you've never said anything much beyond a word or two except the one time."

"There's no reason to say more, is there? You and Grandfather and Mother know, and no one else should." Alucius put down the brush and patted Wildebeast on the shoulder. "There, fellow. Now for some grain."

"But . . . when the collars failed, why . . . why didn't the troopers all revolt?"

"Some did. Some joined my company. But they were all former captives. Why would the others revolt? I suppose some did, but not that many. Life wasn't that bad there, and everyone had a good place to live.

The only really bad thing was that Talent officers could kill anyone who wore a collar from a distance, and most of those with collars were men. With that gone, and men having more say in matters, why would people want to leave their homes or destroy things? They might even learn to fight better without the collars."

"It bothers you," Wendra offered.

"What does?"

"You've talked to me about how much better most people lived in Madrien and how shabby Iron Stem looks."

Alucius left the stall and closed the half door behind him. "I'd like to think that people would treat others better, but the place where they were treated best used force to require it. It doesn't give me the most hope." He took Wendra's arm after he closed the stable door, and they left the stable and began to walk back toward the stead house, arm in arm. Even though it was almost night, the way was bright enough for a man who had the night vision of a herder, so that even full dark, without either moon in the sky, appeared as early twilight might to others.

"I don't want you to go back," she said quietly. "I know you have to, but I worry."

"I worry, too." Alucius laughed. "It's been quiet, except for raiders and bandits."

"Grandfather Kustyl says that the Reillies who left the Westerhills are moving back in, and that, before long, they'll be raiding steads again."

Alucius nodded. Wendra's grandfather knew a great deal. As one of the closer neighbors—close being over ten vingts to the north—Kustyl often stopped by to chat with Royalt, and had for years.

"They might, but there are fewer of them, and they probably won't have to raid for a few years. By then, it might be some other poor captain's problem." He stamped his boots on the porch to remove the thin dusting of snow, then used the boot brush, first on Wendra's boots, then on his own.

Once inside, they cleaned up in the washroom, where the hand pump squeaked with every downstroke, and where the water was cold enough to leave Wendra's hands bluish.

When they entered the kitchen, Royalt was already sitting at one end of the long table. He looked at Lucenda, standing by the heavy iron stove. "Told you they wouldn't be long."

Alucius's mother smiled indulgently before she seated herself at the table and inclined her head to Alucius. "If you would . . ."

Alucius bowed his head. "In the name of the One Who Was, Is, and Will Be, may our food be blessed and our lives as well, and blessed be the lives of both the deserving and the undeserving that both may strive to do good in the world and beyond." The words of the ancient blessing disturbed him, although he'd come to understand more of their import. Even at his age, he'd seen enough to discover that it was often hard to determine who was deserving and undeserving, simple though it might appear at first glance. The Matrial had brought prosperity and peace to the entire western coast of Corus, after more than a thousand years of bloodshed and anarchy. But it had taken more than four generations of oppression of men, and the use of silver torques that could kill a man at the whim of any woman with Talent. Who had deserved what, for how long, and why? He still was uncertain.

Lucenda stood, as did Wendra. Wendra began to hand platters and dishes from the serving table, while Lucenda ladled a sauce that simmered on the stove over a large platter.

"Marinated stuffed fowl with the orange sauce and lace potatoes! You're giving Alucius quite a send-off supper," Royalt said.

"He deserves it," Lucenda said. "Wendra and I decided he ought to have a meal to remember on that cold ride back to Emal."

Wendra smiled sweetly at Royalt, though her eyes twinkled, and added, "And you won't enjoy it at all, I imagine."

Alucius almost choked on the mouthful of ale he was swallowing.

"Alucius," Royalt protested, "once you leave, I'll be at their mercy. I'm but a poor herder."

The other three laughed.

"You've never been at anyone's mercy," Alucius said, adding the cheese-lace potatoes to his platter.

"And let's not hear about proper respect, not tonight," added Lucenda.

Royalt offered an exaggerated shrug of helplessness.

Alucius took a bite of the fowl, then smiled at Wendra. "It's good. You made it, didn't you?"

Wendra blushed.

"She did. She cooks better than I do," Lucenda answered for the younger woman. "And she's gotten almost as good with the looms and spinnerets."

Left unsaid was the fact that, except for her father's total lack of Talent, Wendra might well have been raised on a stead herself and learned all the equipment as a child. But it was clear to Alucius that she had enough Talent to be a herder herself, if not so much as he had, and, once he finished his militia obligation, he intended to teach her the herding aspect of the stead as well.

There was silence for a time as the family ate.

"Talked to Kustyl last week." Royalt finally spoke. "He said that the price of summer nightsilk in Borlan was going for fifteen golds a yard."

"That's for nightsilk that hasn't even been loomed?" asked Wendra.

Royalt finished his biscuit before nodding. "Not ours, though. Always some smaller herders who are short on coin, can't face the risk. So they agree to a fixed-price delivery with one of the cloth brokers. Broker tries to sell them for more in the futures market. If he can, he's made money, with no risk."

"What if the herder can't deliver?" asked Wendra.

"He'll likely lose part or all of his flock," Alucius replied. "Broker will take it, then sell the animals to other herders."

"We haven't had to buy any in years," Royalt said. "Did once, twenty-five years back. Gray flux killed off almost ten prime ewes. Didn't have much choice. Didn't like it, though."

Alucius hadn't heard about the gray flux, but there was always something he hadn't heard, once his grandsire started talking about the past.

"The price wouldn't be that high unless the traders think we'll have trouble," Lucenda said. "The weather hasn't been that dry, and the winter that cold." She looked across the table at her son. "Is the Lord-Protector looking north?"

"I haven't heard anything, and Colonel Clyon visited Emal two weeks before we left on furlough. There's more talk about when the Lord-Protector's lady might expect an heir."

"They've been married less than a year, and already they're asking?" inquired Wendra. "Doesn't he have brothers, if that's what they're worried about?"

"He has two brothers, as I recall," Lucenda said. "But neither is married. Not that the Lord-Protector's next eldest brother isn't considered capable."

"You mean, sufficiently ambitious and bloodthirsty?" asked Alucius dryly.

"Who told you that?" Wendra looked at Alucius.

"The colonel let that drop some time back. He said that the current Lord-Protector had more sense than his younger siblings, but all were to be watched."

"Clyon's a good man, but he's getting along," Royalt said.

Alucius nodded. "Majer Weslyn is doing more and more."

"You think he's a good man?"

"Majer Weslyn? He does what the colonel wants, but . . ."

"He's not as strong?" asked Wendra. "Or he'll do what the Council wants if anything happens to Clyon?"

"I worry about that," Alucius admitted. "The head of the Iron Valley Militia has to be able to stand up to the Council. Clyon does."

"It's too bad you can't be colonel," Wendra said.

Alucius laughed gently. "I'm too young. I'm the youngest captain in the entire militia."

"And you've seen more than any of them," Wendra said staunchly.

"It doesn't work that way. Besides, I'd rather be a herder."

The faintest frown crossed Royalt's forehead, an expression— accompanied by a feeling of worry that Alucius could not ignore.

Wendra glanced from her husband to his grandsire, but she didn't speak.

"What else did Kustyl say?" asked Alucius.

"The Council borrowed over six thousand golds from the Landarch of Deforya during the fight against the Matrial. They didn't want to raise tariffs, but they haven't been able to pay the interest, either, and they can't pay even that back without raising tariffs. After four years, the back interest is almost another three thousand golds. Kustyl said he'd heard that the Lord-Protector has bought the note from the Landarch. The Landarch had to sell it because he's got troubles of his own. The Lord-Protector has raised the interest on the note because the Council hasn't made the payments. Some say he's even sending an envoy from Tempre. There's a faction in the traders that wants to accept being a province of Lanachrona, rather than come up with a fifty percent increase in tariffs."

"That much?" marveled Alucius.

"They'd do that?" blurted Wendra.

"Aye . . . some would," Royalt replied.

"They're like Gortal," Lucenda added. "So long as they can turn a gold, it matters not what happens to others."

"What do you think will happen now?" Alucius looked to his grandsire.

"That . . . I don't know. You've seen Madrien, and so far what you thought would happen there has. The Matrites can still protect themselves, and that leaves us, Deforya, and the grass nomads as the places where the Lord-Protector might wish to expand Lanachrona. He already has Southgate. I can't see him spreading the Southern Guard across the Lost Highway and a thousand vingts of grassland."

"Deforya or us, then," Lucenda concluded.

"Or both," suggested Alucius. "In time, anyway."

Royalt shook his head slowly. "It's not as though we could do anything now—or that anyone's going to ask us. We're only herders." He smiled at his daughter. "You said there was some pie?"

Alucius was staggered at the thought that the Council might surrender the independence of the Iron Valleys over such a debt, enormous though it was. Staggered by the revelation, but not surprised by the Council's actions . . . or lack of forethought.

3

Alucius woke in the darkness, knowing that he had to rise. His winter's-end furlough was over, and he had to report back to the outpost at Emal. The ten days of the last week had flown by all too quickly, and now he had a three-day ride ahead of him; he had to leave a day earlier than his men and squad leaders would so that he would be there as they reported.

"I wish you could stay longer," Wendra whispered, snuggling against him.

"So do I."

For a time, Wendra clung to him before he kissed her and said, "It's a long ride."

"I know."

Alucius eased out from under the heavy quilts and headed from what had been the guest bedroom across the back corridor to the washroom. The water coming from the hand pump in the washroom was like liquid ice, and shaving left his face chill. When he returned to the bedroom, Wendra had pulled on trousers and tunic and her heavy winter jacket. She sat on the edge of the bed, watching as he pulled on his nightsilk undergarments and his captain's uniform.

Then she stood and embraced him again. They kissed for another long moment before she turned slightly and pressed the black crystal of her ring against the crystal of his herder's wristband. For an instant, warmth and closeness enfolded them, and they clung to each other.

Wendra stepped back to let him finish dressing, but did not sit down, standing at the foot of the bed. Once he was dressed, he reached down and shouldered the saddlebags, then lifted the rifle from the high wall rack. Except for what he had on, and his personal toiletries, he'd packed the saddlebags the night before.

He wore the heavy cartridge belt over his militia winter parka. While he did not expect trouble, if he encountered it, he'd need the cartridges in easy reach. The rifle was his—but met militia standards, which meant that it was designed for use against sanders and sandwolves, with the magazine that held but five cartridges, each thicker than a large man's thumb.

Wendra accompanied him out of the house, carrying the basket of travel fare. As they walked through the darkness toward the stable, a darkness that was more like early twilight to Alucius, she said quietly, "It's colder than yesterday. You'll be careful?"

"I'm always careful, dear one. Even in Madrien I was careful."

"I worry."

Alucius worried, too, although he had less reason to do so than he had when he'd first been conscripted years before in the middle of a war. Still . . . Corus was an unsettled place, and there were raiders and brigands, even if there were no battles. Yet.

After saddling Wildebeast and slipping the food from the basket into the top of his saddlebags, he turned to Wendra and wrapped his arms around her. "Just another four seasons, and I'll be here all the time."

She did not speak, but lifted her lips to his.

After the embrace and kiss, Alucius pulled on the skull mask of night-silk that shielded his entire head, with only eyeholes and slits for nose and mouth.

"You look dangerous in that," she said with a faint smile.

"I don't know about dangerous, but the nightsilk keeps my face from freezing. I'll have to take it off at sunrise, or someone will think I'm a brigand." He led Wildebeast out of the stall and then from the stable out into the chill air of a winter morning three glasses before sunrise.

In the west, just above the horizon, the green-tinged disc of Asterta was setting. The larger moon—Selena—had set a glass after sunset the night before. Alucius closed the stable door and mounted. "I'll walk you back to the house."

"I can—all right." She turned and began to walk back to the house, Alucius riding beside her.

Once Wendra stood on the porch, Alucius turned Wildebeast.

"You *will* be careful," Wendra said again, looking at her husband.

"I will," he promised. "You take care as well."

Wendra nodded, as if she dared not to speak.

After a long moment, of just looking through the darkness at her, he turned his mount toward the lane, heading southwest, swallowing as he did.

He understood her fears, her concerns.

So much had happened. Three years earlier, he had been conscripted into the Iron Valleys Militia. He'd served in the militia as a scout, then had been captured at the battle of Soulend by the Matrites and forced by the Talent-torque welded around his neck to serve as a captive trooper in the Matrial's forces. He'd discovered his own Talent-abilities, broken the power of the torques, and returned to the Iron Valleys at the head of a company of other captives—only to discover that the price of freedom was to become a militia captain over that company. Now, after a little more than a year of service since his return, in command of the Twenty-first Horse Company, he had just less than a year before he could return to the stead, and the life of a herder—and to Wendra.

As he rode past the outbuildings, he turned and looked back at the stead house. Wendra still stood there watching. He waved, not knowing whether she might see his gesture in the darkness, and he could not tell whether she did or not.

He had ridden less than a vingt from the stead buildings when he sensed the others. There were four men—none with Talent, for his Talent revealed that the being of each was blackness without the flashes of green that revealed herder Talent or the flashes of purple that revealed the only other kind of Talent in people that Alucius had come across.

He slowed Wildebeast into a walk, letting his Talent-senses reach out to locate those who waited. They were waiting in the low wash less than two hundred yards from where the stead lane met the old high road that ran from Eastice south through Soulend, then through Iron Stem to Dekhron. Two were on the north side, and two on the south, all of them less than twenty yards from the road—a clear ambush.

Alucius could also sense the grayish violet of the sandwolves, doubtless waiting to see if there would be carrion left for them. Alucius smiled grimly behind the skull mask. There would be carrion.

He continued to ride until he was less than two hundred yards from the ambush site. In the darkness, far enough away in the now-moonless night that none of the men would see him, he reined up, dismounted, and tied Wildebeast to one of the posts marking the stead lane, then took the rifle from its holster, holding it in his left hand.

Moving as silently as only could a man who had been both herder and scout, he slipped through the quarasote, using his night vision and Talent-sense to make his way to the wash on the north side of the lane.

He hoped he could use his Talent to stun the men, then sever their lifethreads, rather than using the rifle. But he had to get within yards to use Talent that way, and there was every chance that one of them might hear him. So he held the rifle ready as he eased toward the northernmost of the ambushers. When he reached the edge of the wash, only about a yard and a half deep, he slid down onto the lower ground and began to follow the wash south.

He froze as he heard the faintest of sounds. Remaining silent, he listened.

". . . thought I heard something . . ."

". . . scrats probably . . ."

". . . not at night in winter."

". . . quiet . . . he'll be along . . ."

Alucius edged along the chest-high miniature bluff toward the men, rifle ready, still hoping not to use it, especially not at first.

A good half glass passed before Alucius reached a gentle curve in the edge of the wash, a position from where he could sense the nearness of the closest man. He paused. Then he reached out with his Talent-senses—and struck with full force at the man's yellow-brown lifethread—a thread invisible except through Talent-senses.

There was but the faintest gasp, then a muted thump, and the reddish-tinged void that signified death washed over Alucius.

"Silyn . . . you there? Silyn?"

Ignoring the whispered inquiry, Alucius kept moving, until he was less than ten yards from the second man, where he once more extended his Talent and struck, wincing as the death-void swept across him.

Then, for several moments, Alucius stood silently, shuddering, and feeling the perspiration gathering beneath the skull mask, despite the chill and the light night wind that swirled around him, with the iron-acrid scent that always accompanied any wind on the stead that came out of the northeast and off the Aerlal Plateau. Finally, he took a long and slow deep breath, then crossed the ten yards of the wash to the western side, where he climbed out and silently began to circle west and south toward the remaining two men.

The second pair were far closer together, less than three yards apart and lying prone behind quarasote bushes on the edge of the far shallower section of the wash south of the depression, where the stead lane dipped and ran through the infrequent watercourse.

Neither even turned as Alucius Talent-struck.

Alucius had to sit down, with his legs over the crumbling edge of the wash, breathing heavily and shuddering. He'd killed with his Talent before—but never more than one person at one time. He'd had no idea that the effort was so great—or the reaction so violent. But it explained why those with Talent didn't make that much of an impression on the world, especially since there were few who had great Talent. He doubted that he could have used his Talent against a fifth man—not if he wanted to remain conscious.

After a time, he stood, slowly, and walked back to the first pair of dead men, rifling through their wallets and winter jackets to see if there happened to be any sign of anything that might say why they had tried to attack him. All he found that indicated their motivation was five golds in each belt wallet, in addition to some silvers and coppers. He took the golds, but left the lesser coins. Then he trudged back to the first pair, where he found nothing revealing, except five golds more in each wallet.

He took a deep breath and made his way through the darkness toward Wildebeast, his Talent-senses still extended. The sandwolves were closer, perhaps a vingt to the west, across the ancient eternastone high road. Only when he reached the stead road, and Wildebeast, did he concentrate on the image of carrion, of food for the sandwolf pack. Then, with a grim smile, he mounted.

He frowned. His Talent indicated someone was riding toward him— quickly. He relaxed slightly as he sensed the green-shot blackness that was his grandsire. Rather than ride on, he waited.

Within another quarter glass came a voice.

"Alucius?"

"I'm here. I'm all right."

"I can tell that now. Wasn't sure what had happened until I was headed out here. Was certain something had. Could feel you were worried. So did Wendra. We both caught that. Not like you. You just called the sandwolves," Royalt observed, reining up on the stead road. "I didn't know anyone could do that."

Behind the skull mask, Alucius grinned raggedly. "Someone told me not to tell anyone. Herders don't tell, remember?"

"You can do more than that."

Alucius ignored the statement. "There were four of them. I don't think the sandwolves will leave much. They're hungry." He eased Wilde-beast toward his grandsire and the gray that the older man rode, then extended his hand. "They'd been paid in gold. Five golds each. Use it for the stead."

The twenty golds clunked into the older man's hand.

"I left the silvers and coppers in their wallets," Alucius said.

"What do you think about their mounts?" asked Royalt.

"They're tethered. Leave them where they are. I thought you and Kustyl could find them and the bodies—or what's left of them—early tomorrow. I was going to ride back to the stead and tell you, but you've saved me the trip. I'd guess that the four, whoever they were, were trav-elers who got lost in the dark and had the misfortune to run into hungry sandwolves."

"That's what Kustyl and I will say. But I'll get the mounts now. Wouldn't want to lose them to the sandwolves. Waste of good horses." After a pause, Royalt asked, "Do you know who it could be?"

"If Dysar were still alive . . ." Alucius said slowly. "But I can't think of anyone else. You said Wendra felt it, too?"

"She wanted to come. I thought it was better she didn't."

Alucius nodded. "She has Talent. She might show more. You ought to take her out with you."

"I will. I'd thought about it."

Left unsaid was the understanding that the stead needed a herder, and, in Alucius's absence, should anything happen to Royalt, there would be no one else to herd the nightsheep—unless Wendra could. The last woman herder had been Royalt's mother, the last woman with Talent in Alucius's family. Alucius didn't know—or hadn't asked, he cor-rected himself silently—about any female herders in Wendra's family.

After another silence, Royalt said, "You'd better get going, before the sandwolves get here. Kustyl and Wendra and I . . . we'll take care of things."

"Thank you."

Once more, Alucius turned Wildebeast westward, leaving his grand-sire behind once more.

In less than a fifth of a glass, he was traveling southward on the ancient high road. The gray eternastones, laid down at least a millennium before, remained unmarked by the passage of time or traffic. Within a day, any few scars that might mar the gray stone surface vanished. In the darkness the gray stone emitted a faint glow perceptible only to those with Talent, a line of illumination that ran straight as a rifle barrel from Soulend to Iron Stem.

As he rode, Alucius pondered the attempted attack. Why would anyone wish him harm? He was the most junior captain in the Iron Valley Militia. His death would not turn the stead over to anyone outside the family, not while his grandsire and mother and Wendra still lived. He had never been involved in trade. His only skill was that he was perhaps the best battlefield captain in the militia. He was certainly the most experienced, if not through his own desires.

Yet there was no war, and, so far as he or Royalt knew, none in sight. From the brief words he had heard, the would-be killers had either been from the southern half of the Iron Valleys, from Deforya, or from Lanachrona. While the Lanachronans might wish a less effective militia in the Iron Valleys, Alucius couldn't see how his death would affect anything. He'd been a captive Matrite trooper when the militia had repulsed the Matrites—if with some earlier help from him and the Lord-Protector of Lanachrona.

All Alucius could come up with was the idea that the ambush meant he was in a position to do something, or to stop something—or no one would have bothered with trying to kill a lowly captain. The question was whether he would recognize whatever it was before it was too late, and that might be difficult because he hadn't the faintest idea of what he was looking for.

A glass passed before, in the darkness, he could sense the dustcat works, the long wooden sheds that confined the animals, kept and groomed for the dander that provided exquisite pleasure when inhaled—and which made gold and gems cheap by comparison. He'd only met Gortal a handful of times, and not in years. Even when he had been much younger, Alucius had found the man who confined the captured dustcats and sold their dreamdust to the traders of Lanachrona cold, almost without spirit, for all of Gortal's manners and fine clothes.

The scutters who labored for Gortal would do almost anything to be around the big cats, just to inhale the vagrant dreamdust, and it was said that the women scutters made those who served at the Pleasure Palace seem virtuous. It still amazed Alucius that people would destroy themselves so—and that Gortal could accept the golds that came from such degradation.

Then, he reflected ruefully, golds affected everyone. The traders of Dekhron had pressured the Council to reduce the size of the militia in previous years, almost inviting the Matrial of Madrien to attack, all because they had not wished to pay the tariffs necessary to support a strong militia. In the end, they'd paid more by having to expand and equip the militia rapidly—and they'd been forced to borrow the golds—a debt it appeared they could not repay. And, once more, right after the war, they'd pressured the Council to reduce the size of the militia—and the tariffs that could have serviced that debt.

Were there those on the Council so much like Gortal that they would do anything for a gold? In the chill, Alucius snorted. From what he'd seen, there was little difference, except that Gortal was probably more honest.

4

Alustre, Lustrea

The workshop walls were of pale green marble, but the floor was polished pink-gray granite, as were the pillars. There were no wall hangings, and the windows were but narrow slits in the walls. Set well away from the workbench was a solid black square table, sturdily constructed of lorken, and upon the table was a thick glass mirror, also rimmed in lorken.

Sweat poured from the face of the thin young man who looked over the silver-rimmed circular mirror set in the middle of the table. As he concentrated, the silver of the mirror was replaced by ruby mists, which swirled.

"Well?" asked the man in silver and black, standing over the table—and the engineer.

"This is but makeshift, my lord Praetor. It is not truly a Recorder's Table. There are none left in the east." The man did not meet the older man's eyes. "I said it might function as one."

An image swirled into being out of the mists, the image of a young man dressed in silver.

"That is Tyren," stated the older man.

Another image appeared—that of a slightly younger man, with silver-blond hair and wearing the blue leathers of an Illegean and mounted upon a white stallion. This image was silvered, and wavered in and out of focus. A third and fainter image appeared, almost a shadow image of a third figure, one wearing some type of herder garments. After a moment, a fourth image appeared—the face of a young woman or a girl, but, it too was shadowed and even fainter than two that had preceded it.

Then . . . the last three images vanished—all at once.

Almost as suddenly, the mirror shattered, spraying fragments around the room. A thin line of blood appeared on the forearm of the younger man, and the older man carefully picked several shards from the folds of his silver cloak.

"What does it mean, Vestor?" There was a pause, and a hard laugh. "Besides showing your limited ability?"

"Compared to the accomplishments of the ancients, Praetor, my abilities are limited, but that is because I am young and have not had the time or the resources to enhance them on your behalf. No one now alive could have turned a mirror into a replica of one of the ancient Recorder's Tables, albeit a poor replica."

"Is there not one Table left anywhere in Corus? Of the score the records recall?"

"There is one. I can sense it." Vestor lifted his thin shoulders and dropped them. "Where it might be, that I cannot say, except it is likely to be somewhere to the west of the Spine of Corus."

"And you cannot construct one that might last more than a fraction of a glass?"

"They must be linked to nodes within the earth, Praetor, and I have yet to find where such a node might be or how to create such a link."

"Then . . . this must do. For now." The Praetor's cold glance fell on the engineer. "So tell me—instead of saying how great you will be—what meant all those images."

"I could but guess, Praetor."

"Then guess."

"Young Tyren is indeed fated to find and carry the dual scepter and to lead Alustre to greatness in reestablishing the Duarchy in power over all of Corus, but . . . he will face challenges from the other three."

"Shadowy challenges? Or faint ones? Why were their images so indistinct?"

"Because, I would surmise, that all may have the ability to call up Talent. They have not, or I could not have summoned them in the mirror. They may never, but they have that ability."

"We must find them and eliminate them. *You* must find them."

"One wears the leathers of a rider of Illegea. I would surmise, although it is but a guess, that it is Aellyan Edyss. The second is a herder, possibly from the Iron Valleys, although he could be anywhere in Corus. The third—and faintest—is a girl, perhaps a young woman. She may not even have been born, so faint was that image." Vestor's eyes met those of the Praetor but did not flinch from the glare he received.

"You *will* create another mirror, and you will watch for those dangers."

"Each one will shatter after use, I fear."

"No matter. You will only use them when I am here, then."

"And what of the golds for the equipment for your armies?"

"Oh . . . you will have that." The graying Praetor smiled coldly. "We will need them to conquer Illegea, Aellyan Edyss or not."

5

Alucius glanced back over his shoulder, looking westward in the twilight along a snowswept road that was visible only because of the three-yard-tall black poles on each side, each pole a hundred yards from the next. He could see no one following him, not that he expected to, since his Talent-senses revealed nothing living nearby—except for him and Wildebeast.

He looked at the way ahead, guiding Wildebeast to the right as the road made a sharp turn southward for the last two vingts before it reached Emal, descending through a natural cut in the river bluffs that followed the curve of the river.

After removing the skull mask, Alucius wrapped his black wool scarf more tightly around his face as he rode into the chill section of the road where direct sunlight reached but for a few glasses in winter. The sun had already set behind the river bluffs to the west, flat stretches of grasslands in four of the five seasons, but in winter an expanse of snow swirled into drifts by the unrelenting wind off the Aerlal Plateau, less than twenty vingts to the north.

Most of the troopers returning from furlough would travel the lower road along the river, but Alucius preferred the bluff road, cold as it was, because it took a full day and a half less than riding south to Dekhron and then taking the river road back east-northeast to Emal. As it was, even by the bluff road, the ride from the stead to Emal was a hard three-day ride, and could be as long as five days, if the roads were muddy, because once Alucius left Iron Stem and the eternastones of the high road, the way eastward was by the local clay roads. Winter travel did offer one advantage. The roads might be rough, but they were frozen as hard as the stones of the high road.

After Alucius passed through the cut and reached the flat section of the road below the bluffs, he could see the town less than a vingt away to the south, perched on a higher section of ground, a low bluff overlooking the now-frozen River Vedra. The arched stone bridge that crossed the narrows to the matching bluff on the south side was the only safe crossing of the river, except in winter, in the more than three hundred vingts between the point where the river gushed from beneath the headwall of the Aerlal Plateau—some one hundred and twenty vingts generally east-northeast of Emal—and Dekhron itself. The Lanachronan community of Semal, that clustered around the south end of the bridge, was scarcely more than a hamlet, and the Southern Guard had stationed but a single squad there to guard the bridge—mainly to collect tariffs from what few traders there were. The pale off-white limestone walls of the hundred or so dwellings at Emal faded into the snowy backdrop of the fields on the bottomland barely above the flood levels of the river. On the other hand, the steep-pitched slate roofs—stark and dark— stood out, almost floating on an endless sea of white. Thin trails of smoke wound into the darkening silver-green sky.

Alucius rode past houses shuttered tight against the cold and the bitter wind off the plateau, acrid-iron bitter—as always. Glimmers of light escaped through cracks in the shutters, and the smell of burning coal made the northeast wind even more bitter. As Wildebeast carried Alucius down the main street, his hoofs crunched on the packed snow, snow that was more than knee high beside the houses.

The militia outpost stood at the south end of Emal, just above the river, on the low bluff that passed for a headland, guarding the high-arched and narrow stone bridge that spanned the Vedra. The outpost itself—unlike those in the north—was walled. The walls were not of finely dressed stone as in Madrien, but rather of crude blocks of all sizes and colors wedged and mortared in place. The ironbound oak gates of the outpost were open, and a single sentry from one of the two squads of the Third Foot stationed at Emal stood watch in a guardhouse just outside the gates.

The ranker stepped out of his shelter as Alucius neared the gates, his eyes peering through the dimness, then catching the militia winter parka.

"Captain Alucius . . ." Alucius slowed Wildebeast and took in the other, catching his self-identity, and adding, "Nyllen, isn't it?"

"Ah . . . yes, sir. Couldn't see you in the darkness, sir."

"Have you seen anyone from Twenty-first Company?"

"Three or four came back today, sir. Senior Squad Leader Longyl came in, too. They're in the barracks."

"Good." Alucius nodded and rode past the gates toward the stables.

A squad leader walked out of the duty room at the end of the barracks and across the end of the courtyard to the sentry.

"It was Captain Alucius, sir," Nyllen said to the squad leader, adding in a lower voice that Alucius should not have been able to hear. "Does he recognize everyone?"

"Pretty near, Nyllen."

Alucius reined up outside the closed stable door and was about to dismount when the door slid open. He dismounted and led Wildebeast into the comparative warmth of the stable while the ostler closed the door behind them.

"Cold evening it is, sir," offered Vinkin, the head ostler at Emal, both for Twenty-first Company and for Fifth Company. "Some wondered as whether you'd be making it tonight. I said you'd be here. Weather doesn't stop an officer who's a herder."

"Not this time, anyway," replied Alucius with a smile.

"There's grain and water waiting, Captain."

"Thank you, Vinkin." Alucius projected the slightest sense of gratitude and appreciation.

The ostler bowed his head in response.

Twenty-first Company had the stalls on the north side of the long stable, with the first stall being the captain's. At times, Alucius definitely appreciated that perquisite of rank. This was one of those times.

Wildebeast shook himself, then *whuffed* when Alucius led him into the stall and started to unsaddle him.

"I know. It was a long and cold ride. Let's hope we'll have a few days before someone wants a patrol."

Wildebeast didn't respond to the comment, not that Alucius expected that of the stallion.

Once he'd finished with his mount, Alucius shouldered his saddle-bags, picked up his rifle from where he had leaned it against the stall wall, and closed the stall door. He crossed the stable, nodding to Vinkin as he neared the small access door to the courtyard. Once he closed the door behind him, he started across the frozen clay of the courtyard toward the headquarters building, scarcely larger than a small sheep shed, for all that it contained rooms for three company officers, two rooms for visiting officers, and a conference room, a common wash-room, and a kitchen and small mess for officers and squad leaders.

He stamped his feet on the porch, but since there was no boot brush, that was the best he could do to get the snow off his boots and trousers before stepping inside into the entry area. A single oil lamp cast a dim glow.

Another officer, wearing a black wool sweater over his tunic, appeared in the archway on the far side of the entry hall. "Glad to see you, Alucius."

"Good to see you, Feran. I'm glad the journey's over. It's cold out there."

"You took the bluff road, didn't you?" Even in the dimness of the hall, the lines radiating from Feran's eyes were deep enough to show his age—a good fifteen years older than Alucius.

Alucius nodded as he moved toward the hallway where Feran stood and along which his own quarters were located.

"You herders. If I took that road, they'd find me in a block of ice come spring." The career militia officer smiled ruefully and shook his head.

"It's two days shorter. That's half a week more I can spend with Wendra."

"Lucky man, there."

"Anything happening I should know about?"

"We got a dispatch from Majer Weslyn on behalf of the colonel—something about the need to watch for raiders from Deforya sneaking over the river to the east."

Alucius raised his thawing eyebrows.

"I know," said Feran, with a laugh. "What's there for raiders to take east of here? But that's what it said. Nothing else, really. Not that affects us. There was a notice that there had been several Squawt raids west of Rivercliff."

"There haven't been any Squawts there in generations." Rivercliff was some sixty vingts downriver from Borlan, and the Squawts had been driven west and north generations earlier. Rivercliff had even remained well within the borders of the Iron Valleys at the height of the Matrite War. "Sounds like Lanachronan raiders under Squawt colors."

"You don't think it's a Matrite tactic?"

Alucius shook his head. "They don't think or operate that way. They wouldn't send out a raiding party of all men right now. They'd worry that some would defect. Even when the collars worked, they almost never had scouting parties of less than eight."

"Don't like that . . . Lanachronans, I mean."

"I don't, either." Alucius paused. "When are you getting furlough?"

"Tomorrow—if most of your company gets back. The colonel wants all outposts at full strength before the turn of spring." Feran stretched. "I'd better let you get settled. You look sanded."

"I feel sanded," Alucius admitted. With a nod, he headed for his small officer's room.

His spaces were all of three yards by four, with a bunk against one wall, a narrow wardrobe, two footchests—one for his clothes and one for records, an armless straight-backed wooden chair older than Alucius himself, and a cramped writing desk. The single narrow window was shuttered tightly, but the edges of the shutters were dusted with frost, and Alucius's breath steamed in the chill room.

After using the striker to light the lamp in the wall bracket, with a little boost from his Talent, he unloaded the rifle and placed it in the wardrobe, then unpacked the saddlebags and smoothed out his clothes, hanging his three sets of uniforms in the wardrobe. While he unwound the scarf and loosened the winter parka, he did not take them off.

Then, Alucius sat down at the small desk in his tiny room to write a letter to Wendra. There might not be a messenger headed west for days, but that didn't matter. He'd learned that he needed to write when he had time, not when messengers were there. As it was, the messenger would have to leave the letter at Kyrial's cooperage in Iron Stem, and that meant it might be weeks before his words reached his wife.

He took out the copper-tipped pen from his kit, and the portable inkwell. After a time, he began to write.

Dearest Wendra,
The ride here was long and cold, but I was fortunate in not having to brave a winter storm. Already, I miss you and wish we were yet together, walking, or even working on the stead . . .

While Alucius had little news for her, he recalled all too well the years when he had had much news and no way to write.

6

Twenty-two men rode eastward along the river road, two scouts well ahead and out of sight, and then Alucius, Zerdial, and the rest of first squad. Alucius had left his senior squad leader, Longyl, at the post and in charge of the other squads.

The patrol followed the tracks of fifteen or so riders.

"Their tracks are headed both ways, sir," Zerdial observed. His breath steamed in the the cold and clear midday air.

Alucius glanced at Zerdial—the thin squad leader for first squad. At times, Alucius hadn't been certain that the young squad leader would mature fast enough to keep holding the position, but with Alucius's help, Zerdial had grown into the job—as had Anslym, the second squad leader. His other three squad leaders—Faisyn, Egyl, and Sawyn—were seasoned veterans.

"They're already back across the river," Alucius said. "They crossed, went west as far as Tuuler. They turned back there and came this way to somewhere ahead. Then they retraced their path along the road and crossed back into Lanachrona." He had a good idea of why the riders had gone farther east, but he wanted to see if he happened to be right. He did not Talent-sense anyone close by, besides his own men, and he would have been most surprised if they had found the riders.

"The scouts did report that there were tracks both ways on the ice, sir." Zerdial frowned. "They didn't raid Tuuler."

"There's little enough to raid, and the houses are stout stone," Alucius pointed out. "Most folk here have militia rifles."

"But . . . why . . ."

"They're not here. Let's just see if they went so far as the second cataract." Alucius gestured to the road ahead. "It's not that far."

"Yes, sir."

The first two weeks after Twenty-first Company's return to duty had gone by slowly, very slowly, each ten-day week feeling twice as long. The third week had begun the same way, and while Alucius had not accompanied every squad he had sent out on patrol, he had accompanied about half the patrols, and on one other occasion, the patrols had found the tracks of riders who had crossed the frozen section of the River Vedra from Lanachrona, then returned.

As first squad continued to ride eastward, Alucius studied the road and the scattered trees between the road and the fields to the north. To his left, on the south, was the river, less than fifty yards wide. The ice, which farther downstream had been thick enough to support a wagon team, was clearly thinner, and less than a half vingt ahead, Alucius could see breaks and cracks in the ice, and even one small spot of open black water.

On the north side of the road, beyond the trees, the snow-covered fields were untracked, unmarked by man or mount. Only the road and, at times, the shoulder held hoofprints. Half a glass passed, and Alucius could hear a low rumbling in the distance, coming from upriver, somewhere beyond where the river curved northward for a time before turning back eastward. The center of the river was largely clear of ice, although the edges and banks were ice-encrusted, but the black water was so smooth it almost looked like a dark mirror.

The tracks of the riders continued eastward, and so did Alucius and first squad, along the banks of the river. Only traces of ice remained near the banks, and a steamy fog rose from the black water.

"Sir?" ventured Zerdial. "Why would they keep going eastward, then turn back? Past here, there's no ice and no way to cross."

"Think about it, Zerdial," Alucius said.

As the column rode around the gentle curve, where the road followed the river, the low rumbling turned into a far louder roaring that filled the air, with enough force that the branch tips of the scattered junipers along the river road were already bare of the snow that had fallen the day before.

"Sir!" Zerdial gestured to the pair of scouts ahead, who had ridden off the road and almost down to the edge of the river.

When the squad reached the scouts, Alucius nodded to Zerdial.

"Squad halt!" ordered the squad leader.

Alucius glanced upriver, even as he urged Wildebeast to the right and down to the riverbank, where the scouts waited.

Less than a vingt upstream was a rocky escarpment, over which jet-black water steamed as it dropped a good hundred yards into the pool below. For more than a hundred vingts above the falls and for a good four vingts below the cataract, the river was ice-free, running rapidly over the rocky shallows, with foglike vapor rising from the water. Roughly three vingts westward, the riverbed deepened, and the ice cover began. By another four vingts farther south, the ice was solid enough to hold a wagon team, and it stayed that solid all the way westward until slightly north of Tempre.

Alucius reined up short of the scouts.

"Looks like they watered their mounts here, sir!" Elbard, the older and stockier scout, shouted to make his voice heard over the roar of the cataract. "Probably early this morning, maybe before dawn."

There were also boot tracks in the already ice-crusted snow at the edge of the river, more than just a few.

"It looks like they filled their own water bottles, too," Alucius suggested.

"Yes, sir."

"No tracks east of here?"

"No, sir. They watered and turned back west."

"Thank you." Alucius nodded to the two. "We'll be heading back to Emal now."

"Yes, sir."

Alucius rode back up the slope to the road, where he reined in Wildebeast beside Zerdial. "We'll head back now."

"Yes, sir." Zerdial cleared his throat. "First squad! To the rear, ride! Scouts to the van position!"

The captain and the squad leader rode along the shoulder until they were at the head of the double-filed column that was first squad.

Once first squad was settled back into an easy pace westward, Alucius turned in the saddle and looked at Zerdial. "What do you think?"

"They came up here for water. That's at least an extra glass of riding each way." Zerdial frowned. "It would spare them the time it would take to chop through the ice, but why couldn't they just stop for water at one of the hamlets on the other side?"

"Why indeed?" asked Alucius.

"They didn't wish to be seen, sir?"

"That would be my guess, Zerdial."

Alucius had figured that aspect out almost immediately, but what bothered him was that he couldn't figure out why the riders hadn't wanted to be seen. The tracks made it clear that they had come from Lanachrona, and none of people in the hamlets on the Lanachronan side would have cared or said anything if the riders were Southern Guards. That meant that they weren't—or that they weren't in uniform. But brigands would have had far easier pickings to the south, and, despite the warnings from Dekhron, Alucius had trouble believing that Deforyan raiders would have traveled almost three hundred vingts—through the coldest section of the Upper Spine Mountains in winter—to raid some of the poorest hamlets in the Iron Valleys—or the one town with a militia garrison. He also didn't like the idea of Southern Guards not being in uniform.

Neither possibility was one that he liked, and that meant that, if the tracks continued, winter or not, he'd have to shift the patrol schedules to before dawn to see what he could find out.

7

Tempre, Lanachrona

The Lord-Protector, his face appearing a good ten years older than when he had taken office three years before, walked briskly into the plain marble-walled room, hidden deep beneath the palace, a structure erected generations earlier with great care not to disturb the ancient room and what it contained. He glanced at the Table of the Recorders, a device appearing more like a dark lorken-framed table than the artifact from the Cataclysm that it was. The Table's shimmered surface appeared but to be a mirror. It was not.

The silver-robed Recorder stood on the far side of the Table, waiting.

"You said you have finally discovered something about the mysterious officer whom you thought had brought down the Matrial," offered the Lord-Protector.

"I will call forth what I have discovered, Lord-Protector. You may be both surprised and amused."

"Amused? Is anything amusing in these times?" The Lord-Protector frowned, but stepped to the Table and looked down.

The Recorder cleared his throat softly, then concentrated on the ancient glass. The mirrored surface that appeared but fingerspans thick was replaced by ruby mists that looked yards in depth, mists that swirled before dissipating to reveal an image.

A tall and broad-shouldered officer in the black of the Militia of the Iron Valleys rode along a snowy road, flanked by two squad leaders. Although the captain was only slightly larger than the others, his presence, even through the Table, conveyed an impression of authority and command, making him seem far larger and older than he was. In addition, around his image flickered an aura of green and silver, and at times, he vanished entirely.

"He is in yet another uniform. Is he a mercenary?"

Before replying, the Recorder took a deep breath and allowed the image to vanish, to be replaced by a mirror that but reflected the ceiling. "I think not, Lord-Protector. For whatever reason, he was captured by the Matrites. From what I can discern through the Table, he was born the heir to a herder family in the Iron Valleys, and, because of his Matrite service, involuntary as it was, has been required to serve more time in the militia. He currently commands a horse company at Emal."

"And their Council of idiots does not know this?"

"No, Lord-Protector. He has doubtless used his Talent to avoid their discovering such."

"I do not like that he is a militia officer. Can you do anything through the Table?" The Lord-Protector went on, answering his own question. "Of course not. The Table is useful for gathering information, and that is all." He looked down at the blank surface, then back at the Recorder of Deeds. "Continue to watch him, and let me know should he accomplish anything that I should know."

"Yes, Lord-Protector." The Recorder inclined his head slightly, then straightened.

"It is better not to act when it is not necessary, but . . . we may have to act otherwise. We may indeed." Without another word, the Lord-Protector stalked from the small marble-walled chamber.

The Recorder glanced at the blank silver surface that had once more become a mirror. His face was impassive, despite the darkness in his eyes. Once the Lord-Protector had left, he again beheld the Table, his face bathed in a faint purple glow that radiated from the images he had called forth.

8

Outside the headquarters building, a howling wind blasted what otherwise would have been a light snow against the stone walls and shutters. Every so often, a particularly violent gust pushed cold air and puffs of white past the windows and inner and outer shutters.

On that dreary Duadi, barely into yet another winter week, Alucius sat at the table in the officers' and squad leaders' mess, looking at the stack of papers before him. There was a sheet—or more—on each man in his company, and the company captain had to make a seasonal report on each, then send the reports to militia headquarters in Dekhron. Since winter was already more than half-over, despite the snowstorm outside, and since Alucius was not sending out any patrols in the blizzard, he had decided to use the time to work on the seasonal reports. With the stepped-up patrols he had in mind, time for reports would be scarce in the weeks ahead. Even short handwritten statements took time when the company captain had to write a hundred on the troopers and five on the squad leaders—except that since Twenty-first Company was understrength, Alucius only had to write ninety-four reports on troopers.

There was a knock on the door.

"Yes?"

"Sir," said Longyl, the senior squad leader, "you sent word for me?"

"I did." Alucius gestured to the chair on the other side of the small mess table, waiting until the older squad leader had seated himself before speaking. "I'd like your thoughts on Reltyr. I've already had a few words with Faisyn."

"I'd rather not say much, sir."

"Neither did Faisyn, and I can understand that," Alucius said quietly. "He's got a wife outside of Wesrigg, doesn't he?" He was trying to use his Talent to pick up feelings . . . clues. While he could have talked to Reltyr directly, he disliked going around both the senior squad leader and Faisyn, his third squad leader. "She's worrying him."

"Yes, sir, but he's a good trooper."

"Most of the time. Unless someone baits him about her? Is that what happened? Or didn't she expect him to return from Madrien?"

"Both, sir," Longyl admitted.

"You don't think discharging him will help, then?"

"No, sir. More likely he'd kill her and the fellow hanging around her."

"What have you and Faisyn told Reltyr?" asked Alucius.

"Told him that he still had a job to do, and that he had a choice. He could stay until his term's up and get his pay and mustering-out bonus, or he could stay in and get the re-up bonus. Or he could walk out now, get caught and flogged for abandoning duty, maybe shot dead for desertion."

"You think he'll stay in line?"

"For now."

"Do you want me to draw him aside and tell him that I know times are hard for him, but that he's a good man, and that we need him?"

Longyl fingered his chin, squared the broad shoulders that topped a stocky, barrel-chested torso, then spoke. "I'd not be suggesting, Captain . . ."

"But it might help because he knows I'm married, and you're not, and he might feel I understood?" Alucius added, after a moment, "I'd have to tell him that we'd discussed his situation."

"Still might help. Might tell him that you're watching."

"I'll talk to him this afternoon." Alucius concealed the sigh he felt. In the end, so much came down to fear. He was the captain who had the reputation of seeing more than he did, of surviving more than he had, and of being the one no one wanted to anger or upset—for all that he'd never raised his voice in anger or ever violated militia—or, in the past,

Matrite—regulations. Of course, he'd bent more than a few. "What about Ashren? How is his arm doing?"

"Much better, sir. Looks like it will heal fine."

Alucius only had questions about two of those in third squad, but that was two more than in the first two squads, because he'd been forced to watch the first and second squads more closely. Faisyn, Egyl, and Sawyn were experienced squad leaders, and Longyl had been a great help. Alucius looked at the older man for a moment, then asked, "What do you make of the tracks across the river?"

"Someone's scouting." Longyl pulled on his left earlobe for a moment.

Alucius waited.

"I'd say it has to be the Southern Guard, but they don't want anyone to be able to prove it's them. If we were fighting, I'd say that we'd be seeing an attack." Longyl studied Alucius.

Alucius smiled, faintly, knowing that Longyl wanted Alucius's opinion, but didn't want to ask—a sign that Longyl wasn't absolutely certain. "They're scouting, and they're probably Lanachronan—or paid by the Lord-Protector."

"Sir, there was a message about Deforyan raiders . . ." ventured Longyl.

"That was sent from headquarters almost a month ago. No one's actually seen either the riders or the scouting parties." Alucius nodded. "Is third squad up to a patrol before dawn? Tomorrow, if the snow lets up?"

"I'll tell Faisyn to have the men ready."

"He might want to inspect their rifles. If we run into these brigands, or whatever they are, they may need them." Alucius grinned momentarily. "Don't have him tell them that, yet. Just that the captain expects their rifles in working order whether they're riding in a blizzard or a downpour."

Longyl grinned back. "Yes, sir. What time?"

"Three glasses before dawn. First squad will accompany us as well. I'll tell Zerdial shortly. You get to hold the post."

Alucius could sense the squad leader's resignation . . . and acceptance. Although riding out before dawn in winter was miserable, Longyl preferred action to post duty, but someone had to be in charge of the squads not on patrol. And since the early-morning, midday, and late-afternoon patrols hadn't found anything but cold trails, Alucius needed to take the patrol this time. "If we don't find anything, I'll have fourth squad out the next dawn, with second squad . . ." He stood.

So did Longyl. "I'll pass the word, sir."

"Make sure that they've all got their scarves and full undergarments." Alucius paused. "If you'd ask Egyl and Zerdial to come over?"

"Yes, sir." The squad leader nodded, then turned and left.

Alucius reseated himself and took out the sheets that held the past reports on Egyl's fourth squad. Outside of the vague reports on nonexistent Squawt raiders to the west and the supposed Deforyan raiders around Emal, neither he nor Feran had received any more information or instructions from militia headquarters. He feared he understood why. Given the uneasy peace between Lanachrona and the Iron Valleys, the Council certainly wouldn't want Colonel Clyon sending out messages warning about hostile Lanachronan activities, but Clyon did what he could to alert his all-too-few captains and companies.

Then, if Alucius happened to be reading the veiled messages correctly, and if he did run into Lanachronan Southern Guards in Deforyan or brigand guise . . .

The young captain shook his head. If . . . *if* that happened, he'd decide when he had to, based on the situation.

9

Lyterna, Illegea

Deep within the Vault of Lyterna, two men stood before the wall—a creation that few had seen over the past millennium, and one that fewer still would have believed could exist, for it was both a relief sculpture and a mural, the brilliant and varied colors seeping from within the very stone, rather than having been painted over the marble. Yet the wall appeared to have been carved from a single block of stone, for there were no lines that revealed joints.

The scene depicted a squadron of twenty Myrmidons, each of the ancient enforcers of justice seated upon his blue-winged pteridon, each pteridon flying below high clouds, each pteridon's beak of glittering blue crystal, and each Myrmidon carrying a blue metal skylance. From each lance, a ray of blue light shone down upon the ranks of an army drawn up upon the grasslands. And flames created by those rays of blue light were consuming all the soldiers of that massive army.

The younger man—the white-blond man in blue—studied the wall silently for a time before speaking. "It is truly a work of art. So lifelike. So perfect. One could imagine it had been created yesterday."

"It represents what was . . . and what might yet be, Aellyan Edyss," replied the white-haired councilor and guardian of the Vault. "If you have the will to make it so."

"If I have the will?" Edyss's voice was not shrill, nor querulous, but inquiring, not quite humorously. "How should I present my will, then, to make it so?"

"Address your desire to the wall, Aellyan Edyss, as directly as you can."

The younger man squared his shoulders and, eyes open, looked directly at the ancient flight leader of the Myrmidons. He did not speak, but his figure shimmered, silver-clad.

Abruptly, a section of the wall silently swung back, revealing a passageway.

Edyss looked at the dark opening, then at the older man. "A test?"

"All life is a test."

The warleader inclined his head to the councilor. "If you would, Councilor?"

The older man stepped through the oblong opening a yard wide and two high, and the nomad warleader followed. Once Edyss had passed the opening, it closed behind him, and the two walked in total darkness for a moment, until the councilor flicked on a light-torch and then handed a second to the younger man.

At the end of a marble-walled passage—also without seams—the two stepped into a vast dark hall. Edyss pointed his light-torch upward. The narrow beam revealed a smooth and flat stone ceiling, without detail, that looked to be more than forty yards above. He turned the beam to the right wall, playing it slowly away from him. The wall appeared to consist of featureless blue-tinged marble, within which were set at regular intervals a series of recesses, each roughly ten yards wide. Set back in each recess a yard was a flat expanse of what appeared to be blue crystal. The crystal rose but five yards, and the space above the crystal was empty all the way up to the high stone ceiling.

"If I might ask . . . Honored Councilor?"

"It is the Hall of the Last Myrmidons—or the first." The white-haired man's steps echoed softly in the vastness as he turned toward the first recess on the right.

Without questioning, Edyss followed, until the two stood before the flat crystal.

"Shine the light-torch and see what you will see."

Aellyan Edyss turned the light-torch upon the crystal wall. The crystal had looked far darker in the dimness and from a distance, but it was almost clear, and only lightly shaded with the merest hint of blue. On the left side was a small alcove, set into the crystal itself, an alcove roughly the shape of a man, but without any figure inside. Farther back in the solid blue crystalline mist, embedded within it, was a shape, one with massive blue leathery wings folded back, and with a long cruel blue crystal beak. The eyes were also of blue crystal, and they glittered like gemstones—or the blued crystals that had powered the lost skylances of the original Myrmidons. For all their glitter, for all their stillness, they held a dark intelligence. Set just below the thick neck and above the shoulders that anchored the wings was a blue leather saddle.

"Is this a mausoleum?"

"No. Just before the Cataclysm, the head of the Myrmidons created this. The crystal blocks the passage of time, of anything. When the crystal is dissolved, the pteridon will be as alive as it ever was, waiting for his new master and rider."

"How do I release them?" Edyss turned to the councilor.

"You must agree to bind yourself to the pteridon, as its master and rider, for so long as you both shall live. That is all."

"And none have agreed to do that?"

"None have united both Illegea and Ongelya before you, and there has been no need. As the guardians of the grasslands, and the protector of the Vault, we do not wish to see Lyterna fall under the Praetor and the iron bootheels of Lustrea—or the Lord-Protector of Lanachrona. There may be another such as you, but he has not come forward to claim the heritage, and you have."

Another item caught the attention of Edyss. "Is that . . . a skylance of the Myrmidons?" He gestured to the shimmering blue length of metal set in a holder beside the arrested figure of the pteridon.

The white-haired guardian smiled. "It is. Each skylance can only be borne and used by the pteridon's rider. It draws its power from the sun and the world, but the ancient texts state that it will take several weeks to regain its full potency."

"What of . . ." Edyss frowned. "Do pteridons mate?"

"The texts are silent on that, but I would judge that they do not, but are creatures created by the ancients from beyond."

"Not by the Duarches or their minions?"

"The Duarches used what they found, and they used it as wisely as they knew how, but most was a legacy from the ancients. All that has endured is what they created anew—the high roads, a few buildings—"

"Except for these pteridons," Edyss stated. "Are there any more?"

"Not that we know. Just these twenty. You must use them wisely."

"I will do what I can. That is all any man can do."

"That is what the Legacy requires." The councilor raised his hand. "We do not have all the words of the Legacy, but these are those we do have." He cleared his throat and stated,

> "In those ages, then, will rise a leader,
> who would reclaim the glory of the past,
> and more, as he would see it, in the sun,
> to make sure the dual scepter will always last."

"Is there more?" asked Edyss, honest curiosity in his voice.

"There is, but we do not know those words. They were writ in the stone, once, there." The councilor pointed his light-torch back to the wall above the passageway through which they had entered the hall. "But long before we found this hall the words of the two stanzas below the ones I recited were chiseled away. It is said that the Legacy was a long work, with sections chiseled and spread all over Corus, so that none would know all the words until Corus was once more united."

Aellyan Edyss smiled. "Then we must begin." He walked toward the man-shaped alcove. "Is this the one for the leader?"

"It is."

Aellyan Edyss stepped into the alcove, and the crystal block embracing the pteridon and the skylance began to glow.

The councilor swallowed and watched as the crystal shimmered, then dissolved into a thick blue mist.

10

In the chill of a Sexdi morning, in the darkness two glasses before dawn, the two squads rode quietly eastward from Emal, hoofs sometimes clicking on the frozen clay, at other times crunching and packing the new snow that would have been hoof deep, had it fallen more gently. Instead, the wind had swirled the dry white powder into knee-high drifts in places, and left the road clear in others. The gale that had buffeted Emal earlier in the week had died down to a light but bitter wind out of the northwest, with but a hint of the iron-acridness of the Aerlal Plateau.

While he was wearing the fleece and nightsilk undervest, Alucius still wished he had on his nightsilk skull mask. Instead, he wore the heavy black wool scarf and carried two rifles, a perquisite of being the captain, since he knew that he'd have little time to reload in the darkness—if they found the raiders.

The patrol on Tridi had found nothing, not even any signs of tracks, nor had those on Quattri and Quinti, but Alucius had decided that Twenty-first Company would keep searching until they found those who had been traveling the back roads. The patrols would also keep the company alert—and those troopers who weren't patrolling on a given day thankful for the comparative warmth and rest.

The two squads with Alucius were second and third squads, and Anslym and Faisyn rode beside Alucius, Faisyn on the left, Anslym on the right. The column was already almost ten vingts east of Emal, within two or three vingts of the hamlet of Tuuler. On the south side of the road, down a gradual slope, was the River Vedra, its frozen surface also covered intermittently with swirled snowdrifts.

Through a darkness illuminated slightly more than normal by the half-disc of Selena, Alucius continued to scan the road ahead, the frozen river, and the snow-covered bottomland fields to his left—both with his eyes and his Talent-senses.

"You think we'll find raiders this time, sir?" asked Anslym in a low voice.

"Sooner or later," Alucius replied. "Even if we don't, the men will learn what a winter campaign is all about." He paused, then added, "Why do they need that? Most everyone's time will be up by next winter, but that won't hold if the Iron Valleys get attacked. The Council will extend terms and conscript more recruits, and probably a third of your senior troopers will get pushed into being squad leaders in other companies."

"The way things are going," Faisyn said quietly, "that wouldn't surprise me."

"Because the Council has reduced the number of companies in the militia?" asked Anslym.

"They've always done that," Alucius said. "Troopers cost coins. If the Council had funded a militia large enough to warn off the Lanachronans, much higher tariffs would have fallen on the large traders in Dekhron. Since the Council is largely formed of such traders, the Council would not have passed an increase in tariffs that took many coins from the larger merchants. If the Council tariffed the small crafters and holds, they wouldn't have the coins to buy the goods of the large merchants. Either way, the merchants and traders who control the Council lose coins."

"There's another thing," Faisyn pointed out. "Conscripts don't get paid much for the first year."

"So . . . the Council waits until everyone knows there's a problem, then conscripts more troopers?" concluded Anslym.

"And they hope that the experienced companies can hold off whoever attacks until they can train and bring in more conscripts," Faisyn said. "That's why the colonel could persuade the Council to keep Twenty-first Company. Our pay is less than that of any other company with as much experience."

"We're about to earn it," Alucius pointed out. In the stillness and the winter cold, his Talent reached farther, and he'd been sensing something ahead. He'd finally been able to determine that somewhere ahead were riders—more than the ten to fifteen whose tracks Twenty-first Company had seen almost a week earlier. "There's a hint of mist or fog over the river to the east, and I think there are tracks there. I can't be sure yet, but I think we're going to run into those riders." Alucius looked through the dimness first at Anslym, then at Faisyn.

"What do you want us to do?" asked Faisyn.

"We're less than a vingt from Tuuler. You know the back lane on the north side of the town?" Alucius asked the older squad leader. "The one that goes to the north and right below the bluff?"

"Yes, sir."

"You take third squad on that lane. It joins the river road about a vingt east of the hamlet. It's likely the raiders will probably have passed you coming west by the time you get there. If there are tracks on the river road showing that, you turn west and follow them. You'll need to be ready. If they haven't reached you, you wait well back until they do pass, or until we come east on the river road. We'll set up an ambush in Tuuler. If we're successful, the stragglers should come back toward you. If you can, make sure none of them escape."

"Yes, sir."

Alucius turned in the saddle toward Anslym. "We'll take second squad into Tuuler—all the way through the hamlet to the eastern side, just short of the low rises on the road there. Half the squad will set up with you on the southwest side, and the other half will be with me. There's enough snow that the raiders should stand out against the white, even before dawn. We'll set up an angled cross fire and charge them." Alucius smiled, grimly, although he doubted either man could fully see his expression in the dimness.

"Charge—" Anslym broke off his involuntary exclamation.

"There are two possibilities," Alucius replied. "They're truly raiders, and they'll ravage our people. Or they're someone else's troopers posing as raiders. If we can catch them by surprise, do you think it's a good idea to let either one go?" He paused. "I'm going up to talk to the scouts." Alucius urged Wildebeast forward.

Behind him, Faisyn laughed, softly. "That's what captains are for, Anslym. That's what they get the golds for. If he's wrong, he has to face the colonel. Even if he's right, and I'd never wager against him, he'll have to explain."

As he drew his mount up toward the two scouts acting as the vanguard, Alucius knew that Faisyn had said what he normally wouldn't, in an effort to make things clear to the younger squad leader before they encountered the raiders.

"Sir?" asked the younger scout as he saw Alucius ease up beside him.

"Karstyn, I want you to move out to a good vingt on the main road. Be quiet. We've got reports of raiders, and there are signs that they may have crossed the river. If you see or hear anything, move back here, but silently. If you don't hear anything, wait for us at the crossroads in the middle of Tuuler, and watch all the dwellings and shops."

"Yes, sir."

"Waris . . . Squad Leader Faisyn will tell you where he wants you to go. Third squad will be circling north of Tuuler. Check with him."

"Yes, sir."

Alucius turned Wildebeast and headed back toward the main column, swinging back in ahead of the two squad leaders. After Faisyn passed his instructions to Waris, and the scout headed out, Faisyn and Anslym and their squads rode silently behind Alucius, the only sounds those of hoofs on stone or frozen clay, and the occasional *whuff* of a mount.

Another quarter glass passed before second squad reached the first holding on the western side of Tuuler. Alucius turned. "Faisyn . . . the lane heading north around Tuuler is just ahead. Swing off from the rear when we pass."

"Yes, sir." With a raised hand, the older squad leader turned his mount back toward third squad.

After he passed the lane, Alucius looked back several times, as if to make sure of the squad's movements, although he Talent-sensed the departure of third squad as clearly as if he had seen it in broad daylight.

"Anslym." Alucius motioned for the squad leader to join him.

"Sir."

"You remember the drills on single targeting? We're going to do that here. Your men—you'll take the right file, and I'll take the left one—will be lined up in a partly concealed position on the southwest side of the road. Your troopers are each to take aim at a different raider, the northernmost trooper to the northernmost raider. If they're in a double column, they're to fire at both men in that rank, the nearer one first. We'll be firing from more of an angle, but we'll be doing the same thing. Pass the word, then report back. Make it clear. We won't have time to go over this later."

"Yes, sir."

Second squad was nearing the crossroads that served as a square and center of Tuuler before Anslym rejoined Alucius.

"All set, sir."

"Good."

Karstyn appeared out of the dimness, riding toward the two at the head of the column. "Sir . . . all quiet, except at the shop on the left ahead. They're up awful early."

Even more than a glass before dawn, Alucius could see glimmers of light through the shutters of the small shop that served Tuuler as a dry goods store, factorum, and chandlery, glimmers that indicated lamps had been lit. He could also sense that at least two people were awake in the shop. "Too early for honest work. Anyone out? Any riders?"

"No, sir."

"Good . . . and thank you. Fall in behind us, for now." Through his Talent, with second squad far closer to the raiders, Alucius could discern that the strangers were riding in a double column, with even files and ranks, trooper-style. That alone told him that they weren't common raiders, if they were raiders at all.

Past the center of Tuuler, the scattered dwellings were dark, and Alucius could smell only the faintest hint of woodsmoke or coal smoke, a good sign that those in the houses had not yet risen.

On the eastern side of the hamlet, the road followed the river, curving slightly south, rising ever so sightly, just enough to conceal riders on either side. The oncoming raiders were less than two vingts away.

Alucius leaned toward Anslym. "You see that orchard there on the right? Station a trooper beside each tree, as close to it as he can get while mounted. They won't be able to see the orchard because of the rise to the south, not until they get within about a quarter of a vingt. But don't have your troopers fire until I give the order."

"Yes, sir."

"Rifles ready, Anslym. Pass the word."

"Rifles ready . . ."

"Now . . . right file with you, left with me."

"Second squad, left file, to the captain. Right file to me," Anslym ordered.

"Second squad, left file, follow me," Alucius commanded.

The nine troopers followed Alucius off the road and toward a low shed. He reined up behind the shed and went down the line, explaining. "We'll wait behind the shed until the last moment. Then, at my command, we'll ride out and do a quick wheel and fire, single-target style, first man at their first rank, second at their second . . ."

"Yes, sir."

Alucius stationed himself at the head of the single file, where he could remain mounted and appear to be peering around the corner of wooden shed. To the left of the single file, to the north and toward the Plateau, another hundred yards away, was a house, but he doubted that those inside, even if they heard and saw the troopers, would be likely to raise any alarm.

Before long, the faint sound of hoofs slipped through the darkness, a sound Alucius alone could hear, and a confirmation of what his Talent-senses had already revealed.

"Stand ready," he hissed.

Another fraction of a glass passed, and the raiders neared the orchard.

"Column forward." Alucius kept his voice low, waiting until all his troopers were clear of the shed. "Wheel in place. Second squad! Fire at will!" Alucius projected both his voice and a sense of command.

The chill air cracked apart under the almost simultaneous volleys from the north and southwest of the road. The militia force fired a good three volleys before a single lighter series of *cracks* came from the raiders.

As the voids of death and the agony of the wounded raiders swept over Alucius, a grim smile flicked across his lips. The glass after glass of training had clearly paid off.

"Withdraw! Back!" The command was in the Lanachronan dialect. That scarcely surprised Alucius.

Once he was certain that the raiders had turned, he eased Wildebeast back toward the road.

"Second Squad! Re-form!"

"Re-form on the captain!"

Alucius quickly reloaded with the speed of long practice and habit. Still, quick as the squad was, the last of the surviving raiders had vanished over the crest of the river road before second squad began the pursuit. That was fine with Alucius. There was no sense in riding into the volleys from third squad.

As second squad rode past the ambush site, Alucius made a quick and rough count of the dead—ten or eleven, and one raider dying. Once they dealt with the remaining raiders, they'd have to return and claim mounts and weapons, and deal with the bodies.

Less than two vingts past the rise, there was a swirl of men and mounts, outlined against the snow of the bottomland fields, with the sound of metal against metal and only a few reports from rifles. Most of those still mounted were the militia troopers, but the remaining raiders fought with a quiet ferocity.

"Sabres at the ready!" Alucius ordered. "Charge!" He had his own sabre in his left hand, although he was equally adept with it in either hand, unlike the rifle, where firing left-handed was definitely superior.

With Alucius at the point, second squad swept into the back of the raiders. In moments, most were down, one way or another.

As he studied the chaos of riders and riderless mounts, and the dead and dying raiders and troopers, Alucius could sense two riders turning and breaking away, driving their mounts off the road and across the fields toward the river. With some of third squad's troopers covering the road and trying both to stop the raiders and to corral the surviving mounts of the raiders, Alucius dared not use his rifle.

"Second squad! With me!" He urged Wildebeast forward, not looking back, but knowing at least some troopers would follow.

Less than halfway to the river, the lagging rider looked over his shoulder, then to the river, before he abruptly slowed and turned his mount.

Sensing fully the fatality within the raider—the resignation to death and the desire to take others with him as he reached for the rifle—Alucius lifted his own weapon, forced himself to concentrate, and fired. It took three shots before the void of the raider's death washed over him.

Within moments he was past the dead raider's mount and nearing the snow-covered underbrush at the edge of the river.

The single remaining rider had spurred his mount onto the ice of the river.

Alucius reined up at the edge of the river, quickly changed rifles, and focused all his will and Talent on the fleeing raider.

Crack!

The single shot was enough.

Alucius turned in the saddle to the two nearest troopers. "Skant, Noer . . . go and bring him back. We can use the mount if you can catch it, but we'll need the body and his rifle."

"Ah . . . yes, sir."

"I'll be back on the road, checking with the squad leaders." Alucius guided Wildebeast back uphill, through the crusty snow toward the river road, his herder hearing taking in the comments from the two.

". . . forgot how good he is with that rifle . . ."

". . . not even dawn yet . . ."

". . . see why they tried a night raid . . ."

"Didn't do 'em much good."

Alucius wasn't certain about that. Sometimes, failed raids had purposes, too. He just hoped that there was some evidence, but the fact that the raiders had all fought to the death was another indication that they weren't ordinary brigands.

Faisyn and Anslym were waiting on the road, overseeing the marshaling of the captured mounts.

"Did we lose anyone?" Alucius asked.

"Two, sir," answered Faisyn. "Silper and Daern. Gill took a slash, but he'll be all right."

"Sond took a bullet in his left arm. Shattered the bone," Anslym reported. "Stopped the bleeding, but I'm not sure how it'll heal."

"Have you got it splinted?" asked Alucius.

"Best we could, sir."

"Any survivors from the raiders?" In the grayness just before dawn, Alucius looked from Anslym to Faisyn.

"No, sir."

"Did any others escape?"

"No, sir," offered Faisyn. "Can't find any tracks, and no one saw any except the two you chased down."

"We'll need to search the bodies. Keep anything that might shed light on who they were. Then dump them at the edge of the fields to the north—where the sandwolves can get them." Alucius looked to Anslym. "I'd like to take a look at Sond's arm."

"He's on the north side of the road, there."

Alucius and Anslym rode toward the wounded trooper.

Even before he reined up, Alucius could sense the shattered bone.

"How are you doing, Sond?"

"Have to say . . . hurts, sir."

Alucius eased Wildebeast closer to the trooper's mount. There wasn't any infection yet, and the sections of what remained of the bones were lined up. Alucius fingered the splint, then let a trace of his Talent flow. He looked at the trooper, struggling to hang on to consciousness. "Looks like it'll take a while to heal, but, with luck, you'll keep the arm."

"Felt the bone go, sir."

"You'll make it, Sond." Alucius projected confidence, then turned. He couldn't afford to spend too much Talent that way, but it was unlikely that he'd have to use his Talent extensively for several days, and he owed what he could give to his troopers.

"Anslym . . . detail someone to ride with him, watch him, and keep him alert."

"Yes, sir."

Alucius reined up slightly to the north of where the squads had trapped the raiders. From what he could see, they had not worn uniforms, but with the near-identical gray woolen riding coats and black winter caps, they might as well have, although Alucius knew of no troopers in Corus who wore black and gray. He doubted that there were any.

The rifles the raiders had used were neither the heavy five-shot weapons used by the militia nor the lighter ten-shot weapons used by the Matrites. Nor were they Lanachronan, but something else.

All the circumstances indicated trouble ahead, and while he guessed the cause of the trouble lay with the Lord-Protector, it was only a guess. He could hope that what his troopers were gathering would provide evidence, but he had doubts that the evidence would point southward. The Lanachronans were far too devious for that.

He took a deep breath, feeling the chill, despite the lightening of the sky in the east with the coming of dawn. The squads still had a ride of several glasses back to Emal, with all the captured gear—and the wounded.

11

A glow that shone through the ground fog to the east signified dawn as the second and third squads of Twenty-first Company formed up to begin the ride back through Tuuler to Emal. It had taken more than a glass to gather together the fifteen captured mounts, those that had not scattered, and the weapons and personal effects of the raiders, but all were packed on the fifteen horses.

"Column forward!" Alucius ordered.

"Second squad! Forward!"

"Third squad . . ."

Alucius was more than a little worried. With the weapons they had carried, the riders they had killed had certainly not been traders. Nor had they carried anything that would have absolutely identified them. Their wallets had contained coppers and silvers, but no golds—except for that of one gray-bearded and hard-faced raider, whose figure and face looked far more like that of a trooper than a brigand. His wallet had held ten golds—an enormous sum for a raider or a brigand.

The young captain looked at the road ahead, a road now covered with hoofprints and tracks, despite the frozen clay. In places, there were splotches of blood, and in others, the carcasses of a few horses, too heavy to move easily.

"We didn't take that many casualties," Faisyn said from where he rode on Alucius's left. "For raiders, they seemed surprised when we attacked."

"They didn't expect an ambush in the middle of the night," Anslym pointed out.

"You're both right," Alucius said. "We're going to stop at the chandlery shop in Tuuler." Sensing Faisyn's puzzlement, he added, "Someone was up and had a fire going when we passed through, and that was two glasses before dawn."

"You think the raiders were headed to get supplies there?"

"We'll see."

As Alucius and the two squads passed the shed behind which he had set his part of the ambush and reached the outskirts of Tuuler, he could see the smoke rising from the chimneys of most of the scattered dwellings. Farther toward the crossroads, several dwellings had even opened their outer shutters to let light in, and a woman in a sheepskin jacket was standing on a side porch, throwing a bucket of water out onto the snow of the side yard. She looked at the riders, and the black winter riding parkas of the militia, and hurried inside, banging the empty bucket on the doorframe as she did.

Alucius looked toward the crossroads ahead, then spoke. "Anslym . . . take your squad to the back side of the shop. Have them with their rifles at the ready. I don't want anyone leaving."

"Yes, sir."

"Third squad will cover the front, while I go inside," Alucius told Faisyn. "I'd like to talk to the chandler."

"How many troopers do you want with you?" asked Faisyn.

"Four should be enough, I'd think, with the squads outside having their rifles at the ready," Alucius replied.

"Yes, sir. Third squad! Rifles ready! First two ranks, dismount and accompany the captain."

Just as third squad reined up before the chandlery, a man emerged from the door of the cooperage across the street—only long enough to take in the armed riders, and immediately retreat back into the shop.

Alucius dismounted, then climbed the two steps to the narrow wooden porch. The door was unlocked, and he nodded to one of the troopers, who stepped inside before Alucius. Alucius followed him into the shop, far warmer than outside.

The other three followed, sabres drawn.

Inside, at the back of the shop, little more than a large, single-room warehouse, stood two men beside a long bench. From the iron stove set on a small stone hearth next to the north wall radiated gentle warmth.

"I'm looking for the owner," Alucius announced.

"Who might you be?" asked the taller of the two by the bench, a burly man with a square-cut brown beard.

"Alucius, captain, Iron Valley Militia."

"You don't do much these days, Captain, except ride back and forth. It's not as though we're fighting folk, but I suppose you have to do what you're ordered to do." A wide and generous—and false—smile appeared on the man's face, exposing white but crooked teeth.

"I take it you're the owner?"

"You take it right. I'm Cephys."

"Are you usually open this early?"

A frown crossed Cephys's face, then vanished. "We're really not open yet. Usually folk don't show up until two glasses after dawn in winter."

Alucius nodded. "That's understandable. Mind if we look around?"

"Can't say as I like it, but you got four men with blades. Man would be less 'n wise to say no."

Alucius moved toward the bench.

The other man, younger, thinner, stepped back, his eyes wide. Cephys watched the militia captain intently.

"I see you've got some provisions laid out here. Are you expecting someone?" Alucius watched the chandler.

"That's why I was here early," Cephys admitted. "Some traders . . . said they were Deforyan. They came through a couple of weeks ago, said they'd be back on Sexdi this week." He frowned. "Should have been here already."

Alucius could Talent-sense that the chandler was more than shading the truth. "Did you ever see them before?"

"Not until two weeks ago."

The lie was obvious to Alucius, but he let it pass as he looked at the goods laid out in stacks along the long bench. He picked up one of the waxed wedges of hard cheese. "Riding supplies. Most of them made right here in Tuuler. Some even have the marks on them."

"Fellow said he wouldn't take unmarked goods. Said that too many folk tried to pass off shoddy or spoiled stuff on traders just passing through."

"I imagine he would say that," Alucius agreed, nodding.

"You think I'm lying?" Cephys's face stiffened in anger.

"No. I think you're telling the truth . . . this time." Alucius set down another wax-coated packet—one containing strips of dried beef—and turned. "I don't think your traders will be here. Was the one you made the agreement with a gray-haired, gray-bearded fellow?"

"No . . . but he was the one who paid the deposit."

Alucius could sense Cephys's sudden worry.

"We'd had reports of raiders," Alucius said. "So we were out early this morning, patrolling. We ran into some raiders. Most of them didn't escape." He smiled and shrugged. "I just thought you'd like to know."

"Raiders? Said they were traders. Wore good gray coats."

"That may be, but they fired a great number of shots for traders, and when they realized they were trapped, they fought to the death rather than be captured. Traders don't do that." Alucius turned back toward the door. "I wondered why they were headed to Tuuler. Now I know. Good day, chandler."

The wave of consternation and panic that emanated from the chandler told Alucius that the chandler had suspected something was not right, but that he had not known for certain—and that he was likely to be out coins he didn't have.

As Alucius stepped through the door, he caught the muttering of the chandler.

". . . horsedung . . . miserable militia . . ."

". . . careful . . . he's the one . . ."

Alucius couldn't catch the rest of the phrase, but he suspected he knew one of the phrases. Either it was about his being a herder or about his reputation as the killer captain.

He mounted quickly, then nodded at Faisyn. "We can go."

"Third squad! Column to the crossroads . . ."

Alucius turned Wildebeast, thinking. How could he lay too much blame on Cephys when the man was only following the example of the merchants who controlled the Council in Dekhron? He took a slow breath and resettled himself in the saddle.

Even with the sun close to burning through the mist that clung to the river valley, the ride back to Emal would be chill, if not nearly so cold as the ride out had been.

12

Catyr, Lustrea

The white morning sunlight did little to warm the second-floor workroom of the provincial armory. Chill winter winds from the Spine of Corus whistled outside the windows as the angular engineer looked down at the ancient workbench and at the black metal container resting upon a thin sheet of perfect green quartz. The container was approximately two-thirds of a yard long, a third wide, and a third in height. Within were an assemblage of crystals—none red nor pink—small silver metallic objects, and an empty silver bracket.

The thin man wearing the black and silver of a Praetorian engineer adjusted the contacts of a silver bracket and eased the green crystal into place before sliding the cover back over the black weapon. He looked up, then across the workbench at the gray-haired man in the silver vestments of the Praetor. "That was the last one. All ten are ready for battle."

"A good half year later than you had originally promised, Vestor."

"I could not have planned for whatever Talent-anomaly it was that shattered every red and purple crystal in all of Corus."

"No. *That* was not within your control. Have you discovered anything else about that, save that it appeared connected to the death of the Matrial?"

"No, Praetor. Whoever marshaled that Talent has done nothing at that level since then."

"And it could not have been the Matrial herself?"

"It is possible, but I think that would be too convenient an explanation."

The Praetor laughed. "Spoken like a true son of Lustrea. Convenience never operates to one's advantage." After the briefest of pauses, he continued. "I do not understand why your replica devices—the ones that mimic the Tables of the Recorders—show Tyren, and Aellyan Edyss, and even a herder and trooper who has been in three different uniforms in as many years, but they do not ever show the Lord-Protector of Lanachrona as one likely to hold or seek the dual scepter." The Praetor's voice was mild, but steel backed his words.

"I do not know, Praetor," Vestor replied carefully. "I would surmise that might be because Lanachrona is the pivot around which the entire future of Corus will turn, and a pivot is not an actor. Also, the device would not show all those seeking to hold the scepter, just those who might be capable. The militia officer might have the Talent, but not the ambition, while the Lord-Protector might have the ambition, but not the ability."

"Still . . . the Lord-Protector, young as he is, can marshal a force of far greater size and power than can this Aellyan Edyss."

"Aellyan Edyss holds the Council Vault at Lyterna. We do not know what that holds. It is Talent-shielded."

"Could he have devices such as these?" The Praetor pointed at the black metal box on the workbench.

"If he does, he has not yet removed them from the Vault. Even if he does, he may not be able to repair or use them."

"You can tell if he has such a weapon?"

"So long as it is not totally developed and operated by Talent, and so long as you can afford each replica mirror, Praetor. If the weapon is made by Talent and operated by one of Talent . . . then the glass will not show it."

"Are there such weapons?"

"Not since the Cataclysm," Vestor offered cautiously.

"Then those are golds well spent." The Praetor turned and looked in the direction of the small window at the west end of the workroom. "Once the worst of the snows abate, we will begin the campaign to take Illegea. While the high road is seldom fully blocked, with your devices, we will be able to assure that it remains clear for all of our legions. We will come upon this barbarian before he is ready, and before the grass grows high enough to nourish the mounts of his horse warriors. And before he becomes more ambitious." The Praetor added in a cold voice. "His insolence in tariffing our traders is not to be countenanced."

"He does appear insolent," Vestor said carefully.

"Insufferably insolent."

"Will Tyren be with us, Praetor?"

"Not for now. It is not wise to have both the Praetor and his successor on the same campaign. I have kept him well aware of both our plans . . . and your . . . capabilities, Vestor."

"You are most kind, Praetor."

"You mean I am most careful."

"That, as well."

As he departed, the Praetor's hearty laugh filled the armory workroom.

13

A gust of wind rattled the windows of the officers' mess, but Alucius continued to look down at the papers on the table. It was already midmorning on Septi, more than a day after the battle with the raiders, but he really couldn't finish writing his report to militia headquarters until he heard from Haesphes. He wiped the pen clean and closed the inkwell, then stood and walked to the door. Smoke was coming from the chimney of the armory.

With a shrug, and without bothering to don his parka, Alucius stepped out of the small outpost headquarters. For a moment, he surveyed the courtyard, kept free of snow by troopers with shovels—a measure that provided both exercise for the troopers and freedom from endless mud when the spring thaw came. Then he walked across the courtyard to the squarish stone building that was the armory. His boots crunched on a patch of the crusty snow that had escaped the shovels and softened with the momentary thaw of the afternoon before and then refrozen. Officially, winter would be over in another week, but the snow would likely persist for several more weeks, before melting and turning the roads—and everything else—into a muddy mess.

Once at the armory, he opened the door and stepped inside. Despite the heat radiating from the iron stove set against the stones of the south wall, the armory was chill. Alucius looked at the rifles on the armory bench, then at Haesphes, the elderly armorer, who had just returned to the militia outpost that Septi morning. Alucius couldn't blame the armorer for wanting to go to his daughter's funeral, but Haesphes' absence had not been at the most convenient time.

"What do you think?"

Haesphes looked up, then coughed, and cleared his throat, twice. Finally, he spoke, with the thick accent common to those who lived on the upper reaches of the River Vedra. "They're Deforyan rifles, sir, or so much like to them as none could tell the difference."

"You think someone copied them?"

"Not all of them. Five of them have the maker's mark, and Deforyan issue numbers. You can find issue numbers on Lanachronan rifles and Matrite rifles, too. Iron Valleys is about the only place you don't find issue numbers."

"Why didn't they copy the issue numbers? Or put false ones there?"

"Extra work . . . or they wanted to be able to claim that the rifles were copies." Haesphes shrugged. "Good workmanship, though. It's as good as if they were Deforyan, and they make good weapons. That's one reason why Deforya has stayed independent."

"And one reason why the Lord-Protector would like to take it over?" Alucius speculated.

"I'm just an armorer, Captain," Haesphes protested.

Alucius laughed. "You know more than any of us captains, I'd wager, and you've seen a great deal over the years."

"Not so much as you, sir, from what I've heard tell."

"You're older, and you've listened. Who else could make those weapons? You could. So could the Matrite's workshops at Salcer, but I doubt either of you did."

Haesphes pursed his lips, then looked toward the iron stove before turning back toward Alucius. "Elcoyn could. Apprenticed in Dereka, years back, and he's got a place in Dekhron. Probably three or four in Lanachrona could. And, I've heard tell, a good number in Lustrea."

"So . . . either Elcoyn did or someone in Lanachrona did," Alucius said.

"Most likely."

"Is there any way to tell from the rifles you have?"

"Not here. If I watched an armorer, I could see if certain patterns showed in the metalwork and woodwork. Without that . . ." Haesphes shook his head.

"Thank you. Can you keep them locked away? The commandant may want to see them."

"Aye. I can do that."

"Thank you." Alucius paused. "I was sorry to hear about your daughter." He didn't know quite what else to say, although he could sense the older man's sadness. "I wish there were something I could do."

"It was sudden-like, sir. Nothing anyone could have done. But I thank you."

"I wish I could have." Alucius nodded, then turned and slipped out of the armory.

He stopped in the middle of the courtyard, feeling the slight warmth of a white sun that had finally burned through the ground fog of the morning. The wind had changed, and now blew out of the south, far more warmly. If there weren't any more raids in the next week or so, and if the warming continued, there might not be any more after that because the river ice would be breaking up.

Was that the reason why the raiders had been in Tuuler when they were? He frowned, then continued back toward the small headquarters building. He still had to add in the details on the rifles to finish his report to the colonel.

The mess remained empty, and his papers were untouched, not that he would have expected otherwise. He sat down and began to write once more.

He'd written perhaps an additional half page when he heard steps in the corridor. He looked up as the door to the mess opened, and Feran stepped inside, unfastening his parka.

"You're back early." Alucius said.

"Just three days." Feran shook his head. "It was easier that way, even getting up before dawn this morning in Fiente." The older captain extended an envelope with the black wax seal of the militia commandant. "Here."

The outside stated: CAPTAIN ALUCIUS, EMAL OUTPOST.

Alucius did not open the message. "Did you get one?"

"Late last week. The colonel knows my family. He tracked me down in Dekhron. After reading what he sent me, I decided to come back early. I let him know, and he gave me that to bring you." Feran laughed harshly. "Vinkin said you'd had some action."

"Raiders, clad as Deforyans, with Deforyan rifles. Yesterday."

"And?" Feran lifted his eyebrows.

"There were about twenty-five. There weren't any survivors. Third squad lost two troopers, and second and third squads each had one wounded."

"How did you manage that?"

"Ambush two glasses before dawn at Tuuler. They had arranged for supplies there. I'd wondered about that, but we didn't find that out until after it was all over."

Feran nodded slowly. "I see."

Alucius suspected he knew what Feran saw, but asked anyway. "See what?"

"Why the colonel put Twenty-first Company here." Feran offered a lopsided smile and gestured to the envelope. "Open it. I want to see your reaction."

Alucius broke the seal and read the message silently.

Captain Alucius—
The Lord-Protector of Lanachrona has sent a strong statement to the Council. He claims that the Iron Valleys are providing sanctuaries for Deforyan raiders who have been crossing the River Vedra and terrorizing the peace-loving people of Lanachrona. The Council wishes to know why they have not been informed about these events.

As you may recall, I had sent a warning early in the winter about such a possibility. Therefore, at your earliest convenience, I would appreciate a report on the situation, including a detailed summary of the actions you have taken to stop such depredations.

The signature and seal were those of Clyon, Colonel and Militia Commandant.

Alucius looked up.

"In a way, I'm glad we were on furlough," Feran said. "I've already reported on what Fifth Company did in the early winter, and what we plan if the so-called raids continue. But it doesn't look like they will."

"Not for a time," Alucius agreed. "Not until whoever it is learns that they lost everyone." He paused. "I'll write my response, but I think you should look at the weapons and mounts and gear we captured, and send a message with your own conclusions about them. Otherwise, the colonel will get accused of slanting the reports because they come from the one company commander most indebted to him."

"You're probably right. After I get my mount settled . . ."

"You didn't—"

"No. Left him with Vinkin. I wanted to see what you thought."

"Haesphes has the rifles under lock. Vinkin has the mounts in the east end of the stable. I've got the personal effects, such as they are."

"I'll look at them." Feran turned and left the small mess room.

Alucius took a deep breath. Now he'd have to rewrite the report.

By the time he'd redrafted the report and gone to work on the letter to the colonel to cover it, Feran had returned to the mess and begun his own letter.

When Alucius finished the draft of the cover letter, he cleared his throat.

"Yes?" asked Feran.

"Would you read this?"

"Lucky me." But Feran took the draft and read through it, with Alucius standing and rereading it over his shoulder.

Colonel Clyon
Commandant, Militia of the Iron Valleys
Dear Colonel Clyon—
Your message of twenty Duem reached us today. We had only seen tracks of the raiders beginning around the fifth of Duem, and we have been doing our best to track and to corner them.

You will be pleased to learn that yesterday the second and third squads of Twenty-first Company cornered the raiders, numbering almost thirty, and in a predawn attack on the east side of Tuuler, wiped them out to the last man. We have saved all their weapons and other materials. Their rifles appear to be of Deforyan style and manufacture, but more than half their mounts were shod with the iron-star shoes of the Southern Guard. I cannot speculate on how this may have occurred, but we will be especially vigilant in making sure that no other raiders are successful in using the area around Emal as a haven for attacks on us or upon Lanachrona. A copy of my full report on the attack is attached.

After he finished, Feran handed the draft back to Alucius.

"What do you think?" asked the younger captain.

"Smart. You don't draw any conclusions."

"He will, but it's better that way."

"Much better." Feran shook his head. "I can't wait to tell the company that there's trouble on the way."

"Another war, you think?"

"Might not be that obvious. Then, it might. Either way, people are going to be shooting at us."

Alucius knew he was right. He just didn't know who was playing what game. Was the Lord-Protector using the "raids" as an excuse to move into Deforya when spring came, or to take on the Iron Valleys? Or had someone else set up the raids? And if so, who? And why? Could one of the Council? Like Elcoyn? But why?

He had no answers, not ones he could place coins upon.

So, rather than stew about what he could not change, he took out another sheet. He could certainly write another letter to Wendra and let it wind its way from Dekhron to Iron Stem. It would be weeks, in all likelihood, before she saw it, but he'd never forgotten his failures to write once before—and the regrets those failures had engendered.

He glanced down at the silver-rimmed black crystal of the herder's wristband, and the depth of the crystal for a moment, thinking about the matching ring that his wife wore. Then, with a smile, he dipped the pen in the inkwell.

14

Dekhron, Iron Valleys

Two men sat at a small table in the back corner of the noisy café, watching a man with a gitar accompanying a woman dressed in yellow. The dark-haired singer's voice was low and sultry, yet carried through the low-ceilinged room.

> ". . . Selena was full with faith and light,
> so long ago, on that summer night,
> when you swore that you'd be true,
> but now my heart is filled with rue,
> for loving a man inconstant as the dew . . ."

The round-faced man in a severe blue tunic turned from the singer to his companion, a sharp-featured and white-haired trader, whose fingers tapped on the oiled wood of the tabletop in time to the rhythm of the gitar. The older trader appeared not to notice.

Finally, the man in blue spoke, his voice low. "Tarolt . . . you said those men were reliable."

"They were," answered Tarolt. The white-haired trader's lips drew into a brief and cruel smile. "They died on the task. A pity . . . but at times matters take a course of their own. You should know that, Halanat."

"One man—and they failed? Four of them?" Halanat's eyes traveled to the shapely singer for a moment before returning to rest on Tarolt. "And it has taken you nearly a month to discover what occurred?"

"They attempted an attack in the dark. They were killed and eaten by sandwolves. I do imagine that the sandwolves left very little. They are not wasteful by nature. Or so I am told."

"Eaten, anyway. Who is to say that he did not kill them and leave them for the sandwolves?"

"That may be," pointed out Tarolt, "but there were no bullets found, and their wallets were not touched, nor their weapons, nor their mounts. All were found and returned by one of the local herders, a neighbor of the captain's. The herders are most honest about that sort of matter, you understand."

"He could have used a sabre. They stick together, those herders."

"That could be, but there were witnesses that claim they were killed by sandwolves." The pale-faced Tarolt smiled the cold smile once more. "Nothing has been lost. They are dead."

"Except for the captain."

"But even if he did kill them, he would not know why they were there. Or who had sent them. And, should he be bright enough to guess, he will certainly see the more obvious possibilities . . . the action against him might even persuade him not to be so supportive of the colonel. Or not to follow his grandsire and that old fool Kustyl so blindly. He might even come to see that the alliance is most necessary, and that will only lead to weakness among these Coreans." Tarolt tapped his fingers briskly again. "He has no evidence, and there is no one who would believe a mercenary renegade, and even less would anyone understand what is truly at stake."

"Those who serve him know better."

"But few others. Very few. We will continue to do what we can to erode the colonel's position."

"What of the captain? Are we to—"

"We will let others do what they can, now. If they fail, then we will see."

"And Weslyn?"

"Without the colonel, he stands alone. He will do as the Council wishes, and they will do as we wish."

Halanat nodded in agreement.

Both men returned their scrutiny to the singer.

15

Nearly a week had passed since Alucius had dispatched two troopers with his message to Colonel Clyon. The clouds had broken, and the sun had poured out warmth on the River Vedra valley. The wind had continued to blow out of the south.

Alucius stood outside the headquarters building in the mild air, waiting for Bakka, the first squad scout. The courtyard of the outpost was dusty, because there had been little snow to melt within the walls. Outside the outpost, the streets of Emal were shallow rivers of mud, as was the river road.

The troopers of fifth squad were taking a break from the blade drills, a break given after Alucius had seen Bakka ride into the courtyard. Most of them stood in the sunlight, breathing heavily from their one-on-one drills with covered sabres.

The scout emerged from the stable, glanced around before catching sight of Alucius, then headed toward his captain.

"I'm sorry, sir, but it took a time to brush all the mud off my mount."

"That's fine," replied Alucius. "I imagine there was a great amount of mud."

"Yes, sir."

"What did you find?" asked Alucius. "Besides mud?"

Bakka glanced down at the dusty clay of the courtyard for a moment, then at the captain. "There weren't any signs of anything, sir. I looked over the riverbanks good, like you said, but I didn't see any signs of rafts or boats, or anyone watering loads of mounts. No wagons tracks, or hoofprints along the shoulders of the road. No new tracks around the place where you ambushed the raiders. I rode around Tuuler. That's where it was the muddiest—"

"What was the mud like there?" asked Alucius.

Bakka grinned sheepishly. "Well, sir. I was thinking that it might be because they'd had riders. I was real careful. Even checked the back lanes. Reason it was so muddy was because someone had left open the gate on one of the irrigation ditches and when the water started to rise . . ."

Alucius laughed. Then he frowned. Could that have been a way to cover tracks? He shook his head. He doubted that even the most adventurous trooper leader or any brigand would go to that trouble. One of the problems with being a captain was a growing suspicion of everything.

The other aspect of being captain that Alucius hated was not being able to do his own scouting. As captain, he could no longer scout, not out alone by himself, where he was most effective, and he had no one who was anywhere near as good as he was. So often he felt almost blind in relying on his scouts, even as he did his best to coach them.

"Sir?"

"I'd wondered . . . never mind." Alucius offered his captain's professional smile. "Thank you, Bakka. Report what you told me to your squad leader. Carry on."

"Yes, sir." Bakka nodded and turned.

Alucius looked out over the walls toward the silver-green sky to the east and the faint hazy clouds that suggested that the warming would continue for at least another day. Then he turned at looked northward at the towering ramparts of the Aerlal Plateau.

Although he had his own ideas, he still had no firm answers or proof as to why anyone would want to raid Tuuler—or even create the impression of using Tuuler as a staging base. Nor did he have any response from Colonel Clyon, and he wasn't sure which bothered him more.

He turned and walked back toward the center of the courtyard, nodding toward Sawyn. "Fifth squad! Break's over. We'll go to two on one, now."

At least, Alucius reflected, he'd keep sharpening his company's weapons skills.

16

Borlan, Lanachrona

The majer in the blue-and-cream uniform knocked on the door, then straightened his tunic nervously.

"Come on in, Ebuin." The captain-colonel was sitting behind a dark oak table desk, but rose as the more junior Southern Guard officer entered and closed the door behind him.

"I have a report, sir."

"What's wrong now?" asked the captain-colonel.

"Sir?"

"You always smile when you have bad news, and you shift your weight from foot to foot. You need to break that habit." The captain-colonel's smile was open and friendly. "Sit down and tell me about it." He reseated himself and waited.

Majer Ebuin sat on the edge of the straight-backed chair, looking squarely at his senior officer. "The marauder squad . . . it's disappeared. From what our informants in both Emal and Dekhron can tell us, the Iron Valleys Militia wiped them out to the last man."

"To the last man? That seems . . . extreme."

"They ran into the militia's Twenty-first Horse. The captain—the one you had expressed concerns to me about—reported to militia headquarters that he had run into a group of Deforyan brigands. Apparently, none of them survived his attack."

"Your sources are good?"

"The same as always, sir."

"And none of them escaped? He must have gone out determined to destroy them." The captain-colonel nodded, then tugged at his earlobe. "He is a determined type. We had reports that he was rather good. I had been assured that some other . . . efforts . . . might have solved that problem, but they didn't work out either. I'm not as pleased as I could be. The Lord-Protector doesn't like bad news, and that means that Marshal Wyerl doesn't. And we don't want to make the marshal unhappy."

"No, sir."

"Your idea of using Deforyan rifles was a good touch, though." The captain-colonel's open smile returned. "Have you any other ideas along those lines?"

"Make an attack at Emal from the east—with two companies. The attackers should be attired in the tunics of Deforya."

"Why would we want to do that?"

"You can test the strength of the Iron Valley Militia, perhaps weaken it—and blame the attack on the Landarch of Deforya."

"Not a bad idea—unless we lose more troopers, and that would be likely against the Twenty-first Company. If we go against the Fifth, we would not lose so many, but there wouldn't be much point in that, now, would there? Besides, we may need those troopers in the future. We would rather do without their captain, however."

"We know the patrol schedules, and we can make sure that the captain of the Twenty-first gets information to put him in the right place."

"I'm sure you can, but we can't go around having Southern Guards attacking the Iron Valleys—even in Deforyan tunics, and even if they annihilate this . . . problem. And it would be even more embarrassing if someone were to be captured. And explaining . . ." The captain-colonel shrugged. "You understand."

"Can you give me leave and the funds to hire two hundred mercenaries?" asked Ebuin.

"That might be possible, if you can make sure that whoever hires these brigands speaks in the dialect of the Deforyans. It will take a week or so to gather the Deforyan golds, also." After a moment, the captain-colonel added, "You might see if your agents could hire a sniper or two. Or three. We'd really rather keep the troopers. They could be useful in the east, if it comes to that."

"Yes, sir."

17

In the dim glow of a single oil lamp in the small mess room, well past sunset and the evening supper of excessively aged and baked mutton, Alucius and Feran sat on opposite sides of the table, Feran's leschec board between them. The first two weeks of spring had passed, and the mud that had covered almost every thoroughfare and lane had finally begun to disappear, either into dust or damp packed clay.

"We still haven't heard anything from the colonel," Alucius said, moving his lesser pteridon.

"You're going to win again," Feran said resignedly. "I don't know why I play with you. You can spot me your soarer queen, and three foot-warriors, and I still can't beat you. You could have made a small fortune if you'd played when you were a ranker."

"That's why I didn't. It's why I don't play for coin," Alucius replied, almost absently. "Why do you think the colonel hasn't replied?"

"Maybe he has. If the roads west of here are as bad as ours are . . ."

"Three weeks is a long time."

"What could he say?" countered Feran, his voice turning ironic as he continued. "Captains, thank you so much for confirming that mischief is afoot and for embarrassing someone so dramatically. Of course, I can't say that officially, and if I make any guesses, it will upset either the Council, the Lord-Protector, the Landarch of Deforya, or perhaps all three."

Alucius laughed, heartily. "Thank you! That's the best explanation you could have made, and probably the most correct."

"If it is," Feran replied dourly, "I'll be a captain here or at Rivercliff until I receive a stipend, and that's another ten years."

"You want to be a majer like Weslyn? Or Dysar?"

"I could do as well as Dysar did. Anyone could have. He was the kind that makes sour peaches taste good," Feran pointed out.

"The Council liked him."

"Of course they did. He didn't want to spend coins on weapons or training or replacement mounts. He arranged for the worst and cheapest provender, unless it was provided by one of his family's friends. Weslyn tries, in his own way. We actually have a few spare mounts, now."

"And the food usually isn't spoiled."

Feran tipped the sander king sideways on the leschec board. "I don't see any point in continuing the game." He shook his head. "You think life is one big leschec game?"

"I'd hate to think so," Alucius replied. "It's played too badly for that, from what I've seen."

"But do we see everything?" countered Feran as he began picking up the pieces and replacing them in the battered wooden box.

"I'm sure we don't, but there's an awful lot of waste in what I've seen."

"Sometimes, I wonder."

"Don't we all." Alucius stretched, then stood. "I ought to get some sleep. I'm going out with fifth squad in the morning."

"At dawn?"

"We're forming up at dawn."

"When we take over the patrols next week, we're not going that early," Feran promised.

"It has its advantages. We see more, and the men get more time off when we get back."

"I'd rather get more sleep."

"Go to bed earlier," Alucius suggested humorously as he turned toward his small room.

"You herders . . ." Feran laughed again.

18

By the third week of Triem, the roads around Emal were actually usable, with farmers and peddlers occasionally traveling into town. Alucius and Feran had been able to send out road patrols without it taking a half day to travel three or four vingts, although the patrols had revealed nothing untoward. The rankers of the Third Foot squads, charged with bridge duty and collecting tariffs—always small—and nominally under Feran's command, had reported nothing strange among those crossing the bridge to or from Semal.

In the sunny late-Quattri afternoon, with a light breeze playing across the courtyard of the outpost, the two captains were standing outside the headquarters building, watching as their troopers unloaded the three supply wagons that had finally arrived from Dekhron, along with the two returning troopers that Alucius had sent with his report almost a month earlier. Alucius and Feran had already locked the two pay chests into the small strong room before returning to monitor the remainder of the off-loading.

The two troopers walked from the stable toward the captains. They had tried to brush the dust and mud off their uniforms, but from their boots and their trousers below the knees, it was clear that parts of the river road were still quagmires.

"Captain . . . we have three messages. Two are from Colonel Clyon. That's one for each of you, and one . . ." Firtal grinned as he extended an envelope to Alucius. "It's personal-like, sir, I wager."

Alucius returned the smile and reached for his wallet, extending six coppers, three for each trooper, the going rate for such "unofficial" messages. "I'll probably appreciate the last one most, Firtal."

"Seeing as it looks to be from a woman, sir."

"My wife," Alucius said with a smile.

"Thought as much, sir, when the herder brought it to me."

"Do you remember what herder?"

"Said his name was Kustyl, and since he had business in Dekhron, he brought this from his granddaughter. Remembered that, sir, cause he didn't look old enough for a daughter you'd be . . . well . . ." Firtal flushed.

"He is, believe me," Alucius said. "And he's a good herder, one of the best." Alucius grinned. "And we've not been married but a year."

"No wonder you were looking for that message," Feran said.

The troopers smiled more widely.

"Enough," Alucius said, mock-gruffly. "We'll need to read the messages from the colonel first." He wasn't looking forward to that message, one way or another.

"Yes, sir." Firtal and Doonan nodded and stepped away, trying hard to keep the smiles from their faces.

Alucius tucked the message from Wendra inside his tunic and broke the black wax seal of the colonel's message. Feran opened his as well. Both captains read silently, as the troopers continued to unload the wagons.

The colonel's message was brief, and the heart of it was in two short paragraphs that Alucius read twice.

At the moment, the militia is running short on both coins and supplies. While I trust that the pay chests, the ammunition, and the provender that accompanies this message will not be the last, as commandant, I cannot promise any quick resupply. I have presented the problem to the Council, and I am confident that they will act upon it with due deliberation, given the gravity of the situation.

The Council has also asked me to convey to all officers of the militia the seriousness of the present situation. For this reason, the

Council requests great caution in any maneuvers or actions that could be mistaken as hostile actions. Because of the seriousness of the finances of the Iron Valleys, I will state the situation more directly. Do not fire upon anyone unless they fire upon you first, and do not undertake any actions which you cannot successfully complete within the supplies and ammunition at hand.

Alucius winced. His grandsire and Kustyl had certainly foreseen the problem. Alucius still had problems believing that the Council could have let the situation get that bad.

He frowned. Then . . . that could be the reason. Only if the situation were untenable . . . Was that why Kustyl had been in Dekhron? Wendra's grandfather had always known more than Royalt, and Alucius had wondered how. Now, he had a good idea.

"What are you thinking?" asked Feran.

"That we're going to end up as a province of Lanachrona after all," Alucius said.

"How do you figure that?"

Alucius shrugged. "We've just been told—I'm guessing your message is the same as mine . . ." He let the words drop off and handed his to the older captain.

Feran glanced over what Alucius had handed him, then nodded, and handed the missive back. "Same words. Only thing different is the address." He glanced toward the wagons being emptied. "We got more supplies than usual."

"I'd wager that the colonel got them on account, before the Council told him there were no more coins."

Feran glanced down at his own missive, then looked up. After a moment, he walked to one corner of the headquarters building, then back. He stopped and stared at the younger captain. "I don't like your wager." His voice was rueful.

"Do you think I do?"

"Those coin-pinching, offal-swilling, sluts' sons . . . Fifteen years I've given them, and it's come to this?" Feran's voice was low and bitter.

Alucius could understand all too well. He was lucky to have made it back to the Iron Valleys, where he had a family and a stead. Had he still been in Madrien . . . he would have faced what Feran might. "It might not."

"You wouldn't wager your family's stead on it, would you?"

"No. But, if it comes to that, we could lose it. We almost did when they raised the tariffs during the Matrite War."

"Those spawn of a dunghill . . . those . . ." Feran shook his head slowly.

"Whatever it is, it hasn't happened yet."

"It will." Feran's laugh was more like a bark. "You don't look that surprised. Do you have any idea why?"

"Not for certain. I'd heard that the Council borrowed six thousand golds to keep the militia going during the Matrite fight—and that they reduced the tariffs so quickly after the war that they didn't have enough to repay the loan."

"Who would lend them that?"

"The Landarch of Deforya, or so I was told. Except he sold it to the Lord-Protector."

"Asterta save us . . . What I said about the Council was generous." Feran's lips tightened. "And that message means that we'll be seeing Southern Guards on our lands, and we can't do anything?"

"I don't know," Alucius said thoughtfully. "If they're pressuring the Council, I wouldn't think they'd do that."

"You're right. The Council might be that stupid, but the Lord-Protector isn't." Feran glanced toward the south wall of the outpost, in the direction of the river and of Lanachrona. "Why would he offer that caution?"

"In case we do have to fight later?" Alucius suggested.

"That would follow." Feran turned. "Can you watch the unloading? I need to go off and think."

"I'll take care of it." Alucius understood Feran's consternation. The older officer had worked his way up through the ranks and had served the militia long and loyally—and was seeing that everything he'd done and risked his life for might well be thrown aside. Alucius had done the same—but not so willingly, and certainly not for nearly so long.

Once Feran had slipped back into the building, Alucius slipped the missive from the colonel into his tunic and slipped out the one from Wendra.

Dearest one—
You are so thoughtful to write, even when I know you have much to do, but it is a treasure to see your words upon the page . . .

Your grandsire has taken me out with the flock a number of times now. He was surprised to learn that the rams would follow my lead and instructions, and so was I. I can see even more why you so love the stead, and I love you the more for your love and kindness, knowing and seeing what I have seen . . .

Alucius smiled to himself. She was a herder. He'd felt it, but he hadn't known for certain.

. . . the harder part has been learning to handle the rifles to your grandsire's satisfaction, but I actually hit a sander and drove it off . . . even before your grandsire rode up . . .

A sander? In the late winter?

Grandpa Kustyl and your grandsire both have asked me to tell you to act with great care, for the financial arrangements about the large note taken out in Dekhron have come to pass as you were told, and pardon me, but you will understand if I do not spell out the details, for herders should not. You should be most prudent with your personal goods as well, for we may not be able to send you any . . .

Alucius paused and reread the lines. They would not have sent him personal goods in any case, but the words were there as a reinforcement.
Feran was right to be worried.
Alucius looked back at the graceful letters upon the page. Despite the

clear warning and the ominous tone, he was glad to have received the missive, and glad once more that he and Wendra had been able to share what brief times that they had, and glad that he had seen how special a girl had been at a gather so many years before.

19

On the Septi three days after the arrival of his letter from Wendra, Alucius was up early, unable to sleep, and rather than toss in his blankets, he washed and dressed well before dawn and made his way from his quarters out into the darkness of the courtyard, past the sentry from the second squad of the Third Foot, who acknowledged him with a challenge, and then out onto the deserted cobblestone causeway to the bridge.

He walked slowly, silently, stopping short of the foot of the bridge. He looked out into the clear sky, with the full greenish disk of Asterta hanging well above the river bluffs to the west of Emal. Asterta—the ancient moon of the horse goddess, half of the duality—with Selena—that the ancient Duarchy had embodied. Balanced duality, the goddess of war and the goddess of peace, sharing the heavens, and for millennia, or so the ancient texts and roads proclaimed, that balance had brought prosperity. But had it?

From what Alucius had seen in his short life, he wondered about the truth of those ancient legends.

He looked down from the moon at the black surface of the river, flowing westward toward Dekhron. Kustyl had been in Dekhron, and Wendra's letter had been about more than love and longing. It had also been clear enough in suggesting that times were unsettled and likely to become more so—and that the Council had been unable, or unwilling, to take the steps to repay the debt they had incurred in the Matrite War.

While the Landarch of Deforya had no real way to require repayment, and doubtless knew it, that lack of ability did not apply to the Lord-Protector of Lanachrona. The only real question in Alucius's mind was how exactly the Council would sell out to the Lord-Protector. The traders in Dekhron, and those few others all along the Vedra, probably had more in common with Lanachrona than they did with crafters of Iron Stem and the herders of the north, and the nightsheep herders were few and far between across the arid quarasote plains. Alucius doubted if, even with wives and children, they numbered more than five hundred. And five hundred could do little against the thousands in Dekhron, and the tens upon tens of thousands in Lanachrona.

He turned toward the bridge itself, where nothing moved. There was but a single bridge guard at night—although there was a large bell atop the guardhouse with which he could summon aid—and the iron gate was locked. The gate was tall enough to accommodate a rider and wide enough for most wagons, although at times some traders had been forced to disassemble their wagons and slide the wagon beds through sideways. The gate was also far enough out onto the bridge, if on the south side, that while an individual *might* be able to climb over or around the barbs on its extended edges, that individual certainly would not have been able to carry much in the way of goods. Neither the Iron Valleys nor Lanachrona was that concerned about individuals. Both wanted the tariffs from the others' traders or from any goods crossing the river.

Alucius suspected that the real purpose of guards and gate was to force those traders with goods of greater value to travel through Dekhron and the smaller city of Salaan on the Lanachronan side of the River Vedra. The Lanachronans probably didn't care that much, since little enough trade came to the eastern arm of the Iron Valleys, but the traders who made up the Council of the Iron Valleys cared greatly enough to keep two horse companies and two squads of foot stationed in Emal.

On the far side of the bridge and river, there were no lights in the hamlet of Semal, not a one, and Alucius had seldom seen any there, except early in the evening, and certainly none late at night or well before dawn.

The faintest of silver-green radiances washed over him from his left, and he turned, slowly, sensing the clean greenness of a soarer. But for a moment, she hovered there, a small womanly figure with wings of silver-green light that extended yards from her shoulders. Then she was gone, as if she had never been.

Not a message, not a thought, not even a gesture . . . but Alucius shivered. Soarers had only appeared for him when his life had changed or was about to change. Then, he reflected with a self-deprecating smile, he had already known his life was about to change. He just wasn't sure how.

20

Lyterna, Illegea

Shadows still cloaked the redstone spires of the Council Vault, even as the harsh white early-morning light of the sun poured over the peaks to the east that composed the Spine of Corus. Against the shadows, the timeworn crimson stone spires, carved ages before out of the cliffs, stood out as a hard red.

Legions of the new Myrmidons, all in their blued armor, stood on the steps leading up to the Vault, but they faced westward, looking down upon the polished redstone plaza beneath those steps. Upon the plaza were twenty pteridons, creatures from before the Cataclysm, formed into a wedge. Beside each blue leather form stood a rider, wearing the blued armor that had not been seen in Corus since the Cataclysm. Each rider held a length of shimmering blue metal, the ancient skylances once carried by the original Myrmidons.

Beside the lead pteridon stood Aellyan Edyss, his silver-blond hair glittering in the morning sun, his arm raised, holding the skylance overhead. He jabbed the lance skyward once, then turned toward his pteridon, slipping the skylance into the holder that extended forward of the saddle. Then, with a mighty leap, he vaulted into position astride the pteridon and settled himself into the blue leather saddle that seemed invisible against the pteridon's hide.

In turn, the pteridon leaped forward and spread its wings, wings that suddenly stretched more than twenty yards on each side, and with strong strokes bore Aellyan Edyss aloft.

A single explosive cheer echoed from the new Myrmidons arrayed on the steps of the ancient Vault.

One after another, the remaining pteridons lifted off from the shimmering expanse of polished stone below the Vault and, following Edyss, circled upward into the spring sky, higher and higher, until they reformed into a wedge that arrowed southward.

From just forward of the pillars of the Vault, the councilors watched, their mouths slightly parted, as the wedge of pteridons swooped down at the targets to the south, targets that flared into blue flame as the narrow beams of blue light struck.

21

Another Quattri came and went, another week, another ten days of increasing warmth and dust, and continued quiet in Emal and upon the roads in the eastern part of the Iron Valleys. On Quinti, Alucius took fourth squad east beyond Tuuler, up along the river road toward the second cataract, not that he expected to find much of anything. He and Egyl rode side by side at the head of the column, and two troopers acting as scouts were more than a vingt ahead, well out of sight around the gentle curve in the river road.

As if following a celestial glass, once spring had turned, the snowfalls had stopped, and the skies had cleared, and there had not been a drop of moisture falling across the entire river valley for almost a month. The light breeze picked up the road dust, and even at a walk, the squad's mounts left a trail hanging in the air that followed the riders.

Alucius wiped the faint grit from his damp forehead and looked at the curve in the road ahead, the shed to the left, and the orchard to the right, with the small green leaves of spring already cloaking the branches of the apple trees and the faint perfume of the last white blossoms lingering in the air. There was not a single sign that barely a month before there had been a skirmish—or ambush—along this section of the road.

Alucius could sense the roar of the distant second cataract, and he glanced toward the river, running high enough that the underbrush along the normal shoreline was a good yard underwater.

"There's been talk around, sir," Egyl said cautiously. "Things like the men might not get paid, and that we'll all be put out of service. That'd include those with more 'n a few years."

"I've heard the rumors," Alucius said. "We got the pay chests almost two weeks ago, and there's enough in them for spring and summer, and sometime into fall. I don't see us going short on pay anytime soon."

"That's good to hear, sir. Still . . . Captain Feran's been quiet, too. Jissop says that's not a good sign, and he's been a squad leader with Captain Feran for almost four years."

Alucius considered. What could he say? Finally, he said, "You're right. There has been talk, but there are always rumors. There always have been. It's not secret that the Council has always been hard-pressed to come up with funding for the militia." He forced a shrug. "It's something the militia has always had to live with."

"What do you think will happen, sir?" Egyl pressed.

"I don't know. There are some traders who think we should become part of Lanachrona. There are others who don't, and there are some of each who sit on the Council. I know that the colonel doesn't favor that, but I've heard that the Council still owes a large sum that they borrowed from the Landarch of Deforya in order to pay for supplies and troopers during the Matrite War. They'll probably have to raise tariffs to pay that off, and that won't set well with anyone. How it will all turn out—your guess is as good as mine."

Egyl laughed. "I'd not be thinking so, sir. You've always seen things the way they would be. That's why I asked. You're not saying, and I'd be think-ing that you're as worried as Captain Feran. Would I be wrong in that, sir?"

Alucius turned in the saddle and looked at Egyl. "No, I am worried. But until we know what's likely to come down, I can't say what might be the best to do. There are times to act, and there are times when it's best to wait. This is a time to be prepared for anything—and to wait."

"You think we'll be seeing attacks by the Southern Guard?"

Alucius shook his head. "No. We might see an attack by someone else, but not by the Southern Guard."

"There's no one else on this border, sir."

"We ran into raiders who were supposed to be from Deforya, as I recall, less than a month ago."

"I see your meaning, sir."

Alucius hoped they wouldn't see any more attacks, but he could also see that attacks by "outsiders" would be a way to put more pressure on the Council—to force the militia to use resources it really couldn't afford. "We'll just have to be alert and see what happens. That's all we can do."

He just hoped that would be enough.

22

South Pass, Spine of Corus

Vestor rode into the chill wind, following directly behind the vanguard of the Praetorian Legions, a small cart drawn by a single horse behind him, each chest within the frame of the cart contain-ing one of his devices. A second cart remained well guarded within the main body of the foot companies and horse troopers who filled the high road for more than three vingts back toward Catyr. Despite the clear skies and the full sunlight, Vestor wrapped the heavy fleece-lined jacket around his slender form more tightly, trying to ignore the cold creeping up from his legs toward his lower thighs.

"It's a warm day for early spring here," offered the Praetor heartily as he reined in the silver charger beside the engineer's smaller gray mare. "You should feel it in winter."

"If it is all the same to you, Praetor, I would rather not," Vestor replied. "I was raised in Lysia and never have adjusted to the cold."

"You'd never make a Praetorian Guard, then."

"No, Praetor, I would not. I fear I must remain an engineer."

The Praetor, ruddy-faced in the cold, his iron gray hair blown back by the wind, laughed. "Then best you remain a good one." He paused. "You are certain Aellyan Edyss has discovered no ancient weapons in the Vault?"

"No, sir. I am not certain. I have destroyed two glasses looking for such, but, as I have told you, if there is much Talent involved, the glass will not show it. I can say that he has no weapons such as ours, or as those of the Matrites."

"Does that woman still rule Madrien?"

"The woman who had been the chief assistant to the Matrial? She does. She styles herself the Regent of the Matrial."

"And no one has said anything?"

"Who can understand the people of the west?" Vestor replied.

The Praetor snorted, then looked up as an overcaptain rode swiftly down the side of the high road toward them, reining in and turning his mount. "Praetor, there is a nomad scout ahead. He perches like a mountain cat on the cliff on the north side of the road."

"How far ahead, and how far off the road?"

"Perhaps a vingt ahead, and less than half a vingt to the north, but the cliff is a good hundred yards of sheer rock."

The Praetor looked to Vestor. "Could not your device destroy such?"

"I would think so."

"Then let us see."

"We will need to reach a high spot where we can look directly at the nomad," Vestor pointed out.

"You will be able to see him from the side of the road ahead, there." The overcaptain gestured toward a shoulder on the north side of the high road, wider than the few yards that bounded most of the high road, and roughly a half vingt farther along the road to the west.

Once they neared the area, wider and somewhat flatter than the road shoulder before and after it, the Praetor gestured, and the column slowed to a halt.

Vestor rode his mount onto the crusted and packed snow. He turned in the saddle and, with the lead he still held, stopped the cart horse, awkwardly. After the engineer dismounted, a trooper had to ride over and take the reins of the engineer's own mount as the mare started to wander toward a shiny patch of ice that looked like a puddle of water.

The Praetor looked westward, noting, "The nomad is still there."

Vestor ignored the byplay as he unfastened the heavy oak tripod from the side of the cart and set it on the uneven ground, adjusting and readjusting the legs until it was solid. After that, he extended the retaining brackets at the top of the tripod and screwed them in place. Only then did he return to the cart, where he slid back one of the wooden panels in the top of the cart and extracted a black metal object, oblong in shape, nearly a yard in length, and a third that in height.

With the ease of practice, he slid the device into the retaining brackets and tightened the clamps. Once the device was firmly anchored, he slid back the apertures on the top to let the sunlight fall on the power crystals.

"How long before it is ready?" asked the overcaptain quietly.

"When the crystals glow," replied Vestor, using the small telescope attached to the left retaining bracket to sight the device at the nomad, who remained nearly motionless on the cliff top ahead, still watching the column of the Praetorian Legions.

After a time, Vestor slid one of the side levers forward, and a beam of red-limned light flashed from the discharge crystal. To the west, perhaps ten yards below the cliff top from which the nomad watched, a line of steam flared from one of the icicles hanging from rocky overhang. The lower half of the icicle, sheared from the upper by the heat of the beam, plunged into the depths below. The nomad leaned forward, looking down.

Vestor resighted, then brought the beam up and across in a slashing motion. The red-limned beam of light sliced evenly through the nomad, cutting through the blued armor on his chest as if it had been blue-silver cotton. A pink haze sprayed across the snow, and the rider split into two parts. His mount half reared, then collapsed.

Vestor swallowed convulsively.

"Wonderful! Wonderful!" the Praetor exclaimed. "Now he won't be able to report anything to Aellyan Edyss."

The device began to hum and Vestor, swallowing yet again, quickly slid back the power lever and closed the apertures.

"Why did you do that?" questioned the overcaptain.

"Because the crystals within would vibrate, then disintegrate. Depending on the temperature, the dampness of the air, a device may work only for a short period, or for a much longer one. That is why we needed so many."

"It is good that you recognized that," offered the overcaptain.

"The engineer is very good at recognizing limitations, Overcaptain," the Praetor said. "Perhaps you should check and see if there are any more scouts lurking in the cliffs. It would do little good to kill one and then have two others report our presence."

"Yes, Praetor, sir. Right away."

Vestor began to unclamp the weapon from the retaining brackets, then slid it clear and returned it to its storage space in the horse cart.

"You are most adept at that, Vestor," observed the Praetor. "One might actually think that you came from a family of cannoneers."

"Thank you, sir." Vestor quickly disassembled the tripod and restored it to its place on the side of the handcart, then glanced around, before seeing the trooper holding the reins of his mount.

"But one would never think of you as a horse trooper," added the Praetor, with his hearty laugh.

Even after they resumed their journey, none of them looked forward at the pink-sprayed snow at the edge of the cliff top to the west.

23

A light wind blew through the open shutters of the mess windows, a Londi afternoon breeze cooler than the warm days of the previous week, but not chill. Despite the high clouds, no rain had fallen, and Alucius doubted that any would, not with the wind coming out of the northwest. As he stood across the table from Feran in the mess, Alucius looked at the missive that had arrived moments before, carried by two militia troopers from headquarters at Dekhron. Feran held a similar missive, which he had already opened.

After a moment, Alucius broke the seal and began to read.

Captain Alucius—

Earlier this spring, you received word that, as a result of financially parlous times, the Council requested that all company commanders show great care in the use of their resources. While the militia has been told that a resolution of this difficulty is being developed, supplies are at close to the lowest level in many years. Therefore, you are requested not to engage in any sustained or lengthy training exercises and to refrain from arms practice with cartridges until further notice.

There will be no dispensation for local recruiting to fill vacancies in companies, and any request for a stipend for troopers nearing the time of completed service must be deferred until the turn of harvest.

Please acknowledge with a brief response to accompany the
messengers who carried this to you.

The seal was that of the commandant, but the signature was that of
Majer Weslyn, with the words "acting commandant" penned beneath
the signature. Alucius wondered why Weslyn was acting commandant,
and he hoped that such was merely temporary. Colonel Clyon was the
only one of the senior militia officers in whom Alucius had any confidence for the ability to stand up to the Council.

After a moment, Alucius went back over the short set of instructions
again, but he could not read anything into them except the Council's
desperate frugality and continued lack of understanding of the importance of the militia. He would certainly acknowledge the missive, not
that he had a choice. And he would seal up and send back his latest message to Wendra, even if he did not have time to add more than a quick
note to the bottom of what he had already written to his wife.

Across the table, Feran was mumbling to himself. ". . . a seed-oil
works . . . all the idiocy . . . stupidity . . ."

Abruptly, the older officer thrust the missive he had received at Alucius. "Would you read this? Can you believe it? First, they threaten to
cut our supplies and pay, and now I get an order to take the entire company thirty vingts down the river road for three weeks to a hamlet no
one's ever heard of—except us—because some trader's afraid that his
precious seed-oil works may be threatened."

Alucius handed his own orders to Feran, then began to read what the
older officer had received.

Captain Feran—
In view of your length of service with the militia, and your great
understanding of the importance of handling matters with both
dispatch and tact, you are hereby ordered to take Fifth Company,
immediately, that being the morning after receiving these orders,
to the town of Fiente. There you will contact Trader Yussel. The
militia has received word that a raid on the seed-oil works is
highly likely. Inasmuch as the seed-oil works provide much of the

support necessary for militia goods and supplies, the Council has strongly recommended that a company be dispatched to make sure that no ill comes to those works.

You will spend three weeks in Fiente, unless you receive additional orders to the contrary. You are to exercise great caution to make sure that no harm comes to the works.

Earlier this spring, you received word that, as a result of financially parlous times, the Council requested that all company commanders show great care in the use of their resources . . .

Alucius nodded. The remainder of Feran's instructions were the same as his, word for word, as were the signature and seal lines. He handed the orders back to Feran and received his own in return.

"We have to go off and protect a seed-oil works. Can you believe that?" asked Feran. "Just who is going to attack that?"

"Lanachronans disguised as raiders?" suggested Alucius.

Feran shook his head. "They've got far better oil works all over Lanachrona. More likely, someone on the Council—this trader whatever his name is—wants to show that he has power over the militia."

"I worry about the signature," Alucius said.

"The signature?" Feran looked down. "Acting commandant? Sander offal! As soon as the colonel goes somewhere—or gets sick—the Council's twisting Weslyn's arm."

"Let's just hope he's only sick or away."

Feran froze for a moment, then shook his head. "We'd better hope it's only that."

"I'm sure it is." Alucius was sure of no such thing, but there was no point in saying that. Time would tell, one way or another. He also wondered what sort of resolution was being worked out by the Council. That veiled reference bothered him as much as Weslyn's signature as acting commandant.

Still . . . he had a response to write—two in a way—and he might as well get on with it. He turned to head to his own quarters to get pen and inkwell and paper, and the missive to Wendra.

Behind him, Feran continued to murmur under his breath.

Abruptly, Alucius turned and walked out to the courtyard, looking around for the two messengers. One stood talking to Egyl, near the corner of the building.

Both looked up as Alucius approached.

"Sir?" asked Egyl.

Alucius looked at the messenger. "Trooper . . . I wonder if you might have some information. About the commandant—Colonel Clyon. The instructions you delivered were signed by Majer Weslyn as acting commandant. Is the colonel ill?"

"Why . . . yes, sir. He's been suffering a terrible flux for the past few weeks. That's what the majer said."

"And you haven't seen the colonel around headquarters?"

"No, sir. We'd wondered, but when the majer told us . . ."

"Thank you." Alucius nodded.

He turned and walked back toward his own quarters. The colonel seriously ill? Or being made seriously ill? The timing was too coincidental, and he liked it not at all—even if he could do nothing at all about it. Feran would like it even less. Of that, Alucius was most certain.

24

Northeast of Iron Stem, Iron Valleys

Wendra reined up the chestnut mare and listened.
Her eyes went eastward toward the front of the flock, where Royalt rode, and the Aerlal Plateau well beyond. After a moment, she turned her head toward the straggler ewe and her lamb—less than fifteen yards to her south. Her brow wrinkled. Then she turned the chestnut farther south.

The faintest shimmer of reddish tan glinted in the low morning light from behind a thicker clump of quarasote.

Reining up quickly, she slid the heavy rifle from its holder, cocking it and bringing it to her shoulder in a smooth motion that was practiced but not yet quite instinctive. She watched, waiting.

After long moments, the sandwolf streaked toward Wendra, a blur of tannish red, and the long crystalline fangs glinted in the morning sun.

She squeezed the trigger. *Crack!* She recocked the rifle and fired again, missing. Her third shot tore into the chest of the beast, and the sandwolf staggered, then fell, less than two yards from the mare.

Wendra recocked the rifle, holding it ready as she continued to survey the quarasote plains around her. She could hear the hoofbeats of Royalt's mount, but she kept checking the terrain until she saw the second sandwolf, more than thirty yards away, behind a more distant and larger clump of quarasote. Again, she waited.

The second sandwolf peered from the side of the quarasote, then turned, and bounded to a second clump of quarasote, before vanishing into a gully so small that Wendra could barely make it out.

"I don't see any more," Royalt said as he reined up.

"I can't either," she replied. "But only two . . . ?"

"Sometimes, the younger ones hunt in smaller groups." Royalt, his own rifle ready, glanced at the dead sandwolf on the red and sandy soil. "That's a young one."

Wendra measured the dead animal with her eyes. "It's more than two yards long, and that's not counting the tail."

"Full-grown, they can run to almost three yards." Royalt smiled. "You did well. They're harder to hit than a sander."

Wendra glanced back toward the flock, then aimed her eyes at the straggler ewe. "Get moving." She tried to project the kind of authority that Royalt and Alucius did.

After a moment, the ewe nosed the lamb, and the two began to trot toward the main body of the flock.

"You've got the touch, Wendra."

She smiled faintly. "If we could just do that with people. Some people . . . anyway," she added quickly. "Like the Council." She flicked the reins gently, and the mare began to walk toward the flock, still moving eastward toward the plateau.

"Aye. That could get worse." Royalt eased his mount up beside Wendra's mare as the two herders moved closer to the flock. Both continued to scan the quarasote, even as they talked.

"If Clyon doesn't recover from his illness?"

"*If* it is an illness."

"You think someone on the Council would go that far?"

"At times, I wonder if there's anyone on the Council who wouldn't. They're all more concerned about how many golds they can put in their strongboxes this year than whether they'll have any at all next year. We could shear every nightsheep down to the bare skin and make more nightsilk this year . . . but half of them would die over the year, and then where would we be? Herder who doesn't look to the future doesn't have one. They've never liked Clyon 'cause he keeps reminding them about the future."

"How can they be that stupid?"

Royalt laughed, roughly. "Look around, Wendra. Most people are like that. Oh, they talk about planning for tomorrow, working . . . but then they get an extra silver and it goes for more ale, or a fancy scarf, or a shinier knife . . ." He shook his head.

Wendra glanced back at the fallen sandwolf.

"Leave the sandwolf. Can't use anything."

She nodded, looking toward the flock ahead and the Aerlal Plateau beyond.

25

In the indirect light of late spring, Alucius studied the map spread on the mess table. After a time, he took the ancient calipers and measured the distance on the map—from Emal to the high road between Salaan and Dereka. He wrote down the figure, then measured the distance as a raven might fly, from Aelta to Emal, writing that down as well. As he did, he wondered how Feran was doing on his travels to Fiente, since Fifth Company had left the day before.

Thrap. At the knock on the door—or the doorframe—to the officers' mess, Alucius looked up to see Zerdial standing there. "Yes?"

"Captain . . . there's a fellow here, says he needs to speak to you. He's an old farmer. He says it's important."

Alucius stood. "Did he say why?"

"He's from across the river . . . He asked for the herder captain. He said he had to talk to you. I think he talked to one of the bridge guards, too, but he knew that it was you he wanted."

"I'll be right there." Alucius gently folded the old map and weighted it in place with one of the histories he had brought back to Emal Outpost from the stead. He'd read the history—*The Wonders of Ancient Corus*—once already and was rereading it more thoroughly.

When Alucius stepped out into the warm and hazy spring sunshine, he saw a man standing beside the wall with Zerdial. The stranger was a gaunt figure of a man, with thin gray hair, wearing a worn and patched sheepskin jacket and equally worn brown trousers. His boots had been stitched and restitched, and his face was wrinkled and weathered. Because he wondered why a stranger would seek him out, Alucius studied him for a moment with his Talent, but nothing seemed odd, and the man's lifethread was a deep brown, rooted somewhere close to the southeast, clearly that of a man deeply tied to the land nearby. Alucius wasn't sure, but those with deep commitments appeared to have lifethreads that were a solid color—herders were almost always a solid black.

"You are the herder captain, sir?" The older man's eyes lingered on Alucius's dark, dark gray hair, and he nodded.

"Yes, I am." Alucius slipped back his tunic sleeve to reveal, if but momentarily, the black crystal wristband, just below the form-fitting nightsilk undergarment that was more effective than mail against sabre slashes. "The squad leader said that you wished to see me. How can I be of help to you?"

"You look like a captain, and you feel like one. Yet you would see me?" The older man had an unspoken question.

Alucius could sense that, impoverished as the peasant farmer might be, he was proud. Alucius smiled as gently as he could, then said, "Few would ask to see a captain if they did not have something to say. You have traveled far. How could I not see a man who has done me that honor?"

Abruptly, the farmer lowered his eyes.

Alucius hoped he hadn't gone too far, but the man's pride seemed to be all that he had. He waited, not pressing.

Slowly, the older man looked up, and his eyes met those of Alucius. He nodded. "You are young for a captain. Yet you are far older than those with more years." He swallowed. "I have little, but I have worked hard. I have never asked for anything except the fruits of my land and my hands."

"You have worked hard. I can see that," Alucius replied, ignoring the impatience radiating from Zerdial. "You do not like to ask of others, but I will hear what you have to say, and if I can, I will do what should be done." Again, Alucius was operating on his interpretation of the other's feelings, which included a sense of righteousness, and anger, but an anger not directed at Alucius, for all that the farmer's accent proclaimed him Lanachronan.

"You have already done that, Captain." The farmer paused, not quite meeting Alucius's eyes as he continued. "I am the one who owes you. I owe you for the vengeance I could not take, Sir Captain," replied the gray-haired man.

Amazed as he was by the man's statement, Alucius could sense the absolute truth in the man's words. "I'm glad whatever I did you found acceptable, but since I am not aware of the details, would you mind telling me?" Alucius tried to project warmth and assurance.

"I will. You would not know, for all this happened on the south side of the river, where I live. Where we lived. My daughter, and her husband, and their children . . . we are from Saubyan. The raiders who were not raiders, the ones who wore gray, who hid in gray. They crossed the ice, and then they raided our hamlet. I had a daughter. They thought she was comely, and she was." The man stopped, swallowed, then went on slowly. "Her husband protested, and they shot him, and they struck me with a rifle." He pushed back the worn hat to reveal a scarred gash that ran across the top of his forehead. "They used my daughter ill, most ill. None thought I would live. My daughter did not, and Busyl did not. My wife is long departed, and my son went to find his fortune in Borlan. I must work the fields alone and raise two bairns, and the eldest is but six." He held up his hand. "I do not ask more of you, Captain. None in Lanachrona lifted a blade or a rifle. You had them all slain, did you not? And you slew a half score yourself."

"I killed some of them," Alucius admitted. "None of them survived."

"I cannot give you what I would wish. I am a poor man. I owe you, and my only payment is what I can tell you. There are more raiders. They wear red, red tunics all alike, of a kind I have never seen, and some have strange long rifles, and I have listened. They think I am old and feeble and deaf, but I am not. They talk about the herder captain, and they are waiting for the runoff to go down. They have built rafts to carry provisions . . ."

Alucius nodded. "I did not know this, and I thank you. Might you be able to tell me how many of them there are and where they intend to cross the river?"

"I have counted almost two hundred. They have talked about crossing the shallows. That is but two vingts to the east of the bridge, where the river widens. They will use heavy ropes and swim their mounts across in the night before dawn. I cannot say on what day this will happen, but I do not think it will be long."

Alucius inclined his head to the farmer. "It is I who owes you. So do the people of Emal, though none will tell of this." He looked over the shoulder of the farmer at Zerdial, and said, "None."

"Yes, sir," murmured the squad leader.

Alucius turned to the farmer. "You rose early and traveled far. Could I at least offer some bread and some cheese for your daughter's children, so that they will not suffer more?"

"I could not . . . for myself."

"I know that," Alucius said. "But for them."

The man looked down and gave the faintest of nods.

Alucius looked at Zerdial. "If you could find some loaves and a wedge of cheese . . . from the cooks. Tell them I'll take care of it."

"Yes, sir." Zerdial slipped away.

"Do you just tend the fields, or do you have livestock?" Alucius asked.

"The raiders, they slaughtered the two ewes, but they left the cow, and they were so noisy that they could only catch one of the hens." The older man laughed. "That was one reason I knew they were not true raiders."

Alucius nodded. "A true raider would have had the hens in the pot first."

"You are a herder, are you not?"

"Yes. My stead is to the north, and my wife and my mother and my grandsire tend it now. We have a flock of nightsheep."

"Yet you are a captain now?"

"For a time yet. My grandsire was a captain, and so was my sire. He was killed by raiders when I was a child."

"Would that there were more who know the land who carry the rifle and the blade."

Both men looked up as Zerdial crossed the courtyard with a cloth bag.

Alucius slipped a pair of coppers from his belt wallet and extended them to the farmer. "These are a token, just a token, one for each child, for when times are hard."

"I could not . . ."

"They are but a token," Alucius repeated. "Were I to offer truly the worth of what you have provided, neither of us would be pleased."

The farmer laughed harshly. "You, too, are a proud man."

"Yes," Alucius admitted. "It is a fault of mine."

The farmer took the coppers, slipping them into slots on the inside of his stained leather belt. "May all officers have your faults, Captain."

Alucius took the bag from Zerdial. As he presented it to the farmer, he could tell that the cooks—or Zerdial—had been generous. "Perhaps you should tell the others in your hamlet that you received these as payment for helping a herder." He grinned. "It is true."

The farmer bowed. "Only for the children."

"Only for the children," Alucius agreed. He nodded to Zerdial to accompany the farmer past the gate and the guard.

The captain stood and watched as the two crossed the courtyard. He waited until Zerdial returned.

"He's across the bridge, sir."

"Good."

"You gave him two coppers. Just coppers."

"Anything more, and he would have been insulted. Also, he can explain two coppers. How would he ever explain a silver?"

Zerdial looked toward the outpost gate, then southward before turning his eyes back to Alucius "Sir? How did you know?"

"Because almost everyone dislikes troopers, or stays clear of them, in any land I know. Anyone who would seek me out either wished me well or great ill. He was too humble to wish me ill, and too shy. So I had to make him feel less uncomfortable and more at ease." That, reflected the captain, had been the easy part. Figuring out how to handle a force equal to two horse companies—and then doing it—would be far harder.

Although Alucius went back to the mess, and his maps, he had the feeling that whatever was about to happen wouldn't be that far away, because the troopers in Deforyan red were being paid, and someone in the Southern Guard was looking the other way. The pay wouldn't last, and the Lord-Protector couldn't afford to keep his eyes averted long.

Yet whatever Alucius did, he'd have to do alone. Even if Feran were in Emal, Alucius could imagine what Feran—or any officer—would have said about his heeding information from the unnamed farmer. "A farmer told you this? A Lanachronan farmer? And you're going to believe him?" Then too, there was the possibility that the farmer had been deliberately misled.

Once again, to conceal his Talent, he would have to find a way to deal with the problem in a logical fashion.

By the glass after the midday dinner for the troopers, he was ready, and had summoned his squad leaders to the officers' mess.

Alucius glanced around the room, looking first at Longyl, and then at each of the squad leaders, one after the other—Zerdial, Anslym, Faisyn, Egyl, and Sawyn.

"I've been thinking . . ." He paused. "We haven't done any full company maneuvers since last fall. The most troopers we've had together at a time is two squads. As I've told most of you, I don't know what's likely to happen this year, but if we do have to fight any pitched battles, against the Southern Guard, especially, we'd better be prepared to do it. We probably won't have much notice. It often doesn't work that way." Alucius smiled. "And I'd be very surprised if they came across the bridge."

"How would they come, do you think?" asked Zerdial.

Alucius gave the young squad leader credit for asking the right leading question.

"I'm not their commander, but they'd either come in winter, across the ice, or now, across the shallower sections of the river. That could be the shallows east of the bridge. The water there is only a bit more than two yards deep, and only in the middle of the river. Or they could come on the back trails through the marsh five vingts west of the bridge, then move across the low isles there. They'd only have the main channel to cross, and that's less than twenty yards wide." Alucius paused, cleared his throat, and went on. "They might even do both, trying to split Twenty-first and Fifth Companies. They'd also have more troopers than we would, at least two to one, maybe more."

"You think this is really going to happen?" asked Sawyn.

Alucius smiled. "Think of it this way. It happens, or it doesn't. If it happens, and we're ready, then we'll ride away. If it doesn't happen, all that we lose is some time and effort. But if it happens, and we're not prepared . . . do you want to be the squad leader at that time?"

Sawyn didn't have to think long about that, Alucius was relieved to see.

"What do you want us to do?" asked Longyl, ever the practical one.

"This afternoon, I'd like you to send your scouts to the eastern crossing point. They're to observe the area and to draw rough maps of where the Lanachronans could cross, either by raft or by swimming their mounts. The squad leaders are to go with them, but no one else, and I'd like you to watch the river in a way that you're not seen from the far side. If . . . *if* they have ideas, they may already be watching. They may not, but it's good practice. If they know we're watching, then they might change their plans." Alucius paused. "We'd have more time, and the bluff as a defense point, if they came from the west. All of you are to think about where you would place the company for the best effect— either above the shallows or to the west of Emal."

"Yes, sir."

"There's one other matter," Alucius said. "We'll probably have to post a sentry on our side of the shallows. So give a thought to where that post should be." He glanced around the small room once more, before concluding. "We'll meet here with the scouts right after supper."

After the six left the room, Alucius went back to his maps and calculations.

26

Alucius was up early on Octi, well before sunrise, riding alone along the river road, eastward toward the shallows. Although he had the observations of five scouts and their squad leaders, as well as Longyl's thoughts, he still felt he needed a better feel for the river at the shallows, the land, and what might already be happening. He also did not wish to draw attention to his concerns by riding out during the day, and although Vinkin would doubtless not say anything, Alucius doubted that the duty sentries would be so circumspect. But for him to ask for their silence would guarantee that everyone would know he was deeply concerned.

In the darkness before dawn that was little barrier to a herder's night vision, he finally reined up on the shoulder of the river road nearest the so-called shallows. There he sat astride Wildebeast and studied the banks, the shallows, and the far shore, and beyond, both with his eyes, and with his Talent-senses.

He was relieved not to sense any mass of troopers on the far shore, but there was a small group of men sleeping beyond the levee on the southern side, and Alucius suspected they were scouts or an advance group for the attackers—whoever they were. That meant that he would have to post his own sentries later in the day.

After taking a long slow breath, he considered the land and the river. The river was wider than either upstream or downstream, nearly a hundred yards, but shallower, with only a space of twenty yards where the main channel was more than a yard and a half deep. One advantage Alucius could see was that the main channel ran far closer to the southern shore. The attackers would see that as an edge, because they could cross the deeper water close to their own side and farther from the rifles of any defenders. From Alucius's view, that meant that there would be more riders in the water, with nowhere to go except into his own fire—if he waited until the bulk of the attackers reached the northern shore.

The grass running down from the river road to the water's edge wasn't that high yet, barely over knee length, and certainly not high enough to cover a squad of men, except on their bellies, and Alucius didn't like giving up mobility, especially when his company had to face twice that many.

He eased Wildebeast closer to the river.

The ground within ten yards of the river was still very soft, enough that a horse's hoofs would sink deeply, and after the first squad or so, the ground was likely to be very slippery. Alucius glanced to the southern bank. There the grade was steeper. With the recent days of mild and dry weather, he could hope that the attackers would not realize the difference, or that the soft ground extended much farther on the north side.

He checked and probed the ground as he moved back, until he was satisfied that he knew where the footing was firm and where it was not.

Then he considered where he could place his squads . . . based not just on what he thought but what his squad leaders had suggested the night before.

The sky was turning light gray-green when he turned Wildebeast back toward Emal, and while the men behind the levee on the southern bank had awakened, they certainly were not preparing for an attack in the glasses immediately ahead.

But the attack would come within the next handful of days. Of that, Alucius was certain.

27

Lyterna, Illegea

The space in the Council Vault was called the small-
est hall, and it was almost fifty yards in length and fifteen in width, with
ceilings easily ten yards high. Walls and ceilings were of polished redstone, but a redstone that did not reflect light, for all its apparent shine
and shimmer. The ancient brackets no longer held light-torches, as they
had in the days of the Duarchy, but oil lamps whose light created a pud-
dled glow on the thirty or so Myrmidon officers gathered on and around
the stone dais at the north end of the hall.

Aellyan Edyss paced back and forth as he spoke, occasionally stopping and gesturing. ". . . we have word that the Praetor's forces are moving through the South Pass. They have a device that can melt the ice and
also cut through armor." The nomad commander looked across the
ranks of his subcommanders. "It takes almost a quarter of a glass for
them to set up the device. We will attack the devices with the pteridons
and the skylances before they can bring them to bear. Once their devices
are destroyed, then you will attack."

"How many horse troopers does the Praetor bring?" asked an older
commander, with tinges of gray in his sleek black hair.

"Most are horse troopers, but they cannot ride and fight as well as we
do. We would judge that they bring six thousand riders. You each are
worth two of them. So we outnumber them." Edyss smiled. "Also, they

will not expect an attack from the skies. None have done so in the generations upon generations since the Cataclysm."

"When do we leave?" asked another, younger, captain.

"Tomorrow at dawn. The Myrmidon Horse will ride south toward the point where the Lost Highway emerges from the Spine of Corus. You should arrive there two days before the Lustreans do. We will not leave for several days because the pteridons can travel faster. I wish to see if there are other weapons here that we might use."

"We have enough to destroy them!" came from the back of the group.

"We do indeed," replied Edyss. "But the more tools and weapons we have, the more we can take with fewer losses, and the sooner all of Corus will be ours. Is that not our destiny and our right?" He raised a clenched fist. "Is it not?"

"Destiny! Destiny!" The chanted word rolled through the smallest hall, like the thunder of a great storm sweeping off the Spine of Corus and down across the plains of Illegea.

28

Three days passed from the Octi when the Lanachronan farmer had delivered his warning. It was late on Londi afternoon before the Twenty-first Company scout hidden in the blind on the northern shore slipped back through the grass to his mount and rode back to Emal to report that a number of riders had briefly appeared on the levee on the southern shore of the shallows.

Three glasses before dawn on Duadi, another scout reported activity on the southern bank. Shortly thereafter, Alucius and Twenty-first Company rode eastward along the river road, through the moonless darkness, under a sky filled with stars that shed little light on the way ahead, not that Alucius needed any. Still, he was all too conscious of the fact that his men would be firing through the darkness, and he hoped that the river's surface would provide enough of a contrast. He had taken the quiet liberty of bringing two rifles and extra ammunition for himself.

Alucius had also slipped on the nightsilk undervest over his undergarments. That gave him three layers of nightsilk, with padding in between two of them, across his chest and torso, and a single layer on his arms and legs. The nightsilk wouldn't do much for his head, but, since he had the vest, there was certainly every reason to wear it, and none not to.

As they neared the curve in the river road immediately to the west of the shallows, Alucius turned in the saddle and ordered, in a voice pitched just enough to carry, "Silent riding. Pass it back." He couldn't hear the whispers past the first few repetitions, and, if he couldn't, he doubted that the attackers across the river could. He looked ahead, but the road was clear, except for a single scout posted on the back side of the road, and barely visible, even to his night vision and Talent-senses.

Another half vingt farther on, he reined up next to the scout. "Waris?"

"Yes, sir?" The scout's voice was low. "They've got riders bringing ropes across. Did just a bit ago, leastwise."

"Are they going to put in posts to anchor them?"

"Looks that way."

"We'll form up and wait. Let us know when they start to cross in force." Alucius could have slowed or turned back the attack by stopping those who were setting up the rope guides, but that wouldn't have accomplished much except warning off the attackers to another time and place, when Alucius had less supplies, and probably fewer men and less ammunition.

He turned Wildebeast, rode back to Longyl and the individual squad leaders, and said in a low voice, "Form up as planned."

There were nods in the darkness, and the five slipped away, quietly enough, Alucius hoped, that they and their squads would not be heard as Twenty-first Company waited. Longyl eased away and into position between squads one and two, as all the squads re-formed on the lower ground on the north side of the river road, where they could not have been seen from the river, even in full light.

Alucius took a position at the front of third squad, where he'd be in the middle, and most able to use his night vision and Talent to the greatest advantage in the early volleys. Before long the sound of sledges could be heard, dull, measured clunks against heavy wooden posts. Then they died away.

Faisyn, mounted beside Alucius, leaned toward the captain. "How much longer, sir?"

"Waris will let us know," Alucius murmured back, "once the first riders of the main body of riders are nearing the shore."

Alucius let his senses range across the river. The attackers had two ropes—or cables—running across the Vedra, and each was attached to a heavy wooden post sledged into the river bank roughly five yards up from the water's edge. Two half squads of mounted raiders were stationed ten to fifteen yards up the gentle slope from the shoreline, each group above one of the guide-rope posts.

Beside Alucius, Faisyn shifted his weight in the saddle, clearly worried that Alucius was waiting too long.

A figure on foot slipped over the crest of the road and ran toward Alucius. "Sir! The first raiders—the main body—they're about fifteen yards offshore."

"Twenty-first Company! Squads to firing positions!"

"Third squad, to firing position!"

"First squad . . ."

"Second squad . . ."

As the commands were called out, Alucius rode forward immediately, knowing Faisyn's third squad would be behind him, up the north side of the road, over the road, then ten yards below the shoulder. There he reined up Wildebeast and slipped the first heavy rifle from its case.

Within moments, Faisyn was beside him. "Ready, sir."

Below, Alucius could see, through the darkness, the guards posted above the guide posts turning and peering uphill.

". . . someone's up there . . ."

". . . more than a few . . ."

Alucius checked around him. First squad wasn't quite in position, but there wasn't time to wait. "Twenty-first Company, fire!"

"Get into position, first squad! Fire!" Longyl's voice rode over the other commands.

"Third squad, fire!"

"Fourth squad . . ."

The initial volleys were aimed at the half squads stationed at the river's edge, guarding the posts to which the guide ropes were attached. Alucius fired five shots, Talent-willing each shot at a raider, then shoved the rifle into the holder, and reached for the second rifle. He was on his seventh shot before there was a single *crack* in response.

By the time he emptied the second rifle, most of the guards were down. As he reloaded the second rifle, Alucius called out. "Twenty-first Company! At the men in the river! Fire!"

"Third squad, at the men in the river! Fire!"

"Fourth squad . . ."

"Second squad . . ."

The first raiders were reaching the northern bank of the Vedra, and the others in the shallower water spurred their mounts forward, but the water was deep enough, and the bottom muddy enough, that even in the shallower water near the shore, the horsemen were having trouble clearing the river. As Alucius had hoped, there was enough contrast between the river and the raiders that each raider stood out like a dark cutout target.

Alucius finished reloading both rifles and began to fire once more. While he knew he was hitting most of those raiders he aimed at, there was enough of a sweep of death scything through the raiders in the river below that he could not tell for certain exactly how accurate he was, although he was well aware that he was contributing a disproportionate amount to the death toll. No one would know, and that was definitely for the best.

He reloaded a third time and continued to fire, but there were fewer targets nearing the northern bank of the Vedra. There were a handful of muzzle flashes, one from the shoreline, and several from the water, but Alucius didn't hear or sense any bullets coming near him as he continued to fire through the darkness that was more like early twilight to him, picking off raider after raider as the attackers neared the shore.

Around him, from the corners of his eyes, he could see the flashes from the heavy Iron Valley rifles, as well as hear the deeper-sounding reports from each shot.

Almost without thinking, he reloaded once more and continued firing.

The more distant raiders began to turn their mounts back to the southern shore, trying to cross the deeper water of the main channel. One rider was swept under the guide ropes, and he and his mount struggled to get to shallower water.

Despite the withering fire from Twenty-first Company, perhaps ten or fifteen raiders had managed to get onto the bank. But they were having trouble making their way across the wet and slippery ground—as Alucius had planned. As he glanced up to see the eastern sky graying, he realized that the fight had lasted longer than he'd thought.

He aimed at the lead rider and squeezed off another shot.

Abruptly, fire slammed into his right shoulder, and Alucius felt himself nearly twisted from the saddle. He could barely hang on to the rifle, even though he was firing left-handed, as always. He did manage to right himself in the saddle and holster the rifle. His entire chest and shoulder was both numb—and a mass of fire—simultaneously.

Stars flashed before his eyes, and he could barely see. He steadied himself with his left hand on the pommel of the saddle. Each breath hurt.

"Withdraw! Back across the river. Withdraw!" That command came from the southern shore of the River Vedra. "Withdraw!"

Alucius just hoped that he could hang on until he was certain that the raiders had indeed withdrawn.

"Are you all right, sir?" That was Faisyn, easing his mount up beside Alucius in the faint light of dawn. "Seemed like most of their shots were aimed at us, maybe at you."

"I think so . . . we'll see in a bit," Alucius replied. The pain wasn't getting any worse, and he wasn't quite so light-headed. He remained in the saddle, waiting for the dawn to reveal the full extent of the carnage.

Already the handful of raiders on the shore had turned their mounts back, and the river was mostly empty, although a number of Twenty-first Company troopers continued to fire. As Alucius watched, another raider clutched at his chest, then sagged in the saddle. One shot hit a horse that collapsed into the main channel, dragging its rider down with it.

Faisyn glanced at the ammunition belt that Alucius wore, a belt that held mostly empty leather loops and but a few cartridges. "You let loose a lot of rounds, sir."

"As many as I could," Alucius admitted. He lowered his eyes to his shoulder, taking in the small rent in his tunic. Through the gash in the black fabric, he could see at least one splash of metal flattened against the nightsilk outer layer of his undervest. He had no doubts that, without the vest, he would have already been dead.

Alucius gently cleared his throat. "Twenty-first Company! Cease fire!" Even calling out the command hurt, and it was probably unnecessary because the river and the northern shore were clear of any living raiders.

As the sky lightened, the extent of the carnage became more obvious. There were at least fifty bodies in the shallow eddies just below Twenty-first Company, and almost that many on the slopes above the bank. Alucius could see others farther downstream.

Cleaning up the mess was going to be another problem—and seeing if there was any real evidence to prove that the raiders were Deforyan or otherwise. Alucius shifted his weight in the saddle—and winced.

"Are you sure you're all right, sir?" asked Longyl, reining up beside Alucius, his voice showing concern.

"I've been better, but I'm not bleeding. I am going to be very sore."

"At least some of them were shooting at you. Even I could tell that from over where I was. Do you know why?"

"They probably felt that if they took out the commander, you'd break off or not fight so well," Alucius suggested. "I can't think of any other reason they'd shoot at the most junior captain in the militia—or that they'd even know that." He would have laughed, but he knew laughing would hurt, and doubtless would for days, if not weeks.

"They weren't raiders, then," Longyl said.

"Mercenaries, I'd guess. Another way for the Lord-Protector to put pressure on the Iron Valleys and yet be able to deny that he is."

"You think so, sir?"

"It's only a guess," Alucius said tiredly. But he knew it was more than that. "We need to get on with things. Have the men collect the weapons and the stray mounts, those that there are. And pass the word to the other squad leaders."

"Yes, sir."

Glad he could rely on the senior squad leader, Alucius looked to the south bank of the Vedra. As the sun cleared the river to the east, flood-

ing the land and water with green-tinged white light, Alucius could see
no sign of living raiders, just the bodies everywhere, including one
caught in the guide ropes, being tugged at by the current. Low mutter-
ings from troopers, the heavy breathing of some horses, and a few moans
were the only sounds.

Breathing shallowly, Alucius continued to watch from the saddle,
scarcely moving, as the troopers combed the bank and the river's edge.

29

On Tridi morning, Alucius could barely move. He stood,
bare to the waist, in the small washroom he and Feran usually shared,
looking at his chest and shoulder, purple and black from his breastbone
to one side and from his shoulder to below his bottom rib. From what he
had been able to tell from the metal splashed across his nightsilk-
covered undervest, he'd actually been hit twice, almost at the same time.
He suspected professional snipers, but he still couldn't account for why
anyone would take the trouble. He was the most junior captain in the
militia. He'd made it more than clear he did not intend to remain in the
militia. He had no personal ties or influences to anyone on the Council
or among the senior militia officers—or to anyone of power.

Yet someone had tried to ambush him outside his own stead, and someone—presumably the Lord-Protector of Lanachrona or someone high in
the governing councils of Lanachrona—had tried two attacks on Emal.

Alucius suppressed a wince as he began to wash up and shave, still
thinking about the attack of the previous day and what he had put in the
report he had dispatched to militia headquarters—and what he had not.

Again, there had been little evidence on the bodies, which he had
reported. But the rifles and coins and the thirty captured mounts might
help raise some funds for Emal Outpost. As a detached company com-

mander, Alucius did have the ability to sell off goods captured in battle, although he had to account for the sale and the use of the coins. He had not reported either the goods captured or his plans for them.

He frowned. Perhaps he had been targeted by the Lanachronans . . . but not in the way he had thought. Perhaps they had sought out the most junior and isolated captain so that they could demonstrate the weakness of the southern borders. If that were so, though, that meant someone else had set up the attack outside Iron Stem.

With a slow sigh, Alucius dried his face. Either way, he had to watch himself. He just hoped that he'd have a few weeks before something else happened. He needed time to heal, and even though he had some healing Talent, it didn't work that well on one's self.

Talent never did.

30

Nothing happened, beyond the usual patrols and garrison requirements, during the week and two days following the attack. There was no rain, and the roads got dustier, and the local farmers complained. A few more bodies washed up along the riverbank, and two more abandoned raider mounts were turned in, surprisingly. Alucius suspected that there were more that would never show up, but he couldn't blame the finders. Emal and Tuuler were far from well-off locales.

The bruises on Alucius's chest and upper abdomen faded into a dull yellow and blackish purple. The worst of the soreness subsided, and there was no sign of the "Deforyan" raiders. Nor were there any messages or dispatches or orders from militia headquarters. Alucius did have to write reports on the five militia troopers killed in the fight, and shorter entries in their files on the six who were wounded. He did not make any notes about his own comparatively minor injuries.

On Quattri afternoon, he was crossing the courtyard after making an unannounced tour of the company barracks, when he saw militia troopers—Fifth Company—riding through the outpost gates, with Feran near the front.

Although he wanted to know why Fifth Company had returned early, he did not approach Feran, but retreated to the mess and the spring seasonal reports on each trooper, reports that he had begun the day before. He was glad, still, that he was left-handed, because he remained sore, and some of that soreness extended down into his right hand, although the worst had long since passed.

When Feran finally entered the mess, Alucius looked up from his reports, but did not rise as he spoke. "I didn't expect you back so soon. I thought they'd keep you wandering around Fiente for at least a month so that the majer could tell the Council how much the militia cared about its traders and their seed-oil works."

"We got word to head back here about three days ago." Feran grinned. "They said that the raiders had attacked Emal." He looked around the mess theatrically. "I don't see any damage."

"We caught them crossing the Vedra at the shallows before dawn," Alucius said blandly. "I thought they might try something like that. So I had sentries out. There were two companies. It was dark, but they showed up pretty well against the river. We found ninety bodies, and the local people here have found another fifteen washed downstream. So far."

"You don't like leaving survivors, do you?" asked Feran.

"The fewer survivors, the less you have to worry about fighting them again," Alucius pointed out. "Also, they were wearing Deforyan tunics and carrying Deforyan rifles, but they were mercenaries. They even had a few snipers."

"Are all herders like you?"

"I'd guess so." Alucius paused. "You have something in mind, don't you?"

"I'd always thought of herders as standing back, watching their flock, intervening and protecting when they had to. You're more like a lead nightram. You always lead from the front."

"What else was I supposed to do?"

"That's what I mean. Herders don't risk themselves that much. At least, that's my impression."

"I had to do something that would stop them from trying again." Alucius waited. "We can't afford too many fights. Twenty-first Company is already too low on ammunition."

"The supplies . . . the coin thing with the Council worries me," Feran said slowly. "Have you heard anything?"

Alucius shook his head. "I made a deal with a factor coming through Semal. I sold him all the Deforyan rifles we got. It wasn't what you'd get in Borlan or Dekhron, but I got sixty golds out of it, and another fifty for the mounts. With the twenty golds' worth of coppers and silvers we got on the battlefield"—Alucius grinned—"the ones that some of the men didn't get first, that should add another month to what we have for payroll and supplies."

"You . . ." Feran laughed. "A herder and a trader. You could be dangerous, Alucius."

"The regulations say that an officer on detached outpost duty can dispose of property acquired through the militia's lawful duties, so long as he accounts for its collection and use. I did keep the ten best mounts, though, for spares, and replacements."

"Have you told the acting commandant that?"

"As I recall . . ." Alucius said slowly, his eyes twinkling, "that is part of the year-end report."

"By then, it won't matter," Feran pointed out.

"Would you wish me to write a report at a time that is contrary to militia regulations?"

The older officer laughed. "How could I possibly insist on something contrary to regulations?"

After a moment, Alucius asked, "Have you heard anything about Majer Weslyn or the commandant?"

"No. The orders I received at Fiente were signed by Majer Weslyn, still sealed as acting commandant, and the troopers who delivered them only knew that Colonel Clyon remained very ill."

"Before . . . he was just ill."

"I know. It doesn't look good."

The two exchanged knowing glances.

31

Borlan, Lanachrona

Ebuin straightened his tunic and stepped through the door into the small room. He closed the door behind him and stood stiffly before the dark table desk and across from the captain-colonel of the Southern Guard, who remained seated behind it.

After a moment, the captain-colonel gestured. "Sit down, Majer."

Ebuin sat, on the front edge of the chair, his eyes not quite meeting those of his superior.

"Well?" asked the captain-colonel.

"The mercenaries made the attack two glasses before dawn the Duadi before last. They reported no sign of the Twenty-first Company before they crossed the river. The plan was to take the river road and move westward to the edge of town, station snipers, and cut down the captain when the Twenty-first Company appeared, then withdraw, unless engaged."

"I take it that the plan did not work as designed." An amused tone colored the captain-colonel's voice.

"No, sir. Less than a third of the mercenaries survived," Ebuin reported.

"Fewer than fifty out of a hundred and ninety? Exactly how did that happen?" asked the captain-colonel. "If you would explain . . . ?"

"Somehow, he knew. He had his company waiting. It was almost pitch-dark. Neither moon was up. His timing was perfect. They'd watered the bank, somehow, because the first riders got slowed by the mud, and most of the rest got cut down in the river. Only the last few squads escaped."

"In the river and in the dark, and they shot that many?"

"Yes, sir."

"You had enough mercenaries for two companies . . . Two." The captain-colonel leaned forward. "How many casualties did Twenty-first Company take?"

"Less than a handful. Two of the snipers claim that the captain was hit full in the chest, twice, and it did not even slow him down."

"He is a herder. He was doubtless wearing nightsilk under his uniform."

"Nightsilk may stop a bullet, sir, but it does not stop its impact. He should have suffered broken bones, as if he had been hit with an ancient lance in the chest."

"We could use a captain like that." The captain-colonel smiled, ruefully. "There are so few."

"What else—?" began Ebuin.

"For better or worse, this effort is over. The vulnerability of the southern borders of the Iron Valleys has been shown."

"Sir?"

"That is an order from the Lord-Protector, Majer. What you did was not totally successful, and not as successful as either of us would prefer, but it accomplished what the Lord-Protector needed, and he is not displeased."

"Yes, sir." Ebuin could not quite conceal the relief in his voice.

"Not as pleased as he should be, but not displeased. Do you understand?"

"Yes, sir."

"I am not totally pleased, either, Majer, but I believe we were both most fortunate, and we should count ourselves well acquitted. At times, it is best to let the soarer queen reign."

"Yes, sir."

Both officers nodded, if for different reasons.

32

Alucius and Feran had just finished their uninspiring and overcooked mutton supper when the duty guard knocked on the doorframe. "Captains, messengers for you." After a moment, he added, "Looks bad, sirs." Then he was gone.

Feran looked at Alucius. Alucius shrugged. They both walked out into the courtyard, filled with shadows cast by the late-afternoon sun. Two troopers had just dismounted. They wore the green sashes of messengers, but the sashes were crudely trimmed with black.

Alucius had no doubts about what message they brought.

The shorter trooper stepped forward. "There are two for each of you, Captains." He extended the missives, first to Feran, and then to Alucius. "From militia headquarters."

One of the missives was edged in black, and sealed on the outside in black wax as well. Alucius opened it, aware that he was being watched from a number of places around the courtyard, as was Feran. The main text of the carefully written note was short.

> It is with great sadness that the militia announces the death, after a lingering illness, of the commandant, Colonel Clyon. The colonel devoted his entire life to the Iron Valleys Militia, to its success in safeguarding the peoples under its care, and its efforts to ensure the full and free flow of trade to and from the Iron Valleys. In tribute to this remarkable officer, a month of mourning

126 L. E. MODESITT, JR.

is hereby declared for all militia outposts. All officers will wear black mourning bands.

The signature was, of course, that of Majer Weslyn as acting commandant.

Alucius looked up from the missive. "Thank you, troopers. We will miss the colonel." He nodded to Longyl, who had eased his way toward the group. "If you would see to the messengers, Longyl. They've ridden a great distance with tragic news."

"Yes, sir."

Neither Feran nor Alucius spoke until they were back in the small mess, alone.

"We knew it was coming," Feran said. "Doesn't make it any easier." He looked at the second, unopened message. "Hate to even think about opening this."

So did Alucius, but they both looked down, then opened the missives they held. Alucius read slowly and carefully.

The past few years have been difficult and trying times for the Militia of the Iron Valleys. The efforts it has taken to obtain coins, provisions, ammunition, and other supplies required to maintain the militia have been enormous, and Colonel Clyon accomplished much against odds that were overwhelming, it can be stated without exaggeration. This struggle has taken its toll, both on the colonel, and upon the militia and the people of the Iron Valleys.

The officers and troopers of the militia continue to face such odds with honor and with the ability for which the militia is justifiably known throughout all of Corus. One company, although outmanned by well-armed attackers with more than twice its numbers, recently repulsed an attack and did so with minimal casualties. That attack came less than two months after another attack of similar intensity. These attacks illustrate that we live in an unsettled time, and, because we do, once more, as the new commandant of the militia, I must call upon you and your troopers to maintain the high standards and unending vigilance that have been the militia tradition throughout the generations.

I look forward to working with you to continue that proud tradition.

Alucius's message was signed by Weslyn as colonel and commandant. Below the seal and signature, in the different hand that had signed the message, presumably Weslyn's, another brief line had been written: My commendations on a job well-done! Twice!

The younger captain refrained from snorting. At least, Weslyn knew Alucius had done something. Alucius waited until Feran had finished reading his own message before asking, "Did you get the 'honor and tradition' message?"

"Oh, that was clear enough. The part that bothered me was about the toll taken."

Alucius nodded. "A hint, you think?"

"More than a hint." Feran shook his head. "And there's nothing I can do, not with five years to go before even a short-coin stipend. You can get out in less than a year."

"If they let me," Alucius countered.

"They'll let you. They don't want to pay anyone any longer than they have to." Feran laughed.

Alucius laughed as well, but he had his doubts. Still, there was little that he could or should say, in anything that might get back to Dekhron. He had a message already written to send to Wendra, but he decided against dispatching what he had written. Instead, before the messengers departed in the morning, he'd write a much shorter note, merely conveying his love and the news of Colonel Clyon's death. He had no idea who might be looking at what in the days and weeks ahead.

33

West of South Pass, Illegea

The Praetorian Legions rode and marched westward along the high road and passed through the cut in the red cliffs—carved with the forgotten abilities of the Duarchy long before the Cataclysm—that marked the western end of the South Pass. The overcaptain of scouts rode along the shoulder of the high road toward the Praetor, slowing his mount as he neared, and announced, "The nomads remain drawn up on the hills to the north a good four vingts west of here, Praetor, and we have scouts on the rise facing them. They have not moved."

"The position where the Legions will form is less than two vingts from theirs, is that not correct?" The Praetor looked westward, checking the clear silver-green sky, then the rolling plains that spread westward into the distance, split by the dark gray of the high road, the one called the Lost Highway, for reasons buried with long-past generations.

"Yes, sir."

"That is well within the range of your devices, is it not, engineer?" asked the Praetor, looking back at Vestor, who rode beside the cart horse that pulled the first third of his equipment.

"It is," Vestor replied.

"You should be ready to set up all ten of your devices when we reach there, without delay."

Vestor looked at the Praetor. "There are tripods but for six, Praetor."

"I will have the other carts sent forward, along with the archers you trained, and you will set up six, and have the others open to the sun and ready to replace those. The nomads will certainly not give us time to replace the devices once they experience them in battle." The Praetor frowned. "In battle, one must have all ready to use at once. One may not get a second chance."

"Against grassland nomads?" Vestor blurted.

"We were all grassland nomads, or some such, once," the Praetor replied dryly, turning his mount so that he could call back his orders. "Bring forth all the carts of the engineer!"

Vestor stood in the stirrups, just to stretch his legs for a time, swaying from side to side before he dropped back onto the leather of a saddle that felt like iron. He kept riding, silently.

In less than a glass, only slightly past midday, the Legions had arrayed themselves across the rise, waiting. In the center of the Praetorian forces, just to the east of the highest point on the ridge, where the Praetor's banner flew, Vestor finished setting up the sixth tripod and adjusting it. Then he began to place the crystal weapons in each tripod.

"Praetor!" At the urgency of the call, Vestor looked up from the second tripod, held steady by an archer as the engineer slid the device into the restraining clamps. Vestor looked to the north. He expected to see the nomads advancing, but their lines remained motionless. All he could see was a flock of large birds, hawks perhaps, rising in the distance behind the nomads.

"Praetor!"

At the second call, Vestor focused on the birds, for there was nothing else moving. He swallowed as he saw, truly saw, the creatures climbing into the sky, with their long blue wings, and the men upon each, so small compared to the pteridons they rode that they looked like dolls. The flying creatures had to be pteridons, although Vestor had never seen one except as depicted in ancient drawings, or in the figures of a leschec set.

"Pteridons . . ." he murmured. "Pteridons . . ." The glint of blue metal caught his eye, blue metal in the hands of the pteridon riders. Abruptly, he rushed to the carts. "Hurry! We must get the devices ready! You must aim them at the pteridons!"

"Pteridons?" asked one of the archers. "There aren't any—"

"There are now!" snapped the engineer. "What do you think those things are?"

As quickly as he could manage, he placed the rest of the devices in their tripods, and tightened them in place. He glanced to the north, into the silver-green sky, and at the pteridons that swept southward toward the Praetor's forces.

"Once they cross the middle of the valley between us, fire your weapons!" Vestor stationed himself at the tripod on the eastern end. There he raised the device and swung it toward the oncoming pteridons and their riders. He pushed the firing lever forward. The device hummed, and red-limned light flashed skyward—missing the pteridon at the point of the wedge. He swung the beam again, and this time, sliced through the wing of one of the giant fliers on the flank. For a moment, he watched as the pteridon cartwheeled out of the air, throwing its rider clear, a nomad in blue who spun like a doll in the sky before plunging earthward. Then he forced himself to aim at a second of the fliers. Again, he missed, as he did a third time.

The pteridons were now almost overhead, and dropping into a near vertical dive—right at him. An eerie scream rose to the west. From the corner of his eye, Vestor thought he saw a blaze of blue flame shoot skyward. Something blue flashed above him, and the heat was like a furnace, but passed quickly—except that another blast flared to his left.

A high whine started, and began to climb. Vestor threw himself to the ground, as did the archer immediately to his left. Before either quite settled on the green spring grasses, fragments of metal flew around and past them. Vestor looked at his left arm, then eased a small splinter of metal from his tunic and out of his arm, although it had barely broken the skin. Another burst of blue flashed over the hillside, and the screams of agony shivered the air once more, with another wave of heat, and the sickening stench of burned flesh.

Vestor lurched to his feet, and glanced at the tripods. Where the two farthest to the west had been, blue flames had flared, and were beginning to subside. The tripods—half-collapsed—were sticks of charcoal.

The third tripod had vanished, the archer nowhere in sight. The next two tripods—and their archers—were untouched. Vestor looked up.

The pteridons had swept past, and were turning for another pass.

"Aim ahead of them! Just a bit!" Vestor followed his own advice . . . and missed. He readjusted . . . and saw another pteridon go down, and then another, its wing severed by one of the other archers. The lead flier and its rider were less than a hundred yards away, when Vestor managed to slice through the long neck of the beast to the left of the leader. For some reason, he had trouble focusing on the leader.

Then more blue fire swept across the ridgetop, and Vestor threw himself to the ground, feeling the air turn furnacelike where he had been standing moments before.

When he staggered up, he discovered he was the last one standing, and his tripod was the only one erect. He glanced to the west, but where the Praetor and his banner had been was nothing but a mass of blue flame, and greasy white-and-gray smoke.

The device on his tripod was beginning to whine, and Vestor slammed the apertures closed and spun the clamps open, before pulling the device from the bracket and running to the cart to try to get a replacement before the pteridons turned once more.

He glanced up to see another group of fliers sweeping from the northwest, and flames flaring across the entire ridgeline. As the flames and the lines of blue light that fed and created them flashed toward him, he dived and rolled for the back side of the hill.

A combination of overtaxed crystals and skylance flames exploded, pushing him into a series of rolls that tumbled him a good hundred yards downhill.

For a time, he just lay sprawled on the damp grass.

"Engineer! Is that you?"

Vestor struggled into a sitting position, then made out an officer—the overcaptain of scouts, riding toward him, leading a mount without a rider.

"You want to see Alustre again, mount up. The Praetor's dead, and those things—"

"Pteridons," Vestor said involuntarily. "They're pteridons."

"Whatever they are. They're burning everyone to cinders. Don't think they'll do well in the pass. Not enough room for them to get close. The marshal's ordered everyone to retreat to the pass."

Vestor struggled up into the saddle, one-handedly, realizing belatedly that he could move neither his left hand nor his arm. Then he rode after the overcaptain. He did not look back.

34

On the last Quinti before the turn of summer, in the dry and dusty midmorning, under a sky of blazingly clear silver-green, Alucius rode eastward along the river road at the head of the second squad. A half vingt ahead rode a pair of scouts, and to his left rode Anslym. Although it was barely midmorning, Alucius found himself blotting his forehead with the back of his tunic sleeve, wiping away both sweat and grit, and having half emptied one of his water bottles.

"Haven't seen a trace of raiders in almost a month, sir," Anslym said. "Think we'll see any more anytime soon?"

"I wouldn't think so," Alucius replied, "but common sense said that the two groups we fought off shouldn't have even been out here." He shook his head. "I hope we don't see any. We've only got enough ammunition for patrols, and not a stand-up battle against raiders."

"Has Colonel Weslyn sent any messages about ammunition and supplies?"

"Nothing new except a reminder to be very careful about both . . . and a statement that both powder and sulfur are once more getting hard to come by."

"The sulfur comes from Lanachrona, doesn't it?"

"It does," Alucius said, glancing ahead at a plume of dust, before looking back to Anslym once he saw that the dust had been raised by a farmer's oxcart headed westward toward the squad, presumably to market in Emal. "It's always been a problem. I'd hoped the new Regent for the Matrial would encourage trade with the Iron Valleys, in goods like sulfur, but it hasn't happened."

"The Madriens don't like to trade that much, do they?"

"They don't have to trade as much as we do. They produce more different things. They don't care for most lands in Corus." That was being generous. From what he'd seen, Alucius wasn't sure that the women of Madrien had much use for any other land in Corus. Pushing that thought away, Alucius looked toward the River Vedra, his eyes traveling over the eddies in the black water. Eddies? He turned and studied the river more closely, seeing not just the eddies near the shore, but the two yards or so of drying mud on the shore below the matted grass and low undergrowth that marked a shoreline that, after the spring runoff, seldom varied much. He couldn't recall seeing the water level that low, especially so early in the year. That meant there hadn't been nearly the usual snowfall up on the Plateau. With no snow or rain to speak of in two months, and none in sight, and the river already so low, the outlook for the crops wasn't good—on top of everything else.

"Sir?"

"I was thinking about rain," Alucius admitted. "If we don't get more, then the farmers won't have good crops. By next winter, food will cost much more, and tariff revenues will be even lower because people will be buying less."

Anslym frowned.

"Lower tariffs mean fewer coins for the militia—and we're already short of things."

"Most of the men—"

"Are scheduled to be released at the turn of the year. But they probably won't get release bonuses, the way they have in the past, and they might even get out a month early—with no pay for that month, and they'd be going back to families, and farms and crafts that will be having trouble feeding the people there." Alucius added, "That's if we don't get more rain. But it's still early in the year, and that could change."

The way matters were going, Alucius wasn't about to wager that the Iron Valleys would get more rain. Or that the Lord-Protector wouldn't find a way to use the drought to Lanachrona's advantage.

35

Tempre, Lanachrona

The younger man in the violet-blue tunic looked up from the Table of the Recorders. An expression of annoyance crossed his narrow lips before he spoke. "Can you recall that scene again, Recorder?"

"As you wish, Lord-Protector. I had thought you should see this."

"I don't know what I am seeing," muttered the younger man.

The ruby mists swirled and revealed a scene as if observed from the sky. Two forces, each on a ridgeline, faced each other. To the south of the southerly force was a great high road that ran east and west, vanishing into the Spine of Corus to the east and disappearing into the rolling hills to the west.

The Lord-Protector studied the scene in the Table of the Recorders, intently, for he had not believed what he had seen the first time. Again, he watched the two forces. As before, a flare of flame, tinged with silver, appeared near the banner of the southern force, a force with livery of black and silver, or, in some places, silver and gray. Then a second flame appeared. Before long, the entire crest of the hill was in flames, and the forces in disarray, retreating hastily back along the high road back behind the redstone cliffs.

The Lord-Protector looked to the Recorder of Deeds. "I saw flames from nowhere, blue flames, that destroyed an enormous force. The other force did not move at all. Some of the flames were tinged with silver, and that means that they were called forth by Talent." He paused. "But . . . how can anyone call forth that much flame? And where were those who did so?"

"You did not see all that happened," explained the gray-haired Recorder. "Blue was always the color of the Myrmidons of the Duarchy, and their skylances created blue flames. That is what the records claim."

"I did not see any pteridons or any skylances. The only blue I saw was the livery of the northernmost force—and flames from nowhere," the Lord-Protector pointed out.

"No . . . that is all the Table showed you. It cannot show creatures of Talent, or great users of Talent."

The Lord-Protector rubbed his forehead. "Would you make yourself clear? I have little time for games and riddles."

"I believe that Aellyan Edyss found—somehow—pteridons in the Council Vault, protected against time. Or he has found the secret of creating them. They are creatures totally of Talent, and the skylances are weapons totally created by Talent. You could not see either, because the Table cannot show them. You could see the results, the uncontrolled fires, and the rout of the Praetorian Legions."

"You are certain?"

"I am certain that he has some Talent-based creatures and weapons. Whatever they are, they did what you saw."

"So . . . I have this . . . Regent of the Matrial to the west, with her crystal spear-thrower. I have to the north an officer in the Iron Valleys Militia that your Table shows as a danger to me, although it cannot say why, and now I have Aellyan Edyss to the west with creatures of such Talent that they can rout an army far larger than any I could field without stripping every outpost in Lanachrona."

"The Table shows what is, Lord-Protector."

"The matter with the Iron Valleys Council is not resolved, and yet it may take weeks or months for them to understand that they have no real choice." The Lord-Protector massaged his forehead with his right hand.

"Now, with this, I cannot afford to fight in the north, no matter how long I must wait, otherwise."

"Perhaps both the threat of power, and the offer of benefits . . ."

"Benefits?"

"It could be that there is something else, still, that might help persuade this Council and yet enhance your power." The Recorder paused, then asked, "Have you not said that the Militia of the Iron Valleys has many companies that are the equal of the Southern Guard?"

"Yes. I would not say such too openly, but all know it is so. Especially the one commanded by the herder captain."

"Perhaps you should make them—and him—your ally. Would not an ally be better than a foe? They have a militia they cannot afford to pay and support for a defense they would not need, were you to offer them guarantees of their liberty and freedom to trade."

The Lord-Protector's head jerked up. "Not a bad thought, but how . . . ?"

"That, Lord-Protector," replied the Recorder of Deeds, "I cannot say. I can see how the pieces might fit, but you are the leader who must discover how to encourage those involved to see it as you do."

"Or as they would like to see it," mused the younger man.

After a time, a slow smile crossed his lips. He stood slowly, nodding to the Recorder as he left the small, marble-walled chamber.

36

Late in the day on the first Quattri of summer, a single wagon, half-loaded, had arrived from militia headquarters—carrying the entirety of the supplies for the next season. With the wagon had come a short missive from Colonel Weslyn explaining that and apologizing for the shortfall, but citing the inability of the Council to raise enough tariff coins to provide more. Half a wagon, Alucius reflected, for two months. More than half the supplies had consisted of flour and dried beef. There had been but four cases of cartridges, two for each horse company, and none for the two squads of foot, and Twenty-first Company had gone through close to four cases in the one battle against the raiders.

The only cheerful aspect of the supply delivery had been the message from Wendra, which Alucius had slipped inside his tunic to read when he had a quiet moment.

That moment finally came after supper, when in the dying twilight, he sat on the ancient chair in his small room and broke the seal on the message.

My dearest Alucius,
I am writing this quickly, because Grandfather Kustyl is riding down to Dekhron to see some traders. He said that he could deliver my words to militia headquarters and make sure they got to you.

We just received your latest message. That was the one about Colonel Clyon's death and about your battle with the raiders. Your grandsire had already heard about the colonel. He was deeply saddened, and said to tell you that. He also said that he was not surprised about the raids. He is hopeful they would be the last for a time because of everything that has happened.

Alucius nodded. His wife and his grandsire shared the same views as Alucius did.

We were both glad to hear that you were not seriously wounded in the battle and that all is now well . . .

Alucius frowned. He had not said anything about his injuries. Then he glanced down at the black crystal of his herder's wristband. Of course, Wendra had known that he'd been hurt.

The spring shoots on the quarasote are smaller and shorter than usual. That didn't affect the nightwool we just finishing shearing.

Unless we get more rain later in the summer, their coats won't be nearly so strong next year . . .

Your grandsire is letting me take the flock to the southern sections of the stead, now, by myself, if only for part of the day. Sometimes, we trade off. That lets him work on the equipment in the mornings, then I help your mother with the carding and the spinnerets in the afternoon . . .

A sander got one of the ewes two weeks ago, and left a ramlet. I remembered the story about Lamb and decided that, if you could nurse him through when you were only five years old, I certainly could manage. The first nights were hard, but he's now taking the bottle well, and he's going to grow up strong.

Alucius smiled to himself. He'd said that she'd make a herder, and she was. He just wished he were there to share in that joy. But then, he reflected, would she have discovered what she truly was had he been there?

I must close so that Grandfather Kustyl can take this. I look forward to seeing you when I can, whenever that may be. All my love goes with you . . .

For a long time, he looked at the words on the page, reading and rereading them, especially the last lines.

37

On a late Septi midmorning two weeks after the supply wagon arrived, Alucius was conducting mounted sabre drills with second squad—one-on-one. Longyl had first squad on the flats to the east, working on maneuvers.

The sun was pounding down on the outpost through the silver-green sky on another cloudless day—when the militia trooper wearing the sash of a messenger rode through the gate of Emal Outpost. Despite the swept stones of the causeway, the messenger's mount still raised dust.

"Stand down!" Alucius ordered, and turned Wildebeast toward the messenger, who had reined up outside the small outpost headquarters building. He brought Wildebeast to a stop several yards short of the dusty trooper.

"Captain Alucius?"

Alucius nodded.

"I have dispatches for you and Captain Feran. Each has to be hand-delivered to each of you, sir."

Alucius was spared having to call for the older officer because Feran stepped out of the headquarters building.

"Captain Feran?"

"None other," Feran said.

The messenger leaned forward in the saddle and extended a dispatch to Feran, then eased his mount toward Alucius, handing the sealed missive to him, almost as if he didn't want to get too close to the younger of the two officers. "I'm to wait for a response from each of you."

Alucius turned and motioned to Anslym, then waited as the squad leader rode across the courtyard.

"Anslym . . . if you would arrange for the messenger. He'll be staying tonight, and leaving in the morning."

"Yes, sir." Anslym looked at the trooper. "Please follow me."

The slender trooper glanced at the officers.

"You'll have a response by muster tomorrow," Alucius promised.

"Yes, sir."

Feran and Alucius watched as the messenger followed Anslym toward the stables.

"He doesn't want to stay around," Feran observed. "That's not good."

"I don't think I'd want to be a militia messenger right now," Alucius added. "There can't be that much good news to deliver."

"You don't think this is good news?" Feran chuckled as he looked up at Alucius.

"Do you?" Alucius paused, then broke the seal and opened the dispatch. "Might as well read what else has gone wrong."

"You're such an optimist," Feran said, still holding his own dispatch, unopened.

"Compared to you . . . yes."

Alucius's eyes skimmed over the standard salutation and focused on the text.

As most of you know, the Iron Valleys incurred heavy debt during the Matrite War. The Council could not raise tariffs quickly enough to cover the cost of paying the militia and providing ammunition and other supplies, and was required to borrow heavily from other lands. Because of poor weather and adverse trading conditions over the past several years, the Council has not been able to raise the coins necessary even to pay the interest on that debt, and there are no coins left in the treasury to pay troopers and officers past the turn of harvest, little more than a month away. Unfortunately, raids by brigands and others are continuing, and within weeks it will be impossible to protect the people of the Iron Valleys. The Lord-Protector of Lanachrona has also expressed strong concerns that, without an operating militia, the northern borders of Lanachrona would be open to raids of the sort that had occurred earlier this year until the brigands were killed by the militia. He noted that Lanachrona would be forced to station more companies of the Southern Guard along the River Vedra and might well be forced to pursue such brigands into the Iron Valleys, as well as destroy any sanctuaries within the Iron Valleys. This would not be a good situation for either the people of the Iron Valleys or those of Lanachrona.

Under these circumstances, the Council met in a series of emergency negotiations with representatives of the Lord-Protector of Lanachrona . . .

Alucius winced. Even though he had predicted something like this coming, seeing it in cold black letters was still a shock.

. . . and worked out an agreement of union between Lanachrona and the Iron Valleys. A summary of the main terms is attached.

The Iron Valley Militia will remain as a separate unit, under the Council, but it will be called the Northern Guard. All troopers and officers will remain on the rolls and will continue to be paid, and all companies will be supplied regularly. Later this summer, after the commanders of the Northern Guard and Southern Guard meet, there may be other changes announced, but all commitments to present militia troopers and officers will be fully honored . . .

One of your tasks will be to explain to the people of Emal and the surrounding area what has happened, and to reassure them that, for them, nothing has changed. No Southern Guard detachments or forces will appear. The Council will still promulgate laws for the Iron Valleys. Tariffs for farmers and small crafters will not change much. The only increase will be one part in twenty-five, and that was a tariff increase already approved by the Council to pay off past debts. One great advantage will be that tariffs will no longer be levied on Lanachronan goods carried into the Iron Valleys or those of the Iron Valleys carried into Lanachrona.

You are requested to respond in writing by declaring your allegiance to the militia, henceforth the Northern Guard, as now governed for the Lord-Protector by the Council . . .

Alucius glanced over the second sheet, but the main terms of the agreement were as noted in the cover dispatch. He looked at Feran, waiting until the older officer finished reading, then asked, "What do you think?"

"We've been sold out, and there's not a sanded thing that we can do." Feran snorted. "Do you know what I'm supposed to do?"

"No."

"I'm supposed to remove the guard posts on the bridge and the iron gate. Anyone can cross anytime with anything."

"I suppose that's not bad," Alucius offered.

"No, that part's not bad. And for a while, nothing terrible will happen. Not right away. But basic tariff levies on crafters and artisans and farmers will go up in a year, and then more in another year. Then maybe they'll change our uniforms to look more like the Southern Guard, and pretty soon, the senior officers will be from Borlan or Tempre."

"So?" asked Alucius. "Is that any different from right now? Majer . . . Colonel Weslyn might as well have been born in Borlan."

Feran laughed, but there was an edge to his voice. "Maybe . . . maybe . . . We'll have to see, won't we?"

Alucius wasn't looking forward to that, or to telling his troopers, although he knew they were solid and would stand behind him. He just hoped he could continue to do his best for them.

38

Under the faint light cast by the oil lamp in the mess, Alucius sat at the table, looking at the blank sheet of paper before him, about to start another letter to Wendra, since he had dispatched the last one with the messenger who had brought the news of the forced union of the Iron Valleys with Lanachrona. Because the night was hot, he'd taken off his tunic, but not his undertunic. All the windows and shutters were wide, and every so often a fly or mosquito hummed toward Alucius. None of them actually landed on the herder.

Feran cleared his throat. Wearing only trousers and a frayed undertunic, he stood barefoot in the doorway from the quarters end of the building, which held the two small rooms for each of them, plus two others for visiting officers, although there hadn't been a visiting officer in at least the last year.

Alucius looked up.

"Don't know how you do that," Feran said.

"Do what?"

"Mosquitoes. If I close the shutters, I can't sleep because it's too hot. If I leave them open for the breeze, the mosquitoes come in and eat me. They hover around you, but they never land on you."

Alucius shook his head. "They don't like herders. We taste bad." That was the only explanation he was about to give, since he didn't want to admit that he was using a fraction of his Talent to keep from getting bitten.

"You deserve some advantages for having to grow up there, I suppose." Feran slipped into the chair on the other side of Alucius. "Too cold and barren for me. Sander near died when we had to fight through the winter at Soulend. Thought I'd never get warm again."

"I don't mind the cold," Alucius admitted, setting down the pen, "and I like the openness. You know that. That was the hardest thing about being a Matrite trooper—always being with other troopers, never being able to get away."

"You still take rides by yourself."

Alucius nodded. "The troopers understand. They laugh about their herder captain when they think I'm not listening."

"The men took this all pretty well," Feran said. "Better than I did, I'd wager."

"They're getting paid, and they wouldn't have, and they've been told that they can stay if they want to and leave once their commitment is over. And they won't have to fight the Southern Guard. It could have been worse," Alucius said. "We didn't lose a war, and no one is invading the Iron Valleys." Not yet, he thought to himself.

"No, we just lost the peace . . . and the ability to do things our way," Feran said dryly. "What do you think is going to happen? The Lord-Protector isn't just going to let us sit here and collect our pay. Not for long."

"Probably not. What do you think?"

"If he had his way, he'd disband the militia. That won't happen, not for a while. I'd guess we'll get shuffled around, and some may get an incentive to leave early." Feran leaned back in the chair and brushed away an insistent mosquito. "If the Lanachronans were still fighting the Matrites, we might find ourselves riding west again, but I don't see that happening, not this year."

"No. The Lord-Protector took Southgate and the high road from Tempre to the port at Southgate. Some of the militia companies might get road patrol duties there. Without the Matrite troopers riding the high roads, the Lanachronans have to be patrolling the roads, or we'd be seeing raiders out of the Dry Coast. Maybe something like that."

"That would be better than going north," Feran said. "The Lord-Protector might make a stab at Klamat, to get the timber trade, maybe even take over Northport."

"I'd guess that won't come for a few years," Alucius suggested. "He'd have to send Southern Guards across the Iron Valleys. He promised not to do that."

"You really think he'll keep his word?"

"Not forever. But he will for a year or two, perhaps longer."

"Why? We couldn't do that much about it."

"You're right. We couldn't. But he promised. And how will all the other rulers around take it if he immediately breaks a written agreement? The Landarch, the Regent of the Matrial, or even the traders of Dramur? They'd never agree to anything they didn't have to, and they'd ask for more golds or conditions. No . . . he'll wait until he has a good reason, then he'll say times have changed." Alucius laughed. "Times always change. He just has to wait."

"I still worry . . ." Feran stood.

"So do I," Alucius admitted. "But I don't know what to do about it."

"It's getting cooler. You think we'll get rain?" Feran walked toward the door.

"I hope so, but it's still clear outside."

"No rain then. See you in the morning."

"Good night." Alucius sat back in the chair. Despite the difference in their ages, Feran was the only friend he'd really made since he'd been a boy and talked glass after glass with Vardial. Now Vardial was stationed somewhere in the southwest, along the Vedra, and Alucius hadn't seen him in years.

Then, Alucius reflected, his life hadn't exactly been the kind to allow many friends, not when the nearest stead had been almost ten vingts away. He might have made friends when he'd been a conscript, if it hadn't have been for Dolesy—and then having been picked as a scout. And being a Matrite captive trooper and later a squad leader hadn't made finding friends easy there.

He smiled. He enjoyed talking to Feran. That was one of the best parts of duty at Emal.

39

Tempre, Lanachrona

The Lord-Protector walked to the window of the private study and gazed out through the misty rain, looking out on the River Vedra.

"You're worried about something, aren't you, dear?" The woman who spoke could not have been called beautiful, or pretty, for her eyes were too large, and her nose too sharp, although her voice was firm, yet melodious. "Is it the forced union of the Iron Valleys? Still?"

"What else could I do? You were right, and the forced union was far less costly than a war, even if accomplished with the tacit threat of such. In time, if our rein is light, they will forget, or at least accept. Even so, we are stretched too thin with the western campaign. Yet if we had not acted against Madrien after the Matrial's disappearance, we never would have been able to take Southgate. The nomads are stirring to the east, and sooner or later Deforya will fall, and then we would lose the other high road to the east. In the Iron Valleys, only the herders have any strength, and they are becoming fewer every year. With the traders in Dekhron controlling their Council, the Iron Valleys would always have been weak."

"Until someone else invaded them, as the Matrial attempted."

"The forced union was the best course, but I still worry, dearest," the Lord-Protector admitted.

"That is not it, Talryn dear. You have talked of the Matrites and the Iron Valleys and the problems they have created before. Is it that herder officer? You have pondered over him far too much, given all the other difficulties you face." She straightened from the smaller desk where she had been writing.

"He is the key to something. That I can feel, and yet I cannot say what it might be, except that the Recorder likes him not at all, much as he dissembles."

"I would say that is something in favor of this officer. Perhaps a great deal, even if he is from the north."

"You don't care for Enyll, do you?" The Lord-Protector turned and walked toward his consort, circled behind her, and stood with his fingers on her shoulders, his thumbs kneading the muscles beside her shoulder blades.

"That feels good, but you need not . . ."

"I know I need not, but it is something that I can do for you that has little to do with being Lord-Protector. You were saying about Enyll?"

"I had said little." She smiled mischievously.

"Say a little more, then."

"Enyll has such a desire for knowledge that he would sacrifice anyone to discover—or rediscover—the source of a new power or the design of an ancient new weapon. He thinks less of all those who do not know what he does. I would call it the arrogance of knowledge."

"In that, he is arrogant," the Lord-Protector replied. "Yet that thirst for knowledge makes him valuable."

"It also makes him dangerous and unpredictable."

"That, too." The Lord-Protector laughed. "You are better than any of my ministers and marshals at seeing to the heart of matters."

"You do not mind . . . my other deficiencies."

"We are young, and what will be, it will be. I would rather have you as you are than anyone else as they might be." He bent and kissed the back of her neck, gently.

40

Little more than a week after Alucius and Feran had sent their replies back to Colonel Weslyn, a squad of militia troopers rode through the Emal Outpost gate, again in the afternoon, as Alucius was drilling a squad, this time, fifth squad.

The squad leader rode straight to Alucius. "Sir? You're Captain Alucius?"

"Correct, squad leader. How might I help you?" Alucius didn't like unannounced squads appearing at the outpost, especially after the last message, the one declaring that the Council had surrendered an independence dearly purchased with years of sacrifice.

"We're the advance guard for the commandant. Colonel Weslyn."

"The colonel is riding to Emal Outpost?"

"Yes, sir. He will be visiting all the outposts along the river."

"How long before he arrives? And how many are with him?"

"About a glass, sir. Just another squad, sir."

"If you will excuse me, my senior squad leader will be with you in a moment."

"Yes, sir."

Again . . . Alucius had the feeling that he was being treated with far greater care and courtesy than the average captain. Either that or the colonel had problems everywhere and had instructed that all officers be treated with great courtesy.

Alucius alerted Feran first, then set to work with Longyl to assure that

Twenty-first Company was fully mustered out, as if for inspection—in formation, with full summer uniforms.

The courtyard was crowded, with Fifth Company on the north side and Twenty-first on the south, and through the open gates, Alucius could see that a number of townspeople had gathered and were watching. Both Alucius and Feran were mounted and waiting when the colonel rode through the gates at the head of another squad, accompanied by a captain Alucius did not know, the black banner of the commandant following.

"Twenty-first Company, all present and awaiting inspection," Alucius announced.

"Fifth Company, all present and awaiting inspection . . ."

"Captains, you do us honor." Weslyn was tall and blond, his face tanned, his smile ready. He inclined his head briefly.

"Not so much as you honor us, sir," returned Alucius, thankful in a way for the training in handling such situations that he had inadvertently gained as a Matrite squad leader.

Feran merely nodded.

"We will make the inspection brief." Weslyn laughed softly. "It has been a long ride."

True to his word, the inspection was brief, and the commandant offered only complimentary comments to a handful of troopers.

Once done, he turned his mount to Alucius and Feran. "If you would not mind, Captains . . . we would like a moment to wash up before we eat, and, at that time, discuss why we are here."

"Yes, sir. The quarters for visiting officers are ready, sir, although they are not large."

Once the commandant had dismounted and turned his mount to a trooper from the squad that had accompanied him, Alucius turned. "Twenty-first Company! Dismissed to the outpost!"

"Fifth Company! Dismissed to the outpost," Feran followed.

Alucius and Feran turned their mounts to Vinkin, something Alucius normally would not have done, but he wanted to talk to Feran before they met with the commandant.

The two officers slipped to one side of the courtyard in the shade and well away from the barracks and the headquarters building.

"What do you think?" Alucius asked.

"He's visiting every outpost on the river. That means change. We'll all be moved or put under Lanachronan command . . . or something. What else could it mean?"

Alucius nodded. He also had no doubts that the squad leader of the advance guard had been ordered to tell them that. "We might as well go wash up ourselves and see what he has to say."

The colonel was waiting in the small mess when the two captains joined him and the captain accompanying him.

Alucius had forgotten that Colonel Weslyn stood half a head taller than Alucius himself. Only a handful of men were that much taller, and few were both taller and broader across the shoulders. Colonel Weslyn was both. With his silvering blond hair, his square jaw, and piercing blue eyes, he presented an impressive appearance as he stood in the small officers' mess.

Alucius scanned the colonel with his Talent. Not to his surprise, Weslyn's lifethread was amber brown and ran southwest, certainly not the lifethread of a northerner or a man likely to understand herders.

"Greetings, Alucius, Feran," said the colonel, his voice full and deep.

Alucius nodded politely. "Greetings and welcome to Emal Outpost, Colonel."

"Greetings," Feran echoed, his voice barely verging on politeness.

"This is Captain Shalgyr, who is acting as my aide for this tour." Weslyn nodded to the almost squat and black-haired officer.

"We're pleased to meet you," Alucius said.

Feran nodded.

"We might as well sit down," Weslyn said.

"The meal will be here shortly," Alucius noted, nodding to the cook, who had peered out from the small kitchen. "I fear it will not be up to the standards of Dekhron."

"Dekhron is not up to its own standards lately." The colonel paused, then went on with a smile. "I don't imagine either of you expected to see me in Emal."

"No, sir," Alucius admitted.

"Times have been difficult, but I hope that we are past the worst of that now, but I had thought it might be better to discuss matters over a meal, less formally, if you will." Weslyn paused as the serving girl, the cook's daughter, appeared with two mugs of ale, which, following Alucius's eyes, she placed in front of Weslyn and Shalgyr, before departing and immediately returning with two more mugs. "I do not know that official dispatches could have told you how dangerous our situation was. The debts incurred by the Council, with interest, had reached ten thousand golds."

Feran swallowed, started to speak, then stopped without a word.

"That was so great a sum that all the tariff revenues for several years would not have covered it."

Alucius suppressed a frown. From his rough calculations, the annual budget of the militia was around five thousand golds, and surely there were other expenditures?

"The Council could not devote all the tariff revenues to repaying or even paying the interest on that debt. In fact, as we had written you, we did not have the funds to pay or supply any companies past summer. The lack of rain, and the probable crop failures to come made matters worse. The coins were originally borrowed from the Landarch of Deforya, but he needed repayment, and so he sold the debt to the Lord-Protector." Weslyn shrugged. "You could see where that left the Council. There was no choice, and now we must work out the arrangements."

The serving girl delivered a platter of mutton smothered in white gravy, a second one of lace potatoes, a compote of early apples drizzled in honey, and two baskets of bread.

Weslyn served himself before asking, "Does either of you have any questions?"

"We'd just like to know where that leaves our troopers and us," Feran said politely.

"I can understand that. We have all felt that way," the colonel replied. "I don't know that you have heard, but the nomad ruler of Illegea—his name is Aellyan Edyss—has conquered Ongelya. More important, we have received word that he has routed the forces of Lustrea near the South Pass and killed the Praetor. While the Praetor's son is well respected, and will certainly become the new Praetor, it is highly unlikely that he will immediately undertake another attack on the nomads. We understand from the Lord-Protector that Aellyan Edyss is riding to the northwest. The Landarch of Deforya is greatly concerned that Edyss is bringing his forces into position to attack Deforya."

"Why not Lanachrona?" asked Feran bluntly. "That's northwest as well."

"Because he will gain more by taking both the north and south passes to the east. He already controls the South Pass to Lustrea. If he takes Dereka, he will hold both high roads, and both passes. Also, Deforya is an easier target than Lanachrona."

"I don't quite see how that affects us, or even the Iron Valleys," Feran stated.

"No, not directly. But . . ." Weslyn drew out the word, then smiled. "As I have explained, the militia is in great debt to the Council and, now, to the Lord-Protector. The Lord-Protector has agreed, as my earlier dispatch informed you, to accept the militia as the Northern Guard of Lanachrona. Further, he has agreed to assume all back pay owed, and to ensure that all stipends will be paid to troopers and officers alike."

Alucius had a cold feeling about where the discussion was headed, but he waited, listening.

"Because the southern border of the Iron Valleys will no longer need to be patrolled, the outposts along the eastern part of the River Vedra will be closed . . ."

Feran nodded. "You want us to volunteer to do some dirty work elsewhere to keep our stipends?"

Weslyn went on without looking directly at Feran. "The Council had to agree to several terms as part of the agreement with Lanachrona. As you may know, the organization of the militia is unique in all of Corus. By comparison, all equipment and all mounts used by the Southern Guard belong to the Lord-Protector. That is also true in Madrien and in Lustrea, and even in Deforya. The Lord-Protector finds himself assuming responsibility for the debts of the militia, yet there are no . . . assets to speak of. In addition, he has pledged not to station any of the Southern Guard in the Iron Valleys for the next twenty years. In return for these conditions, he has asked the newly established Northern Guard to provide four horse companies—under their own officers, of course—for service with the Southern Guard in defending the borders of Lanachrona."

Alucius repressed a nod.

Feran snorted.

"We felt that far less dislocation would be involved if those companies that were already going to be displaced were among those assigned." Weslyn smiled at Alucius. "In addition, the Twenty-first Company has a reputation for effectiveness, and the Lord-Protector specifically requested that you be among those companies. Unless, of course, you would choose to buy out your service time—all four years as a captain, which would be four times the rate of a herder conscript, since your service is not yet complete."

Alucius didn't have to consider that provision for long. A conscript's buyout would have taken half the revenues from the stead for each year. A captain's buyout on those terms would destroy the stead. "We will serve as requested."

"I had thought you might." Weslyn turned to Feran. "There are two possibilities for Fifth Company, Captain. You could be assigned to the outpost to be opened at Eastice and charged with ensuring that the high road be kept clear of brigands . . . and provide border guard service along the northern boundaries with Madrien, or you could be assigned to accompany Twenty-first Company."

Feran's lips tightened.

"If Fifth Company went with Twenty-first Company, you would, of course, be under the command of Overcaptain Alucius. That is, unless you choose to leave the Northern Guard." Weslyn took a sip of his ale.

Alucius concealed a wince. Weslyn was clearly trying to force Feran to leave the militia.

After a long moment, Feran presented a smile—a cold smile. "If it's all the same to you, Colonel, I think it's fair to say that Fifth Company and I would prefer to serve with and under Overcaptain Alucius."

For the briefest instant, an expression of surprise flickered across the

154 L. E. MODESITT, JR.

colonel's face before he replied smoothly. "Both the Northern Guard and the Lord-Protector will be pleased to know that two such experienced companies will be defending our borders."

When had Lanachrona's borders become "our" borders? Alucius wondered.

As he cut through the gravy-covered mutton, Weslyn looked at Alucius. "Your promotion to overcaptain will become effective when you leave Emal two weeks from yesterday. I will make sure your insignia are dispatched in time."

"Might you be able to tell us where we will be defending those borders?" asked Alucius.

"Oh . . . I didn't mention that, did I? The Lord-Protector is sending a detachment of five horse companies to support the Landarch of Deforya. Four will be from the Northern Guard, and one from the Southern Guard. It's good to know that the Twenty-first and Fifth Companies will be two of them."

"How . . . or where will we join this detachment?"

"The detachment commander is a Majer Draspyr, I believe. I have your route here, and I will leave it, obviously. You will cross the Vedra here and ride south to the high road and a road outpost there in a place called . . . what is it . . . Senelmyr, that's it. That's where you will meet the majer and the other companies. We brought the new shoulder patches, also. They're really just blue shimmersilk triangles, but they go on your tunics so that the Southern Guard can tell who you are. We can go over the details in the morning, once you've had a chance to think about it."

"What about the outpost?" Alucius asked. "Will the militia close it? Or sell it?"

"The Northern Guard has not decided," the colonel said slowly. "Certainly, if we can sell unused assets, to defer costs, that would be prudent." Abruptly, he smiled again. "That is not bad fare for such an isolated outpost." The commandant glanced at Feran, then Alucius. "Might I ask how you have managed such?"

"As carefully as we could, sir," Alucius replied. "Gravy is not terribly expensive, and allows one the luxury of thinking the meat is less tough than it is, and the apples are a type that does not travel well, and so they are not expensive."

"You two are resourceful. Very good. It will serve you—and us—very well." Weslyn smiled yet again. "Did you know that we are already receiving brownberries in Dekhron? And without tariffs, even the lower crafters can afford them."

Alucius got the message that the colonel had said all that he was about to say. So he listened, and commented politely, until supper was over. After more pleasantries the two outpost captains excused themselves and made their way out into the still-light evening. The sun was poised over the western river bluffs, its white light tinged with green as it dropped toward the horizon. The two walked silently out through the gates and along the causeway until they were certain they were alone.

"I'm sorry, Feran," Alucius said. "I didn't—"

"It's not your fault, and I don't hold anything against you. But I meant it. I'd be sanded if I'd take an assignment where there are only two months out of ten without snow. And they are going to pay that stipend."

"You think Fifth Company . . ."

"They feel the same way. A third of them came from Soulend—or Iron Stem—to get out of the cold. You think they want to serve in a place three hundred vingts closer to the Ice Sands?"

"He decided to promote me to force you out," Alucius pointed out.

"We both got sanded. You couldn't afford that kind of buyout, could you?"

"It would force my family into poverty. They'd have to sell the stead, and they'd still end up owing hundreds of golds."

"That much?"

"Low hundreds," Alucius admitted, "but there wouldn't be any way to pay them."

"Well . . . at least you'll get a few more coins out of it."

A few more coins, and much more trouble. As he watched the sun set, Alucius reflected. Troubles just compounded themselves. He'd gotten captured by the Matrites. To escape he'd had to use his Talent to destroy the power behind the Matrial's torques and kill the Matrial. But to get accepted back in the Iron Valleys, he'd had to stay in the militia, if as an officer, rather than a squad leader. And now he was being sent to fight a nomad conqueror who had routed the army of the largest and most powerful land in Corus.

He pushed away the sense of self-pity. He'd managed to get back alive, when most didn't, and his abilities had been recognized, and he had been able to marry the woman he loved—even if he hadn't been able to spend much more than a month a year with her. With even the thought of Wendra, the wristguard felt warmer.

41

In the hot summer evening, Alucius sat at the small writing desk in his quarters and blotted his forehead with the back of his hand. He was more tired than he'd thought. Still, he needed to write Wendra, and tired as he was, he was too restless to sleep. He picked up the pen and dipped it into the inkwell, slowly putting down words and phrases. After finishing another page in his ever-growing letter to his wife, Alucius read over the lines, conscious that he had best be most careful about what he put to paper.

> The change from the militia to the Northern Guard has not affected the time I am required to serve. That remains the same, but it appears my duties will change. Twenty-first Company has been assigned to an expeditionary detachment being sent to assist the Landarch of Deforya. We will be departing in slightly more than a week. I have been promoted to overcaptain, in charge of both the Twenty-first and Fifth Companies, but I also remain as

commander of the Twenty-first . . . We have been working hard to make sure that our companies are as prepared as possible for the coming ride . . .

Some of the preparations were not what the colonel might have wanted, because Alucius and Feran had made a few decisions of their own, including finding goods in the back of the storerooms that they could sell locally to raise more coins for any supplies they might have to purchase along the way. Neither the colonel nor the Council would have known what was there, or been able to sell it, and so far as Alucius was concerned, that meant that he and Feran were not taking anything, but merely providing for their companies.

. . . Colonel Weslyn was most insistent that one of our first preparations was the sewing of our new blue shoulder patches in place on our tunics. That is necessary, I gather, so that the Southern Guards with whom we will be riding will know that we are all now together. After all the years of hearing of the militia and being a part of it, it is hard to get used to being the Northern Guard. But times change, and we must change with them . . .

Alucius was certain that his family would fully understand the meaning behind the words about Colonel Weslyn, although he doubted that either Royalt or Kustyl could do much. Still, he wanted them to understand exactly what sort of a man Weslyn was—and wasn't.

Nodding, he set the letter aside for the moment, not wanting to write a conclusion until he knew he had a messenger to send it west.

He picked up the old history—*The Wonders of Ancient Corus*—and leafed through the pages until he reached the section on Deforya. Shortly, after several pages, one section caught his eye.

The ancient maps from well before the Duarchy had called the place "the land of great sorrow," and map notes stated that none had lived there in tens of generations . . . Yet the land was well suited for the plumapples and the tart green apples, and indeed there were orchards there, if long abandoned, and the ruins of a large town, with dwellings that had once been of fine stone.

The Duarches Riemyl and Fuentyl could not countenance the waste and offered those who had offended the Duarchy grants of property there, providing that those who accepted remained within the province they renamed Deforya, after the ancient term for a place of plenty . . . All who came into that immense open land were most pleased with the patents on tenure granted to them . . .

The iron mines in the eastern part of the province were discovered during the stewardship of the Duarches Antyn and Brytil, and were made possible by the ingenious waterworks still in use under the Landarches . . .

The "place of great sorrow"? Alucius searched through the history for some time, but he could find no other reference to sorrow in Deforya or anything that might shed light on it. Yet books often did not tell the entire story. Some histories still termed the soarers and sanders as mythological creatures, and he'd never found any mention of them in all the histories he'd read in Madrien—or, for that matter, of the wood spirit who had given him the key to the torque.

Legends often had truth behind them . . . but it was hard to discover the stories, let alone the truth, if you weren't born in a place. Coming from a herder family, Alucius well understood that.

He found his eyelids drooping, then he yawned. He was tired.

Slowly he closed the history and set it on the desk. Then he stood and stretched. Tomorrow would be another long day.

II.

THE DARKNESS OF PTERIDONS

42

From the far side of the narrow stone bridge over the River Vedra, where he was mounted on Wildebeast, Alucius watched as the troopers of Twenty-first rode single file over the bridge from Emal to Semal. Outside of two youngsters perched on an old stone wall behind Alucius, no one in either town appeared to be watching, although there might have been a few peering through shutters. As the troopers rode toward him and began to re-form on the narrow dusty street below the southern causeway, Alucius took a quick glance back at Emal Outpost, its stone walls now holding but two squads of foot, who were to be temporarily relocated to Sudon within the week.

From the walls of the post, his eyes shifted to the bridge. As one of the first acts of "union" visible in Emal, Feran had been ordered to remove the guard posts on both sides of the bridge—and the iron gate. The new masonry looked it, but in a few years it would fade under the weather, and outsiders would never know it had been a guarded bridge. Alucius wondered what people would remember and what they would choose to forget, for forgetting was a choice as well.

He glanced down, checking once more the double brace of rifles in the holders on each side of the saddle in front of his knees. He was doubtless breaking some regulation by carrying two, but he certainly couldn't ride back for another in the middle of a battle. For the same reasons, one of the packhorses carried spare rifles for Twenty-first Company as well.

Once Twenty-first Company was in formation in the dusty, squarish, packed-dirt area to the south of the causeway, and Fifth Company was ready to cross the bridge, he rode forward to the head of the column. "Twenty-first Company! Forward!"

"Forward!" Longyl repeated from halfway back along the column.

"First squad! Forward!"

"Second squad . . ."

Rather than have two companies of horse crowded into the middle of Semal, he and Feran had agreed that Twenty-first Company would ride to the southern edge of the hamlet and wait there for Fifth Company to rejoin them. As he rode along the dusty street, Alucius glanced at the handful of dwellings and the few shops, one a chandlery of sorts, and another a cooperage and carpentry shop. A hundred yards farther south was a smithy.

A gray-haired farmer stood by the wall on the east side of the road, just beyond the small smithy, with two small children, one on each side. The man raised his hand, then bowed his head. So did the children.

Alucius realized that the man was the farmer who had warned him, and he tried to recall the man's name . . . but could not. Almost ashamed, he extended his Talent senses, finally coming up with a name.

"Abyert," Alucius said, reining up Wildebeast short of the man, "I must thank you once more, and wish you and your grandchildren well. It is not likely that I will be returning to Emal, for I have been sent to serve in the east, but my good wishes go with you."

The farmer's face paled at the mention of his name.

"There is nothing to worry about," Alucius said, Talent-projecting warmth and reassurance. He could feel the farmer's relief.

The man's eyes did not meet those of Alucius. He replied, "We will offer our best thoughts for you, Captain."

"Thank you." Alucius nodded a last time, but as he began to ride away, he caught the farmer's words.

". . . children . . . he is one of the great ones, a lamaial even . . . do not forget that you have seen him."

A lamaial? Alucius frowned. The mythical hero or villain who was fated to bring back the Duarchy or stop it from returning? Then he shook his head and grinned. A lamaial? No. Just a herder from north of Iron Stem who only wanted to return to herding—and his wife.

He urged Wildebeast along the shoulder of the road to catch up to Zerdial and the vanguard.

43

Two days of riding the dirt roads south from Emal had left Alucius and Feran—and all the troopers—hot and dusty. North-eastern Lanachrona suffered the same lack of rain as had the Iron Valleys. What crops there were were short and stunted, and in many fields there were brown shoots that had died from lack of moisture. Every wind was filled with fine grit, and even by late morning a haze of dust was everywhere Alucius looked.

About a glass past midafternoon, the two companies reached the outskirts of a hamlet with no roadstones or signs. Fewer than twenty dwellings lay scattered across the south side of a gentle rise and above a narrow stream. None of the wooden-sided houses had been stained or painted in any recent year, and most of the outbuildings slanted. While Alucius had often felt that the clean-lined stone dwellings of Madrien had put the dwellings of the Iron Valleys to shame, the hillside dwellings made even those in Emal look palatial.

"The farther south we get, the poorer the people are," Feran said, from where he rode—momentarily—beside Alucius.

"We're farther from the rivers, and the land probably isn't as rich. No bottomland and not that much water, and no rain . . ."

"How much farther to the high road, do you think?"

"According to the maps, less than five vingts. If this hamlet is Yumel," Alucius replied. "Then we have to ride east on the high road another five vingts or so to the road fort at Senelmyr."

"Feel strange riding up to a Southern Guard outpost."

"We'll send a scout as a messenger well in advance." Alucius's tone was dry.

"What do you think about this business?"

"There's too much we don't know. The Lord-Protector wants something from us, and it's not just to get us out of the way. If he wanted that, we'd all be somewhere on the old north road to Eastice or Klamat. I just can't figure out what it is that we have that they don't."

"We're more expendable," Feran pointed out.

"That's true, but it also means he's got something he wants us expended on, and it's got to be the grassland nomads to the south of Deforya or the Lustreans. Either way, someone is trying to move west, and the Lord-Protector wants to stop them before Lanachrona gets too involved."

"Maybe he's using us to buy time while he consolidates his grip on Southgate."

"That could be." Alucius shrugged. "We'll see."

"So we will." Feran nodded to the rear. "I'm headed back to see how my laggards are doing, and I'll check on the packhorses."

"Thank you."

After Feran rode back along the edge of the road, past Twenty-first Company, Alucius kept studying the road ahead and the dwellings they were passing, both with eyes and Talent. Not a single soul had ventured out of the dwellings in Yumel as the two Northern Guard companies passed through. Alucius didn't blame them. He doubted the people had even heard about the forced union, and blue silk shoulder triangles wouldn't remove the concern about troopers in black moving through traditional Lanachronan lands. Even with stops for water and brief rests, it was midafternoon before the column of riders and packhorses neared the road fort at Senelmyr.

They were over a vingt away when two Southern Guard troopers, accompanied by Waris, the scout from the third squad, rode westward toward Alucius and his vanguard.

"They're expecting us, sir," Waris called.

"Good," Alucius replied. "Thank you."

With that, the two companies followed the Southern Guards back to the road fort. There was no sign of a town. The fort, while larger than

Emal Outpost, was far less imposing, consisting of a brick wall, barely two and a half yards high, and a series of low buildings looking more like sheep sheds than barracks or stables.

A majer in the cream and blue of the Southern Guard stood on the wooden and roofless porch of the first building inside the gates. Beside him was a captain.

"Twenty-first Company! Halt!" Alucius ordered. Then he rode Wildebeast over to where the captain stood. "Overcaptain Alucius, Northern Guard, Majer."

"Majer Draspyr, Overcaptain. It's good to see you and your troopers." Draspyr was blond, blue-eyed, and had a thin scar running along his left jaw, the faintest line of red. He offered a warm and open smile. "Greetings." His voice was a mellow baritone that went with his welcoming smile.

Alucius managed to smile in return, although he was put off by the coldness that lay behind the apparent friendliness. "Greetings, Majer. We stand ready to join your forces."

"We'll talk about matters once you get your men settled. If you would join me here in the conference room, in say a glass." Draspyr nodded to the captain beside him, then to a squad leader who had appeared. "Captain Clifyr and his senior squad leader will help your companies get settled. You and Captain Feran, of course, have quarters here with the other officers."

Clifyr stepped forward exactly one pace and looked up at Alucius. "Sir . . . if you and your men would follow us. Your companies have the barracks nearest the east wall."

Alucius and the two companies followed. Once he was convinced that the barracks and stables were adequate, if barely so, and after he'd settled and groomed Wildebeast, he and Feran followed Clifyr back to the front area of the road post.

The officers' quarters were about the same size as those at Emal Outpost, if sparsely furnished, with only a bunk and an open wardrobe and a small table and a stool. The shutters on the single window sagged, and the bunk mattress was old and thin.

Alucius managed to wash up himself and his dirty undergarments, hanging them from a line he strung between bunk and wardrobe, before heading to the conference room to meet with the majer.

The majer stood as Alucius entered. There was a large map spread on the old and battered circular table, one of eastern Lanachrona and Deforya.

"I trust the quarters are adequate." Draspyr snorted. "If hardly so. Still, they are superior to way stations and camping in the open."

"I am sure we have both seen better and worse," Alucius replied politely.

"Just so." Draspyr studied Alucius for a long moment.

As the majer did so, Alucius used his Talent-sense to pick up the other's feelings—mostly of curiosity, although there was a muted feel of superiority. He waited for the majer to speak.

Draspyr gestured to the map, almost abruptly. "You can see the blue line there. That's the old northern high road. It goes from Borlan through Deforya and the Northern Pass all the way to Alustre. We'll be taking it to Dereka. After that, we'll be on local roads south to the Barrier Range. Our task is threefold. First, we are to provide a presence to assure the Landarch of the support of Lanachrona. Second, we are to determine the degree of threat actually posed by the grassland nomads. Third, if we are attacked, or the Landarch's forces accompanying us are attacked, we are to fight to the best of our ability."

"Do you know whether the grassland nomads are moving northward? And how quickly?"

"The Lord-Protector has received very reliable reports that large numbers of horse companies are riding northwest of Lyterna toward the Barrier Range border with Deforya. It would seem unlikely that they are doing so for peaceful reasons." A cold smile crossed the majer's lips as he looked down at the map momentarily before continuing. "The other two companies of Northern Guards will be joining us either late tomorrow or on Sexdi. Overcaptain Heald will be in charge of that detachment, as well as commanding the Third Company, and Captain Koryt is commanding Eleventh Company."

Alucius managed to keep a pleasant smile on his face and hoped he hadn't revealed the shock. He'd served as a scout, not even a squad leader, under Heald, who was a good, but not outstanding officer. Koryt, far less competent, had been the company commander Alucius had been forced to make a fool of in order to return to the Iron Valleys. Feran was far, far more qualified than either of the other Northern Guard officers, unless they had improved greatly. Alucius reproved himself for the thought about Captain Heald, considering that Alucius himself had certainly improved since he had last served under Heald.

"Do you know either officer, Overcaptain?"

"I've met them both, but Overcaptain Heald is the only one I've seen in action," Alucius replied. "He held off the Matrites near Soulend for almost a season until the Council could send reinforcements." He'd also lost more than half the company, some of the troopers unnecessarily, but Alucius did not mention that.

"What do you know of Captain Koryt?"

"Very little, sir. I only met him for a fraction of a glass sometime over a year ago."

Draspyr nodded sagely. "I've been told that you have the most combat experience, but were the most junior as a captain, before you were promoted."

"That is probably true, sir."

"And that you always get the task accomplished, generally with lower casualties than expected, and . . . shall we say, greater consternation among superior officers." Draspyr's blue eyes twinkled, but the twinkle was not so much of humor as of satisfaction at having delivered a statement containing knowledge that had been hard-won.

"That is also probably true, sir."

"Have you ever directly disobeyed an order, Overcaptain?"

"Only when I was escaping from Madrien, sir."

Draspyr sighed, but the expression was mere affectation. "The chain of command will run from me to you and Overcaptain Heald separately and directly. Neither of you will be subordinate to the other. I believe that is the best way of handling that."

"Yes, sir." It was doubtless the only practical way that Draspyr could see, and, from Alucius's point of view, it was far better than Alucius reporting to Heald.

"We also brought two wagons filled with cartridges for your weapons, Overcaptain." The smile vanished. "Marshal Wyerl had thought about refitting your companies with standard rifles—until he received the reports about the pteridons."

"Pteridons, sir?"

"It appears that Aellyan Edyss has managed to obtain some pteridons. He used them effectively enough to kill the Praetor of Alustre and rout his army. The Lord-Protector and Marshal Wyerl thought that since your weapons are designed to deal with predators such as sandwolves and sanders they might be of equal use against other Talent-cursed creatures."

"They might be, sir," Alucius agreed blandly. "We'll have to see when the time comes." Whether Aellyan Edyss had pteridons or not, the majer thought he did, and Alucius could see no reason for the majer to be deceived. Why he and four Northern Guard companies had been assigned also made a great deal more sense—as did the particular companies assigned.

"You don't sound that surprised, Overcaptain."

"I've learned that in Corus anything is possible, Majer. I've seen the crystal spear-thrower of the Matrial and the silver torques of Madrien—and I've seen sanders appear out of the soil and vanish into it almost as swiftly. We have leschec pieces that are pteridons and legends, and eternal high roads which show no sign of aging." Alucius smiled ruefully. "If the Lord-Protector has solid word that the nomads have found pteridons . . . then I have no reason to doubt him."

Draspyr laughed, a sound which contained actual humor, before he frowned and asked, "Crystal spear-thrower?"

"A weapon which fires hundreds of crystal spears about this long—" Alucius held his hands a half yard apart. "The first one exploded in the battles around Soulend, but one of the Matrial's engineers rebuilt it."

"You have seen that weapon?"

"I was wounded in one of the battles at Soulend where it was used." Alucius could tell that the majer had not been told about the crystal spear-thrower. From what he'd heard and seen of Lanachrona, that did not surprise him.

"It's good that you and your men are used to the unusual." Draspyr glanced up as Captain Clifyr entered the conference room, near silently, and bowed, without speaking. "One last thing—we'll go over commands, early tomorrow, then we'll undertake some maneuvers just to make sure that we're using and understanding the same orders."

"Yes, sir."

"Until after morning muster tomorrow, Overcaptain."

Alucius inclined his head to the majer, then waited for the bow from Clifyr before nodding in return. He left the conference room door slightly ajar as he left, listening.

"Doesn't look that dangerous, sir . . ." murmured Clifyr.

"For all of that youthful and open face he has, Clifyr, he'd turn you and your company into sow sausage in less than a glass. He's a marksman who hits more than half his targets in combat, and that's unheard of. He's a top blade with either hand, and personally killed well over a hundred men in combat . . ."

"Sir?"

"That's from the Recorder of Deeds . . . Now . . . we need to discuss your reports . . ."

Alucius tried to pick up more, but at that point one of the two officers closed the door to the conference room. Recorder of Deeds? Who or what was the Recorder of Deeds? And how would he know about Alucius?

Feran was waiting by the door to his quarters—adjoining those of Alucius.

Alucius motioned for the older officer to join him in the quarters he'd been assigned. He closed the door, but after all the riding, he scarcely felt like sitting.

"What did you find out that we haven't guessed?" asked Feran.

"Things are even worse than we'd thought."

"We knew that. Tell me how they're worse."

"Aellyan Edyss has at least some pteridons," Alucius said evenly.

"Pteridons? You expect me to believe that? They're make-believe . . . mythical creatures . . ."

Alucius shrugged. "All right. Edyss has something that routed the legions of Alustre and killed the Praetor, and has the Lord-Protector worried enough to send five companies of horse to support the Landarch of Deforya."

"If he's that worried, why is he sending any companies at all . . . Oh . . ." Feran grimaced. "Sander shit! Offspring of diseased rats . . . There's only one company of Southern Guards, and the rest are from the Iron Valleys."

"We've got heavier rifles, and he can get a report on what Edyss does, as well as get rid of the best of the militia if Edyss isn't a threat. Even if he is, Lanachrona doesn't lose that much."

"All because that fornicating bunch of traders in Dekhron never had the masculinity to raise the tariffs to pay for the militia . . ."

"Aellyan Edyss might be moving in our direction anyway, sooner or later."

"But we wouldn't be the ones in front if it weren't for those cowardly coin-lovers."

"They've sent two wagons full of cartridges for our rifles," Alucius added. "I'd like to see if we can work out at least some idea of target practice at something in the air—maybe string a line between poles or trees and pull something along it."

"You really think . . . ?" Feran looked hard at Alucius.

"Yes. The majer does, too. He was assigned because he's fairly smart, but arrogant enough not to realize just how dangerous this task is. We're supposed to see if the pteridons are a real danger, reassure the Landarch that the Lord-Protector is his ally, and, if at all possible, either kill the pteridons or discover how."

"They don't want much, do they?"

"You said that you'd do anything to avoid going north to Eastice." Alucius smiled. "I'd say this qualifies as almost anything."

"Next time—if there is one—remind me that the cold isn't so bad." Feran shook his head, with such an exaggerated expression that Alucius laughed.

After a moment, so did Feran.

44

As Majer Draspyr had predicted, the other two Northern Guard companies arrived late on Quinti, when the sun had touched the horizon to the west at the end of a hot and dusty day. Alucius hurried out to meet them as they rode through the gates of the road fort. He had hoped to meet Heald by himself, but the majer was already there, along with Captain Clifyr.

Overcaptain Heald reined up opposite the majer. He still had the deep dark circles under his eyes, and his face was thinner than Alucius recalled.

"Majer, Overcaptain Heald and Captain Koryt reporting." Heald inclined his head.

"It's good to see you, Overcaptain," Draspyr replied. "You made good time."

"We thought it best, sir," Heald replied.

Draspyr gestured toward Alucius. "I believe you may have met Overcaptain Alucius . . ."

"Indeed I have," Heald said warmly. "We served together at Soulend, and I'm very glad to know we'll be working together here."

While Heald's words surprised Alucius, the warmth behind them surprised him even more.

They clearly surprised the majer, who paused before replying, "I am very glad to know that." After another moment of silence, he added, "After you get your men settled, Overcaptain Heald, I'd like a few moments to brief you. In the conference room here. Then, you and

Overcaptain Alucius might want to discuss anything you think useful. Tomorrow, we will be doing some joint maneuvers, and we'll set out on Septi. Captain Clifyr and his senior squad leader will show you where your troopers will be quartered."

"Yes, sir." Heald inclined his head, then looked directly at Alucius and smiled. "It is good to see you."

"You, too," Alucius replied, half-surprised that he meant it.

After Heald had turned his mount and begun to direct Second Company, Draspyr looked at Alucius. "You did not mention that you were friends."

"We've never spent much time together, sir, but we share mutual respect." Alucius didn't feel that was stretching the truth too much.

"That's good. It's useful in an effort like this will be." Draspyr was both concerned and pleased. That Alucius almost could have read without his Talent. "If you will excuse me . . ."

"Of course, sir." With a nod, Alucius turned and walked back toward his own quarters.

A glass later, there was a knock on the door to the small room where Alucius was reading the single history he had brought with him. He stood and opened the door.

Heald offered a friendly smile, if tentative. "Alucius . . ."

"It's good to see you," Alucius replied. "I have to say I was surprised."

"So was I, but you're where you belong. You should have been an officer from the first."

"I don't know that I would have learned what I needed if I had been," Alucius replied, closing the door behind the other.

"That may be, but . . . it's well that you are. Especially now."

After a moment of silence, Alucius asked, "How is Third Company?"

"There aren't too many troopers left that you knew. You were close to Kypler and Velon, as I recall. Velon was mustered out last fall, and he was happy to get back to his orchards and mill. Oliuf was wounded, and his leg was broken. He was mustered out. He'll always limp, but he's all right otherwise." Heald's face turned sober. "Young Kypler . . . he was killed in one of the last fights before the Matrites pulled out of Soulend. I'm sorry."

"I appreciate your telling me."

"Oh, and they made Geran an undercaptain last fall. He's in charge of Seventeenth Company. He's not too pleased that he's being sent to the far north road outpost they're reopening. I saw him in Dekhron, and he sends his best." Heald paused. "Is it true that you wiped out an entire company of raiders last winter, and then reduced two companies to less than two squads later in the spring?"

"We were fortunate."

Heald laughed, heartily. "You've told me that far too often. You make that kind of luck, and it takes hard work."

"Hard work—and luck," Alucius half agreed.

"That's what comes of being a herder." The older overcaptain hesitated. "You were there at Pyret. You know . . . Dysar made my life . . . less than pleasant."

"He never understood the situation you were in." That was true, and Alucius had thought that then, and even more as he'd considered the Soulend campaign in the light of his own later experience.

"He never understood anything except that the militia cost too much," Heald said bluntly.

Alucius laughed.

"No one talks much about it, but the story is that you got him so upset his heart stopped."

"I did get him upset. That's true. And his heart did stop." Not for that reason, but Alucius wasn't about to say more. "He wanted to have us all executed for desertion because we'd been captured or left for dead and didn't have the decency to commit suicide rather than wear a Matrite collar."

"Those as bad as they say?"

"Worse. They quit working, and that was how we could escape. When they were working, any officer could kill any man just by pulling on a little noose on her command belt. If you attacked an officer, you died right there. If you tried to remove the collar, you died, too."

Heald shuddered.

"We were lucky that the collars stopped working, and we ripped them off before they could get them working again. I don't know if they did." Not for sure, Alucius thought to himself. "So we rode for home, and when we got there . . . and finally met with Dysar and Colonel Clyon, I suggested to Dysar that, if he didn't want to treat us fairly, we'd have to seek other redress—like take refuge with the herders." That wasn't quite correct, but close enough. "And then I suggested to Colonel Clyon that after all the trouble we'd gone to—and all the silver collars we'd brought back—that the Council would have trouble if we were treated badly. He agreed."

"And Dysar couldn't stand that thought?"

"He couldn't stand something," Alucius said. "He turned red and fell out of the saddle."

"I'm not surprised. He had a terrible temper." Heald paused. "Anyway . . . after that, things got better."

"Until the colonel got sick and died," Alucius added.

"*If* he got sick."

"We'll never know for certain," Alucius pointed out.

"No, we won't. No matter what we think." After a moment, Heald added, "Oh . . . and Koryt won't be a problem. He turned white when he heard you were here." He laughed again. "I asked him about you, and do you know what he said?"

"I couldn't even guess," Alucius admitted.

"He said that the Council had made a horrible mistake because they'd picked the only officer in the militia who was meaner than a dustcat and tougher than a sander."

Alucius couldn't help but frown.

"Then he said," Heald went on, clearly enjoying himself, "that it was a mistake because they clearly wanted to get rid of us all, and no one could get rid of you. The Council, Dysar, the Matrial, and the Southern Guard had tried, and they'd all failed." The older overcaptain raised his eyebrows. "Is that true?"

"I don't know about the Council," Alucius said slowly. "The others . . . well, I did survive battles against all of them. I was fortunate."

Heald shook his head. "You use that word too much. I recall your first scouting expedition. Somehow, three-quarters of a Matrite patrol died. Was that fortune?" Heald grinned.

Alucius shrugged. He certainly didn't want to be thought of as a solution to everything. "It probably was . . . but we won't have that kind of luck against the grassland nomads."

Heald's face sobered. "I know that. I've got a good company in the Third. Feran's solid; everyone says so. Twenty-first Company is probably worth two, if not more, and Koryt would charge one of those Matrite spear-throwers rather than upset you."

That wasn't necessarily good, Alucius reflected.

"If you tell him to be cautious, he will be," Heald said.

"You'll have to," Alucius said. "Majer Draspyr has indicated that neither of us will be considered senior to the other."

Heald nodded. "I'm not surprised. We both got promoted at the same time. That will work."

Alucius hoped so. "Did the majer tell you about this Aellyan Edyss and his weapons?"

"The pteridon bit? Yes. What do you think?"

"He's telling what he believes is the truth, and I can't see any reason why the Lord-Protector would deceive him about that. It also explains why we're here."

"We're considered expendable in the new and enlarged Lana-chrona . . . and we're used to heavier rifles."

"We're not used to shooting up, though. I was thinking about some target practice with targets pulled along in the air . . ."

"You'd have to have them move fast . . ."

The discussion lasted for well over a glass.

45

The northern high road to the east was long—even longer than the midroad from Iron Stem into the middle of Madrien. Even though the road fort at Senelmyr was more than a hundred vingts east of Salaan, that left more than four hundred vingts to Dereka. After nine days of riding, the companies were just entering the foothills leading to the Upper Spine Mountains that formed the natural barrier between Lanachrona and Deforya, although the actual border was slightly to the east of the midpoint of the range.

Feran and Alucius were riding together, at the head of the part of the column that encompassed both the Twenty-first and Fifth Companies, at that point bringing up the rear, just before the ten supply wagons. The gray eternastone pavement was as unmarked by time as any high road, but dustier than most Alucius had traveled, since there had been no rain along the road, perhaps not since the turn of spring. Alucius and Feran, and many of the troopers, sneezed often.

Alucius glanced at the dark stone peaks rising beyond the hills through which they rode, peaks whose snow-tipped summits towered far above the road ahead, straight as it was in its course through them. "I wish we'd had more time to practice with the moving targets."

"We got the men to think about it. You should have seen the majer's face. But he didn't say anything."

"What could he have said?" Alucius smiled, momentarily. "We still don't know any more than when we left Senelmyr."

"Does the majer know something he's not telling us?"

"I don't think so." Alucius lifted his water bottle and took a healthy swallow. "His troopers are solid, but Longyl was asking around. They've all had problems . . . good fighters, but they don't do well when they're not on duty. Heald told me something like that last night, too."

"So what was the majer's problem?"

"I'd guess that he's well enough placed that he can't be dismissed, but not in the Lord-Protector's favor. Like the rest of us."

"If we succeed in learning something and surviving, all is well and good. If not, well . . . the Lord-Protector has sacrificed five companies for his friend and ally, the Landarch . . . Is that it?" Feran added quickly. "I'd say that's charitable. It's probably worse than that, especially for you."

"Me?"

Feran eased his mount closer to Alucius. "You're a herder. You're more than a herder. I've seen enough." The older officer raised a hand to hold off any objection Alucius might offer. "I've been around. Heard a few things, like the Lord-Protector having folks with Talent who can use a strange mirror to find out things. How else would they know to pick you?"

"Misfortune? Mine?" suggested Alucius.

"It might be, but don't count on people thinking you're just a young and simple captain."

"I can try." Alucius grinned.

"Try all you want. I won't say anything. I'll take any advantage we can get. It's not going to be good."

"No," Alucius agreed. "If our rifles are more useful against the pteridons—or whatever the nomads have—then the Lord-Protector will have an excuse to throw every militia—Northern Guard—company into the fight *if* the nomads head west."

"Will they head west, though?" asked Feran, as if he knew the answer.

"I don't think so. Not for a while. There's a great advantage for them to take Deforya, because they'd hold both passes and control all land trade to the east, but I don't see what they'd gain by attacking Lanachrona immediately."

"This . . . expedition . . . smells worse than a week-old carcass in midsummer. Do you have any ideas about how we get out of this?"

"Outside of defeating ten times our numbers and pteridons, or something just as bad . . . no. Not yet, anyway."

"Keep thinking. You're the bright one." Feran forced a grin.

"Thank you," Alucius replied dryly.

"You're also the overcaptain. I'm just a mere captain, following orders, trying to do his humble best."

"You could spread that a little thicker," Alucius retorted humorously. "I'm not sure how, but, if there's a way . . ."

They both laughed.

46

Alustre, Lustrea

Vestor stood at the second archway into the ancient workshop of the Praetorian Engineers. Behind him glistened the pale green marble walls, and polished pink-gray granite pillars and floors. Thin lines of brilliant summer light flared through the narrow windows. The black-haired man wearing the silver-and-black jacket and silver trousers of the Praetor, scarcely a handful of years older than Vestor himself, walked toward the archway.

Vestor bowed. "Praetor Tyren."

"Engineer." The new Praetor walked into the work chamber, stopping short of the workbench and the narrow tanks on the tables behind it, in which were seed crystals. After studying the benches and the tanks, he turned to the engineer. "I have received a number of reports. They all say that you alone remained fighting the pteridons until your weapons and your archers were destroyed, and that you were burned and barely escaped with your life."

"Yes, Praetor."

"And that your arm and hand were damaged." Tyren paused. "Will they affect your work?"

"I can still do the delicate work and the design, but I fear it may be some time before I can lift much weight on my left side."

"But you can build more of the devices that you used against the pteridons?"

"I have already begun. You can see. It will take time, as I told your father before we left for Catyr. I cannot grow the crystals faster than they will grow."

"Unlike my sire, Vestor, I have time to make sure we do matters with full preparation. You had six of the light-knives, with roughly two replacements for each. Correct?"

"Yes, Praetor."

"We will plan for twenty-five, with five replacements for each. When we strike the nomads again, we will be prepared for anything. I understand that you have one working device remaining?"

"I am using it as a model for the others."

"Good. What about the Table project?" Tyren pointed toward the solid black square table, sturdily constructed of lorken, set well away from the workbenches, and at the thick glass mirror, also rimmed in lorken, upon the table.

"I have discovered a way to measure the forces exerted on the mirrors. Given time, I can at least determine where they can be placed so that we can use them longer without explosion. I am hopeful that this will lead to a working replica of the Tables of the Recorders. But that will take even more time, I fear."

"Do not neglect that, but take the time you require. The new Duarchy will need such, and should you succeed, you will be acclaimed and rewarded above all other engineers in the times since the Cataclysm." Tyren smiled. "You have already given much, often with little reward. I have taken the liberty of making the upper floors of the Northern Tower ready for you. There is enough space for a family there, in great comfort, and your new stipend will support that, should you wish such. If not, you will have the comfort and space to sustain you."

Vestor's eyes widened, if slightly. "You are most kind."

"Most realistic, Vestor. Even engineers who love their work deserve recognition and golds," Tyren went on. "You will receive the green circlet of valor at the next assembly of honors." He nodded, then stepped back. "I also expect continued progress." With a smile, he turned.

Vestor nodded, more to himself than to the departing Praetor.

47

By the following Octi, the five companies were well into the Upper Spine Mountains, far taller than any mountains Alucius had traveled. Even so, the tallest peaks were shorter, he judged, than the Aerlal Plateau. But then, no one he knew had ever tried to climb the more than six-thousand-yard-high sheer walls of the Plateau. As his grandsire had said, years back, after Alucius had dreamed of climbing the Plateau, there were better ways—and far less dangerous ones—to make a fool of one's self.

When Alucius studied the mountains around and above him with his Talent, even in midday he could feel a darkness that enfolded the gray stone slopes, slopes that held far fewer trees than he would have expected. Yet he found no source for the darkness. The trees themselves were all evergreens, bent and twisted and old, and he saw but a handful of younger or smaller pines or firs. Even the few valleys he had seen were almost lifeless, heaped with stones, and with scattered handfuls of stunted bushes.

"The winds must be fierce here in the winter," he said to Longyl, riding beside him.

"Thought that myself, sir. Haven't seen any animals, and only a few ravens. Only one hawk. Can't be much in the way of small game."

"No." Alucius hadn't sensed that much life. Even the barren quarasote plains of the stead, under the Aerlal Plateau, held far more living creatures. "Good thing we've got supply wagons. Be tough foraging here."

"For five companies . . . be impossible, sir."

"Let's hope it's better in the Barrier Range."

"You think we'll be headed that way soon?"

"No one's said, but I wouldn't wager against it."

"Least it's summer."

As Wildebeast carried Alucius to a low crest in the mountain high road, he suddenly sensed a point of dark bluish violet in the heights to the south—a single point. He forced himself to look upward slowly, as if studying the sides of the unnatural gorge cradling the high road, but his eyes could make out nothing. Whatever the creature hidden and watching within the rocks above the gorge might be, it felt similar to a sander. Were there mountain sanders? Alucius had never heard of such, and in his readings had never come across any such reference; but there were few enough references to sanders, and many people in Corus, especially in the southern lands, thought they were mythical or legendary creatures, although herders saw enough of them to know they were far from mythical.

"See something, sir?"

"I thought I did, but it's gone now." Alucius shifted his weight in the saddle, looking forward along the impossibly straight high road and the dry canyon leading eastward.

The history book had made a passing reference to Deforya as an ancient land of great sorrow, and one which had been abandoned by all the inhabitants before the Duarchy. Did the mountains reflect that, or was there something about them that had created that sorrow? He looked to the north, over vingts and vingts of near-lifeless gray stone, then back at the road ahead. Did the emptiness of the mountains really matter?

He didn't know enough to answer his own question. Instead, he looked to Longyl. "How are the mounts doing on water?"

182 L. E. MODESITT, JR.

"So far . . . we're all right, and if we reach that stream tonight, they'll be fine."

Alucius nodded. The sense of the blue-violet mountain creature had vanished, as if it had never been, even without the lingering sense that he felt with sanders on the stead.

48

By Duadi, the combined force was nearing the eastern edge of the Upper Spine Mountains. A glass before, Twenty-first Company had rotated forward to take its place as the first company in the main body, a half vingt behind the Lanachronan vanguard, where Majer Draspyr usually rode.

Less than a vingt ahead of the vanguard, Alucius saw two vertical cliffs of gray stone, rising almost two hundred yards above the high road, each in a single unbroken line. As he rode closer, he could see that the cliffs were even more unnatural than the gun-barrel-straight gorge they had followed for days, for they had been sliced from the heart of a single mountain, creating an opening nearly a half vingt in width, more than enough for both the river to the left of the road and the high road itself to pass out into the high plains beyond.

Alucius wondered why the ancient builders—for it had to have been an artifact of the Duarchy—had not left a much narrower gap that could have been more easily defended. Then . . . he laughed quietly to himself. The Duarchy had been built on unifying Corus, not on creating narrow passes that could have been reinforced to facilitate uprisings or revolts.

"Sir?" inquired Zerdial.

"Just thinking." Alucius gestured at the artificial cliffs ahead. "About how times change."

Zerdial's brow wrinkled, but the squad leader didn't pursue the question.

Once through the massive cut, Alucius found himself looking out at an endless plain, with only the slightest hint of rolling hills. The high road had not dropped more than two thousand yards, if that, from the heights it reached in the middle of the Upper Spine Mountains until it emerged onto the high mountain valley that held the land of Deforya.

Alucius had studied the maps and histories of Corus, and he knew Deforya was bounded by mountains on three sides and by the rampart-like walls of the Aerlal Plateau on the north, and that Deforya was essentially one huge valley two hundred vingts from west to east, and three hundred from the Aerlal Plateau south to the Barrier Range that separated Deforya from Illegea. Knowing that and seeing the endless open valley were two different matters.

As he continued to ride, passing through and then leaving behind the stone gate to the Upper Spine Mountains, another feeling swept over Alucius—one of immense sadness, an emotion that had not come from within him, but from the gray stone mountains he had just left . . . and even from the plains ahead. A feeling from those beings he had never seen, whose Talent-colors of maroon-violet had felt so similar to those of sanders, yet were not? And why would a sander—or whatever the mountain creatures were—be sad, or show sadness? Or were there other reasons for the sadness?

He glanced to his left. The river that had flowed through the ancient stone channel beside the high road for the last fifty vingts was now carried completely by an eternastone aqueduct, an aqueduct more than twenty yards wide, whose graceful arches were already almost five yards higher than the high road it paralleled.

"Never seen anything like that, even in Hieron," said Zerdial quietly.

"They didn't need aqueducts in Hieron; but it took as much effort, if not more, to build the river levees and roads there," Alucius pointed out.

"Not as much as it did to cut the high road all the way through the mountains, did it?" Zerdial asked politely.

"About the same, I'd guess. The levee roads are on both sides of the river, and they run for over a hundred and fifty vingts, and they probably had to dig fairly deep to put in foundations. Here, they just cut away stone."

"Just?" asked Longyl, easing his mount up beside Alucius on the left.

"Just," Alucius affirmed with a laugh. "It's always easier to build by removing. It's like carving. You cut what doesn't belong away. When you build anything, first you have to dig deep enough . . ." He stopped and shook his head. "You may be right. We don't know how they did it. If we were doing it today, this"—he gestured back toward the artificial gorge and then to the aqueduct "—would be easier."

"How far is Dereka, sir?" asked Zerdial, clearly wanting to change the subject.

"About thirty vingts. We won't make it today. Besides, we're supposed to stop at a border post another few vingts or so to the east. We might have to wait there, until the Landarch sends for us. The majer wasn't sure."

"Didn't tell him enough, did they?" asked Longyl.

"That doesn't change from land to land," Alucius suggested. "They never tell those doing the fighting enough." As he finished speaking, Alucius concealed a frown. Even away from the mountains, his Talent registered the continuing sense of sadness.

49

On Tridi, the combined force left the outpost early, escorted by a half squad of Deforyan troopers in crimson uniforms, strikingly similar to those worn by the second raider company that Twenty-first Company had destroyed in late winter. The sky was clear, the white sun bright, the silver-green sky clear, and the day was pleasant, perhaps because of the higher elevation of Deforya, with a light breeze out of the north.

The high road and the aqueduct continued due east. Every so often Alucius looked to the north, but the aqueduct remained solidly there, having risen only a few yards over the vingts since the outpost. At intervals of roughly two vingts, circular eternastone pipes ran down from the aqueduct and into the ground, the water they carried reappearing in functional square stone fountains on the north side of the aqueduct and on the south side of the road. From the fountains, open stone channels ran parallel to the orchards. Rather, Alucius thought, the orchards had been planted paralleling the watercourses.

At times, there were hamlets around the fountains, and each dwelling looked exactly like every other dwelling—oblong, with brownish red shutters, walls of plaster over stone, and old slate roofs. While the houses were well kept, Alucius saw none that looked new. At other times, there were not even dwellings, only the orchards.

By midafternoon, what had first appeared as a golden haze where the road met the horizon had resolved itself into the first view of Dereka. Rising out of the green golden grasses and above the neat rows of the apple and plumapple trees that filled the orchards lining both sides of the high road and aqueduct were golden stone buildings, as well as three glistening green towers that reminded Alucius of the tower in Iron Stem. Even from a good five vingts to the west, the sharp and clean edges of the buildings were clear, as was their size. Many had to have been a hundred yards or so on a side.

As Alucius and the column of troopers rode closer, smaller structures— dwellings, shops, stables—became visible, and while they were also of stone, the stone was of a yellow shade, and the lines were not as sharp and clean.

The aqueduct and high road continued straight, effectively splitting the city into two sections, northern and southern, with half the ancient structures to the north, half to the south. The dwellings on the fringe of the city were of the yellow stone as well, but far more crudely cut, and the roofs were of split slate, much like those of the Iron Valleys. Some of the side streets were of stone, but most were packed dirt and dusty, and more crowded than in any city where Alucius had been—but none of the people thronging the side streets ventured onto the high road. Some of their comments did, although Alucius had trouble at first with the dialect, an oddly accented form of Lanachronan.

". . . black . . . the northerners . . ."

". . . Landarch . . . bought them . . ."

". . . don't need outsiders . . . just take up water . . ."

"No . . . sent by the young Lord-Protector . . . rather fight here . . ."

". . . no fight at all . . . rock spirits will finish the grass-eaters . . ."

Close to the middle of the city, the Deforyan escorts turned south onto a paved yellow stone road, into which years of wagon wheels had carved grooves almost a handspan deep. The vanguard and then the rest of the column followed.

Alucius studied the ancient buildings, whose lines were straight and clean. The windows were oblong, without shutters. The slanted roofs, some of them fifty yards high, were of the same polished golden stone, without any chinks between the roof or building blocks. The one structure directly to the east of the main street on which they rode was vacant, and Alucius wondered why. Was it gutted on the inside, the way the green tower in Iron Stem had been? Or were there other reasons?

They continued to ride south, nearing a second ancient and massive building, at least three hundred yards in length. There, from a staff before a wide circular drive and entrance, in the light afternoon breeze, flew a red banner, rimmed in gold, and featuring a golden half-moon and a full and smaller green moon under an arc of four eight-pointed stars. From the northern end of the structure rose a tower with the shimmering green stone finish that made it a duplicate of the one Alucius had passed so often on his way to Iron Stem growing up.

"Must be the Landarch's palace," Longyl suggested. "Looks like it's been there a long time."

"Gold eternastone," Alucius said. "It's mentioned in the histories, but they don't say anything about Dereka being built of it. There wasn't any that I saw in Madrien."

"Ah . . ." Longyl offered apologetically.

"You saw it?"

"Yes, sir. There were some buildings made of it on the outskirts of Faitel. Center of the place was a big circular lake, black water. They say it was created in the Cataclysm, but they didn't tell us how. Maybe two vingts back from the black lake, there were buildings, sort of like that one."

"That's interesting." It was more than interesting, and it fit, but Alucius couldn't say why, just as he hadn't been able to figure out the meaning of Hieron's construction in the beginning.

The iron gates to the palace were open, but guarded by a half squad of mounted troopers, who did not move as the column rode past and toward another ancient structure, far lower, if as long, that was farther south on the western side of the main street and surrounded by a stone wall two yards high. The gates to the city fort were guarded by two sentries, in open wooden posts.

Directly inside the gates was a large paved courtyard, but the stones were old and cracked, although the cracks had been filled with mortar and the joins between stones had been repointed, if not recently. At the western end of the courtyard was the long ancient structure, and in the center on the lower level, a stone platform with a balustrade extended some ten yards into the courtyard.

"Form up by company, left to right, centered on the platform!" Draspyr's orders bellowed across the courtyard.

Twenty-first Company, in the middle of the order of march, ended up directly in front of the stone platform. Then all waited as the ten wagons creaked into the courtyard and came to a halt. Alucius glanced back over his shoulder. The five companies—more than five hundred troopers and officers—and the wagons covered only half the courtyard.

A tall man, dark-haired, with a square-cut beard and wearing a crimson uniform with silver epaulets and silver collar insignia of crossed sabres over an eight-pointed star, stood at the front of the platform, behind the stone balustrade. The platform was tall enough that his head was a yard and a half higher than those of the mounted troopers and their officers. "Welcome to Dereka and Lancer Prime Post, and greetings on behalf of the Landarch." He looked to Majer Draspyr. "Your presence, and the friendship which it betokens, are most appreciated. You have had a long journey, and I would not wish to prolong it unduly.

There is a welcoming feast for you in several glasses. Your troopers will be feted in the troopers' hall, and you, Majer, and your officers will dine with the Landarch in the Great Banquet Hall . . ."

It took a moment for Alucius to adjust to the accent, but the words were familiar enough.

". . . the stables are ready, and so are your quarters, so that you may care for your mounts and refresh yourselves." He gestured, and from the building behind him appeared ten men in crimson uniforms, the equivalent of squad leaders, Alucius judged, walking out into the courtyard, two toward each company.

". . . and now . . . a word with you and your officers, before you begin your preparations."

"Officers forward!" Draspyr ordered.

Alucius eased Wildebeast toward the platform, reining up beside Feran. Heald slipped his mount next to Alucius, while Koryt reined up alongside Feran. Clifyr took the end.

"I am Submarshal Ahorak, the Assistant Arms-Commander of Dereka, and I am pleased to see you. You will all be quartered in the visiting barracks. There are officers' quarters at the north end, more than enough for you all. There is an officers' café in the headquarters building here, on the lower level, and it is open from one glass before dawn until midnight every day . . . Tomorrow morning . . . we will have a briefing on what we know of the nomads' movements, and on Quinti you will be on your way south to join our border guards . . ."

Alucius listened to the brief explanation, keeping a pleasant smile on his face, but studying the submarshal all the time. Ahorak had no traces of Talent, and behind his pleasant façade were condescension and arrogance, probably because he had to welcome a mere majer, Alucius judged, realizing that, by sending only a majer the Lord-Protector had delivered yet another message.

". . . You, Majer, as the commander of this force, will sit at the high table with the Landarch, and, if you will supply the names and ranks of your officers, they will be seated at the long table of the Deforyan Lancers, with its officers . . . no weapons at table . . . not even sabres . . ."

After another set of instructions, Alucius followed a Deforyan squad leader to the officers' section of the stables, where he saw to Wildebeast before walking back to the building that held the visiting officers' quarters. The quarters were on the upper level of the barracks, and close to luxurious. Each chamber was walled in marble, with inside shutters on the windows, and had a wide bed with a thick mattress, as well as a writing desk and a large armoire, and plenty of wall pegs for gear, even a rack for rifles. The floors were polished granite, but with a large woven cloth rug beside the bed.

In addition, rather than having a common wash chamber, each officer's room shared a large washroom, containing a tub, with one other chamber. There were even two spigots to the tub, one admitting warm—not hot—but warm water. After talking matters over with Heald, quietly, Alucius and the other overcaptain had agreed it was best that each take a chamber shared with their captain counterpart.

Alucius enjoyed getting thoroughly clean, and, after Feran bathed, and before Alucius fully dressed, washing out his other undergarments and riding uniforms.

In time, two open carriages took the six officers from Lancer Prime Post to the Landarch's palace. There they were escorted down a long great hall, thirty yards in height, and fifty wide, supported by golden eternastone pillars that exuded antiquity, for all that the hall was spotless, the polished stone floor bright enough to catch the reflections of the officers. They then made their way into the even larger Great Banquet Hall, with similar pillars and ceiling, and with crimson hangings draped between the pillars on each side of the hall.

The high table was on a dais a yard above the floor of the rest of the hall. The tables set up below the dais covered but the front third of the banquet hall. While Majer Draspyr was escorted away, Alucius found himself seated between two Deforyan officers in crimson dress uniforms with the silver epaulets. Heald was seated across from him, and two places more toward the head of the table.

They had barely reached their places when a functionary in gold stepped forward and rapped a heavy staff on the stone of the dais. Then the Landarch appeared, wearing not crimson, but a dark green trimmed in gold. He was not a large man, and his face was thin, but even from twenty yards away Alucius could sense the presence he projected, but without Talent.

"To the time eternal, to the One Who Is, and to the Unknown, as all three are and have been forever!" The Landarch inclined his head in the silence, then added, "And to our friends from the north and west who have most generously offered their services against the scourge of the south. There are no speeches tonight, and no toasts! Just wine and good food and friendship!" With that, he turned and walked to his place at the middle of the high table, seating himself.

Immediately servers appeared, all young men.

Alucius glanced around, realizing that he had not seen a single woman since he had entered the Landarch's palace. He focused on using his Talent, knowing he might feel overwhelmed, but he had to know more than his eyes were telling him. He took in the lifethreads of all the men in the banquet hall, and almost all were of a rust red, a shade that conveyed an ancient sadness or sorrow, or something close to it. Did the lands hold those feelings and pass them on? How?

"How did you become an officer in the . . . Lanachronan forces?" asked the overcaptain across the table from Alucius, a man who looked even younger than Alucius was.

Alucius had to take a moment to refocus his attention on the words addressed to him before he could reply. "I was captain in the Iron Valleys Militia when the Council agreed to become a part of Lanachrona. Shortly after that I was promoted to overcaptain." Sensing a certain frustration from the other even before he had finished speaking, he added, "I had served some time at that point."

"I fear . . . I was not clear. In most cases, how does one . . . become an officer? By birth, or schooling . . . by appointment from the Lord-Protector . . . ?"

Alucius nodded. "I cannot speak for the officers of the Southern Guard. What is now the Northern Guard, those of us in the black uniforms, gets its officers in several ways. Personally, I was raised as a herder—"

"The landholding kind?"

"Yes," Alucius admitted. "We have a large stead north of Iron Stem in the Iron Valleys."

"You are a younger son, perhaps?"

"No. I'm the oldest. My family does not believe that a herder can hold the respect he must have unless he has served in the . . . Northern Guard." He'd almost said militia, because the habits of a life did not change easily, especially when he was trying to slant his answers while still being truthful.

"And have you seen much . . . combat?" That came from the older overcaptain to his left, Gheranak, according to the calligraphed name placard before him. He sat beside Heald and nearer the head of the table. His words were matter-of-fact, almost as if he already knew.

Alucius replied. "It is hard to compare, but I have been told that I am among those with the most combat experience in the Northern Guard."

The face of the younger officer across the table expressed polite disbelief.

Heald started to open his mouth, but stopped as Overcaptain Gheranak, who had asked the combat question, gestured. "Overcaptain Shorak." The words from the older overcaptain were measured, level. "I read the report on Overcaptain Alucius this morning. It is rather interesting. He was seriously wounded in a battle against the Matrites and left for dead. Although he was captured, within little more than two years he not only recovered from a head wound considered fatal, but escaped. He brought back an entire company of troopers, defeating four Matrite companies in the process. He has twice wiped out raider bands outnumbering his forces by two to one. It is also interesting to note that he has always led his men from the front rank." The older overcaptain inclined his head to Alucius. "I beg your pardon, Overcaptain Alucius, but it is often difficult to state one's own accomplishments without being considered boastful."

Alucius nodded in return. "Thank you. I did not know that my life story had been sent ahead of me." He was as much surprised that the older overcaptain had been telling the truth as he knew it as that the officer knew Alucius's background.

"Ah . . . it was not, but the Landarch has his own sources."

Heald concealed a frown, then glanced at Alucius, who smiled back, ruefully, getting the slightest shrug in return.

The younger overcaptain looked near ashen, far more than Alucius would have expected. "I beg your pardon, Overcaptain."

"You need not be overly concerned . . . if you merely sought information," Alucius said with a smile.

The young overcaptain paled further, than took refuge behind a goblet of the amber wind.

"Shorak here . . ." said the officer to the right of Alucius, "he still has a bit to learn about the way other lands handle their forces. He'll learn."

"I fear I know nothing of the structure of your Lancers," Alucius admitted. "So little that I couldn't ask an intelligent question. Perhaps you could enlighten me."

"I'm Feorak," the officer said, grinning at Shorak. "You see, Shorak. That's the way you do it." Then he looked at Alucius. "You've killed a lot of men in battle, haven't you?"

"Enough," Alucius admitted.

"There's an air about experience. Hard to miss when you look," Feorak said, as much for the benefit of Shorak as Alucius. "You asked about the Lancers. We have twenty-five companies, and five are always on border duty. Five more are going with you on Quinti. Regret I won't be one of them. Now . . . structure. Officers all come from families that can provide an education for their sons. Usually younger sons of landowners, like Shorak and me, but could be merchants or clerks. We get a year of intensive training at the Lancer Academy. The rankers get three months. Companies look to be organized like yours, but twenty-four in a squad, and five squads in a company. Overcaptain in charge of each company, and a captain under him, with a senior squad leader and an assistant senior squad leader, and then a squad leader for each squad, with a senior ranker for each subsquad of twelve."

Alucius nodded. The organization alone told him much. "Are the nomads your biggest problem, or is that something new?"

"We haven't had much problem with the nomads for almost a generation. They weren't even united until this Aellyan Edyss came along. There are all sorts of raiders and clans hidden in the Spine of Corus, to the east of Aelta, and that's where most of the Lancer companies have been. There are still ten out there now."

"So . . . after we leave, there will only be five companies here in Dereka?"

Feorak nodded. "Most Deforyans aren't that worried about the nomads. They feel that we're protected by the spirits of the mountains. No one has ever invaded Deforya, not even before the Cataclysm."

"Spirits of the mountains?"

"No one has ever seen one, but we've found raiders, even nomads, dead on the slopes and in the passes. Without even a mark on them." Feorak shrugged. "No one can explain it, but . . ."

Alucius nodded. "If it works . . ." He took a bite of the meat he had served himself from the platter. It was tender, covered with a plumapple glaze, and only lightly seasoned, but not a kind of meat he had eaten before.

"It's plains antelope," Shorak offered tentatively. "Do you like it?"

"It's very good," Alucius replied.

"They come from the southeast, below the high road before it enters the Northern Pass. It's hard to come by, but it's always been the favored meat at banquets, for generations back."

"Even before the land was Deforya? Or has it always been called Deforya?" asked Alucius, keeping his voice indifferent.

"So long as the histories run, it has been Deforya, land of prosperity and plenty, protected by the very mountains themselves . . ."

"Are the mountains why you're not worried about Aellyan Edyss?" asked Alucius. "He did rout the Praetorians and conquered Ongelya."

"He has not crossed the Barrier Range," Shorak offered. "No one ever has. Not in force."

"Not yet," Feorak added with a laugh.

"We passed vingt after vingt of orchards," Alucius offered, taking a sip of the amber wine, but only a sip.

"Our orchards are known all across Corus . . ."

Alucius listened, only occasionally asking a question.

Some two glasses later, Feran, Alucius, and Heald found themselves in one of the carriages headed back to their quarters. None of the three spoke on their carriage ride, nor until they were crossing the courtyard toward the officers' quarters, under the twin moons of Selena and Asterta, neither new nor full.

"How do you feel about Dereka? What does the place feel like to you?" Alucius asked, almost idly, looking first at Heald, then at Feran.

"Old," said Feran. "It's like they're living in a time generations back." He laughed softly. "They seem happy with it."

"Happy? You think so?" Happy or resigned?

"Happy as any folk," Heald said. "I feel like people are watching us all the time. They knew all about all of us." He added in a low voice. "Gheranak even knew about the crystal spear-thrower. After he told everyone what you'd done, he asked me about it, about what it could do and whether anyone else could build one."

"The captains around me were asking why the raiders had used Deforyan uniforms," Feran added. "The ones who attacked Tuuler, you know?"

"They didn't find all that out from the Lord-Protector, or the majer," Alucius pointed out.

"That's not good," Feran suggested.

"It may not be so bad," Alucius replied. "Think about how we got here."

Heald nodded, understanding both what Alucius had said and not said. Dereka was clearly a place where the walls had both eyes and ears, if not more.

50

Tempre, Lanachrona

The Lord-Protector walked into the conference chamber and seated himself at the vacant seat. He looked over the two marshals and the Recorder of Deeds. "Recorder . . . if you would report?"

"The herder overcaptain is in Dereka. What do you expect from this gambit?" asked the silver-clad Recorder of Deeds, his voice flat. His eyes were dark circles in a face that had become ever more white since winter.

Following his words, silence extended around the conference table, then deepened. No one spoke.

After a time, the Lord-Protector smiled, if faintly. "My dear Recorder, that is the first time ever that you have spoken sharply to me. I trust there is a reason for such."

"There is, Lord-Protector. I fear greatly that you may be unleashing more than you realize. You wish stability for Lanachrona, but the Table is now almost unable to show the herder captain. This is less than encouraging when you have no—

"I have been married less than a year, and I do have brothers."

"I beg your pardon, Lord-Protector. That was not what I meant. I was referring to the Table. You know what it means when an image is not shown."

"It means, my dear Recorder, that I was right. Aellyan Edyss has his pteridons. We have sent our Talent-weapon as well. They will fight in Deforya or in the Barrier Range. Either way, we win. If the overcaptain prevails, we commend him, and send him back to being a herder, and that is what he wants. And he will be grateful for such. If he shows signs of wishing battle glory, we may even promote him to majer and send more forces to him so that he can attack and conquer the nomads. That will also keep the good Colonel Weslyn looking over his shoulder. If the overcaptain does not prevail, I am certain he will create far greater damage to the nomads than Aellyan Edyss can imagine. That will give Edyss great pause about attacking us in the near future, and it will also bind the Landarch, if he holds Deforya, closer to us."

"You do not think this captain will turn his forces against you?" asked Marshal Alyniat.

"Not so long as he is a herder with a stead, and with a mother, a grandsire, and a wife. The stead is his life. It is for all herders." The Lord-Protector smiled, coldly. "And if anything should happen to his stead or *any* of them, I would do far worse to whoever caused it to occur than you can possibly imagine. I do not like good tools being damaged through pettiness."

The two marshals nodded acquiescence. The Recorder shivered imperceptibly.

"What of the nomads?" asked the Lord-Protector.

"They are scouting the passes to the north, between Illegea and Deforya. They are also gathering supplies," the Recorder replied. "As you know, the Table does not reveal the pteridons, but there has been no sign of further destruction."

"Good." The Lord-Protector turned to the older marshal. "How long will it take to build up the forces necessary to move from Eastice to Northport?"

"The Recorder's Table shows that there are but two Matrite horse companies north of Harmony. We will have what we need to take Northport in less than two weeks. We should have Harmony by the end of harvest. After that, the fighting will be most intense and difficult. It is possible we might reach Arwyn before winter."

"Then we will consolidate our position before winter, wherever that may be. We will not make the mistakes the Matrial did." The Lord-Protector turned to Alyniat, then the Recorder. "You will be sure to report on any movements of Matrite troopers?"

"Yes, Lord-Protector."

"Is . . . Do you think that moving troopers west . . . ?" Wyerl did not finish the sentence.

"No. It is not absolutely certain. But Aellyan Edyss is a nomad. He thinks of plunder and golds. That is why he wants Deforya and control of the Northern Pass. If we strike in Madrien now, we can gain control of all major ports on the coast except Hafin, and, in time, we can defeat the Matrites. We already control most of the high roads, and golds are now flowing from our tariffs at Southgate."

The two marshals nodded once more.

51

Alucius could feel the coolness of smooth tile under his feet. He looked down and discovered he wore but simple under-drawers, rather than his nightsilk undergarments. As he raised his eyes, a woman with shimmering black hair, violet eyes, and flawless white skin, clad in less even than Alucius wore, stepped through the archway opposite him, swaying toward the herder, smiling, beckoning, suggesting that all manner of delights were within his reach. Yet Alucius hesitated, stepping back, feeling a deep chill from somewhere.

The woman beckoned once more, and Alucius edged farther backward.

A bolt of purple flame appeared at her fingertips, then flared from her fingers. He threw up a sabre that had appeared in his hand. Flame sprayed past him, the heat so intense it was like an iron mill. He could smell hair burning, his hair—

Alucius jerked upright from the wide bed in the ancient stone-walled officers' quarters in the barracks of the Lancers of Dereka, barracks whose walls, at least, dated back to before the Cataclysm. In the darkness that was more like twilight to him, he glanced around, but he could neither see nor sense anyone within the room, perfectly silent except for his own ragged breathing. He swallowed, then moistened dry lips.

Why the Matrial—or the image he had of her? He had not had that dream since right after he had killed the Matrial. Why now? He hadn't even thought of the former ruler of Madrien, except perhaps in passing, in weeks. Was it being surrounded by ancient structures? Or the sense of sorrow that permeated Deforya?

After swinging his legs over the side of the bed, Alucius stood. He walked to the window and opened the shutters slightly. Below, the courtyard was empty. Then he turned. He still needed sleep, and he'd regret not sleeping all too much on the ride that lay before Twenty-first Company.

As he slipped back under the thin blanket that was all he needed on the cool summer night, he tried not to think about the reasons behind the dream. He also worried about Wendra, although he couldn't say why the dream had called up those concerns, and he wished he had a way to write her, or, better yet, that he could return to the stead. But that return, he knew full well, was months away—and only if he and his company survived.

52

On Quinti, Alucius was at the head of Twenty-first Company, riding southward out of the city of Dereka toward the misty peaks of the Barrier Range, barely visible in the distance beyond the orchards and grasslands. The road south was not of eternastone, but it was paved—at least for the first five vingts out of the city and for as far as Alucius could see. Paved or not, it was dusty. Since Twenty-first Company was fourth in riding order among those from Lanachrona and the Iron Valleys, and since the Deforyan forces were up front, there was enough dust that Alucius found himself wiping the fine grit off his face and forehead almost every vingt.

Longyl rode beside Alucius. "No aqueducts or orchards along this road, but the ground looks the same. Wager they could grow plumapples here, too."

"They probably could, if they had water and people to tend them."

"There were a lot of people in Dereka," Longyl mused. "They weren't garbed all that well, either."

"Some of the buildings were empty, the old ones," Alucius pointed out.

"I didn't see any new ones." Longyl laughed.

Neither had Alucius. He also realized something else. With all the briefings and meetings on Quattri, and the need to clean and repair gear, they'd effectively been kept busy enough not to really explore Dereka.

For almost a vingt of travel, he considered what he and Longyl had just talked about, the few words he'd overheard from the streets about water, the painful lack of experience of Overcaptain Shorak.

Then he turned to Longyl. "You're in charge here for a bit. I need to talk to Captain Feran for a few moments."

"Yes, sir."

Alucius eased Wildebeast out along the shoulder and headed back toward Fifth Company, noting the narrow-bodied wagons and packhorses stretched out for half a vingt behind Feran's last troopers. Transferring the ammunition and equipment from the wider Lanachronan wagons to those of the Deforyans had also been a complication, but the majer had assured them it was necessary because the road to the Deforyan outpost in the Barrier Range was too narrow for the wider wagons.

Feran lifted his arm in greeting as Alucius neared and swung his mount alongside the older captain. "Coming back so you can swallow even more dust?"

"You know how I love dust," Alucius said with a smile. "I was thinking. About the supper with the Landarch."

"Best food we're likely to have until we get back home."

"Probably." Alucius paused. "You were sitting with the captains. What were they like?"

"We had a better time than you did. Most of them were long-termers like me."

"Most . . . or all of them?" Alucius asked.

"All probably . . . or so close as not to make a difference. Why?"

"Some of the overcaptains were younger than I am . . . years younger. They came from the families of large landowners."

Feran nodded. "The captains really command the companies, you think?"

"In most cases. I'd say they run the companies, the way the senior squad leaders run the Matrite companies."

"If it works . . . ?"

"I'd wager it works a great deal more effectively than if the overcaptains actually gave commands. Or at least the junior overcaptains."

"Does this have anything to do with the nomads?" asked Feran politely.

"If we're fighting with the Deforyan Lancers, it does. It also explains why Heald and I got promoted. One reason, anyway."

"Oh . . ." Feran shook his head. ". . . son of an underweight sow!" The exclamation was low, but carried to Alucius. "All they've ever done is chase small bands of raiders, and now you're telling me that there aren't any brains in the overcaptains?"

"No . . . I'm saying that you can't tell. They all have their rank because of family, and some might have brains, but until we get into a fight, we won't know."

"That also tells me why the overcaptains don't like talking to me," Feran went on. "I'm just a poor working officer, not the son of a landowner."

"I'm considered a failure, because I'm an older son of a landowner who is an officer," Alucius pointed out with a laugh. "They only answer my questions when they have to."

"You know . . . Overcaptain Alucius," Feran said ruefully, "every time you start to think, I end up getting worried. Couldn't you have just let me think everything was going to be all right? At least for another day or so." Feran's expression turned mock-mournful.

Alucius laughed. So did Feran.

What else could they do?

53

Alustre, Lustrea

Vestor looked at the green circlet on his collar, the token of valor, then down at his weakened left arm. His lips tightened, and he smiled, coolly, his eyes going to the narrow windows and the silver-green sky they revealed.

He walked to the main workbench, where he inspected and tightened several silver clips on the assemblies within the black metal containers, assemblies that would hold crystals. After a short time, he moved to the crystal tanks, where he surveyed the progress there. Casually, he eased around the end of the last tank to the smaller workbench in the corner, a space easily overlooked.

For a long moment, he stood over the bench, then slid back the green quartz surface to reveal a polished and silvered metal circle, recessed beneath the oak that held the quartz top. He took several deep breaths. After a time he concentrated, staring deeply into the ruby mists that appeared, tinged somehow with both purple and pink.

Amorphous dark shadows, suggesting figures, appeared, then vanished, and immediately, a section of a diagram appeared.

Even as he concentrated on memorizing the diagram, suspended against the multicolored mists, Vestor's eyes flicked intermittently to the amber crystal affixed to the side of the metal mirror.

The amber crystal began to glow, and Vestor stepped back from the workbench, just as it shattered. The once-polished surface of the metal appeared tarnished, as if by fire, but had neither deformed nor cracked. Vestor replaced the quartz cover slab, quickly, then took out the engineers' markstick and began to sketch and write out all that he had seen in the metallic mirror.

His right hand was deft as he transferred all that he had seen. When he finished and beheld his handiwork, a smile of modest satisfaction appeared—momentarily—vanishing as he set down the markstick and used his good right hand to massage the left forearm he had leaned on while he had been copying the diagram.

His eyes dropped to the green circle. ". . . hardly enough . . ." But the words were so low that not even an observer behind the nearest wall, had there been one, would have heard.

54

Four days later, the ten companies, followed by supply wagons and packhorses, were riding single file along a narrow trail in the middle of the Barrier Range, whose slopes, while not nearly so steep as those of the Upper Spine Mountains, were far drier and composed of a combination of ancient lava and red sandstone. The road had turned from stone into the dusty trail two days earlier. At first, it had wound through sandy red hills, covered with outcroppings of black rocks, occasional growths of cacti that made the quarasote hills of the Iron Valleys look lush, and scattered thorn trees with silver leaves that were sparse and smaller than a child's little finger.

The thorn trees had vanished once they had reached the actual mountains, but the cacti had remained, although they were even more scattered and more ancient. Overhead, the sun was white and hot. Except at the two waystations, where there were springs, there had been no sign of water anywhere, and few signs at all of animal life, except for scratlike creatures, and the occasional ravens, circling for carrion. On both sides of the trail loomed reddish gray peaks, peaks without a hint of either vegetation or moisture.

With the narrowness of the trail-like road, Alucius understood all too well why the Deforyans used packhorses and narrow-bodied wagons to bring supplies—and the fact that they did so, and apparently had for generations, gave him a greater understanding of why the Lord-Protector worried about Deforya falling to the nomads, because it would be so difficult to retake from a superior force.

"No wonder they call it the Barrier Range," Longyl said from slightly behind and to the left of Alucius.

"We aren't even to the middle of the mountains," Alucius replied, wiping away even more of the fine and gritty red dust that seeped every-where. There was no breeze at all, and the dust rose and hung in the air, waiting to cling to the troopers and officers. Once more, Twenty-first Company was riding fourth in the contingent from the west, and that meant ninth out of ten companies. Only poor Feran was eating more dust. "Not quite anyway."

"Don't see why the nomads would even want this land," Longyl said.

"They don't. They want Dereka and the high road and the trade that travels it. They already control the southern high road to Lustrea."

"Seems like we're always being sent out to save one bunch of traders or another some golds." Longyl shook his head. "You'd think that this Aellyan Edyss would have some better use for pteridons than taking lands to get more golds."

"Maybe he does," Alucius said, "and maybe all the traders can't imag-ine him wanting anything but golds. But . . ." He paused for a moment, then went on, "if he does, that makes it more dangerous for us, because he'll want Deforya whatever the cost."

"You think he wants to claim the dual scepter? I always thought that was just a story."

"It is a story, or a legend, whatever you want to call it," Alucius said. "No one's ever seen it. That's what my grandsire said, years ago. But everyone thought pteridons were a legend, too."

204   L. E. MODESITT, JR.

"I wish they'd stayed a legend," Longyl replied. "You know, sir, things are never dull around you. Not for long."

"We could use them being dull," Alucius replied. "For a good year. Starting now."

"They won't be," Longyl prophesied.

Alucius agreed. He didn't think that matters would stay dull, not for more than the time it took to reach the southern side of the Barrier Range where the Deforyan patrol camp was located. Recalling the references to the mountain spirits, Alucius had been scanning the areas beside the trail frequently, but without success.

He'd been unable to detect any sign of either the blue-violet creatures he had sensed in the Upper Spine Mountains or of any other large living beings. He also realized that the sense of sadness or sorrow he had felt in Deforya—and which had seemed to dissipate as he had ridden south— was gone. In its place was . . . nothing. Rather, the lifewebs were sparse, and the sense of aliveness that underlay most land through which he had traveled was gone. Even the Upper Spine Mountains had felt alive, if subdued. Until he had reached the Barrier Range, Alucius wouldn't really have thought about the difference.

"Something's going on up there." Longyl stood in his stirrups. "They're stopping."

"Column halt!" Alucius called out the order, even before he heard the order.

Before long, a trooper appeared. "Overcaptain, sir, all officers to the front."

Longyl glanced at Alucius.

"We'll see," Alucius said. "Have them stand down and make sure they drink." He eased Wildebeast forward, then around the trailing troopers in Eleventh Company.

He had to ride over a vingt along the winding trail before he reached the head of the column. There, the majer over the five Deforyan companies and Majer Draspyr waited, mounted and facing the other captains and overcaptains.

"Majer Weorynak," began Draspyr, "requested this brief meeting. Behind us is the body of a nomad scout. We believe he was a scout. The majer will have a few words to say once you have ridden by and taken a good look at the nomad."

Alucius was the next to last to ride up to the side of the trail, with only Feran behind him. There were two bodies there—one of a man and the other of his mount. Both desiccated figures looked to have spent weeks—or years—in the heat and dryness, yet the glittering blue breastplate of the nomad held but the slightest coating of dust. The nomad had been dark-haired, but surprisingly fair-skinned, wrinkled and weathered though his face had been—and young. The mount had been a gray, but had been reduced to skin and hair shrunken around bones. The two lay in a heap as if they had been struck down instantly. The rider's right hand still grasped a rifle, as if he had just lifted it clear of its holder. While similar to both Matrite and Deforyan rifles, it was not quite the same, and the steel of the barrel was more obviously blued.

Alucius rode past, then returned to the others, silently. After Feran pulled up beside him, the Deforyan majer cleared his throat.

"This trail was empty when the last dispatch came through here, no more than four days ago," Majer Weorynak said. "You can see what the spirits of the mountains can do to a man who rides alone. It is advisable to ride at least in pairs." He turned his mount away, as if to indicate that he had offered all that needed to be said. The Deforyan officers also turned their mounts.

"That's all," Draspyr announced. "Back to your companies."

Alucius eased Wildebeast around and started back down the trail toward Twenty-first Company, reflecting. The Matrites had also had a policy against scouts going out alone. At the time, he'd thought it was just another way to keep torque-wearers under control, but had there been another reason—one never voiced. Or was it coincidence?

He had almost reached Twenty-first Company when he heard a voice behind him.

"Alucius?"

At Feran's call, he slowed Wildebeast and eased to the side of the trail in the space between Eleventh and Twenty-first Companies.

"What do you think?" Feran asked.

"The same as you do, I'd wager. Whatever did that might be able to pick off single troopers, but they won't do much against larger forces."

"Column forward!" came the command from the south.

Alucius gestured to Longyl, who repeated the order.

Alucius and Feran had to ride shoulder to shoulder as they continued along the dusty incline.

"First . . . pteridons, and now these . . . spirits," Feran said.

"I'm more worried about the pteridons," Alucius replied. "The Deforyans have dealt with the spirits for generations. No one's seen pteridons since the Cataclysm—not until now."

"You think that whatever it was that killed the nomad might be helpful? Reduce the number of nomads?"

"I don't know." Whatever had killed the man, Alucius knew, was rare, and there weren't that many. That he could tell from his Talent, and he had doubts that the creature or creatures could stop an invasion of thousands of nomads backed with pteridons.

For that matter, he wondered, not for the first time, what sort of tactics he or anyone could use against well-armed riders, backed by flying creatures that had already routed one of the largest forces in Corus.

55

Tempre, Lanachrona

The Recorder of Deeds stood alone in the marble-walled room deep beneath the palace of the Lord-Protector, his eyes fixed on the Table of the Recorders.

The mirrored-silver surface swirled and was covered in ruby mists. Then, out of the ruby mists, mists that had taken on a purplish black tinge, appeared the commanding figure of a man, tall, broad-shouldered, with violet-red eyes, alabaster skin, and black hair. Behind him was a hall with pink marble walls, golden columns, and deep purple hangings trimmed in gold, a hall that resembled one of the few antique illustrations left of the now-vanished great halls of Elcien or Ludar.

The Recorder of Deeds studied the chamber, and the man, who smiled as if he knew he was being observed. Then the scene vanished, to be replaced by the view of a single page, half diagram, half text.

The Recorder squinted to make out what was displayed. As he read, his eyes widened, and he frantically reached for a sheet of paper, finding only a message tucked inside his silver vestments, which he flattened on the wood beside the glass, turning the reverse side up. Using the blank reverse side and a markstick, he began to copy the document, and the words beneath the clearly ancient illustration.

Sweat poured down his forehead. Several times, he had to blot the salty perspiration away from his eyes with his upper arm and sleeve as he feverishly continued to copy what the Table displayed.

In time, shivering and shuddering, his vestments and undergarments soaked, he released the image displayed in the table and staggered to the single chair set against the ancient wall, seating himself with a heavy thump. But his eyes, tinged with the slightest hint of purple, glittered as he read what he had copied, even as he massaged his aching forehead.

56

Another two days passed before the ten companies rode into the Deforyan fortress post on the southern edge of the Barrier Range. Black Ridge was a wide ledge set atop a dark outcropping of ancient lava. At the back of the ledge—the north side—rose a thousand-yard-high cliff—nearly sheer—while the southern side of the ledge

ended in an equally sheer drop to the grasslands below. The flat section
of the ledge itself was almost two hundred yards wide, and close to a
vingt in length, with the entry trail at the eastern end. The western end
of the ledge just halted where the sandstone curved forward, leaving a
sheer drop from more than a thousand yards above to the grasslands
below and a stone wall rising another thousand yards skyward.

Alucius worried about the position. While there was a narrow trail
down to the grasslands, and while the cliffs made attack difficult, there
was only one way back to Dereka. Why hadn't the ancient builders created an alternative? Or had they been confident that they would never
need another way out?

Both stables and quarters had been chiseled or cut out of the layer of
red sandstone that formed the higher cliff at the back of the ledge. One
set of stables was at each end of the areas that had been chiseled or cut
out of the red sandstone. From the rounded edges of the doorways and
arches, Alucius could tell that they had been tunneled out a long time
ago. He could also see that wide arcing areas of the red sandstone
around and above the arches were slightly darker than the other areas,
but only around the archways and the very few windows cut into the red
stone. He glanced farther to the west, but there were no such dark areas
in the section of the cliff where there were no tunnels and arches.

"The stables are inside the large arches on the east end, the quarters
on the west end . . ."

Following the orders, and after waiting for the companies that had
arrived earlier, Alucius directed Twenty-first Company toward the stables. The five Deforyan companies stationed at Black Ridge before were
forming up to head back to Dereka, almost as soon as Fifth Company
had begun to stable their mounts.

When he had seen to his troopers and their mounts, and made sure
that there was sufficient feed and hay—some probably gathered from
the grasslands below—Alucius stabled Wildebeast in the section reserved
for officers. He was leaving the stables when Feran stepped up beside
him.

"They could hardly wait to leave. I'd say that means that the nomads
are getting ready to attack, but I can't believe—I guess I can, but . . ."

"That their commander let them leave?" Alucius raised his eyebrows.

"We're here. Why would they want to lose another five companies in the Barrier Range? They'll claim they'll fight to protect Dereka if the nomads get that far."

"Dereka . . ." muttered Feran. "I suppose so. It's the only thing of value we've seen—except the orchards."

Captain Clifyr walked toward the two, gesturing toward the second archway from the west end, cut into the red sandstone. "The officers' quarters are in there. You can take any space that's vacant, but it's two to a room. As soon as you can, the majer would like to meet. There's a conference room just inside that same archway."

"Thank you, Captain." Alucius nodded politely, then shifted the saddlebags on his shoulder, and with a rifle in each hand, headed for the indicated archway.

Feran matched his steps. "I still don't much care for him."

"He does what the majer wants."

"Maybe that's why."

The officers' quarters amounted to small windowless cubicles little more than three yards by two, set along a corridor with a surprising high ceiling—almost three yards high. Each had two bunks, but was doorless, with a shelf above the head of each bunk, and a series of pegs above the foot. Alucius doubted that both men could dress at the same time.

"Which bunk do you want?" Feran grinned. "After all, you have the rank."

"I'll take the one on the left." Not that it made much difference, since they were identical. After quickly setting his gear on the shelf, Alucius slipped out of the confined space and walked farther down the corridor. Just short of the end was a vertical air shaft from which poured cooler air, creating a flow of air from the back of the corridor forward. Beyond the air shaft was a bathing chamber, with a small fountain, clearly fed by some sort of underground source.

Alucius turned and headed back toward the conference room, and Feran joined him.

Captain Clifyr was already in the conference space, which held a long sandstone table carved from the cliff itself, if reinforced with wooden braces in places, and covered with layers of some sort of varnish or finish. A good dozen stools, none of them of recent construction, were set around the table. The single window, with actual shutters, had been closed, although Alucius could feel the warm air seeping through the shutter slats.

Alucius and Feran took stools and waited. Shortly, both Heald and Koryt appeared, and then Clifyr slipped out, returning in moments with Majer Draspyr.

The four former militia officers stood. Draspyr motioned for them to take their stools once more, then unrolled a map and weighted it down with small stones produced by Clifyr, before looking over the officers once more and beginning. "According to the Deforyan commander who just left, the nomads are encamped some ten vingts to the south, along a small stream—the only stream—in this part of the Barrier Range. He has not seen any sign of the pteridons, but, according to the information I received before we left Borlan, in the attacks on the Praetorian forces the pteridons did not appear until sometime shortly before the battle.

"We will begin patrols tomorrow. Patrols will consist of two squads, each squad from a different company. Until we have more information, I am requesting that each of you accompany the squad you choose for patrols. Tomorrow, the patrol companies will be the Twenty-third Company of the Southern Guard and the Twenty-first Company of the Northern Guard. On Tridi, it will be Third and Fifth Companies, and on Quattri Twenty-third Company and Eleventh Company. Once you are clear of the cliff here, you are to split into subsquads, and search the areas on the map here, as indicated . . ." Draspyr pointed. "The first section . . ."

Alucius noted that Twenty-first Company was assigned the section that took in where the nomads were supposed to be camped.

"You are to gather information about possible routes to and from the nomad encampment, sources of forage for mounts, places suitable for battle, and places unsuitable. Any information about the nomads, their mounts, and their weapons is particularly necessary . . ." Draspyr continued for a good fifth of a glass before stopping and asking, "Now. Do any of you have any questions?"

Alucius cleared his throat. "Sir?"

"Yes, Overcaptain?"

"Did any of the Deforyan officers mention why they were sending back five companies when a nomad attack might be imminent?"

"No, they did not, Overcaptain."

Alucius could sense the majer's anger at the question, or at the Deforyans, and he merely replied, "Thank you, sir."

"Sir?" asked Heald. "Do we have any information on the numbers of nomads?"

"I regret that we do not, since the Deforyans did not send any scouts down into the grasslands. Or not very far."

That didn't astonish Alucius, although it did surprise both Koryt and Clifyr.

"Sir?" asked Feran. "Are the Deforyans here just to hold this base? Or am I missing something?"

"I think, Captain Feran, that you have grasped the situation. We cannot, however, say much about their orders, since they are under the command of the Landarch, and they have kindly allowed us to share their quarters and provided supplies. We are almost here on sufferance, it would appear." Draspyr straightened. "I will see you all in the officers' mess shortly."

"They have one?" murmured Feran under his breath.

Alucius waited until the majer had left. "They'd have to have one. Otherwise, the officers would have to eat with mere rankers."

"They couldn't do that," Heald said quietly. "They don't even like eating with career types."

Clifyr was straining to hear without seeming to do so.

Alucius turned toward the Southern Guard captain. "We were considering what sort of mess they might have here."

"It's actually quite suitable," Clifyr said. "Enough chairs and tables for close to forty, and a well-equipped kitchen."

Feran and Heald smiled and nodded.

"Thank you," Alucius replied, waiting for Clifyr to leave.

"This really smells like sander shit," Feran finally said. "We're supposed to scout, and fight, and . . . the Deforyans are just going to sit up here and see if the nomads attack?"

"They won't attack here," Heald said. "They'll just ride around Black Ridge and head for Dereka."

"We'll have to see," Alucius replied. "Starting tomorrow."

The others nodded, not happily, but then, Alucius wasn't exactly pleased, either.

57

South of the Barrier Range, Illegea

In the cool of evening, nearly a score of Myrmidon war-leaders had gathered in the largest tent in the encampment, and half the panels had been lifted to provide air. They sat cross-legged on the thin but elegantly woven carpets circled around the stool on which Aellyan Edyss was seated. Outside in the gathering twilight, some of the younger Myrmidons had also gathered, far enough back from the light cast by lamps set on posts pounded into the ground so that their faces could not be seen.

"We are the riders of the wind," Edyss said, his voice stating the obvious. "We ride the wind either upon our mounts or upon the pteridons, and nothing stands before the wind." After a pause, he continued. "The westerners believe that all we live for is plunder. Plunder is good." He grinned. "It is very good. But it is not enough. For generations, the easterners and the westerners have ridden the great road through our lands, doing as they please, scorning us. Even now, they scorn us. Up on the black ledge, there are ten companies of troopers. There have always been five. Now, the Lord-Protector of Lanachrona has deigned to send a mere five companies. Do they think so little of us that they believe five more companies—a few hundred weak westerners with rifles—can stop us from reclaiming our destiny?"

A low and rumbled "No!" rose from the warleaders.

"For generations, the weaklings of Deforya have trusted in the mountains to keep them safe. They believed that we could never act together. They have high grasslands, and they have few horses. They have water through all the year, and yet they huddle in a handful of towns and cities. They control the northern high road, and yet they reap little gain from it. Are they guardians of the land? Do they celebrate the sky and life? Do they deserve the land they hold?"

"No!" rumbled forth once more.

"The westerners . . . in their arrogance, they will come down from the mountains and they will scout. For a time . . . let them, but watch what they do and how they do it. We will only attack if they near our camp. They will see how mighty our force is, and they will hesitate. While they hesitate, and before they can summon more of their troopers, then we will attack them . . . and the despicable Deforyans." Edyss stood, his eyes blazing, his gaze catching the eyes of every warleader in turn.

In the silence that followed, he seated himself once more on the stool.

"How do we know that the Deforyans or their allies in black do not have a weapon like the Lustreans did?" asked one of the older horse commanders, his weathered face emotionless.

"We do not know," Aellyan Edyss replied. "But we will find out before we bring all the pteridons to battle. We of the grasslands can be as cunning as the great grass serpents, when the need is there. If they do have such a weapon, we will creep up the mountain in the darkness and overpower them while they sleep." He laughed. "We may do that anyway."

"What of the spirits in the mountains?"

"What of them?" asked the blond-haired commander. "The grasslands have their spirits, and they are far more numerous than those of the mountains. Have you once feared to ride your horse because of grassland spirits?" His laugh was open, yet mocking.

The man who had asked the question looked down, and more laughter rang through the tent.

"We have already destroyed the greatest army raised in generations," Edyss went on. "If we strike when our enemies are weak, and choose the time and place of our battles, you will see the banner of the new Myrmidons fly above Dereka, and within your lives above far Alustre and Tempre, and even Hieron and Southgate. Corus can be ours. It will be ours . . ."

In the darkness beyond the tent, smiles appeared on the shadowed faces of the younger Myrmidons.

58

Early on Duadi, right after muster, Alucius and the third squad of Twenty-first Company led the patrols down from Black Ridge on a trail cut from the black lava sometime in the distant past, a trail that was even more narrow than the one across the Barrier Range. Switch-back followed switchback, and while the exposed stretches were clear, the protected niches just beyond each switchback were piled high with fine dark sand that spilled onto the trail in places.

Alucius was near the lead, with just two scouts before him. Even after they had traveled less than a vingt, he could see that there were no hoof-prints or footprints on the trail, just rodent tracks and occasional bird trac-ings, and one slithering trace that indicated a largish snake. But he could sense nothing with his Talent—except for his troopers and their mounts.

At the bottom of the cliff trail, as Alucius and third squad waited for Captain Clifyr and his first squad, Alucius studied the nearly sheer cliff. So far as he could tell, there was no other way to Black Ridge from the grasslands—not directly. There were other defiles and gorges heading northward, and it was certainly possible that the nomads could use them to bypass the sheer cliff and circle back along the supply trail, but the four-man guard detail could certainly hold off any attack up the trail long enough for reinforcements to cross the open two hundred yards from the barracks to overwhelm any attackers—except perhaps at night, when they would not be able to see the attackers against the shadows and dark stone until they were within a few hundred yards.

He decided to make that point to the majer on his return—after he had experienced how hard the ride was back up the narrow and ancient trail.

The grass that covered everything was still the full green of early summer, spraying out of thick root clumps that protruded a finger's width from the ground. Each clump was separated from the next by perhaps two handspans. In most places, the grass had reached a level waist high on a grown man, tall enough to conceal a scout hidden in it, but not tall enough to hide a standing man or mount. Where the grass was thinner, Alucius could see the tannish remnants of the previous year's growth, although there was little enough of that. Were there beetles or insects that consumed the dead growth the way the shellbeetles went after dead quarasote?

Captain Clifyr rode to meet Alucius well before the last of the squad from Twenty-third Company cleared the narrow trail. He inclined his head as he reined up short of Alucius. "Overcaptain."

"Captain. How did you find the descent?"

"It's steep. The footing is good, except for where there's sand." Clifyr paused. "How would you like to handle the return rendezvous?"

"I don't think we should plan on that. We'll be heading farther west," Alucius said. "We should make sure we each have our full squad before coming back, but one of us could be waiting here for some time, and that would just make whoever it is a target."

"The majer wants everyone back—"

Alucius looked at Clifyr, and said quietly, "You can do as you think best. We will probably take longer. You can wait here at the bottom or head back up. If you're not here, and there aren't tracks heading back up, we will make a quick search."

Clifyr frowned, then nodded. "As you wish, Overcaptain."

"It's not something we can plan that well. You'll do fine," Alucius said, using a touch of Talent to project reassurance and confidence. "We'll see you late this afternoon." Then he turned Wildebeast back toward third squad.

As Clifyr marshaled his squad, Alucius reined up beside the third squad leader. "Faisyn . . . we'll ride together until we get to a point where we're opposite that next canyon to the west. Then, you'll head south from there. You take the left file, with Waris as your scout, and I'll take the right file and Deuryn. You're clear on the area to travel? And how far south you'll go?"

"Yes, sir."

"Don't stop for very long when you take breaks, and keep in mind that we'll be tracked, at least from a distance, by the nomads. They could attack at any time. I don't think they will, but they could." Alucius laughed softly. "I've been wrong before, and I wouldn't want unnecessary casualties because you took my word. With the Lanachronans and the Matrites, we had some idea how they fought. Here, we don't have any idea."

"But you think they'll feel us out?"

"I'm fairly sure of that. What I don't know is whether feeling us out is attacking immediately to see how we defend ourselves or watching and then attacking."

Faisyn nodded.

"Patrol forward!" Alucius ordered.

Two glasses passed before they reached the higher ridge overlooking the narrow stream that emerged from the Barrier Range through a narrow defile a vingt to the north. The ride had been slower than Alucius had thought, because the grass was thicker, and there were no signs of any trails. Once they had reined up on the crest of the ridge, Alucius studied the terrain once more.

Below them, in the gentle swale, the stream meandered in a southwest direction. From what observations Alucius and the majer had made and from the fires they had seen the night before, the nomads had camped on the southern side of the stream close to seven vingts farther to the southwest.

Alucius gestured to the squad leader, riding to his right. "Faisyn."

"Sir?"

"Remember. You go south and then east from here. You're not to go any farther west than you already are. And when you get back to the base of the trail, you're to wait there, but in such a way that you can ride up it immediately if you're threatened. You'd be exposed until you get to the first switchback, but you could hold that against a company."

"Yes, sir."

"Head your subsquad out. We'll see you later."

Alucius watched for a time until he was certain that no one was following, not that his Talent could sense, before he turned Wildebeast and started down the slope to the stream. The stream was only three yards wide, with a mud-and-clay bottom, but clear and nearly a yard deep.

After refilling water bottles and watering their mounts, they headed up the slope on the far side. About halfway up, Alucius sensed riders to the south, barely at the range of his Talent.

"Dueryn!"

"Yes, sir?" The scout rode up alongside Alucius.

"We're nearing the edge of the territory the nomads patrol. I'd like you to trail us a bit and keep a close eye out to the south."

"Yes, sir."

As Dueryn turned his mount, Alucius beckoned to Velmyr, an older trooper.

"Sir?"

"I'd like you to ride ahead, not far, about fifty yards, and give a yell if you see anything."

"Yes, sir."

Alucius doubted that even half a glass had passed before Deuryn returned and eased his mount up beside Alucius. "We're being followed, sir. There's a bunch of nomads about a vingt to the south on the next rise, the one on the other side of the stream. Mostly, they're staying below the crest on the far side."

"How many?" asked Alucius.

"I'd say only five or six."

That number matched the feel that Alucius had gotten from his Talent. "Then we don't have to worry about an immediate attack. They'd have to ride down, and then up against us anyway. But keep watching and let me know if anything changes."

As Dueryn turned his mount, Alucius tried to stretch his Talent sense to the south. He gained a feeling of many men somewhere beyond the stream, but the vagueness of the feeling meant that they were at least three or four vingts distant. But there was something, someone, directly ahead.

"Velmyr!"

"Sir?"

Alucius did not speak, but gestured for the trooper to return, then motioned for him to ride beside him.

"What have you seen?" he asked, as the patrol followed the ridgeline toward the southwest. They were now a good two to three vingts south of the cliffs that marked the southern edge of the Barrier Range.

"Grass, sir, and more grass. Might be some riders ahead—out on the horizon on the other side of the stream. Saw a few dark spots . . . but only a few times."

"That wouldn't surprise me." Alucius could sense that a single nomad or scout lay in the green waist-high grass, a hundred yards ahead.

"Patrol halt!" He reined up with the order to the half squad patrol. Did he want to reveal that they knew?

"Quiet," Alucius said, studying the grass ahead. "There's someone or something in the grass ahead. From the way the grass was moving against the wind, it's either a grass-cat or a nomad scout."

For a time, the patrol remained motionless, the only sounds those of the mounts breathing and the occasional creak of leather as a trooper shifted his weight in the saddle. Alucius thought. He really didn't like shooting someone, and he didn't want to avoid the area. If they rode closer, someone would get shot, probably one of his men.

"You can either stand up or get shot!" Alucius finally called out.

There was no response. Alucius didn't sense fear, but something more like contempt. He took a long slow breath as he pulled out the heavy militia rifle, cocked it and aimed. He fired slightly wide of the hidden figure.

There was no response. "The next shot will be for you!" Alucius recocked the rifle.

The sense of arrogance remained, and the nomad stayed hidden.

With a sense of regret, Alucius fired again. *Crack!*

Even with the sense of pain that washed back over Alucius, he could feel no fear, and no response, but a gathering of resolve. So when the nomad leapt to his feet with his own rifle, Alucius was ready with his third shot. Before the nomad could squeeze the trigger on his weapon, he pitched forward into the grass, the red-dark void of death washing over Alucius.

". . . sander shit . . ." came a faint murmur from behind Alucius.

Alucius scanned the area, with eyes, ears, and Talent, but could sense nothing near, although there might be a horse in the low wash farther south. "Patrol forward!"

He reined up opposite the dead man and dismounted, then quickly searched the body, finding only a few coins, which he left, but neither maps nor anything else beyond what any trooper might carry. Leaving the body in the grass, he remounted and gestured for the patrol to continue.

". . . didn't see the grass moving . . ."

". . . because you're not a herder . . ."

". . . herders are scary . . . never want to upset 'em . . . story is that back when he was a ranker years ago, three guys jumped him in the dark, and he killed all three with his bare hands . . ."

Alucius wanted to shake his head. It had been in training, and there had been only two, and he'd flattened both without damage—although he could have killed them as easily. He hadn't had to, though, and they'd been stupid enough to get killed in the early skirmishes over Soulend.

"Keep an eye out!" he ordered, as much to stop the murmurs as anything.

They continued southwest for another glass and a half before Alucius called a halt. The bands of nomads on the opposite ridge had become more numerous—Alucius and the others had spotted four separate groups, but none held more than four or five riders.

With their numbers increasing, and with a squad at risk, he wasn't about to head farther or to cross the stream to get any nearer to the nomads, not in a new land where he was learning and where they would be clearly outnumbered in any skirmish.

From his Talent, he could tell that the majority of the nomads were where they had been reported, and in the late afternoon, the smoke from the cookfires confirmed that. The acrid odor that drifted northward on the hint of the breeze confirmed another suspicion—that the nomads were not using firewood for their cookfires. Then, they couldn't have been. From what Alucius had seen there were neither trees nor brush suitable for that.

On the return, Alucius kept checking with his Talent, and the scouts

Dueryn continued to report, but the nomads who trailed them remained a good vingt to the south, shadowing them all the way back to the bottom of the trail up to Black Ridge where Faisyn and his half squad were waiting, along with two troopers from Twenty-third Company, who immediately started up the trail once they saw Alucius.

59

Three more days of patrols had changed nothing, except that more nomads shadowed each patrol. Alucius was eating breakfast in the sandstone-walled officers' mess, seated on a sturdy wooden chair that was doubtless older than he was. Before him, on a chipped crockery platter also of antique vintage, was an omelet stuffed with cheese and some form of meat, with a mixture of dried apples and plumapples on the side—prepared by the Deforyan cook brought along with the supply wagons.

The only officers in the mess were those from the west—Feran, Clifyr, and Heald. Koryt had left a few moments earlier, as had Majer Draspyr. Deforyan officers, Alucius had observed, rose somewhat later.

"How long before they attack, do you think?" asked Heald.

"Today . . . tomorrow. No later than the day after," Feran suggested.

Alucius swallowed the bitter ale that came with breakfast and took a last mouthful of the omelet, but did not offer an opinion as he finished off the dried fruit.

Feran glanced across the table at Alucius, as if to ask his opinion.

Alucius shrugged, although he shared the older officer's views that any attack would be soon in coming.

Majer Draspyr appeared in the archway—flushed. "Get your men armed and ready! Have your squad leaders form them up on foot out front! Then meet me in the conference room!"

"Yes, sir." Alucius stood. He could have sensed the majer's agitation even without Talent.

"Today, I'd wager," muttered Feran under his breath as he also stood.

"You'll pardon me if I don't take that wager," Heald replied.

Alucius let the others head toward the barracks directly. Instead, he loped out of the mess and toward the overlook of the ledge, twenty yards to the right of the half squad of Deforyan troopers, who just stood looking to the south. For a long moment, Alucius gazed out. Three columns, each vingts long, rode northward. The center column was headed toward the trail at the base of Black Ridge. After another look, he hurried toward the sandstone archway that held the section of barracks where Twenty-first Company was quartered.

Longyl was already waiting for him. "Told the men to stand by, sir."

"Good. Have them form up by squads on foot in front of the barracks area. With full arms and as many cartridges as they can carry. The nomads are setting up for an attack. It could be a very long day." Alucius paused. "Keep them as close to the back cliff as you can."

"Ah . . . yes, sir."

"We can move forward when we need to." Alucius didn't explain further, because he feared the explanation wouldn't have made much sense, since it was based more on feelings than on anything he could explain. "I'll meet you there. I have to meet with Majer Draspyr first."

"Yes, sir."

He hurried back to his room and picked up both rifles, as well as both cartridge belts, before heading back outside. In front of the entrance to the officers' quarters, he paused, looking southward. In the sky, circling up from nomads' camp, were distant black specks. Alucius thought. The nomads' camp was a good six vingts from Black Ridge, yet he could see the wings of whatever flew upward, and he could see them clearly. Nothing he had ever seen was big enough for that. He turned and headed back inside to the conference room. He wasn't the last, since Captain Koryt followed him inside.

As Alucius seated himself, Draspyr glanced pointedly at the pair of rifles Alucius carried, but said nothing for a moment. Then he began, "From what we can see, the nomads have more than fifty companies' worth of riders. I have not seen the rumored pteridons—"

"They're out there now," Alucius said. "They're circling the nomad encampment."

Draspyr nodded impatiently. "So we must face thousands of nomads and magical creatures. I have ordered Twenty-third Company to take positions along the front of the ledge immediately, but we will rotate that duty. The Deforyans have dispatched their five companies back along the trail. They will take positions at places where the nomads cannot easily attack . . ."

Alucius had his doubts about that aspect of the strategy, but decided against voicing it. Draspyr wasn't about to listen.

"The rest of you have your companies standing by just inside the barracks and stables, by company. I leave it to Overcaptain Heald and Overcaptain Alucius as to how you will arrange your troopers, but request that they hold themselves in readiness in a fashion that does not tire them and so that they will be prepared to move into the front positions as necessary. I will be visiting all companies as I see fit." He nodded briskly. "That is all."

After the majer stepped out, hurrying toward the front of the ledge where the Twenty-third Company was arranging itself, Heald stepped toward Alucius. "How do you want to do this?"

"One company in each barracks corridor and two—Twenty-first and Third—in each stable corridor?"

"Sounds good to me."

"With double cartridge loads and all rifles loaded," Alucius added. "If they do get to the top, we may have to fire from the corridors and places with windows."

"I'd thought that. Hope it won't be for a while."

Alucius turned to Feran. "Have Fifth Company take the barracks corridor."

"We'll be ready."

The two stepped out into the open morning air, where Alucius looked southward, into the sky. The pteridons were still circling over the nomad camp, but were now a good thousand yards higher than Black Ridge and climbing. "We'd better get everyone in position." He moved quickly toward the space before the barracks, Feran walking beside him. As they neared Twenty-first Company, Feran stepped away and hurried toward Fifth Company.

"Twenty-first Company, all accounted for and ready, sir," Longyl reported.

"We're to be ready to reinforce or replace Twenty-third Company. In the meantime, we're to form up by squads inside the middle stable arch."

Longyl raised his eyebrows.

"There's no sense in being out in the open." Alucius gestured skyward toward the pteridons, who had formed into a long line headed northward toward Black Ridge. He counted eleven.

Crack! Crack! The troopers from Twenty-third Company began to fire over the side of the ledge.

There was a dull *clunk* on the cliff wall well above Twenty-first Company, and then a grayish blob of metal that had been a bullet dropped onto the sandy stone just behind the last trooper in fourth squad.

"Twenty-first Company! Re-form in the archway to stable number two, by squads, first squad forward! Move!"

As Twenty-first Company re-formed, Alucius glanced along the front edge of the sandstone cliff holding quarters and stables. Fifth Company was almost clear, and even Third and Eleventh Companies were moving inside the cliff structures. Only Twenty-third Company was exposed, but most of the troopers were in prone positions along the edge of the rocky black ledge, firing down at the advancing nomads.

Once the rest of Twenty-first Company was inside the stable archway, Alucius joined them, standing beside the right wall of the high arch. The Lanachronan troopers continued to fire downward, and bullets continued to flatten themselves against the cliff. Many lodged there, but a number continued to drop onto the stone below like intermittent lead hail.

Longyl stepped up beside Alucius. "Would more troopers out there help, sir?"

"The nomads can only ride up that trail single file." He glanced to the east, where the road or trail from Dereka wound out of the Barrier Range. "I'm more worried about being taken from behind. Maybe you should send out Waris and Dueryn . . . to see what's happening along the trail. I'm not all that trusting that the Deforyans have done what the majer thought."

Longyl looked blank.

"They're supposed to have been covering the trail so that we don't get encircled." Alucius glanced eastward. "I have doubts."

"I'll send Waris and Dueryn out immediately, sir."

"Get them out of here quickly," Alucius said.

Longyl vanished, and almost immediately the two scouts reappeared, leading their mounts.

Alucius smothered a rueful smile. Longyl—or Faisyn—had anticipated the need for scouts—more than he had. Still, he watched as the two rode along the front of the sandstone escarpment and disappeared around the cliff edge on the trail that led back toward Dereka.

Longyl reappeared.

"Good thinking," Alucius said, turning to the senior squad leader.

"Sir . . . what's that?"

A line of bluish flame swept across the western end of the troopers firing down at the nomads riding up the trail toward Black Ridge. So intense were the flames that Alucius could feel the heat from where he stood next to the stable openings. He stepped back involuntarily. The westernmost troopers in blue and cream turned into blackened figures almost instantly—including Captain Clifyr, whose figure pitched forward, twitching.

Behind the wave of flame swooped down a blue-winged creature—easily ten yards long from the tip of its beak to the end of the tail, a little over fifty yards above the ledge. In a saddle just forward of the wings sat a rider, leaning forward with a metallic blue lance, from which flared more of the blue flame.

As the pteridon passed, Alucius ducked out of the stable archway and scanned the sky. There were no more of the pteridons nearby, although he thought that one was turning to the west, ready to sweep down on Black Ridge to follow the first. He glanced out to the ledge where half a company remained—flat on the stone, still firing downward.

No one was ordering anything. Carrying one rifle, Alucius sprinted forward. "Take cover! Back to the barracks and stables!"

Several of the troopers looked up.

"Back to the cliff!" Alucius snapped. "Now!"

Slowly, ever so slowly, the Lanachronans began to move.

"Move!" Alucius bellowed. "Unless you want to be blasted into charcoal!"

That worked. The remaining troopers sprinted toward Alucius.

Alucius glanced up, seeing a shadow coming out of the early-morning sun. He sprinted back toward the stable archway.

The last four or five troopers were engulfed in flame, and Alucius felt the heat on the back of his neck as he scrambled under cover. Once inside the stable archway, he turned in time to see another pteridon sweep past, little more than thirty yards above the flat expanse of Black Ridge.

"Overcaptain!"

Alucius turned.

"I didn't order that," Draspyr growled. "They weren't your troopers, Overcaptain. With no one guarding the trail, the nomads will be on us."

"Once they reach the top, they're exposed as well," Alucius pointed out. "We station our men at every door and arch. We'll try to bring down the pteridons from there first." Then he added, "Their captain was killed by the first pteridon. If they'd stayed there, Majer, they'd all be dead by now."

Draspyr looked past Alucius at the faintly twitching blackened forms, then swallowed. After a moment, he said. "I . . . beg your pardon, Overcaptain. Carry on." With that, he turned away.

Alucius looked out from the archway once more as another pteridon swept by, barely fifty yards above the front of the ledge, so close that Alucius could make out the dark-haired rider and the blue metallic lance he carried—even as Alucius aimed, and fired.

Although he *knew* he had struck the blue-winged creature, the wings continued to beat as the pteridon vanished from his sight to the east.

"Aim for the riders!" he ordered. "Pass it on." Then he felt stupid, because he'd never ordered the company into firing order. He turned to Longyl. "Put first squad here in the arch in two ranks."

"First squad to the fore! Two ranks, first rank, fire from your knees!"

Another pteridon swept in from the west, and Alucius was ready. His shot hit the rider. The rider slumped in the blue saddle, and the pteridon wheeled, moving rapidly southward. Impossibly . . . one of the clawed forefeet reached up and plucked the blue metallic lance from the air as it slipped from the hands of the dying or dead rider.

Alucius wiped his steaming forehead. He had the feeling that the pteridon would be back—with another rider.

More blue flame lashed across the flat ledge, beginning about twenty yards from the red sandstone cliff holding the quarters and stables and moving southward. Alucius frowned, trying to figure out what that meant.

"Here they come!" Longyl called.

Alucius shifted his concentration to the edge of the ledge where the trail ended—or began. Several nomads had just appeared there, turning and urging their mounts forward.

"Twenty-first Company! On the nomads!" Alucius ordered. "Fire!"

He aimed for the lead mount and fired. *Crack!* The horse went down. Then he went for the second rider's mount. The rider urged his mount over the fallen horse, and Alucius's shot missed. The next one didn't. With the fire from the other companies, the rush of nomads halted.

For several moments, no other nomads appeared, and Alucius used the time to reload, even though his magazine wasn't empty. The heap of dead riders and mounts at the end of the upward trail would certainly slow progress there, enough, Alucius hoped, that the troopers could pick off the nomads as fast as they could get up the narrow trail. But the standoff was only temporary—until the flanking columns of nomads reached the trails leading back to Black Ridge.

Another swath of blue flame swept across the open area of black stone, catching one Lanachronan trooper. Alucius wondered what the man had been doing out in the open, but it certainly wasn't the time to ask.

Alucius was ready as the next pteridon swooped. While his troopers were firing at the nomads—and keeping them from gaining the open ledge—he aimed at the pteridon's head. Again, while he *knew* he had struck the beast, there was no sign of any wound. His second shot slammed through the rider.

Once more . . . the same thing happened. The pteridon reclaimed the blue metallic lance and wheeled back toward the nomads' camp.

For a time, there was an uneasy quiet across Black Ridge. No more nomads appeared at the edge of the ledge.

The nomads couldn't have decided to withdraw. It was barely midmorning, and they far outnumbered the defenders.

As he reloaded, Alucius considered. Unless they could stop the pteridons, they were doomed. They might be anyway, but it was certain with the blue beasts. Repelling bullets the way they had . . . that meant that they were certainly Talent-creatures. What would work against Talent? He'd been so rushed that he hadn't really thought.

The purple crystal of the Matrial had repelled bullets and sabres, and only the sense of darkness that lay beneath the lifewebs had helped there. But he couldn't get close to the pteridons, not against the blue flame that came from the metallic skylances. Could he somehow create that shell of darkness around a bullet that he fired? The way he had enveloped the crystal in darkness?

He concentrated on wrapping darkness around the bullet of the cartridge in the heavy rifle's chamber. Then, rifle in hand, he eased out from the stable archway.

"Sir . . . there's one of those beasts . . ."

Alucius turned, seemingly in slow motion, toward the pteridon that dropped out of the sky toward the ledge, although it felt as though the blue-winged monster was headed straight toward him. The rifle came up, and he fired, concentrating on both aim and a last infusion of that lifedarkness into the cold lead of the bullet.

The pteridon wobbled in the air.

Alucius recocked the rifle and fired again—and then again.

A thin shriek—piercing—filled the air, and the beast literally cartwheeled out of the sky, crashing somewhere against the trail below.

"Sir!"

Alucius bolted back toward the stable as a line of blue fire seared across the black rock of the post. Within moments after the pteridon sailed over the empty expanse of black rock between the sandstone cliff and the ledge overlooking the grasslands below, a single rider galloped around the edge of the cliff and made for the stable entrance.

Alucius stepped out from the archway just far enough to fire at the next pteridon. Obviously, he hadn't concentrated on the darkness enough, because, although the pteridon wobbled as it passed, it continued onward. He reloaded quickly, then turned to the scout.

Waris had had to flatten himself against the bay's neck to ride into the stable archway, and he immediately dismounted.

"What did you find?" Alucius asked.

"The Deforyans . . . there's no sign of them." Waris gasped. "Deuyrn's still out . . . checking the west approaches. Lucky . . . there's a canyon to the east . . . nomads have to travel another six, seven vingts before they can circle around. Terrain's rough . . . might take till tomorrow."

Alucius looked out through the archway. Three pteridons were headed directly north, aimed directly at the stable. "Everyone back! Back as far as you can go!"

Alucius lifted the first rifle, forcing himself to concentrate on two things—the lead pteridon's head, and darkness, and more darkness, cast within the bullet in the chamber. He fired, then switched his aim to the second flying monster. He fired twice.

Both pteridons fell, one just as if its wings had collapsed, the other cartwheeling and slamming into the section of the ridge edge where the ill-fated squad of the Twenty-third Company had been incinerated.

Alucius felt, as much as saw, the line of blue flame arcing toward him, and he sprinted and dived behind the archway of the stable.

Flame flared above him, and for a moment, he felt as though he had been in an oven, but as it passed he rolled and brought the rifle back to bear, but the pteridon was out of range.

"He veered off to the west," Longyl said. "You all right?"

"So far."

"How did you manage—"

"Aimed for their eyes," Alucius half lied. He *had* aimed for their eyes.

"Look!" yelled one of the troopers.

In spite of himself, Alucius did. The enormous bulk of the pteridon that had fallen on the ledge just above the trailhead had burst into a bluish flame, like the bursts from the metallic skylances. After a moment, Alucius focused his Talent senses on the blazing creature. He moistened his lips. Behind the blueness was the same evil pink-purple sense that he had felt with the Matrial's torques and with the purple crystal that had linked them.

"Back!" he shouted. "Down."

He barely had flattened himself around the corner of the archway when the pteridon exploded, sending waves of heat across the ledge and into the stable.

Alucius scrambled and found the rifle he had been using, then handed it to Longyl. "Have someone clean it." He recovered his second weapon and eased forward toward the arch.

Waves of blue flame crossed the ledge, but none were within thirty yards of the stable entrance. Alucius looked out with Talent-senses and -eyes.

The remaining pteridons—six of them—were circling overhead, but trying to stay far enough north so that no one could fire at them from the entrance to the corridors. That meant that the lances couldn't reach all the way to the sandstone cliff. Alucius smiled grimly, easing out of the stone archway.

"Sir . . ."

"Just have some of the squad ready to shoot if any nomads stick their heads up over the ledge," Alucius ordered. He eased farther out, then raised the rifle, waiting.

Crack!

Darkness and bullet meshed, and another pteridon's wings folded, but Alucius could not see where the beast fell.

Abruptly, the five remaining pteridons began to circle higher, then head southward.

"Twenty-first Company to the edge of the ledge!" Alucius snapped. "Now! Longyl! Send out scouts along the trail! We'll need a warning if the nomads manage to cross over that canyon or get around it."

Without waiting for an answer, he began to sprint forward. If they could just hold the nomads there, and it was possible—without the pteridons . . .

Less than fifty yards down the trail another company of nomads was approaching. Alucius flattened himself against the ground and began to fire.

Within moments, others were beside him and firing. Longyl slid in beside Alucius and handed him the second rifle. "Thought you'd need this, sir."

"Thank you."

"Thank you, sir."

Perhaps a glass passed, with bodies of men and mounts growing on the trail below, before the remaining nomads began to retreat from the exposed position against the withering fire.

Alucius watched for almost a glass before he eased away, then stood and called out, "Fifth Company! To the ledge! Relieve Twenty-first Company!"

"Fifth Company! Forward!" Feran's voice rang out.

Alucius slipped over to Longyl. "Get the men fed and let them rest. But make sure all their weapons are reloaded and that they replenish their cartridge belts."

"Yes, sir."

"I need to find Majer Draspyr."

Before he went looking for the majer, as the companies changed places, Alucius studied the glasslands below Black Ridge. The nomads were setting up another camp, less than a vingt from the base of the trail up to Black Ridge. Alucius looked to the southwest, but he could see no more pteridons.

With a deep breath, he began to walk toward the officers' section, still carrying both rifles, and the conference room.

Majer Draspyr stood in the stone archway that led outside from the conference room. He looked evenly at Alucius. "Overcaptain . . . you and your men killed four of those monsters and disabled two—"

"The two will be back," Alucius said tiredly. "We killed their riders, but that doesn't stop them." Then he added, "I sent out scouts. One returned. The Deforyans have retreated, and the nomads are working to encircle us. They probably can't manage it today, but they might tonight or tomorrow."

"I was warned about the Deforyans," Draspyr said. "It's hard to believe . . . they'd just turn and run."

"They believe the mountains will stop the nomads, and, if they don't, they'd rather fight defending what they think is valuable."

"You can't defend Dereka. It's too open." Draspyr shook his head. "I must congratulate you, Overcaptain. Your leadership under fire is commendable."

"Thank you, sir." Alucius didn't feel like pointing out that his leadership had been slow, his understanding of the situation slower, and only the Talent-skills he had almost failed to use had held off the nomads. "We'll have to do better. Much better."

"Do you think we should withdraw?"

Common sense screamed, "YES!" Alucius considered as he spoke. "That would be my first reaction, sir. We can't stay here for long, not without support. But there's no water on the way back, except at the waystations, and the nearest of those is more than two days away. And then, too, the nomads are headed that way, and they might well get there before we do. The Deforyans didn't take the wagons with them, and that means we have ample provisions for a while whatever we do. I think we need to see where things stand."

Alucius was also speaking on feel. For some reason, the idea of an immediate retreat to Dereka felt wrong. Very wrong. He just wished he knew why, because he also knew they couldn't stay long at Black Ridge.

"Then you and I should take a short ride," Draspyr said. "With a squad or so, of course. We can see what we might do before we decide."

Alucius nodded. "That might be best." He hoped it was.

60

In the late afternoon, Alucius and the majer rode northward along the narrow trail, with two scouts from fourth squad well ahead, and Egyl and the remainder of fourth squad immediately following. Majer Draspyr had left one squad from Twenty-third Company mounting guard on the trail where it left Black Ridge.

Alucius studied the road and the terrain around it carefully. For the first half vingt north of Black Ridge the trail clung to the mountainside, a ledge generally less than two yards wide in most places, cut out of the sheer stone. While the nomads could not move many men along it at once, the problem was that there was also no real cover for the defenders, and even if they erected a barricade, the best that they could hope for was a standoff, and in the end, they would be overwhelmed when they ran out of ammunition or were starved out. Alucius was looking for better than that.

"Be hard for them to move along here," Draspyr pointed out.

"I'd like to see if there's a place where we could use more firepower, and they would be just as exposed," Alucius replied.

The next section of trail was through a steep cut in the sandstone where the trail widened to almost three yards. While Alucius might have been able to place some snipers above, they would be totally exposed to the pteridons, and there was room for only a comparative handful.

They covered another half vingt, and then another, the trail returning to its previous narrowness and winding upward and clinging to steep cliffs.

As they rounded yet another curve, Alucius looked at the area ahead. The trail went west, then curved eastward, winding back around a low promontory that jutted out into the canyon on the east. The top of the promontory, a stony ridge, was gradual enough that either horses or men could climb it, and less than a hundred yards to the west, the sandstone rose into another cliff wall, arching out in a way that would be difficult for the pteridons to attack effectively.

"That might be promising," Alucius suggested. "We'll have to see."

Draspyr looked at Alucius, but didn't say anything.

"Where that juts out, it's an easy climb to the top, with cover there from this side. I'm going to climb up and see whether what sort of angle it has on the trail to the north."

"This is quite a ways north of Black Ridge," Draspyr pointed out.

"It is, but there's no way they can get behind us."

The majer didn't reply as they rode around the curve toward the promontory.

Once they reached the spot Alucius had mentally marked, one of the spots where the trail widened enough for turns or passage, he lifted his arm. "Patrol halt!" He dismounted and handed Wildebeast's reins to Egyl. "Hope this won't take long." Carrying one of his rifles, he started up the sloping sandstone. Although he skidded and slipped several times, before long he was at the top, where he looked northward.

From there, he could see almost all of the next stretch of trail, which curved westward once more, then back eastward—giving a long field of fire for any troopers on the top of the promontory. At the end of the promontory, where the road made a sharp curve, it was narrow enough that one of the Deforyan wagons, turned on its side and filled with rocks, would provide enough of an obstacle to keep riders from charging or jumping it. Another wagon, placed farther north, could also slow the nomads and make them more vulnerable to fire.

Alucius looked northward again.

A single rider in the colors of the Northern Guard rode southward on the trail, occasionally looking over his shoulder. Even from a distance, Alucius recognized Dueryn. He called down. "We've got a scout returning! Looks like Dueryn. Have him wait for me."

As Dueryn rode toward the patrol, Alucius kept checking, to see just how exposed any riders would be. Except for one stretch of about twenty yards, the sandstone rampart of the promontory would provide a good location from which to defend the road, and a good two squads could fire on the exposed road from a shielded position.

With a nod to himself, Alucius started down the sandstone, carefully. He was mounted and still had to wait for Dueryn.

"Sir? Didn't expect to find you out here."

"Did you locate the nomads?"

"Yes, sir. The canyon here on the east . . . it goes ahead another ten vingts or so, and then just almost stops. They've set up a camp just on the east of a narrow ridge that joins the road. They could cross that to the road tonight, or maybe in the morning. On the west . . ." The scout gave a ragged laugh. "There's a deep gorge. It must go for twenty vingts if not more. There's no way they'll get across on that side."

"There's no way we could get past them?" asked the majer.

"Not on this trail, sir," Dueryn. "From the ridge, they could fire down

on the road with at least three companies, maybe more, and we'd be in
single file. They could also charge across at us."

Draspyr nodded as if he hadn't expected any other answer. He looked at
Alucius. "We'll need to send a company out here as soon as we get back."

"Third Company," Alucius suggested. "We'll have to rotate some,
though." He turned to Egyl. "Leave a pair of scouts here until we can
send out a company."

"Yes, sir." The squad leader turned. "Feshyn and Dorayn! You're to
watch the road until relieved. Any nomads come this way, you get moving and warn us."

Alucius remained at the rear of the column, as did the majer, while the
riders eased their mounts back around on the narrow trail.

"You think the nomads will attack?" asked Draspyr.

"Don't you, sir?" Alucius replied.

"From what I've seen, they will. It doesn't look good."

"No," Alucius admitted. He had some ideas, but he wasn't ready to
say anything, especially to the majer. Not yet.

The rest of the ride back to Black Ridge was quiet, and in the early
evening, the cooks had supper for both officers and troopers, although
there had to be two shifts, in order to relieve the troopers guarding the
ledge and the trail up from the grasslands.

After the evening meal, Alucius gathered the scouts from both Fifth
and Twenty-first Companies in the conference room. "Here's the problem. We can probably hold Black Ridge so long as we have ammunition
and food. But every day we stay here, there will be more nomads behind
us, and no one is coming out to rescue us. Dueryn says that on the west
side of the trail, there's no way for the nomads to reach us. What I want
you to find out is whether there's any other way, probably to the west,
that will bring us back to the main trail north of the nomads. It sounds
impossible, but this entire trail was cut on purpose. I have a hard time
believing that whoever cut it didn't have another way out of here."

Looks passed between Waris and another scout.

"I'd like you to leave as soon as you can see in the morning. You won't
do us any good falling off a cliff at night. That's all."

Once the scouts had left the room, Alucius walked out to the end of the ledge where two squads of Eleventh Company were stationed. Two squads were more than enough to hold the ledge for long enough to summon the other three squads, and that way, more of the men could get some rest during what might be a long siege.

Out of the growing darkness, Koryt stepped toward him. "What do you think?"

"They could attack tonight, or tomorrow or the next day, or anytime in between. I don't see them leaving us alone."

"Neither do I," replied the captain.

"You've got your troopers well placed. We'll be here if they do."

Koryt nodded.

Alucius returned the gesture and headed for his quarters. He thought he ought to try to get some sleep.

Feran looked up from where he lay on his bunk as Alucius entered the dark quarters. "Anything changed?"

"Not yet. The nomads are still down there, and everywhere else."

"They'll attack tonight. They were building up fires."

"Look who's the cheerful one now."

"Get some sleep," Feran suggested, rolling over.

Alucius wondered if he would sleep well—or at all—even after he stretched out on his bunk and could feel his eyes close.

He had barely drifted into sleep when distant shots echoed down the sandstone corridor, and he bolted upright in the narrow bed.

"Attack! All officers and companies forward!"

Alucius yanked on his boots and grabbed both rifles and the ammunition belt. Feran was close behind him.

Once outside, Alucius could hear shots passing well overhead as he made his way to where Twenty-first Company was forming up in the darkness, just forward of the barracks area of the sandstone cliff. Fifth Company was forming just to the west of Twenty-first Company. Again, Alucius was grateful for the night vision that allowed him to see as if it were only early twilight. He frowned. What about the pteridons? Could they see or fly at night?

He cast out his Talent-senses . . . but he could find no sign of the flying creatures.

"Twenty-first Company, ready, sir!" Longyl snapped.

"Thank you, Longyl." Alucius barked out the orders. "Twenty-first Company! By squad! From the eastern end!" Then he walked toward Feran. "You ready to take the middle section?"

"We'll do it." Feran raised his voice. "Fifth Company, middle section!"

"Stay low as you near the edge!" Alucius called out. "Low!"

He watched as the troopers ran, then crawled into position to reinforce the two squads of Eleventh Company. The firing from below became stronger. Alucius checked the skies once more, with eyes and Talent. Still no pteridons.

Alucius sprinted forward and eased his way into a prone position beside a trooper—Ryem, he recalled.

"Sir?"

"Just keep your eyes on the nomads, Ryem." Alucius took aim on one of the lead nomads, less than fifty yards down the trail, then fired.

A sheet of rifle fire sprayed across the narrow trail, already littered with bodies, mostly of men, rather than mounts, indicating to Alucius that the attackers had attempted the assault in stealth and on foot.

Under the intensity of fire by the defenders, the nomads either fell or fell back. How many Alucius had shot, he had no idea, only that he had been effective, but in the darkness, no one would know, and that was certainly for the best.

After a half glass of silence, Alucius eased back away from the ledge and stood. "Twenty-first Company . . . back to barracks!"

"Fifth Company . . ." echoed Feran.

"Eleventh Company . . ." came from Koryt. "Fourth and fifth squads, hold. First, second, third squads, back to barracks until the next watch . . ."

Alucius paused, waiting until the troopers passed him. He looked up into the night sky, still puzzled by an attack without the pteridons. Was it too difficult to fly in darkness, or was there some other reason? As he pondered, his eyes took in the greenish half-disc of Asterta, the moon of war and of the horse goddess. Did the nomads feel she favored them?

Did it matter? He wondered how many more attacks there might be—and whether there really was another way out of Black Ridge. He hoped the scouts could find one, even as he considered, fitfully, how they might be able to attack and evade the nomad hordes.

61

After the attack, Alucius did not sleep well, even though there had not been another attack, and he ended up rising before dawn. He doubted many had slept that well. There were circles under his eyes as he ate a breakfast moments after dawn, a breakfast prepared by the Deforyan cooks. That they had been left behind didn't surprise Alucius, but little about the Deforyans did any longer.

He ate silently, with Koryt, since Fifth Company was manning the ledge posts, and since Heald and Third Company were still on station manning the defenses on the trail to the north. He hadn't even finished when he saw a trooper outside the mess room, looking at him. Leaving his platter, he hurried out.

"Sir . . . Overcaptain sent me . . . lots of nomads on the old road to the north of Third Company . . . maybe ten or twelve companies."

As the messenger spoke, Draspyr appeared at Alucius's shoulder, but the majer said nothing.

"Thank you. Get yourself something to eat, then be ready to ride back. The majer and I will let you know what we're doing."

"Yes, sir." The round-faced trooper nodded, then hurried away, toward the troopers' mess.

"They'll need reinforcements," Draspyr said.

Alucius had a feeling that the pteridons might well be used in the north—or in both places, but he couldn't be in both places. After a moment, he replied. "I'd recommend that I take Twenty-first Company to support Third Company, and that Twenty-third Company and Eleventh Company remain here to support Fifth Company."

Draspyr gave a wry smile. "I thought that might be your answer. It would have been mine."

Alucius thought about explaining and decided against it. "We'll be on our way as quickly as possible."

Draspyr nodded.

Longyl was waiting as Alucius neared the barracks area. "Sir?"

"Have them saddle up. We're headed north to reinforce Third Company. They're under attack." Then he laughed, ruefully, at the inanity of the remark. They were under attack everywhere.

In less than a quarter glass, the company was on the trail northward, with several packhorses, as well, carrying ammunition, water, and some rations. As he rode northward, with the sun barely clearing the sandstone escarpments to the east, Alucius kept scanning the skies, but he had not seen the pteridons. Twenty-first Company had covered slightly more than a vingt when his Talent-sense warned him. He glanced up, and to the west of the cliff, barely visible, were three pteridons flying overhead.

Alucius nodded. He had been able to sense the purplish feel that underlay the pteridons, that strange similarity to the crystal that had powered the torques of the Matrial. Yet he knew the Matrites had not had any connections to the nomads. Was it just that certain kinds of Talent-use were shaded into the purple, and others into the green and black? Why? And was there any connection with the destruction and disappearance of the purple crystal and the appearance of the pteridons?

"There they are, sir!" said Longyl, from behind Alucius.

"Let's hope Heald can get his men under cover." Alucius urged Wildebeast into a faster walk, but he wasn't about to move that much more quickly on the narrow way.

One of the blue-winged creatures swooped downward, and a line of blue light flared from the metallic lance held by the rider. Alucius couldn't see where the pteridon was headed, because his view was blocked by the way the trail curved, but he had no doubts that the creature was attacking Third Company.

As Alucius and Twenty-first Company neared the beleaguered troopers, he could see that the pteridons—four of them—continued to circle and swoop, and send streams of the blue fire downward. He hoped that meant Heald had his men under cover.

Another half glass passed, and, as Alucius rode around another curve, he could clearly see the promontory—clear of troopers, except for two blackened figures halfway down the slope. Heald had been careful enough to watch the skies, and his troopers were lined up flush against the sandstone cliff—safe from the pteridons but unable to cover the road.

While the blue flame from the skylances splashed around the top of the cliff and fifteen yards from the base, the pteridons had not been able to fly close enough to allow their riders a direct aim at the troopers. But the troopers could not fire at either the pteridons and their riders, or at the nomads farther to the north, who were doubtless moving southward.

Alucius also saw Third Company's mounts, in a long line southward, against the cliff wall, also shielded from direct fire from the riders on the pteridons and watched by a handful of troopers. The last of the mounts was only a hundred yards ahead of Alucius. From where they circled high above, if trying to stay out of rifle range most of the time, swooping occasionally, the pteridons or their riders had not yet seen Twenty-first Company.

"Company halt!" Alucius dismounted, and handed Wildebeast's reins to Longyl. "Have them wait here, but have them ready rifles."

"Yes, sir. Ready, rifles."

After taking both rifles from their holders, Alucius walked another fifty yards northward along the narrow road-trail, keeping as close to the cliff wall as he could.

Once he was far enough north so that he could get a clear sight, at least part of the time, on the pteridons, he took his time, watching the patterns, waiting—and infusing the cartridges in the magazine with darkness, the kind of darkness that came from him, from the stead, and from the healthy lifewebs of Corus.

Then, he fired. *Crack.*

The first pteridon tumbled out of the sky, careening downward, before striking the canyon to the north and the right of where Alucius stood. A flare of blue flame erupted—the heat reaching Alucius.

He ignored the flame and concentrated on the second pteridon. That was harder, because the riders immediately changed their pattern and began to climb, circling upward and searching for the source of the attack on them.

Alucius emptied the magazine of the first rifle and had taken two shots with the second weapon before a bullet struck the lowest and trailing pteridon. The wide blue wings folded . . . but Alucius could not see where the beast fell.

A cheer rose from the troopers under the cliff to the west of the promontory. Alucius and Twenty-First Company watched as the pteridons headed southward.

Before the cheer even died away, Heald called out, "Back to positions and ready to fire!"

One of the troopers went down from the nomads' fire as they scrambled back into position.

"Twenty-first Company! Forward!" Alucius ordered.

As Longyl rode forward, leading Wildebeast, Alucius put one rifle in the holder and mounted quickly.

"Good shooting, sir."

"Very fortunate shooting," Alucius acknowledged. "We'll have to take our mounts past those of Third Company, probably all the way to where the wagon blocks the trail."

"Yes, sir."

Alucius couldn't help but feel a little uneasy as they rode past the Third Company mounts, because he was close enough to the edge of the way cut from the solid and ancient lava that he could easily look down, and "down" was several thousand yards of a sheer drop. He pulled Wildebeast in right in front of the first of the Third Company horses, where he dismounted and looked to the young trooper from Eleventh Company.

"I'll watch him, sir."

"Thank you." Alucius climbed up the slope enough to be clear of the trail, then moved eastward, well below Heald's troopers, who were firing almost continuously, then continued eastward, waiting until Twenty-first Company came to a halt below. "First and second squads! Dismount and take your rifles. Up the slope to reinforce Third Company!" Alucius looked at Longyl. "Hold the others here until I see what we need and where."

Longyl nodded.

Alucius scrambled up across the sandstone, but carefully. The entire trail was filled with nomads—on foot—and the first handful was less than fifty yards from the wagon. He knelt just below the crest of the natural stone rampart. "Twenty-first Company! First squad on me! Prone position!" He waited only until the troopers scrambled into position. "Take out the lead nomads! Fire!"

The first volley was nearly instantaneous, and most of the nomads in the first wave dropped. By the third, and far more ragged volley from first squad, none of the lead nomads were moving.

"Second squad! To my left! Interlock with Third Company!"

Heald raised his hand, then smiled. "Welcome!"

"We've got more ammunition below." Not enough. Not nearly enough, Alucius thought, but the nomads didn't have to know that. Not yet.

62

Alucius slowed as he, Heald, and Third Company neared the last fifty yards before the trail turned the bend onto Black Ridge. He didn't like leaving Longyl, but it was unlikely that the pteridons would attack in the late, late afternoon, especially after their hasty retreat, and he needed to find out if any of the scouts had returned—and if there was any other way out of Black Ridge. They had used all too much of their ammunition, and Alucius had no doubts that the attacks would continue. He also had not seen the pteridons circling to the south . . . and he had to hope that Black Ridge had held out against any nomad attacks.

The four troopers standing guard at the bend that led onto the black lava ledge looked at the two officers and the riders behind them.

242 L. E. MODESITT, JR.

"Sirs . . . how are things to the north?"

"They're holding back the nomads for now," Alucius replied.

"Sir . . . there were pteridons here."

"Are they still here?"

"No, sir. They only came by once—this morning. Then they went south. Been two attacks by the nomads since then."

In one way, Alucius didn't like that at all. "How many pteridons?"

"Just two. They didn't stay long, but they got some of Fifth Company. Captain Feran got most everyone clear, then got 'em back in time to stop the attack."

"Thank you." Alucius rode around the last narrow curve and out onto the flat black expanse of Black Ridge. He could see more blackened patches on the ground along the edge of the ledge. After a moment, Feran came hurrying toward him on foot. Alucius pulled Wildebeast to the side and reined up short of the older captain. "How bad was it?"

"Could have been worse. The pteridons only came by once, and there were only two of them. Came in out of dives, and ran a quick flame across the ledge. Almost impossible to get a shot off. Still lost half a squad. Been three attacks from below today. Last two were more just to make sure we were watching."

"Do you know if any of the Twenty-first Company scouts are back yet?"

"There were a couple of riders that came in maybe a half glass back," Feran replied. "One was wounded. That was just after the last nomad attack. I wasn't watching too closely . . ." He shook his head.

"Thank you. I need to see what they found." Alucius hoped they had discovered something. "If they did."

"You thinking there might be another way out?"

"Hoping," Alucius admitted. "But I don't know where."

"If anyone could find it, you can. Let me know." Feran gestured toward the ledge. "I need to check on them."

"I will." Alucius worried, once more, about leaving Twenty-first Company and Longyl . . . but . . . if he didn't come up with something, they were all likely to be dead anyway.

He made his way to the stone archway that gave access to the barracks bays where Twenty-first Company was bunked.

Waris and Dueryn were in the first bay, where one of the Deforyan cooks was binding a dressing over Waris's left shoulder.

"Sir . . . they said . . ."

"Twenty-first Company's still out. I came back to find out if you'd discovered anything."

"Sir . . ." Waris glanced down at the dressing on his shoulder as the Deforyan stepped back.

"How's that wound?"

"Not too bad," the scout lied.

Alucius could sense the waves of pain. "Let's see." He reached out, his fingers barely touching the dressing, and let a trace of his own Talent run over the torn muscle. "That will take a while to heal, but it will." He paused, almost afraid to ask. "Did you find anything?"

"Sir . . . you were right . . . there's another road . . . but there's no way to get to it. Leastwise not that we can see."

"Go ahead," Alucius said.

"Black Ridge . . . it sits . . . it's a big long point of stone, and there are canyons on both sides. I managed to get up a ways. The nomads caught me coming down, didn't realize they were so close, but they didn't know what I was doing. Thought I was spying on them, and they were shooting from below to the east. Anyway, to the west in places . . . you can see a road-trail, just like the one we came in on, but it's so sheer . . . you couldn't climb down. It looks to run along the west side, just like the one we used runs the east side."

Alucius frowned. The upper west end of Black Ridge was a solid sandstone cliff—wasn't it? "You're sure about this?"

"Yes, sir . . ." Waris winced again. "Goes a long way, but you can't see it from the east except from real high and in the afternoon . . ."

Alucius nodded. "Thank you. Just rest for now. You might have to ride later." He glanced at Dueryn. "If you'd come with me . . ."

"Yes, sir."

The two slipped out of the barracks bay and walked along the corridor and out onto the ridge, where Alucius headed west, walking swiftly.

From somewhere, Heald appeared. "Mind if I join you? You look like you have something in mind."

"The scouts say that there's another road to Black Ridge. But they couldn't say how it got here."

"I haven't seen another road. Have you?"

"I have the feeling we weren't meant to see it." Alucius stopped short of the sandstone escarpment that blocked the west end of the flat lava ledge. The sandstone rose more than a thousand yards above him, and it looked solid. More important—it felt solid even to his Talent, as he slowly walked its curving length back toward the stable entrance.

He looked up, his eyes taking in the sweep of the stone above, noting the indentation in the top of the cliff to his left, almost over the western-most archway—the one for the western stables. Whoever had created the tunnels and stone-hollowed rooms had done so symmetrically, so symmetrically that, from the first time he had seen Black Ridge, the lack of a second access had bothered Alucius. He had ignored that feeling, but now he had to follow it. He turned toward the stable archway and walked swiftly to and through it, to the end—the westernmost part of all the tunnels. There, he began to study the back walls, both with Talent and with his eyes.

He could sense the puzzlement from both Heald and Dueryn.

One area—although it looked the same—felt different. Alucius took out his belt knife and scratched the wall. At first, just sandstone plaster fell away, and then, a reddish white powder, and then a huge clump of mortar covered with sandstone. He continued to scrape until he had uncovered the outline of a sandstone block, set amid others.

He turned to Dueryn. "I need four men, with shovels, picks, anything they have or can find."

"Yes, sir." Dueryn hurried out.

"You herders . . ." Heald shook his head.

Alucius continued to scrape away the mortar covered with the red sand, a good imitation of the sandstone itself.

"Overcaptains? What are you doing here? And in the back of the sta-bles?" Majer Draspyr's voice carried more than annoyance.

"Trying to see if we have another way out, where we don't have to fight through thousands of nomads."

"In the stable?"

"I sent out scouts this morning . . ." Alucius went on to explain, ending up, "If there is a road on the west side, it had to have been concealed for some reason, and it has to be on this end of the tunnels." He pointed to the stones he had uncovered. "There's no mortar around them, just over them. That's almost as if they were meant to be removed quickly. I've sent for some troopers . . . and then we'll see."

"You left your company?"

"For just a bit. Twenty-first Company is holding the position. Longyl is a good senior squad leader, but he doesn't know what to look for in something like this. This morning, and early this afternoon, the two companies pushed back the nomads. Third Company had been out there for a solid day, and they'd lost some men to the pteridons. We did manage to down two, and the others left, but that didn't stop the nomads for long. They backed off, and we brought back Third Company. I came back to check to see if the scouts had discovered anything and to arrange for more ammunition for Twenty-first Company."

"There's not that much left," Draspyr pointed out.

"That's why this is important."

"Sir?" came a voice from behind the officers.

The four troopers who followed Dueryn back into the stables had two short shovels, a pick, and an iron bar a yard and a half long.

"We need to get these blocks out of here."

"Yes, sir!"

It only took the four men a quarter of a glass to uncover the rest of the archway filled with rough sandstone blocks and to remove the unmortared blocks—an indication to Alucius that the archway led to the unused road—but only an indication. Even before all the blocks were removed, he could see and sense a tunnel, and cool air began to flood out.

There was indeed a tunnel—one with ancient light-torches in brackets on the wall, the first light-torches Alucius had seen anywhere in Deforya.

"I think we just might have another way back to Dereka." Alucius stepped into the tunnel, wide and high enough for a mounted rider—if with little room to spare—and took down the first light-torch.

The greenish beam revealed that the tunnel continued northwest, and Alucius kept walking. The west tunnel was over two hundred yards long, and there was another blocked archway at the north end, but it was sealed only with square stones not mortared on the outside, because Alucius could see light around some of the stones.

He turned to Draspyr. "I'd like to send a messenger to Twenty-first Company and have them withdraw to Black Ridge."

"We don't know if this road will take us out, Overcaptain," Draspyr pointed out. "Or that we won't meet nomads at the other end."

"We don't," Alucius agreed. "But you just told me that we were almost out of ammunition. If we try the road, we're no worse off than if we stay here, and there's a chance that we'll be far better off."

Draspyr nodded. "Send your messenger."

Alucius looked to Dueryn. "Are you up to it?"

"Yes, sir."

"Longyl is going to have to give the impression that his forces are still there. Try to leave a couple of men in position, occasionally firing, until the others are well clear. Then, they'll have to follow and catch up." Alucius hoped that would work, since the nomads hadn't tried early-night attacks before, but attacked later in full darkness.

"I'll send a half squad from Third Company with him," Heald added.

As Alucius watched the four troopers open the second archway, he could only hope that the road was usable—at least to a point beyond where the nomads were.

Draspyr had already left to organize the withdrawal when Alucius looked out in the late-afternoon light at the narrow way, sandy in places, and clearly not used in years, if not generations. The road *felt* open and solid, but Alucius could only hope that he was not deceiving himself—and the others.

63

The sun had already dropped below the western peaks of the Barrier Range by the time all the companies had been gathered. One of Heald's scouts had also traveled more than a vingt along the western road and reported back to Alucius that the trail was sound that far, if sandy in places, and looked to be in good shape for at least half a vingt farther.

Majer Draspyr and the remnants of Twenty-third Company led the long column, which included only one wagon, with the four Deforyan cooks who had been abandoned, and all the remaining horses bearing ammunition and supplies. Twenty-first Company, set to be the last company, was providing guard duty as the others rode through the stable tunnel and out onto the western road. So far there had been no sign of the nomads moving toward Black Ridge on the other road.

As soon as the last horses had passed through the stable and were waiting in the tunnel, as was Wildebeast, three troopers from Twenty-first Company began replacing the stones in the archway, from the tunnel side. As they worked, Carlis, a slender trooper, swept the stone surface from the front of the stable back toward the tunnel archway.

When he reached the archway, then halfway filled with stones, the others helped him up, and supported him while he swept the area close to the wall, then eased him—and the broom—through the opening, before finishing replacing the stones.

Alucius hoped that, by leaving no tracks in the stable, the nomads would simply look at the stoned-up archway and not investigate farther—or not too soon. The time taken wasn't wasted, because, at the least, the nomads would have to spend some time undoing the stones. The farther that the understrength Northern Guard companies—and the one half-strength Southern Guard company—could travel before being discovered, the better. There was always the possibility of the pteridons finding them, although that was somewhat less because there were fewer pteridons, and because the initial travel was under the cover of darkness. He could hope that the nomads would be more careful with their remaining pteridons—and that they didn't come up with more of the creatures.

Alucius and the remaining troopers repeated the process of sweeping and stoning up the second archway, before moving to catch up to the others on the beginning of the long trip back to Dereka. Alucius hoped that the journey would not be too long, and that it would be very uneventful.

64

South of Black Ridge, Illegea

In the light of midmorning, Aellyan Edyss surveyed the handful of warleaders who stood before him at the base of the narrow trail that led upward to Black Ridge.

"There is no one there? No one at all?"

"You asked for an attack at dawn. We attacked. No one resisted us. We have searched everywhere there. They are not there, but they are not on the trail road back to Dereka. They have vanished as if they never were."

Aellyan Edyss laughed, and his laughter boomed out across the grass-lands. "Then there is nothing between us and Dereka!"

"They have vanished," protested one older warleader. "There are no fresh bodies, and there are no horses. None of our warriors have seen them."

"They are hiding in the rocks, to avoid us, and they will die there, except for a handful that give themselves up and beg for mercy. They will not receive mercy, not after all the years of scorn and all the years when they invaded our lands." The blond leader, whose face had become so fair that it was nearly white, turned and gestured toward the glasslands to the south. "Their lands will also become ours."

"They destroyed many of the pteridons . . ."

Edyss turned slowly, glaring, but could not determine who had uttered the words. "It does not matter. We still have enough and we could take Dereka without a single winged Talent-beast. They have less than twenty companies of horsemen, and they would rather flee than fight. The westerners would fight, but they too have fled. No one else will come to defend the Landarch and his fat landowners."

This time, no one protested.

"Leave a garrison there." He pointed toward Black Ridge. "But not a large one. Ride for Dereka. We will join you on the far side of the mountains."

65

The sky was silver-green and cloudless, as it had been for most of the year, and more red dust sifted upward with each step by every horse in front of Alucius and Wildebeast, although there were only those of the vanguard, because Twenty-first Company was now in the lead. Under the warm late-summer sun, Alucius yawned and tried to stretch in the saddle. After five days of riding, with almost no sleep on the first night, he was sore, and stiff, and tired, although they had found two cavelike waystations, with springs. In the second, they had had to dig away drifted sand to make an entrance and get to the water, but the water had been clear and pure . . . and most welcome.

Following the rediscovered western trail road, the weary troopers and officers had taken four days before they had finally rejoined the main road—through a short tunnel, also filled with an unmortared stone wall at each end. Alucius had insisted that the second stone-filled archway be refilled. Then he had the residue and sand shoveled against it, as if over the years the wind had piled it against the stone blocks. While the Deforyan troopers might look askance, the nomads probably wouldn't, since they weren't that familiar with the road.

The western road had run its separate way long enough that they had rejoined the main road north of the nomads. That had been clear from the lack of recent tracks in the main road. Where the two trails rejoined was roughly where the mountains ended and the red sandy hills and the thorn trees began, although the valley that held both Dereka and the good road was days ahead. Still, the trail had widened enough so that the column could ride two abreast, and there were no traces of nomad tracks in the dust—not so far.

"How do you think the Deforyans will feel about us coming back?" asked Longyl, riding to the right of Alucius.

"They'll welcome us for killing large numbers of nomads, and behind closed doors, they'll complain that we didn't kill enough, and that the Lord-Protector didn't send enough companies. Then, they'll probably want us in the fore of the big battle when the nomads try to take Dereka. Not right in the center, but somewhere close where we can take huge casualties."

"Captain Feran said you were feeling right cheerful, sir. I can see what he meant."

"Like everyone, I'm just tired, Longyl." Alucius felt neither cheerful nor charitable, and he doubted it was just exhaustion. He and Waris and the scouts had managed to save most of the troopers, but the time at Black Ridge and leaving it didn't feel like a victory, or even like much of an accomplishment. He should have followed his feelings about the symmetrical nature of Black Ridge from the beginning. Yet . . . would that have changed anything that much? They couldn't have retreated immediately. Not without being considered cowardly by both the Lord-Protector and the Landarch and facing disciplinary action from Colonel Weslyn and the Lord-Protector. And without facing the pteridons under conditions that had actually favored them, they wouldn't have been able to kill those pteridons that they had.

By killing something like half the pteridons, they had reduced the impact of the deadly beasts. They had killed hundreds of the nomads with losses amounting to slightly more than one company. They'd effectively shielded Dereka and allowed the Landarch time to call in troopers from the northeast—if he would. And they had certainly reduced the risk the nomads posed to Lanachrona and the Iron Valleys.

All that considered, why did Alucius feel so depressed by the situation?

Because he knew that no one would be pleased with the situation? Because they hadn't done the impossible and stopped the nomads? Because they hadn't destroyed all the pteridons? Because there were still more battles ahead with a dubious ally?

Alucius took a deep breath and looked northward. Maybe, once they reached Dereka, rest and food would help his attitude.

He hoped so.

66

Just before midday, with high hazy clouds over Dereka, Alucius crossed the ancient stone courtyard of Lancer Prime Post toward the officers' café. Two days had passed since he and the western forces had returned to Dereka, and while he had gotten more sleep and far better food, as had the troopers, he was still concerned.

The other three officers were already seated at a circular table in one corner of the café when Alucius stepped inside. Although a handful of Deforyan officers were also eating, none was close to the Northern Guard officers, with empty tables around Heald, Feran, and Koryt.

The Deforyan cook, on the other hand, looked at Alucius's uniform as he stood by the low railing that separated the grill and stove area from the tables, and said, "We have some fine chicken here, sir. I can even put lace potatoes with it, and there's a good plumapple wine sauce."

"Thank you. I'd appreciate that very much, and any fruit that you have."

"Yes, sir. I'll bring it right out. You just sit down." With a smile, the cook turned back to the grill.

Alucius crossed the polished stone floor and seated himself at the single empty chair with the others. "The cooks are friendly."

"I think the ones we brought back told their buddies," Heald observed. "It hasn't made the Deforyan officers happy."

"Glad someone appreciates what we did," Feran said, taking a sip from a large beaker of ale. "No one else does."

Low and rueful laughter went around the table.

"Have you seen the majer this morning?" asked Koryt.

"Majer Draspyr has a meeting with the Deforyan submarshal . . ." Alucius paused. "Ahorak, the Assistant Arms-Commander, to discuss the need for the defense of Dereka."

"What is there to discuss?" asked Feran. "The city needs a defense. The nomads are riding this way. They want the city and everything in it. If they aren't stopped, they'll take it."

The cook appeared with a large platter and a beaker of the pale golden ale.

"Thank you." Alucius still couldn't get used to the idea of an officers' mess that was a café where he didn't have to pay.

The cook bowed, then slipped away.

"Their spirits of the mountain didn't do that much," Heald said, after finishing the last mouthful of potatoes. "Not that I could see."

"Alucius did more with the road," Feran suggested.

"Who do you think blocked off that second road? And why?" asked Koryt.

Alucius took a mouthful of chicken, well seasoned and tender, before replying. "I don't know, but it was done a long time ago. I'd guess the western road was sealed off right after the Cataclysm by one of the first Landarches. He probably wanted to make it harder for the nomads to reach Dereka. That's only a guess. Also, by sealing it that way, it meant that they had an alternative that no one knew about. The only problem was that someone forgot."

"Forgot, or just kept secret?" asked Feran.

"Probably kept secret for generations," suggested Heald, "then forgotten." He stopped talking and looked toward the door.

Majer Draspyr had stepped into the café and was surveying the tables. Then, upon seeing his four officers, he walked toward them, past the Deforyan officers and the empty quarter circle of tables around the western officers.

The four stood, and Alucius moved to take a chair from the nearest table. "Would you join us, sir?"

Draspyr frowned, but only momentarily, then laughed, once, before replying. "I think I will. This is as a good a place to meet as anywhere."

Even before the majer had seated himself, a cook appeared at his elbow, setting an ale in a tall beaker before him. "Sir . . . would you like the chicken and the lace potatoes? It's the best."

"Ah . . . yes, thank you."

The cook bowed and hurried away.

Alucius noted the frowns from the Deforyan officers, but said nothing.

"Almost embarrassing," Draspyr muttered. "Couldn't leave them there, cooks or not."

"The Deforyans did, sir," Heald pointed out.

Draspyr raised his eyebrows. "That may be. We're not Deforyans."

"Could you tell us what happened at your meeting, sir," Alucius asked, "if you can, that is. And about the ammunition?"

"I was looking to do that." Draspyr lowered his voice. "First, the ammunition. There's actually a hunting gun used against the plains antelopes that has the same diameter as your cartridges. They have a shorter casing, but the way they're cut can be adjusted. In fact, the armory is already working out the cartridges, and we should have at least several hundred by tomorrow, and perhaps a great number more in a few days. That was the easy part."

Several hundred would help, Alucius reflected, but they needed more like several thousand.

"The nomads are another problem," Draspyr went on. "The submarshal says that the marshal says that the Landarch isn't convinced that there are pteridons." He snorted. "I don't know if that means that Ahorak doesn't think so or none of them think so. Not one of Ahorak's officers saw them. They didn't see them because they were riding away with their lordly tails between their yellow-stained legs."

"Maybe it's a good thing that Twenty-first Company didn't destroy them all," Heald said quietly. "If we'd managed that, then he never would believe us."

"Oh . . ." Feran added, "he's the kind that will claim we didn't destroy any of them and that whatever number there might be that come north . . . he'll say that's how many there always were."

Alucius had thought about both those possibilities, but was happy he didn't have to voice them.

"If we weren't caught in the middle," Koryt suggested, "I'd almost rather see the nomads take over this place."

"Enough," Draspyr said quietly. "We are in the middle, and we have orders to help repel the nomads. If the nomads aren't thrown back . . ." He shrugged and left the sentence unfinished.

As far as Alucius was concerned, the majer didn't have to finish the thought.

"What do the Landarch and the marshal want?" Alucius asked. "Did he say?"

"They speak most politely and elegantly, Overcaptain, and at great length. When they've finished, I'm not certain still that they have said anything." Draspyr lifted the beaker of ale before him, then took a swallow. "That tastes good. Almost as good as a solid vyan vintage, but you can't get those here." He waited until the cook had delivered his meal and left the table before continuing. "Until today, the marshal—the submarshal—was not even convinced that the nomads were coming, but the

Deforyan scouts have reported thirty companies two days south of Dereka. The submarshal suggested that, given the size of the nomad forces, the Lord-Protector might have been well-advised to send more than five companies."

Koryt winced.

"I just told him that we were here and would do our best." Draspyr took another swallow of the ale. "I'd like you all to think about how we might best conduct ourselves in an open-field battle. Talk it over among yourselves, and then we'll meet again tonight after supper. I'm to meet with both the marshal and the submarshal tomorrow morning, when the order of battle—if there is a battle—will be discussed." Draspyr began to eat his dinner.

Feran looked at Alucius, who provided the slightest of shrugs.

What else could they do but try to figure out how to kill thousands of nomads? That, or kill the last of the pteridons and the nomad warleaders, if they could even determine who and where they were amid the hordes of riders.

A rueful smile crossed Alucius's lips. Killing the pteridons *might* be possible. He had monumental doubts about the practicality of the rest.

67

Alustre, Lustrea

The sound of boots on the polished pink-gray granite floor came after Vestor had already been warned of the Praetor's approach by the flashing crystal inset beside the metal mirror. By the time he heard the footsteps, the engineer had already replaced the quartz top to the sheltered workbench, concealing both mirror and crystals, and stepped around the tanks, where he waited for the Praetor, bathed in the hazy light of late summer streaming from one of the narrow-slit windows.

Tyren stopped a yard short of Vestor.

The engineer inclined his head. "Praetor Tyren."

"I have not heard much of late from you, Vestor. I thought I should visit you and hear from you yourself." Tyren studied the engineer. "You have been working hard. Your face is pale, and your hair darker from lack of sun." He nodded. "Yet you look stronger and healthier."

"My health is good, Praetor." Vestor smiled politely. "I am enjoying both the tower quarters and the freedom you have provided me. I have put both to good use. We will have all the light-blades you require by spring, and you will have ten, I would judge, by the end of harvest."

Tyren frowned, ever so slightly, before nodding. "I had hoped that you might have found a way to produce the crystals more quickly."

"I can produce only so many at a time, Praetor, unless you wish me to train other engineers, and there appear to be few who have both Talent and the ability to be engineers."

Tyren laughed ruefully. "We have found none. There are few indeed with Talent in Lustrea in these times."

"There have been few in any time since the Cataclysm."

"So you have told me."

"I have not been idle. As you requested, I have worked upon the calculations and the materials necessary to produce a Table of the Recorders—a true Table. The Table cannot be located in Alustre, because there are no nodes here, nor anywhere nearby."

"Nodes?"

"Beneath the surface of Corus run unseen webs of power. These webs hold the world together. For a Table to work—without exploding— the Table must be assembled in a locale where at least two lines of this power cross, and preferably where three are located." Vestor gestured toward the map mounted in an oak frame and set upon a sturdy easel. With the gesture, he was easily able to avoid looking at the Praetor without seeming to do so. "I did decipher the ancient codes. Alustre, Elcien, and Ludar were once all set upon such nodes, but

Alustre is no longer. There is a good possibility of such a node in or near Prosp."

"There are no other suitable locations?"

"There might be one near Norda . . . or possibly Dulka," Vestor replied, again looking squarely at the Praetor. "Those are the most likely locations."

"How long would it take you to determine such?"

"It would take me longer to travel to each than to determine. No more than a few days in any place where you would like such a Table."

"But we would have to build a suitably strong building . . . would we not?"

"It would not have to be terribly large, and the Table itself would need to be below ground, in order to lock into the nodes and flows."

Tyren nodded thoughtfully. "You have learned much, Vestor, and as your works come to fruition, you will continue to be rewarded."

"Thank you, Praetor."

"Is there anything else you have discovered? Anything that might augment the power of our legions?"

"I may have discovered the keys to an ancient manual in your library that presents other weapons, possibly the secret of the Myrmidon's sky-lances."

"The nomads already have those," Tyren pointed out.

"I beg your pardon, Praetor. They have skylances, but we destroyed half of them in that ill-fated battle. They may lose more—they may have already—when they attack Deforya or Lanachrona. They have sky-lances, but they cannot construct more of them."

Tyren laughed. "You are truly a wonder, Vestor. Truly. You build sky-lances, and I will build you a summer palace in the Acolian Hills—a small palace, but a palace." He paused. "And remember. I have always kept my word."

"That I know, Praetor." Vestor gestured to the crystal tanks. "Would you like to see the latest crystals?"

The two men walked toward the tanks.

68

In the gray light before the dawn of a Duadi morning, Alucius glanced around the courtyard of Lancer Prime Post, now almost entirely filled with troopers, most in the red tunics of Deforya. His eyes centered on Twenty-first Company. They had been fortunate. The company still had ninety troopers. Feran's Fifth Company was down to around eighty, as were Third Company and Eleventh Company. Twenty-third Company had been so badly mangled by the pteridons that Draspyr had reorganized its fifty-two survivors into three squads under a senior squad leader reporting directly to the majer.

The air in the courtyard was hot and still, a courtyard filled with the sounds of mounts breathing, sometimes heavily, the creaking of leather, and voices shouting reports and orders. With his nightsilk undergarments and the herders' vest under his tunic, Alucius felt far hotter than he would have liked, but they had saved his life more than once, and he could always drink more water. He glanced down at the water bottles, then back up, waiting for riding orders.

The first ten Deforyan companies had already wheeled and were riding out of the open gates, headed southward on the main street.

"Twenty-first Company!" called out Majer Draspyr from where he was mounted beside the stone platform where the Deforyan adjutant was calling out the orders.

"Ready to ride," Alucius replied.

"You're next, Overcaptain."

Alucius nodded to Longyl.

"Twenty-first Company! To the rear . . ."

Once the company emerged from the gates, as they turned southward and away from the Landarch's palace and the center of Dereka, Alucius glanced to the north. There the streets looked no different than before, early as it was, with a handful of shopkeepers and larger handfuls of beggars and a few others. Those who were out were not even looking, except with passing glances, at all the horsemen, as if no one knew or cared that thousands of nomads were massing to the south or that fewer thousands of Deforyan Lancers and Northern Guards were massing to meet them.

Longyl followed the overcaptain's glance. "You'd think they'd go somewhere. At least to their homes. Or take the high road east, anywhere away from here."

"Where would they go? They wouldn't be welcomed by any of the landowners. They might even get shot. There's no water, except for what the aqueduct brings, and that doesn't go any farther east from here."

"If . . . and I know it's a wager of the sort too high for odds, sir, but *if* we get through this, I can't help thinking I'll be glad to get back to the Iron Valleys, even under the Lord-Protector."

Alucius didn't much care for the Lord-Protector, but then, he hadn't cared much for the Council that had sold out the Iron Valleys to the Lord-Protector. He certainly didn't care for what he'd seen of those who ruled Deforya, and the evil behind the Matrial's rule had been so palpable that he still found it hard to believe that such evil had governed such a prosperous land and, in its own way, a land that had tried so hard to treat people fairly.

"I'll be glad to get home, too," was what Alucius said. "Our task is to find a way to make it possible." That was looking to be every bit as hard as Alucius had feared it would be.

As they continued to ride southward, a light wind began to blow at Alucius's back, cool for late summer, and just enough to lift the worst of the stagnant hot air within Dereka.

After another quarter of a glass, the column of riders turned and headed east-northeast along a narrower road that formed an arc between the south road and the high road that led eastward toward the Northern Pass, some two hundred vingts farther northeast. From the sketchy briefing he had received earlier, Alucius understood that the nomads had established themselves some ten vingts to the southeast of Dereka, along one of the few streams south of the city. Scouts had been watching every move. With the arrival of four pteridons late in the afternoon on the day before, even the Deforyan officers had conceded that the beasts existed. But just as Feran had predicted, according to Majer Draspyr, they had expressed polite doubt that as many as ten or eleven had attacked Black Ridge.

The majer had said little to the Northern Guard officers about his briefing, but he had said it with clipped words, and even those without Talent had sensed his frustration and anger.

As he rode along the ring road, Alucius reached out with his Talent, but could gain little in the way of impressions because so many lifewebs swirled around him so closely, and because the nomads were at least several vingts away, if not farther. To his right, the knee-high green-tinged golden grass of late summer extended a good two or three vingts to the horizon, the top of a long rise to the southeast.

"You think they'll attack right off?" asked Longyl.

"They can't wait too long," Alucius replied. "There's nothing to forage off to the south, except grass for their mounts, and there aren't that many places where they can get enough water for that horde. Besides, they've got the pteridons and far more warriors than we have troopers, and nothing's stopped them so far."

"We slowed them down. Killed a bunch."

"We're going to have to kill more than that," Alucius pointed out.

"Too bad we don't have rain. That might keep those beasts away," Longyl said. "If the clouds were low."

"We haven't seen any rain in a season," Alucius replied with a laugh. "I'm not expecting any now. Besides, they'd just wait. We're not about to attack a force that big."

He broke off the conversation as he noted that the companies ahead were stopping and wheeling into position perpendicular to the ring road, being positioned by a Deforyan majer. "Twenty-first Company . . . prepare to wheel to position!"

"Twenty-first Company . . ." Longyl echoed.

As the sun seeped over the grasslands to the east, the Deforyan
Lancers and the Northern Guards—and what remained of the one company of the Southern Guard—were drawn up along the central arc of
the ring road on the southeast side of Dereka. Facing endless waves of
grass, they were positioned directly between the nomad camp and the
city, and on the road that could take them swiftly either farther east or
farther south, should the nomads decide to attack from another direction. Each squad in Twenty-first Company was arrayed four deep and
five across—except that it was more like five across and three deep with
a few behind the third rank in most cases. Farther back were five
Deforyan companies, deployed to be able to fill in any gaps or to support against a more directed attack.

Alucius looked to his left, where, fifty yards to the northeast, Feran
was mounted before Fifth Company. Beyond Feran was the majer, and
beyond him, Heald, then Koryt. To Alucius's right was a Deforyan overcaptain and captain he did not know, and then, another fifty yards to the
southwest, another set of officers. The pattern continued for farther
than he could distinguish any individual officers. From what Alucius
could tell, the Northern Guard companies were about four companies
to the north of the center of the formation.

Alucius wondered if the nomads would sweep out of the rising sun,
but another half glass passed, and the sun climbed, and there was still no
sign of any riders anywhere to the south and east.

More time passed, and the light breeze died away, leaving an oppressive calm. Alucius ordered a break, by squads, to allow his men to
stretch their legs and move around.

A single trooper rode along the front of the defense force. "Nomads
sighted! All companies into position! Nomads sighted . . ."

"Twenty-first Company! Ready to ride!"

Alucius looked to the southeast once more. He waited less than a
tenth of a glass when, for a moment, it appeared as though a shadow had
been cast over the grassy rise to the southeast, because darkness crept
across the golden grass. But there were no clouds in the silver-green sky,
and the darkness was the mass of nomad riders, moving deliberately
toward the defenders.

"Check your rifles!" Alucius ordered.

Even before they neared the Deforyans, Alucius could see that the nomad riders were not riding forward as a line, but as a massive wedge aimed at the center of the Deforyan line, although the trailing edges of the wedge clearly overlapped both ends of the Deforyan formation.

"Lot of targets," observed Longyl.

"More than I'd like," Alucius replied.

With less than a vingt between the forces, the nomads slowed, then halted.

Alucius had a good idea why they had halted, and he watched, again waiting.

Four black shapes rose into the sky, from behind the rise over which the advancing mass of nomad riders had ridden. The pteridons circled higher into the sky and turned northwest, aimed directly toward the center of the Deforyan formation.

Unlike the attacks on Black Ridge, as the nomads rode closer, the pteridons also flew ever closer, but they did not swoop, but remained higher. Alucius wondered. Would they attack at the last moment? Why were they so high, and in the center? Because they had learned that only a few of the defenders could hurt them?

There were no commands from the Deforyan marshals . . . no orders.

Alucius could see that the wedge would strike the center well before the trailing edges would near Twenty-first Company.

"Twenty-first Company, left oblique! Prepare to fire! First volley as single target! First volley as single target!"

"Fifth Company, take oblique on Twenty-first Company! Prepare to fire!"

Alucius could feel the ground thunder as the nomads changed from a fast walk into a full gallop toward the center of the line. He watched the distance narrow. At what he judged to be a hundred and fifty yards, he gave the order. "Twenty-first Company! Open fire!"

"Fifth Company! Open fire!"

The first volley tore into the side of the nomad wedge, and scores of nomads went down. The second volley was almost as well-timed, and equally effective. While the third and fourth shots from the company appeared equally effective, the differing rates of individual fire resulted in an almost continuous stream of fire.

Despite the casualties, the nomads kept coming, and the wings of the wedge were now less than a hundred yards from Alucius.

"Twenty-first Company! Re-form! Tight formation! Re-form!" Alucius quickly reloaded then slipped the rifle he had used into the holder. Both were loaded, if he had a chance to use them again.

"Fifth Company! Re-form!"

Alucius glanced up, briefly to see one of the pteridons circling well to the west of the battle, then drop rapidly and swoop toward the center of the Deforyan line from the rear, blue flame blazing. Then he had to concentrate on the oncoming nomads. He pulled out his sabre.

"Twenty-first Company! Charge!"

The tight formation was a smaller wedge, with Alucius at the point of the wedge. Sabre out, he concentrated on both the nomads and creating the image that his company was larger, and more deadly than anything the nomads had seen.

The first nomad nearing Alucius turned straight toward him. Alucius didn't turn Wildebeast, not until the very last moment, when he twisted in the saddle and struck. The nomad had tried the same thing, but hadn't expected the turn to the left, and took a slash across his left shoulder and throat.

After that Alucius let Wildebeast and his training work for him, concentrating only on keeping moving. His left arm felt like lead, and he had the feeling there were bruises everywhere under the nightsilk undergarments.

Then, abruptly, he was riding across open grassland.

He glanced back. Most of Twenty-first Company had broken through the wing of the nomads, and the nomads had continued onward. The tight spacing of the troopers had worked. Twenty-first Company was behind the main nomad formation.

"Twenty-first Company. To the rear and hold." The hold was just to make sure everyone re-formed in place, ready to head back toward the fight. "Forward, fast trot!"

Alucius glanced to his right. Fifth Company had also managed to break through, although it looked as though they had suffered more casualties.

As the two Northern Guard companies rode northward—back toward the center of the battle, Alucius could see what Aellyan Edyss had planned. The Deforyans had thrown all the reserves into the center. That had broken the force of the nomad charge—or rather the nomads had let it break their force—because they had completely encircled the majority of the defenders, with the clear intent of killing them all. And now, the pteridons were swooping into the center of the battle, and blue flames were consuming Deforyan lancers by the score. The closeness of the battle limited where pteridons could strike, but the pattern was deadly. The pteridons were hitting the middle of the Deforyan, where the lancers could scarcely move, and the nomads on the outside were cutting down those who tried to flee from the fires of the skylances.

As he rode, Alucius looked to his left, finally locating Longyl, easing Wildebeast toward the senior squad leader. "We're going to wheel to a line fifty yards short of them and stop. Then we're going to shoot as many of them as we can."

Longyl nodded, almost grimly.

About a hundred yards short of the ill-defined rear of the nomad force, Alucius called out his orders. "Twenty-first Company! Wheel to firing line and halt! To a firing line and halt!"

The line was uneven, but spaced.

"Rifles ready! Prepare to fire. Open fire!"

Alucius aimed the heavy rifle and fired . . . again and again. Then he reloaded.

So intent were the nomads on hacking their way to and through the Deforyans that Alucius and Twenty-first Company and Feran and Fifth Company reloaded twice before what appeared to be a body of nomads close to five companies in size began to break away from the main nomad force.

"Target the nomads to the south! To the south!"

Twenty-first Company responded. A round of withering fire slashed through the attackers, then a second. At that point, Fifth Company turned its rifles on the nomads who were urging their mounts toward the two Northern Guard companies.

"Rifles away. Sabres out! Prepare to charge. Tight formation!"

Against the remaining nomads, although outnumbered, Twenty-first Company was through the nomad formation quickly. Alucius glanced back, but the nomads had not turned, and those remaining were engaged in a one-on-one melee with Fifth Company.

"Twenty-first Company! Halt!"

The survivors came to an abrupt and uneven halt.

"Hold position."

Alucius sheathed the sabre and pulled out the rifle, reloading as quickly as he could. Unless he could do something against the pteridons, everything was lost. It might be anyway, but he had to try.

"Form around the overcaptain, rifles out!" Longyl snapped.

Alucius turned to the north . . . watching, waiting. There were four pteridons. One, clearly larger than the other three, circled higher than they did, and was not attacking the Deforyans. Alucius waited until he could see one of the lower pteridons swoop from the northwest.

He raised the heavy rifle, investing the bullet of the cartridge in the chamber with darkness.

Crack!

The shot was true, and the pteridon shriveled, then tumbled out of the sky, striking the grass to the west of Twenty-first Company with enough force that the ground shook, even though the beast was a good half vingt away.

Flames flared into the sky, and a powerful gust of hot air swept across Alucius.

"Target those riders to the north!" Longyl ordered. "Fire!"

Alucius forced himself to ignore the oncoming riders, waiting for the next pteridon.

Once more, he concentrated and fired . . . and missed, as the pteridon wheeled just as he squeezed the trigger. He fired again, and again. The fourth shot struck the beast's wing, and it shuddered and slowed. Alucius took the second rifle and forced himself to infuse the next bullet with more darkness as he targeted the slow-moving blue-winged creature.

Still, it took two more shots before the pteridon and rider went down, crashing into the edge of the western wing of the nomad forces.

The ensuing explosion scattered and maimed hundreds of nomads, but the formation continued to tighten on the trapped Deforyans.

While Alucius was reloading both rifles, the third pteridon swooped, spraying blue death across hundreds of Deforyans, and was back beyond range before Alucius was ready.

Now what?

Both pteridons were circling higher than Alucius would have liked to shoot.

"You have to try, sir!" Longyl called. "You have to!"

Alucius took a deep breath, then raised the heavy rifle.

He fired four times, and missed.

Could he add Talent-power to the cartridges? He had to do something.

Carefully, oh so carefully, he visualized a long purple line from the chamber through the muzzle and straight to the lower pteridon.

Crack!

Purple flared across his vision, and he blinked, his eyes watering.

A bluish purple fireball exploded, raining flames down on the nomads and Deforyan Lancers below, but mostly on the nomads.

Alucius could barely see.

"You can do it, sir! You have to do it!" Longyl called.

Have to? Alucius swayed in the saddle, then deliberately changed rifles, forcing himself to ignore the nomads who were riding toward Twenty-first Company.

He had to get the last pteridon. The last one . . . somehow. The last pteridon was even higher. He could manage . . . he could . . . he needed the same sort of darkness that he had used to strangle the purple crystal of the Matrial.

Ever so slowly, Alucius raised the rifle, again extending that purplish line of power, underlining it with the greenish darkness he had used against the crystal. Slowly, aiming, sighting, Alucius *willed* the bullet to strike the pteridon carrying Aellyan Edyss, for the rider on that last pteridon could be no other, even before he squeezed the trigger.

As green and black and purple flared across his eyes, leaving him momentarily blind, as the bullet struck the pteridon with an impact that

Alucius himself felt, rocking back in his saddle, blue fire flared outward from the pteridon and its rider in all directions.

As Alucius's vision cleared, silence covered the entire battlefield for a long moment, and the silver-green sky above it, as though time itself had halted. The pteridon seemed frozen, motionless, in the heavens, glimmering in the white light of the midday sun.

Then . . . jagged shards of purpled black replaced the pteridon and rider, shards that sprayed in all directions. Alucius stared, immobilized, as he could see purple shards flying toward him, toward the troopers of Twenty-first Company who had protected him, sheltered him, to allow him to strike at the pteridons.

He couldn't let the troopers die. He couldn't.

He tried to gather the sense of dark greenness, the shieldlike feeling that went with it, but his thoughts were like molasses in winter, like glue already hardening, and he could feel curtains of blue fire—so hot that his hair was crisping—flaming around him.

Alucius made a last desperate effort to weld a shield of green around his troopers, but a blast of air slammed into him, into Wildebeast. He could feel them both toppling backward, and he was unable to get clear of the saddle.

As he was flattened by the blast, green did rise around him, a greenness infused with blackness, a blackness that swept across him and carried him away.

69

Northeast of Iron Stem, Iron Valleys

The two herders rode on opposite sides of the flock, Wendra to the east and just behind the lead nightrams, and Royalt to the west and to the rear of the straggling ewes.

Wendra frowned, and her eyes lifted to the Aerlal Plateau. She shook her head. For an instant, just an instant, had the quartz crystal outcroppings flared green? She studied the Plateau, but could not see any remnant of that greenish light—if there had been any green flare.

Then, as the darkness struck her, she reined up the gray gelding, her face pale. She glanced at her hand, then stripped off the heavy herder's glove. The black crystal of her ring remained alive, and she could sense the energy there. But there was a sense of pain—of agony.

For a time, she just looked at the crystal.

Wendra was still looking at it when Royalt turned his mount and rode around the rear of the flock to join her.

"Alucius?" he asked.

"Alucius . . . he's been hurt, or wounded," the brown-haired woman explained. "I thought there was a flash of green from the Plateau, and then I could feel the darkness, but it was almost as though I'd been burned."

"Burned?" Royalt's weathered face tightened into an expression of worry.

"That's the way it felt—like fire had washed over me. For a moment, I could smell hair burning." Her lips tightened.

"He's alive, though?"

"He is," she confirmed.

"Just pray to the One Who Is," Royalt said slowly.

"And the soarers," Wendra added.

"You think he's a soarer's child?"

"He's always been one."

"That's what Lucenda said." Royalt shook his head. "Don't know about that, but it can't hurt."

Wendra glanced at the ring, warmer than it had been, and then slipped the herders' gloves back in place. Her eyes lifted to the Aerial Plateau once more, and her lips moved, silently.

70

Alucius lay on a bed of blue flame, unable to move, and a dark-haired and alabaster-skinned man with deep violet eyes stood over him, speaking in a resonant voice. Alucius tried to make out the words, but their meaning eluded him.

The man spoke again, patiently, and still his words meant nothing to Alucius.

Alucius strained, concentrating on each word, knowing that each one was important, that he had to know what the alabaster-skinned man was saying, or that he would be doomed forever. But the man vanished in a curtain of blue flame.

Someone groaned, and he was the one groaning. His skin was on fire once more, and waves of redness washed over him.

A shadowy figure placed something cool upon his forehead, and he wanted to thank the person, but he could not, as he was swept away by darkness.

Abruptly, he was standing in a pink-lit chamber, facing a purple crystal that began to spin, faster, then even faster. From the whirling crystal came spears, crystalline spears that were tinged with pink, and tipped with fire.

With each spear that struck him, he winced, and each wince hurt more than the last, until his entire body was a mass of flame.

Beside the spinning crystal reappeared the alabaster-skinned man. His smile was no longer sympathetic, but cold and condescending. He spoke again.

His words tumbled out, each one a pinkish block that floated toward Alucius, and Alucius tried to grasp one, but his fingers closed on emptiness.

With a sad and simultaneously disdainful expression, the alabaster-skinned man vanished.

In his place, between Alucius and the crystal, appeared the blocky form of a sander, and the crystals in his skin glittered greenish black. He lifted a hand and struck the spinning crystal. Purple-black fragments sprayed everywhere. Each, as it struck the chamber wall or Alucius, transmuted into a puff of purple smoke that immediately vanished.

The sander looked at Alucius. He had no mouth, but he spoke, nonetheless. *He said that you should have found a Table. He thinks you would have understood. He is wrong, but that is something you must discover for yourself.*

Then a golden green radiance filled the featureless chamber, and a soarer appeared, delicate, finely formed, especially in comparison to the blocky sander. With the green light that washed over Alucius, the flames that flickered from his body died away, as did the agony.

This time, the darkness that washed over him was cool and comforting.

71

Tempre, Lanachrona

The pale-faced Recorder of Deeds stood back from the Table of the Recorders slightly, watching as the Lord-Protector observed the scene displayed before him.

"You see," gestured the Recorder. "There are the dark uniforms of the Northern Guards, and two companies break through Aellyan Edyss's hordes. That silver emptiness there? That is your herder captain. Notice how many bodies fall before him."

"So? He has always been effective in battle. That is why we sent him." A tone of annoyance crept into the younger man's voice.

"Yes, Lord-Protector. I only ask that you watch closely."

The two men studied the image in the Table, noting the charge by the two companies, then the wheel to a firing line and the carnage as they shot hundreds of nomads from behind. At the same time, the nomads hacked down hundreds of Deforyans, pushing them even more tightly together while blue flames incinerated hundreds of lancers in red in the center of the compressed Deforyan formation. Slowly, a loosely grouped wedge of nomads formed and charged the outnumbered Northern Guards, who had avoided the encirclement. The southernmost company formed into a tighter wedge and rode through the nomads, scattering and killing scores before re-forming, this time into a circle around the shimmering and shifting silver—sometimes a circle, sometimes an oval.

"Now . . . if you would," the Recorder said, "watch most closely." He surreptitiously blotted perspiration from his forehead. His violet-shaded eyes darkened.

"I *am* watching."

Even from the view afforded by the Table, it was clear that something unseen had struck the ground, flattening a broad circle of nomads, and instantly charring them and hundreds of others. Farther to the northeast, another such circle of destruction followed, and then, after a time, a third and even larger circle of similar destruction. Abruptly, hundreds if not a good thousand nomads turned southward and charged raggedly toward the small company of Northern Guards in the circular formation. Just as the nomads were within yards of the Northern Guards, an enormous flare of blue suffused the entire image in the Table, instantly turning black wide sections of riders, but leaving the two circles of Northern Guards untouched—except for a single point of blackness in the center of the Northern Guard formation to the south.

"What . . ." murmured the Lord-Protector, "what did he do?"

"That . . . that I cannot say for certain, but it appears that each blackened circle was the destruction of a pteridon and where it fell. I would surmise that the last was the death of Aellyan Edyss and the pteridon he rode."

"That last fall killed all the nomads around them . . . thousands of them." As the Table blanked back to silver, the Lord-Protector turned to the Recorder. "You say that he survived that?"

"It is most likely, but I can only infer that from what the Table shows. It shows an empty bed, where silver shifts and where people bring food, and watch, and sometimes talk. Their expressions have changed. First, they were silent, and some of the officers were worried. Now, they talk openly."

"That means he will live, but it does not mean more."

"The nomads have withdrawn, all the way to Illegea, and they are making their way to Lyterna, where they will select new warleaders and a new ruler. They would not have done so had the impact not been truly devastating. Even now, the grass is blackened across most of the battlefield."

"What of the pteridons?"

"I cannot be absolutely certain, but . . . it appears that there are no more."

The Lord-Protector laughed, openly and triumphantly. "You see, Recorder. I was right. Our Talent-weapon broke theirs, and he destroyed all their pteridons. Now, should the nomads attack Lanachrona, they will fall to our Southern Guard." He paused. "What of the majer and the company of Southern Guards?"

"I cannot find any trace of Majer Draspyr or Captain Clifyr. They are most certainly dead."

"It is to be regretted, but they served nobly, and one company is not too high a price to pay for such a victory." After a moment, the Lord-Protector added, "The Northern Guard must have suffered great casualties."

"It would appear so. They are far from full strength."

"That is good, also. There will be fewer to cause trouble in the years to come." The Lord-Protector nodded to himself. "And Overcaptain Alucius will be most happy to return to being a herder. We will send a fast messenger requesting that he return his companies to Dekhron . . ." The Lord-Protector broke off his words. "I will wager that the Landarch will request that the honored overcaptain bring his companies back to Lanachrona long before our messenger could possibly reach him."

"You think so, Lord-Protector?"

"The Landarch may be weak, but he is not a fool. Watch him in the glass and see. We will send the messenger, and the message, wherever it reaches the good overcaptain, will request that he present himself to us in Tempre for his reward. But we should let him bring a squad with him, so that he does not feel as if he is a prisoner. What reward? Some golds, and an early return with honor to being a herder."

"You would bring him here, Lord-Protector?"

"That I would. He will see that Tempre is great, and not old and decaying as is Dereka, or Dekhron, and he will also understand that I can be both terrible and grateful. I will find some way to suggest that the entire future of the herders rests on their support of Lanachrona."

"The man is not a man. He is a lamaial, and he will bring ruin upon us."

The Lord-Protector shook his head. "About this you are wrong. He may indeed be a lamaial, but he is young, and he has an attractive wife. He wishes to return to her. We will show our gratitude, but we will make most certain he understands that our support and forbearance from displacing or taxing the herders lies in us, and that without my support, there will be no herders."

The Recorder started to speak, then stopped, before asking politely, "You think this wise?"

"If . . . *if* he is as you say, why would I wish to offend him? If he is not, then time will show us otherwise, and we may act differently. It may also be that the One Who Is has used him as He has used others. I would not offend the One Who Is. Would you?"

"You do not even believe in Him. You have said so, sir."

"That I have, but if He does exist . . . why offend? Why indeed? If the overcaptain is somehow favored by fate or unknown powers, with the other enemies we have, I think it best not to create yet another cause against us. Would you?"

"No, sir. Not in your position, I would not."

"Good." The Lord-Protector walked toward the archway from the underground marble-walled room, then turned. "I may want even more from the overcaptain, but I must consider. He is still a good commander, and far more effective than other junior commanders. Perhaps a short mission somewhere . . . we will see. In the meantime, you will still watch the nomads and the return of the Northern Guard."

"Yes, Lord-Protector. We will watch most closely."

72

More than a week passed before Alucius was fully aware of his surroundings for more than a few moments at a time. He'd been brought back to Dereka, and Lancer Prime Post, but he'd been placed in a large ground-floor chamber reserved for submarshals, and he'd seen the first women—except on the streets—since coming to Deforya. Those nursing him were older women, who smiled encouragingly and said little. At times, he thought he had felt the greenish radiance, but he was never certain, and when he looked, it was gone.

Alucius was propped up in a large bed, set opposite wide windows opening on a smaller rear paved courtyard that always seemed empty. A light breeze from the windows brought the mixed scents of cooking.

There were no mirrors in the chamber, and the nurses had only removed the bandages from his face the day before. Someone had undressed him long since, and his nightsilk undergarments had been washed and pressed, then hung in the large armoire. He wore a nightshirt of soft cotton.

From what he could see, his arms and chest were covered with healing bruises of mottled and faded purple and yellow, and even the slightest movements still hurt slightly. The skin on the back of his hands was peeling away, and there was a layer of pinker skin beneath. His hair had either been cut or burned away, because all he could feel was stubble on the top of his head, as well as on his face.

Feran was the first visitor he was allowed.

"You look much better." Feran grinned.

"I don't think . . . want to know what I looked like." Alucius's throat was dry, no matter how much of the ale on the table beside the bed he drank. Speaking remained hard. "What happened . . . the nomads?"

"You saw . . . you saw what happened with the last pteridon . . . well . . . that was Aellyan Edyss, so far as we could figure. That explosion killed most of his warleaders. Couldn't tell how many nomads, but at least half of them. The Deforyans turned and attacked, and the nomads pulled back and rode south to Illegea."

"Just . . . like that?"

"Submarshal Ahorak—he didn't want to talk to me, but he couldn't talk to you—he said that it had to do with how the nomads rule. The warleaders have to chose their ruler, and so many of the warleaders died. . . . Something like that. We're not complaining."

"What about . . . Twenty-first Company?" Alucius feared the worst.

"Squads on the wings got hit the hardest, first and fifth squads."

"How hard?" Alucius tried to sit up, more, but the blackness and the dizziness threatened to overwhelm him.

"You've got sixty troopers left. Egyl's holding them together pretty well."

"Egyl? Longyl . . . ?"

"The nomads got him just before the fires got them. I didn't see what happened. No one did," Feran said. "Everything around Twenty-first Company got blasted . . . turned to cinders. Think that as much as anything decided the nomads to go back to Illegea."

Alucius managed the smallest of nods. "Fifth Company?"

"We were far enough from you that only a couple of troopers got burned, but we lost a bunch before that. I've got forty-five left."

"What . . . the others?"

"The majer and pretty much all of Twenty-third Company were wiped out. Two troopers left. I put them in Fifth Company. Half of Third Company, but Heald didn't make it, and less than a third of Eleventh Company. Koryt scraped through. Left arm's broken, and a bad slash on his thigh. Looks like he'll make it. Until he's better, Heald's senior squad leader's running both Third and Eleventh." Feran shook his head. "No one thought you'd make it. Uniform was burned off you. Women tending you said that you didn't have a span of skin that wasn't either black and bruised or burned—mostly bruised."

"Herders . . . are tough . . ."

"The nightsilk helped, but I still think anyone else would have died."

Alucius had to lean back on the pillows. "Wildebeast . . . ?"

"That stallion's tough, too. Had bruises and cuts, but he's in better shape than you are." Feran smiled. "He'll be ready to ride home before you will be."

Alucius nodded.

"I told Ahorak that you'd trained your troopers to shoot at flying targets. Told Egyl too. That's the way it is."

"Thank you . . ." Alucius whispered.

"Once you're better, Landarch wants to give some sort of award, then send us packing. Think he figures that few as we are, we shouldn't stay too long." Feran straightened. "I'd better go. You still have some healing to do."

"Thanks . . ." Alucius knew he was repeating himself, but couldn't find anything else to say.

"No. We owe you the thanks. Every trooper who left that field would have died without you, and we all know it. All of us are going to make sure that no one else knows it. That's the way it'll be." Feran smiled. "Just get better. We want you riding up front again."

After Feran left, Alucius looked blankly at the open windows.

73

Alucius stood in a great hall, the like of which he had never seen before. Above him, the vaulted ceiling soared at least fifty yards, a ceiling seemingly of pink marble, fitted together so cunningly that there was not a sign of a join, or of mortar. The walls were of the same marble. Golden columns flanked the entryway and were also set into the walls at regular intervals. Deep purple hangings, trimmed in gold and flowing down from golden brackets anchored in the columns, framed the marble walls.

After studying the chamber, Alucius glanced down. The floor was of polished gold and green marble, each octagonal section of green marble inset with an eight-pointed star of golden marble, the narrow arms of the star outlined in a narrow line of golden metal that was neither gold nor brass. Alucius looked up to see a man appear from nowhere.

The tall figure had flawless alabaster skin, shimmering black hair, and deep violet eyes. He stood in the center of one of the golden stars, wearing a tunic of brilliant green, trimmed in a deep purple, with matching trousers, and black boots so highly polished that they appeared metallic. Less than two yards from Alucius, his violet eyes centered on Alucius, and he began to speak.

The words were deep and resonant, and Alucius understood not a one, although he felt that he should have.

After a moment, the man frowned, then spoke again. "You should have understood the ancient tongue. It may be that, being who you are, you cannot acknowledge that you do."

"Acknowledge?" Alucius felt like a child, where everyone else was talking about matters he was expected to know . . . and didn't. "I'm just a herder and an overcaptain."

The alabaster-skinned man laughed. "Already, you have destroyed two far greater than you say you are, and you are just a herder? The Lord-Protector knows you better than you know yourself. Why else would he pick an unknown captain and send him against the largest mass of nomads in generations? And how else could you triumph were you not greater than you say you are?"

"Luck, and skill, and being able to take advantage of their weaknesses," Alucius replied firmly.

"It takes more than luck and skill to be a child of the Duarchy . . . or to best one. You cannot long hide what you are, not in a world of petty and jealous men. Yet . . . if you continue to act as you are, you will not be the hero who restores the dual scepter and the prosperity of the Duarchy, but the ill-fated lamaial. And if you would be lamaial, you will suffer because you stand against the dual scepter. Few will know the suffering that you will."

Then, Alucius found himself in a darkened chamber, one where the ancient eternastone walls began to move, closing in . . . tighter . . . and tighter . . .

He sat up in the large bed, shivering, his nightshirt damp with sweat. After a moment, he blotted his steaming face, but gently, because his skin was still tender. He sat in the darkness for a time, wondering why he had dreamed once more of the violet-eyed man.

Finally, Alucius eased sideways on the damp sheets until he was again between cotton sheets that were dry and cool. After a time, he dozed off again.

Before long, he found himself in his Northern Guard uniform, riding Wildebeast, digging his heels into the stallion's flanks, urging his mount forward.

Ahead was a pteridon, its rider spraying blue light and flame from the metallic blue skylance across Twenty-third Company. The pteridon and the wall of blue flames were sweeping toward Third Company.

Alucius raised his rifle and tried to aim and fire as he rode, knowing he did not have time to stop and fire, that he had to reach the pteridon quickly. But the flames swept inexorably over the troopers, and the blue-winged pteridon wheeled toward Alucius, so close that Alucius could see the white face and the dark hair of the rider as he aimed his skylance at Alucius and Wildebeast.

Flashes of blue light flared past Alucius, and he could feel his own hair crisping . . . smell it. Behind him, mounts screamed as they were enveloped in flame.

He sat up, soaked in sweat, despite the cooler night breeze coming through the half-open windows.

He recalled the words of the man with the alabaster complexion in the dream. "If you would be lamaial, you will suffer because you stand against the dual scepter."

Lamaial? The legendary character out of the past? What did that have to do with him? He was a herder. Or an officer in the Northern Guard who just wanted to finish his obligation and go back to his stead.

Alucius recalled as well the threat from the man in the dream—that he would suffer as few had. He certainly didn't want to suffer, or to have his family suffer, but he had no idea what he was supposed to do to avoid such suffering. Was doing what he believed to be right standing against the dual scepter? He couldn't believe that his dreams or thoughts were telling him that he was supposed to have let the Matrial strangle men and women through their lifewebs. Or that he was supposed to have let the pteridons and their riders burn thousands of troopers to death and over-run Dereka and whatever other lands and cities might follow.

And . . . besides being the symbol of the ancient Duarchy, long since vanished, what was the dual scepter? The dream figure had suggested it was more, but Alucius, for all his travels and reading, had never run across any references to the dual scepter except as a symbol of the Duarchy, or as a reference to someone's ambition to be a great ruler.

And why was Alucius dreaming of such a figure, with the alabaster skin? Outside of a fleeting glance of the Matrial, a glance he had never been certain he had actually made, he had never seen someone with the violet eyes and alabaster skin. Nor had he ever read of such.

Still . . . the dream figure had raised one interesting question. Why *had* the Lord-Protector picked out Alucius—or any of the others? What did the Lord-Protector know?

Alucius sat up in the bed for almost a glass, pondering, before he dared to try to sleep once more. As he finally drifted off, he held his thoughts firmly on Wendra.

74

Tempre, Lanachrona

The Lord-Protector and his consort sat on opposite sides of the table in the small private dining room. After taking a last morsel of the plumapple mousse and savoring it, he set down the ancient silver spoon.

"Your thoughts are beyond the river, dear," she said with a laugh. "As they often are these days."

"Ah, my dear Alerya, you know me too well." His brown eyes focused on her, and he smiled warmly. "It is good that we are married. You would be a danger otherwise."

"Nonsense. I'd not know you in the slightest, and so would be none at all." She sipped the amber dessert wine. "What concerns you now?"

"Enyll . . . there is something about him," mused the Lord-Protector.

"There has always been something about him," suggested his consort.

"No . . . something different. Before . . . he was always present, even when I did not wish to see him, always pressing to tell me something he had discovered or thought he might. Now, I seldom see him, unless I visit the Table chamber."

"He is hiding something."

"Yes. But what?" asked Talryn. "I have had the best spies search his chambers, his papers. I have had him watched every moment of his day, waking and sleeping. All that he does is reported." The Lord-Protector shook his head. "From all this, what do I discover? That he spends more and more time with the Table."

"Then," she suggested, "whatever he is concealing is hidden within the Table."

"And how can I discover what that might be? I know of none who has the Talent to utilize the Table, save him. And even if I did, would they be any more trustworthy than he is?"

"Perhaps the Table has revealed something he wishes not to disclose. Or, could it be that all the use of the Table has changed him?"

"Either might well be, and where does that leave us? Would the same occur to anyone else, even if we could find another Recorder?"

"Keep watching him, but treat him as though nothing at all has changed. If he has indeed changed, then there will be some action that will provide you a clue as to his thoughts and desires. It may be that, as he is aging—"

"I wonder . . ."

"You wonder what, dearest?" asked Alerya.

"Nothing . . ."

"With you, it is never nothing."

He laughed. "No. You are right, but it is a feeling, and I would not say more until I have seen and thought more upon it."

She frowned.

"You disagree?"

"No. I can understand how you feel, especially as Lord-Protector." She paused. "I give great credence to feelings. If you do not wish to speak of such, because you cannot find the words to match what you feel, that is well and good. But . . . act upon the feelings, if need be, even if you cannot find the words that would reason why."

"Most would caution the opposite," he said slowly.

"Most are fools," she replied. "More often than not, men reason themselves into difficulties more than they reason themselves out of."

"Need we talk more of reason?" he asked, standing from the table and glancing toward the door to their bedchamber.

She shook her head, affectionately, then rose and took his hand.

75

Alucius looked in the mirror, checking his appearance and his remaining uniform. His dark gray hair was the same shade as always, but only a short thatch. His face was thinner and pinker than he recalled, and his beard, he had noted in shaving, tougher. There were faint white lines across his left cheek, but he had no idea how he had gotten them, unless they had occurred unnoticed in the battle or after he and Wildebeast had fallen.

The uniform was a little looser, but not much.

After a last check, he turned and walked from the chamber he had been allowed to keep, even after he had recovered—mostly—from his injuries.

Outside, in the front courtyard, were two squads. One was the third squad of Twenty-first Company, and the other was a squad of Deforyan Lancers in full dress red uniforms. The Deforyan Lancers were formed up at the front, while the third squad troopers, led by Egyl as acting senior squad leader, were drawn up behind Wildebeast.

Wildebeast tossed his head slightly as Alucius neared, then settled down as Alucius projected warmth.

"He's glad to see you, sir," Egyl said. "We all are."

"I'm very glad to see all of you." Left unspoken was the thought that Alucius would have liked to have seen more than the fourteen troopers remaining in third squad. Alucius mounted and settled himself in the saddle.

The Deforyan undercaptain offered a low command, and the Deforyans began to ride toward the open gates.

"Forward!" Egyl ordered, at a nod from Alucius.

After they rode out through the open gates and turned northward, Alucius looked up the main street, but it appeared little different from any other time, with peddlers and beggars and groups of shoppers on each side, but none in the middle, except a boy who sprinted across and vanished behind a group of older women. Without even trying, from the overall feel, Alucius could sense that the youngster had stolen something.

"Do you know why the Landarch wants to see you, sir?" asked Egyl.

"I told you what I know," Alucius said. "He wants to express his appreciation personally. According to Submarshal Ahorak, that is quite an honor."

"More than we got from the Council."

It was, Alucius reflected, but then, they hadn't saved an entire land. In fact, he'd watched his homeland be taken over by Lanachrona because a group of greedy traders cared more for gold than an independent destiny, and neither he nor Colonel Clyon had been able to do a thing.

The ride was short, less than half a vingt northward from Lancer Prime Post to the iron gates of the Landarch's palace, guarded by a half squad of lancers in red. The guard lancers bowed their heads, if briefly, as Alucius rode past.

"Never saw that before," observed Egyl.

"Neither have I," Alucius replied, "but the only other time we were here was for a banquet." He fell silent, thinking about the three officers who had been with him who had fallen. While he hadn't known the majer well, nor cared that much for Clifyr, he definitely missed Heald, and wished he'd had a chance to know him better.

"Sir . . ." whispered Egyl.

Alucius looked up. The entire wall inside the front courtyard of the Landarch's palace was shimmering blue—the blue of nomad breastplates.

"More than a few bits of armor there," Egyl said quietly.

Alucius counted and calculated, trying to do the multiplication and estimation quickly. From what he could determine, there were close to three thousand breastplates on display—more breastplates than the entire Deforyan and western forces combined. "More than the number of lancers and troopers we had, I'd guess."

"Knew that from the beginning." Egyl broke off his words as they neared the entryway.

As they reined up under the covered entryway, Alucius saw Submarshal Ahorak waiting on the steps above the mounting blocks. With him was a white-haired man in the uniform of a full marshal.

Alucius dismounted and handed Wildebeast's reins to Egyl. "I don't know how long."

"That's fine, sir. We'll be here."

Alucius climbed three wide steps and bowed. "Marshal, Submarshal."

"Overcaptain Alucius," Ahorak said, "this is Marshal Seherak."

Alucius inclined his head. "I'm honored, Marshal."

"We are all honored by your actions and accomplishments, Overcaptain."

"Your lancers fought gallantly," Alucius replied, thinking that the Deforyan Lancers had fought bravely, if not terribly intelligently.

"There was much gallantry."

Alucius could tell that the marshal was curious, and just slightly irritated, although he gave little outward indication of anything other than courtesy. Ahorak seemed worried.

"You saw the breastplates of the nomads on display in the front courtyard?" asked Submarshal Ahorak, still conveying nervousness.

"I did," Alucius admitted.

"There are nearly that many in the rear courtyard. The Landarch insisted that they be displayed so that none would fail to understand the greatness of the victory." Ahorak smiled again. "Come. The Landarch is waiting."

With one of the Deforyans on each side, Alucius found himself walking through the stone arches and into the palace. Three Deforyan Lancers led the three along the same great hall that Alucius had been in for the banquet, but they continued past the banquet hall to a stone archway set between dual columns and guarded by a pair of lancers in red, but with gold piping on their tunic sleeves.

The three escorting lancers turned aside, and the doors opened as the three officers neared.

From somewhere came a deep and sonorous voice. "The Marshal Seherak, the Submarshal Ahorak, and the honored Overcaptain Alucius, representative of the Lord-Protector of Lanachrona and the Iron Valleys."

The Landarch was seated in the comparatively small audience hall on a dais of gold eternastone. The high chair was of a golden wood, and carried the presence of great age. As the three reached the steps before the dais, the marshals halted. So did Alucius.

The Landarch stood and took two steps forward. "Overcaptain . . . if you would join me . . ."

Alucius bowed, then took the three steps slowly and deliberately. At the top, he inclined his head again.

The Landarch smiled. He wore the same dark green tunic and trousers trimmed in gold that he had at the banquet.

Alucius could sense that the Landarch's smile was friendly, almost apologetic, but he waited for the ruler to speak.

"Deforya is most grateful to you, Overcaptain Alucius, most grateful indeed. Had not so many lancers seen what you and your troopers did, it would be hard to have believed such. But all have noted that with two companies you broke an entire wing of the nomads, then brought down the Talent-beasts and destroyed half the nomads' numbers." The Landarch continued to smile, but there was a tentativeness behind the open expression.

"You are most kind, honored Landarch." Alucius inclined his head slightly once more. "We came to do our duty, and we did the best we knew how. Many brave men died in that duty, and many were from Deforya."

"They did their duty, and they did so bravely. You and your men went far beyond duty, and you did so to save a land that is not your own." The Landarch gestured slightly with one hand.

A man in red robes stepped forward carrying a red velvet pillow. On it was a golden eight-pointed star, edged in a brilliant green enamel.

"This is the Star of Gallantry. There have been but twenty awarded in the generations since the Cataclysm. This is the twenty-first. I can think of no one more fit to wear it." The Landarch paused. "If, as I have heard, you believe that your troopers deserve it as well, then I ask you to wear it for both yourself and for them."

The functionary presented the pillow to the Landarch, who lifted off the star and fastened it on Alucius's tunic, over his left breast. Then the Landarch gestured again.

A second functionary stepped forward with a carved chest, which he opened and displayed.

Inside were golds, hundreds.

"There are two golds for every man who came to Deforya," the Landarch said. "It is not enough. I do not have the golds that all deserve, and this is but a token, but it is a token given to you and your men, and only to you and your men. I will convey my appreciation to your Lord-Protector in my own way."

"You are most thoughtful, Honored Landarch, and I will be sure to convey your graciousness and your appreciation to the troopers and to the families of those who fell."

"I do believe you will, Overcaptain. Our thanks are most real, for all that they are not as munificent as I would wish." The tentative smile turned ever so slightly more professional and less tentative. "I understand that you will be leaving at the end of the week."

Alucius hadn't heard that, but it gave him another six days to get stronger and make sure that the depleted force had enough in the way of supplies and equipment. "I understand that is the plan, provided we have the necessary supplies and equipment."

"Marshal Seherak and Submarshal Ahorak will make sure that all of your needs will be supplied." The Landarch's gaze fixed on the two below the dais. "All of them."

Both marshals inclined their heads in obeisance.

"We wish you well on your return to Lanachrona," the Landarch added. "We will not forget what you have done." He nodded a last time and stepped back.

Alucius bowed, then stepped down from the dais, at an angle, because he wished neither to turn his back on the Landarch nor to back way. The functionary with the chest of golds followed.

The two marshals escorted Alucius back out of the receiving hall, then through the great hall and back toward the entryway, trailed by the man with the chest.

As they neared the archway leading out of the palace, Submarshal Ahorak spoke. "This afternoon, Majer Wasanyk will see you about any other needs you may need for your return trip."

"I'll look forward to meeting with him, and we appreciate the concern and support."

All three men smiled, expressions of differing degrees of falsity, Alucius knew.

Outside, Egyl and third squad were still waiting, as were the Deforyans.

"Egyl . . . we'll need someone trustworthy to carry that chest back."

"Yes, sir." Egyl turned in the saddle. "Waris, forward!"

The scout took the chest, setting it before him. Then Alucius mounted Wildebeast and offered a last nod to the two marshals on the stone steps above the mounting blocks.

Egyl did not speak until they had left the palace courtyard and were riding southward on the main street, back toward the lancer post. "The star, sir?"

"Oh . . . that. It's the Star of Gallantry. The Landarch didn't want to give out several hundred. So he gave it to me and told me to wear it for everyone."

"I'd wager he didn't put it quite that way, sir."

"Close enough," Alucius said. "And that's what we'll tell everyone."

"And the chest, sir?"

"Two golds for every trooper—or two for the families of those who didn't make it."

"It's something," Egyl allowed.

"The Landarch apologized that it couldn't be more, but he is supplying us with food and more ammunition for the return. He made it quite clear to the marshals that we are to have whatever supplies we think necessary."

"Kind of him." Egyl's voice was dry.

"I don't think we want to overstay our welcome. We've made him very nervous."

"I can see that. Even without what you did, sir, our five companies killed more of the nomads than their twenty-five did."

"The Lord-Protector has something like a hundred companies. I'd guess that the Landarch has the strength of maybe fifteen companies at the moment. I'd be worried, too."

Egyl chuckled. "Did you tell the Landarch about the other road?"

Alucius grinned. "I forgot to mention that. So did Majer Draspyr."

"Sir . . ." Egyl laughed.

"They weren't too interested in Black Ridge. If they're curious enough, they'll find out. We left traces. If not . . ." Alucius shrugged. "We need to get ready. There's a majer coming to see what we need in the way of supplies this afternoon. Talk to all the squad leaders and acting squad leaders. Make sure we have a list of everything that we really need—especially how much ammunition, and spare packhorses and horses for the supply wagons."

"Yes, sir. I'd started on that already."

"Good." Once again, Alucius recalled how fortunate he'd been to have experienced squad leaders like Longyl and Egyl. His face sobered as he thought of Longyl . . . and Heald.

76

In the wide bed that was so empty without Wendra beside him, Alucius turned over in the darkness. Quickly, he sat up, reaching for his sabre. Even with his night vision, the figure standing inside the doorway was dim, and scarcely larger than a ten-year-old child.

Overcaptain . . . you will not need any weapons. You may bring them if you wish.

Alucius frowned. The woman had not actually spoken, and her life-thread was solid green, its solidity unlike that of any person he had met. Yet his Talent told Alucius that she meant no harm. He was still wary.

Please dress and follow me. There is something you should know before you leave Dereka.

Alucius considered, then slipped out of bed and pulled on his trousers, tunic, and boots. He did belt on his sabre. As he dressed, the cloaked woman remained just inside the door, unmoving.

He stepped toward her, catching a sense of amusement as his fingers brushed the hilt of his sabre.

You will not need that, but bring it as you wish. She turned and touched the ancient light-torch bracket, one that had been modified to hold an oil lamp. Noiselessly, a section of the stone wall opened, but only about half a yard.

Without looking back, the woman stepped through the aperture. A yard back inside the opening was another bracket, this one holding a light-torch. The woman pointed to the light-torch. Alucius took down the light-torch and thumbed it on, although he did not need its narrow bright beam to see the steep stone steps on the far side of the small windowless chamber. The steps led straight down. A faint glow suffused all the walls and the floors, and Alucius realized that where he stood had been constructed entirely of gold eternastone.

The small woman glided down the steps, again without looking back. After glancing back over his shoulder to see that the entrance remained open, Alucius followed. He could sense that no one had been in the stairwell for years, if not for far longer, yet there was no dust, and the air was neither stale nor musty. Did the eternastone preserve the air as well? The steps continued downward, for the equivalent of three stories, if not more.

Two yards beyond the bottom of the stone steps was another square stone archway—two stone pillars, topped by an oblong stone lintel. Alucius continued to follow the woman—who was, he realized, somehow akin to either a soarer or the wood spirit who had given him the key to unlocking the torque of the Matrial. Yet she had no wings, and there were no trees nearby, not in Dereka.

Beyond the archway was a long chamber whose high-vaulted ceiling rose a good five yards above Alucius's head. The chamber was more than fifteen yards in length, and about six in width. There were no windows, and the walls were covered with artwork of some sort.

Look closely . . .

Alucius pointed the beam of the light-torch at the mural that ran all the way around the wall, then realized it was not a single mural, but a series of scenes, each two yards long, and a yard in height. The colors were as vibrant and as fresh as the day they were laid down. They had to be because Alucius couldn't have imagined them as any brighter than they were. Each scene was incredibly lifelike.

He forced himself to begin with the first one, to the left of the archway, which depicted a ship without sails, its curved cutwater throwing back water and foam to suggest a great speed. At a jackstaff flew a pennant Alucius had never seen, one with two crossed scepters, both metallic blue, if subtly different in design, set in a sharp eight-pointed, brilliant green star. From the size of the figures at the forward rail, the vessel was close to two hundred yards in length. The star was the same shape as those used by the Landarch, and a match in shape to the Star of Gallantry.

The second panel was of a creature with leathery blue wings, folded back along its body. Beside the pteridon stood a warrior in glittering blue armor holding a blue metallic lance. His face was luminescent white, his eyes violet, and his hair and eyebrows shimmering black.

In the third panel, a sandy-haired and tanned figure stood lashed to a T-shaped metal frame in the middle of a circular stone dais. The man's mouth was open, as if in protest. Above and to the left of the dais was a tall podium or lectern, made of some sort of reflective blue metal. Behind the lectern stood a woman in shimmering blue robes. Her hair was shining black, her face and neck luminescent white, her lips red, and her eyes violet. From somewhere above, blue light played across the figure in the frame, and blue flames had begun to erupt from the man's gray tunic.

Alucius slowly moved the beam of the light-torch from panel to panel, for although he could make out the outlines of each scene without its light, he would have missed the finer details. There were scenes of mighty sandoxes with purple-tinged white skin pulling huge wagons along the high roads at great speed, of cities filled with buildings of gold eternastone and shimmering green towers, of a port filled with dolphin ships, of tanned men and women gathering fruit from rows of trees, overseen by an alabaster-skinned supervisor, of a huge barge headed south on the River Vedra—that location Alucius recognized because the river levees were identical to those he had seen in Hieron, although he saw no sign of a city such as Hieron.

He walked slowly, taking in each of the scenes. He went back and counted. There were twenty-one scenes. Another thought struck him, and he played the light-torch back across the panels. All the faces of those depicted in positions of authority were of that luminous white, and all the white-faced figures shown in detail had black hair and violet eyes.

He turned, as if to ask the spirit-woman . . . but the chamber was empty. He played the light across all the walls and up into the vaulted ceiling, but she was gone.

Alucius turned and walked back up the stone steps, wondering if he had been trapped, if the opening were still there. It was, and he could not but help breathing a gentle sigh as he stepped into the main chamber of his quarters. The opening did not close.

Finally, he twisted the tight-torch bracket upright, and slowly the stone wall closed. Alucius stepped forward and ran his fingers over the ancient stone. The joins were so fine that he could not determine exactly where they were. Even with his Talent, he could not sense anything behind the stone, as if the eternastone blocked his Talent.

Had it been another dream? It had felt far too real. He looked down, realizing that he still held an ancient light-torch, of a kind he had never seen, whose beam created a sharp circle of white light on the stone floor. He thumbed it off and slipped it inside his tunic.

Once more, he looked at the oil lamp bracket, just above his head. After several moments, he reached up once more and turned the bracket. Again, the opening appeared in the stone. He stepped back through the opening, but the long stairwell was still there, leading down-ward. He turned and walked back into the chamber, where he returned the bracket to its upright position. The opening vanished.

Why had the spirit—or had she been a disguised soarer—why had she appeared now, *after* the battles? Why had she shown him the hidden ancient mural? His stomach clenched slightly.

Turning, he glanced out the window and could see the graying of the sky. Rather than try to sleep for less than a glass before dawn, he undressed and went to the washroom adjoining his chamber to wash up and prepare for the day ahead. And to think.

III.

⊰ DARKNESS OF TRIUMPH ⊱

77

Septi had dawned clear and cooler, perhaps foreshadowing the turn of harvest, now less than a week away. The sky above the lancer courtyard was brilliant silver-green, and a brisk but not chill wind blew out of the north. Alucius was mounted, his back to the open gates of the post. Before him, the troopers—consolidated into three companies—had formed up by company.

"Twenty-first Company, present and ready, sir," Egyl snapped out.

"Fifth Company, present and ready, sir," Feran reported.

"Third Company, present and ready, sir!" Koryt was still wearing a splint on his left arm, and a sling.

"Stand easy." Alucius turned Wildebeast and rode back through the opening between Twenty-first and Fifth Companies until he reached the open courtyard behind them. He reined up short of the stone balustrade of the platform where Marshal Seherak stood.

"Overcaptain."

"We stand ready to depart Dereka, Marshal."

"All Deforya wishes you well on your return home." Marshal Seherak smiled warmly. "Your efforts were magnificent, Overcaptain, and your bravery beyond belief."

Without even really trying, Alucius could sense the coldness behind the expression, as if confirming once more how his Talent had become one of his physical senses, functioning all the time, rather than having to be called up through concentration. He could also sense the veiled contempt, as though the marshal felt that Alucius to be a lucky and brainless fool. "We both know, Marshal, that such bravery was born of desperation, carried out with skill, and rewarded by luck." Alucius smiled.

The marshal's smile changed, almost imperceptibly, and he replied, "That may be, but it was bravery, nonetheless."

"We all are placed where we do what we must, sir, and I thank you for your consideration, and for your generous supplies for our return journey. I will convey your courtesy and your regards to the Lord-Protector."

"We are all appreciative of the Lord-Protector's support of an independent Deforya in these times." The marshal emphasized "independent" ever so slightly.

Alucius wished the Iron Valleys had been treated more "independently" by the Lord-Protector, but he had the feeling that Deforya would not be independent that much longer, not with the way the Deforyans fought and the way the Deforyan landowners acted. "I will convey that as well, Marshal." Alucius bowed his head slightly, then turned Wildebeast, riding toward the gates. There he took his place behind the token vanguard, at the front of the main body of troopers.

"Column forward!"

As the force—now almost entirely Northern Guards—rode through the gates and turned northward, Alucius reflected. Half a season before, six officers and five companies had ridden out of Lanachrona, and the companies had all been close to full strength. Now . . . three officers were riding back at the head of three companies little more than the strength of two, he was the senior officer, and everyone was proclaiming a great victory over the nomads, Aellyan Edyss, and his pteridons.

More worrying than that was the visit from the soarerlike spirit, and her guiding him to the hidden chamber. Still wondering whether he had dreamed the visit, he had visited the chamber one last time before he had mustered the troopers in the courtyard . . . but the chamber and the mural remained.

As Alucius rode past the Landarch's palace, the half squad of Deforyan troopers guarding the gates drew up to attention.

Alucius returned the salute with a bow.

"Did you see that?" asked Egyl. "That was the second time."

"I did. They understand what we did."

"You don't think the officers do?"

"Some of the officers do, I'd wager, but most of them are captains. The Landarch does, but he's as much a captive as those captains are."

"Sir?"

"The overcaptains and their superiors are all from landowning families. They control the lands and the Deforyan Lancers, and whoever controls those controls Deforya." Alucius gestured toward the people on the sidewalks and in the shops. "Look. Almost none of them are even looking at us. To them, a trooper is like a lancer. There's no difference. If anything, they're happy to see us leave."

Egyl frowned. "You don't think it's that way in all lands?"

"Not as much." Alucius shifted his weight in the saddle. "In the Iron Valleys, you have the crafters, the herders, and the traders. The traders had the most coins and power, but they had to listen to the others some of the time. In Lanachrona, they have the vintners, the traders, the craft guilds, and the Southern Guard. The Southern Guard has more officers who worked their way up, and that means they owe their loyalty to senior officers and the Lord-Protector, not to those with golds."

"You're worried, aren't you, sir?"

"We've got a long trip ahead," Alucius said. "I'll be happier when we get back to Dekhron."

"Dekhron, sir?"

"Where else do we go? They've closed Emal, and we don't have any orders. I'd rather go to Dekhron than Borlan or Tempre—and Dekhron's far closer." That was another worry, but Alucius was far more concerned about the worries he felt and couldn't even identify.

78

Tempre, Lanachrona

In the darkness, with but a single lamp lit in the ancient underground chamber, the chamber around and over which a palace had later been built, the Recorder of Deeds stepped toward the Table. He shuffled, hesitantly, almost as if his feet were carrying him against his will. His every breath was labored.

Finally, he stood at the edge of the Table of the Recorders. Even in the cool of the night, his forehead was damp with perspiration. His hands rested on the edge of the Table, then grasped the underside of the lorken, as if trying to lift the Table. The Table did not move.

After a time, the Recorder looked down at the mirror surface, then at the ruby mists that appeared. The ruby mists swirled upward, beyond the polished crystal surface, into the dark air, wreathing themselves around the Recorder's face. Even as he turned his head, his body remained immobile.

His entire frame shuddered, once, twice, then spasmed before crumpling into a heap beside the Table.

The mists vanished, and the mirror surface of the ancient Table once more appeared polished and untouched, without even the trace of fingerprints on the edge of either the crystal or the polished lorken around that shimmering surface.

Perhaps a quarter of a glass later, there was a single groan, cut off abruptly. The Recorder rolled over, straightened, then stood, with the grace of a much younger and stronger man.

His eyes lit upon the Table, and a satisfied smile crossed his lips before he turned and walked briskly from the chamber.

79

Alucius glanced to his right, north across the channeled stream to the gray stone slopes rising beyond the artificial canyon that held the high road back to Lanachrona. Ahead, the two scouts from second company were riding up the slight incline of the road toward the point where it crested, beyond which the high road ran flat for a good ten vingts, as Alucius recalled, across a narrow valley that held little besides low brush and stones.

The trees were as infrequent as he remembered, twisted and bent evergreens. There was almost no undergrowth, even near the steams, except for small bushes clinging to life in corners or angles in the stone where dirt and sand had drifted over the ages since the road and canyon had been cut from the heart of the Upper Spine Mountains.

As he rode westward along the high road, the sense of sorrow felt stronger than it had been. Alucius absently patted Wildebeast, considering. Was it that the sensation was stronger, or that he was far more aware of it?

He continued to have dreams—or fragments of dreams—with the alabaster-skinned men and women dominating them. If the ancient frieze or mural under the lancer quarters were accurate, and Alucius *knew* that it was, even if he could not have proved that, then ancient Corus under the Duarchy had been ruled by people like the Matrial. But none of the histories had made mention of that. Nor had he ever heard stories or legends about them.

Then, nothing written about the Matrial of Madrien over the past hundred years had noted her different appearance. Was that something just taken for granted, so unremarkable that none of the ancients had even considered it? Then, too, he had only seen one or two of the pteridon riders, but they had been pale-faced, although not so pale as the figures in the mural. Had some sort of Talent held the riders unaging ever since the Cataclysm? Or did riding pteridons change the nomads who had ridden them?

Alucius had felt, but again could not prove, that the last rider he had downed, and whose death had almost resulted in his own, had been Aellyan Edyss. That argued for the idea that the use of the ancient pteridons made a change in those who rode them. Had the Matrial's torques been a use of ancient Talent-powers that had turned the Matrial pale and violet-eyed? And unaging, as the Matrite officers had claimed?

And what did all that have to do with the spirit-woman's showing him the mural? She had told him that he had to see the mural. But why? What could he do? Did she expect him to kill every alabaster-skinned person he met? Or to be wary of them, as if he would not be anyway?

He tightened his lips.

"You all right, sir?" asked Egyl.

"Still thinking," Alucius admitted. "I keep wondering how Aellyan Edyss got those pteridons, and whether there are any more somewhere. And why they obeyed him and his riders."

"I'd rather not think too hard about that, sir. Just glad that you knew what to do."

A glass later, Alucius was still thinking . . . and more worried. He shifted his weight in the saddle again, not because he was sore, but because he was uneasy. He had not sensed the bluish violet creature so far on the return through the mountains, but the absence of life bothered him more than it had on the journey to Dereka. Even the faint glow of the eternastones of the high road appeared fainter.

Was that because his Talent-senses were sharper and more active? Or because the deadness of the mountains had actually leached out more of whatever power the stones had held? Or just because he was worried more?

By all rights, he shouldn't have been worried. He had survived an almost impossible situation in Deforya, and he was on his way home. He had less than four months left on his obligation to the Northern Guard, and there was no immediate sign of more battles or war. Because of a soarerlike spirit's visit and some dreams, he was worried?

He shivered. Then he frowned. Why was he cold? It was almost harvest, but he was wearing nightsilk undergarments and a riding jacket, and the breeze through the canyon from the west was just pleasantly cool.

After a moment, a red emptiness washed over him. The coldness ahead had caused those deaths—and he hadn't expected such a feeling along the high road. But whatever had caused the deaths of the scouts lay ahead. He turned to Egyl. "Ready rifles! Pass it back."

"Ah . . . yes, sir. Ready rifles. Twenty-first Company! Ready rifles!"

Before Egyl could question him, Alucius asked, "Who are your best marksmen?"

"Waris and Dueryn, of course, and probably Makyr and Fiens."

"Order them forward."

Something lay ahead, and while it was hostile, it wasn't anything like lancers or nomads. What it was, Alucius had no idea, but the coldness and the deaths he did not want to mention left no doubt that it wasn't friendly.

Alucius waited to say more until the four were riding abreast behind him. Then he half turned in the saddle. "There's something ahead. I don't think it's friendly."

"But the scouts—" Egyl began.

"They may not have seen it in time. I want you four directly in a line immediately in front of me, so that you have a clear line of fire. You'll need to be ready as we near the crest of the road."

"Yes, sir."

As the four eased around Alucius and Egyl, the overcaptain checked his own rifles and began to infuse the cartridges in each of his rifles with the same kind of darkness that had brought down the pteridons. Once he felt that each bullet was so charged, he began to slip the darkness of life—for that was the way he had come to see it—into the cartridges of the four who rode before him.

The chill and darkness became more and more oppressive as the column neared the gentle crest in the high road. Alucius felt as though a wall of water lay ahead, ready to break down and sweep them away. Yet . . . what could they do but advance? Retreating before a powerful foe in a narrow canyon was worse than advancing.

Alucius readied his first rifle as he rode. Even before the first six quite reached the crest, there were gasps from the others. Alucius glanced sideways at Egyl. The squad leader's mouth was open, and his eyes were wide.

The twenty-odd creatures that circled in the air ahead were like smaller purplish pteridons, without riders, roughly half the size of the pteridons ridden by the nomads. The claws on their forelegs were longer, metallic blue talons, glinting and knife-sharp. The six creatures blocking the road were worse. Each was close to four times the size of a draft horse, with massive shoulders, a long triangular horn, and scales that shimmered purple.

The two scouts and their horses—or their bloody remains—lay less than a hundred yards ahead of Alucius.

"Aim carefully. Prepare to fire. Fire!" Alucius put his first shot through the eye of the horned creature on the right, then switched to the second, and fired again. Both went down, and columns of blue flame rose from where each had been.

One of the wild pteridons cartwheeled out of the sky, and the others dived toward the troopers. The horned Talent-beasts lowered their heads.

Alucius fired two more shots at the larger beasts. One shot missed entirely. The second plowed into the massive shoulder of the fourth beast, and bluish flames erupted from the wound.

Before him, the four marksmen fired deliberately, and a pteridon exploded in the same bluish flames.

Alucius raised his rifle and used the last shot to aim at the nearest pteridon. While the shot missed, it was close to the beast, and it swerved slightly, and missed Waris by a fraction of a yard. He switched rifles, and fired another shot at a pteridon—and hit it. A blast of blue flame washed toward the front of the column, turning the forearm of Fiens's riding jacket into flame.

The three remaining horned beasts were within fifty yards.

"Fire at the ones on the ground!" Alucius ordered, trying to infuse the cartridges of the marksmen and of Egyl with blackness. Ordering an oblique or a retreat would have been useless. That Alucius knew.

Another horned beast flared into blue flame, but a pteridon swept out of nowhere and slashed Dueryn from his saddle, dropping his body, with long black scars that still burned, on the eternastone in front of the troopers.

Alucius snapped off a shot at the pteridon, momentarily slowed, and was rewarded with another blue explosion. Then he concentrated on the remaining horned beasts.

The last one skidded to a halt ten yards from the front of the column, and Alucius tried his best to throw up the greenish barrier. He had to have been partly successful, because the heat, while intense, merely crisped hair rather than burning exposed skin.

The pteridons redoubled their attacks, striking the column from all angles, slashing and swooping.

Despite the speed of the creatures, slowly, so slowly, their numbers diminished.

Alucius forced himself to concentrate on two things—his own shooting and supplying darkness to the cartridges of those around him. In time—how long it was Alucius didn't know—he shot the last one, then lowered his rifle.

For all the chaos and the slashing attacks, there were fewer bodies strewn on the shoulder of the highway, or amid the column, than Alucius had feared. Far more than he wanted, but fewer than could have been.

"Have the captains report," he said tiredly to Egyl. "Tend to the wounded, but have Waris and your other marksman—Makyr—ride ahead a half vingt—but not out of sight. And have them keep an eye open."

"Yes, sir. Waris, Makyr, you heard the overcaptain." Egyl pointed to a trooper in the column. "Esklyr, ride back and tell the captains that the overcaptain would like their reports." The squad leader looked at Alucius. "Almost got you, too, sir."

Alucius looked down at his right arm. A long rent ran down Alucius's sleeve, cutting through both riding jacket and tunic, leaving the nightsilk beneath shimmering and untouched. His arm was so sore that he could hardly move it. "I didn't notice. I was lucky." In fact, his whole body was shivering imperceptibly, as if he were totally exhausted. He reached down and took out the water bottle, swallowing deeply. The water helped.

As he waited for the officers and the reports, he glanced at Waris and Makyr, but no more beasts appeared. More important, the coldness he had felt was gone, and all that remained was the omnipresent sense of sorrow. Then he turned Wildebeast and studied the stony valley on all sides. There were no traces of any of the Talent-beasts, except for black greasy splotches where they had burned. There were no charred bones, no scales . . . nothing except the residue of intense fires.

Alucius could feel something else—or the lack of something. There was no life at all around them. Even the evergreens, although they looked green, were dead, and would be brown in weeks, if not days.

Then he let out a silent sigh of relief as he saw Feran riding along the shoulder, followed by Koryt. Koryt still had his arm in a splint, and the dressings binding the splint were charred on one side, and Koryt's face was reddened on the same side.

Feran reined up. "Fifth Company, ten dead, five wounded." The older captain was hoarse, his voice raspy.

"Third Company," Koryt reported, "six dead, three wounded."

"Twenty-first Company, sir," Egyl said, "three dead, seven wounded."

Nineteen dead. Alucius paused. "Thank you. You and your troopers handled this well. Most companies would have broken."

"What . . . were . . . those things?" asked Feran.

"I don't know, but the flying ones looked like pteridons. Maybe they were wild pteridons, the kind that the ancients tamed into the ones we saw with the nomads." Alucius considered. "The big ones on the road—they looked like sandoxes would, if they had horns and scales."

"Sandoxes? Like in the legends? How—"

"I saw a picture of one once," Alucius said. "A drawing, really." He moistened his lips, realizing that, outside of the mural under the Derekan lancer barracks, he had never seen a picture. Yet he had known what that creature had been, and it had been so natural to know that he had never questioned how or why he had known.

"I still don't understand why some shots brought them down and some didn't," Feran said.

"Mostly shots from the front of the column," Koryt said. "Saw one of the scouts—Waris, I think—bring down two of those flying horrors."

Alucius was glad for more reasons than one that he'd thought of infusing the bullets of others with darkness. "They had a better angle, but I didn't want the troopers spread out where they could have been picked off one by one."

Feran nodded in agreement.

"We'll need to pack the bodies out of here, those that we can." It was probably a useless gesture, but Alucius didn't want to bury anyone in the sorrowing dead ground in the Upper Spine Mountains. He couldn't have explained why, but as overcaptain, he didn't have to. He would have to explain the losses to the colonel, and possibly write a report that might end up getting sent to the Lord-Protector. He didn't look forward to that, either, but explaining it couldn't be anywhere as bad as what they'd just been through.

80

Northeast of Iron Stem, Iron Valleys

In the late afternoon, the herder rode slowly at the rear of the flock, chivvying the lagging ewes forward, toward the northwest and Westridge, and the stead itself. Wendra had been forced to take the flock farther to the southeast than she would have liked, but the quarasote nearer the stead had far less in the way of new growth.

The lead rams had slowed, and she could sense their apprehension. As she urged her mount forward, she lifted the rifle from its holder, scanning the red sandy ground and reaching out with the Talent-sense still new to her. As she neared the rams and slowed her mount, less than fifty yards ahead of her Wendra saw the faintest puff of sand. In the warm and still late afternoon, there was no wind.

She reined up and took out the heavy rifle, waiting for the sander to emerge, even as she looked back. She did her awkward best to project a warning to the lead rams and was rewarded to see that one of the rams—Lamb's offspring, she thought—snorted and pawed the sandy ground between the quarasote bushes.

Abruptly . . . a green radiance surrounded her, green suffused with black.

Her eyes flicked from the now-boiling ground to the soarer that had appeared less than three yards from her.

You must draw on the darkness within you. Press it into the bullets.
Draw on the darkness . . .

How could she draw on the darkness? What darkness?

This darkness . . .

Wendra could sense a series of threads, black threads twined with green, that ran from her, and from the soarer. Then she understood—and drew upon the darkness.

Then . . . she cocked the rifle and waited.

A purplish mist swirled above the boiling sandy red soil. Then the sander emerged, almost instantaneously—one like no other that Wendra had seen—a creature of blackish purple, rather than of tan and crystal skin.

Crack! The first bullet struck the creature full in the chest, and though it shuddered, it stepped toward the herder and her mount.

Wendra fired again—and struck the creature between neck and shoulder, the point where Royalt had insisted the creatures were most vulnerable. That shot staggered the dark sander, but it took another step.

A third shot, and then a fourth followed.

After the fourth shot, a purplish mist swirled around the sander. Abruptly, the creature raised an arm, but before completing the gesture, it pitched forward onto the sandy soil, one outstretched arm striking the new growth on the nearest quarasote bush.

A short pillar of purple flame exploded upward, then subsided, leaving a rough circle of blackened ground.

For a moment, Wendra held the rifle ready, prepared to use the last cartridge. Then, she reloaded quickly. Only after several long moments did she feel that the sander—or another one—would not return.

Her eyes dropped to the quarasote bush brushed by the strange sander. As she watched, it blackened and shriveled, then disintegrated into a pile of ashes. She swallowed, but her eyes turned to the rams, then the rest of the flock. They were all there, although the lead ram snorted once, as if to tell her that they should move on.

Wendra put forth the feeling of moving, and the rams began to walk to the northeast, giving the blackened ground a wide berth.

She only glanced back once, but the circle of blackness remained.

81

Another three days passed before Alucius led his vastly diminished forces out of the Upper Spine Mountains and into the dry and dusty plains of eastern Lanachrona, where it had rained little or not at all in the season that had passed. The heat was that of full late summer, not harvest, and the dust was fine and pervasive.

While Alucius had hoped to return the bodies to Emal or Dekhron, the heat and the overly rapid putrification had made burial necessary as soon as they had cleared the mountains and reached an area where there was actually soil. There, after looking over the twenty-one graves, Alucius had said a brief prayer to the One Who Is, wondering, not for the first time, whether his prayer was more wish than substance.

They had not seen, and Alucius had not sensed, any more Talent-creatures. He still wondered why they had been attacked. A warning of some sort? Like the dreams? If he had only had dreams—those he could have dismissed—but the hidden chamber and the attacks by wild pteridons made dismissing those concerns impossible. Did the dream figures exist somewhere? Where? Was it that Alucius was some sort of obstacle to someone? It seemed as though he was always an obstacle to someone or something. Except the soarers. Were the soarers and the alabaster-skinned people enemies? Or did both want to use him? He shook his head; he still had no answers.

The majority of the scattered steads that they had passed after that were abandoned, the grass on the rolling rises little more than desiccated stalks, and the small fields mere patches of sandy dust. The waystations had water and little else. For the provisions that Alucius had received from the Landarch, he was more than thankful.

In midafternoon, through haze and dust, Alucius could see a rider ahead, moving toward the column—Waris, who had been one of the two scouts sent forward.

Waris rode back along the high road and turned his mount to come alongside Alucius. "Sir . . . there are four Southern Guard messengers, and they say they have a personal message for you from the Arms-Commander of Lanachrona."

"For me, and not Majer Draspyr?" asked Alucius.

"They were quite clear, sir," replied the scout.

"Ah . . . sir . . . perhaps just the one with the message," Egyl suggested from where he rode beside Alucius.

"Have them all ride to us, but invite the three without the message to join the vanguard," Alucius said.

Egyl nodded.

When the messenger in the blue and cream of the Southern Guard arrived, he managed not to show overt surprise at the reduced forces and their tattered appearance, but Alucius could feel his shock nonetheless.

"We've been fighting for almost a season, trooper," Alucius said dryly, "and we've either been outnumbered or fighting Talent-creatures that haven't been seen since the Cataclysm."

"Yes, sir."

Alucius forced a smile.

"Sir, we were ordered to deliver this to you personally and asked to have you open it immediately." The messenger moved his mount toward Alucius.

Egyl intercepted the flat, sealed message, then leaned sideways and handed it to Alucius.

Alucius took it, broke the seal, and began to read.

Honored Overcaptain Alucius—
Word of your triumph in defeating the grassland nomads and turning back their invasion of Deforya has reached the Lord-Protector. He is most pleased with your success and would wish

to reward you in person, for your leadership, and for your
achievements and for those of the troopers under your
command . . .

Alucius frowned. The last thing he wanted to do was meet the Lord-
Protector.

Therefore, you are to return to Salaan, where you will return any
Southern Guards to the commander of Salaan Post, then to
Dekhron. After reporting to Colonel Weslyn, you are to proceed
immediately to Tempre by the high road, with a full squad of your
own choosing from among those who accompanied you. The
guards bearing this missive will remain with you for the journey.
Once in Tempre you are to report to the Southern Guard
headquarters, and to me personally, before you meet with the
Lord-Protector . . .

The message—or orders—bore the signature of a Marshal Wyerl,
Arms-Commander of Lanachrona, as well as an elaborate gold seal.

To go to Tempre? Why? If the Lord-Protector had wanted to reward
Alucius, he certainly could have done so with far less effort. And if he
had wanted Alucius killed, that, too, could have been done more easily.
By effectively telling all of the Southern and Northern Guard that Alucius was to be rewarded in Tempre, that made his death less likely. Or
did it?

What if he were attacked by brigands along the way? Or was he
becoming overly fearful?

"Sir?" asked Egyl.

"The Lord-Protector is pleased with what we have done, and com-
mends everyone. We are ordered to Dekhron first. After we report there,
he has requested that I bring one representative squad and travel to
Tempre to receive his congratulations in person . . ."

"In person?" blurted the messenger. "That is a great honor."

Alucius feared it was a far greater honor than he wished to receive.

82

The high road west was straight, dusty, untraveled, and long. It took Alucius's tired force a week more after leaving the Upper Spine Mountains to reach the road fort at Senelmyr. There he insisted that they rest for two days, much as he wanted to finish the journey. The small Southern Guard detachment remaining at the road fort was helpful in repairing an axle on one of the supply wagons—helpful, but withdrawn.

Once Alucius and the remnants of four companies resumed their travels, they rode for another five days before nearing Salaan. Just before midafternoon, south of Salaan the high road turned abruptly north, one of the few sharp curves on any of the high roads, and the only one Alucius could recall that did not involve a junction.

Heslyn, one of the guards sent as a messenger, was riding with Egyl, behind Alucius and Feran. "Overcaptain, Salaan Post is just before the bridge over the river."

Alucius turned in the saddle. "How far from here?"

"Five, six vingts," replied Heslyn.

Only when the column was within two vingts of Salaan, the town's low dwellings visible on the northern horizon, did Alucius begin to see more than scattered steads and dwellings rising out of the brown-grassed rises. The only trees were those planted close to dwellings, small orchards of a tree not more than five or six yards tall.

"What are the trees?" Alucius finally asked.

"Apricots," answered Heslyn. "They dry well. We eat many of them."

Alucius couldn't recall seeing dried apricots in Iron Stem.

"They don't send them north," Feran said. "Wonder why."

Alucius shrugged. "Another thing they don't tell officers. Among many."

"You're just finding that out?"

"Along with other things."

Feran chuckled.

Within a quarter glass, they reached the first houses on the southern side of Salaan—low structures with only slightly slanted lean-to roofs, their outer walls covered with stucco plaster shaded an off-white. Windows were narrow slits, without shutters, and none of the houses had front porches, only stoops in front of narrow doors.

"The traders have their dwellings to the west, on the bluff overlooking the river," Heslyn volunteered.

"Of course," murmured Feran.

Alucius looked westward, but could not see over the more modest dwellings.

There were handfuls of people along the high road north of the troopers, but they slipped away, so the troopers rode past houses with closed doors and without people in sight. Those around the central square of Salaan did not vanish, but moved off the high road and the surrounding streets, to the entryways and narrow overhangs of shops— not porches, but areas of shade, from where they watched the riders. Alucius picked out a chandlery, a cooperage, a potter, and, surprisingly, a weaver's shop—as well as an inn. The inn's sign had no lettering, just the image of a tankard. With the exception of the high road, all the other streets entering the square were unpaved.

"Friendly folk," observed Feran.

"Don't suppose the people in Iron Stem or Dekhron would go out of their way if three companies of Southern Guards rode through," Alucius said.

"But they won," Feran pointed out.

Not the people in Salaan, Alucius thought. He had expected Salaan to be a larger place.

"Won't be far, now, Overcaptain," Heslyn offered. "Half vingt or less."

Because Alucius had been ordered to leave Twenty-third Company in Salaan, he had brought forward Sarapyr and Aelyn—the only two survivors of the company. They rode directly behind Egyl and Heslyn.

As Alucius rode northward out of the square, the most obvious structure as they neared the river was the gray eternastone of the bridge over the River Vedra, a bridge Alucius might once have called grand, rising as it did behind and above the low dwellings. But that would have been before he had seen the massive and graceful structures over the Vedra at Hieron, or the stone canyon through the Upper Spine Mountains.

As he neared the structure, he could see that the bridge held a roadway twice the width of the high road, but without the dividing curb of larger bridges. The stone guardhouse on the southern side had not been removed, as Feran had been required to do with the one in Emal, but the gates had been opened wide and chained back, and there were no Southern Guards in evidence.

"To the right, sir, just before the guardhouse," Heslyn suggested.

Alucius nodded to Egyl.

"Column right!" ordered the squad leader.

Alucius turned Wildebeast to the right, down a walled lane barely wide enough for three horses abreast, toward a set of open gates thirty yards away. The two guards by the gate scrambled erect as they caught sight of the riders.

Alucius reined up short of the guards.

"Column halt!"

"Sir?" the voice of the younger guard wavered.

"Overcaptain Alucius, Northern Guard. We're on our way to Dekhron, returning from Deforya, with orders to return those of Twenty-third Company here."

"Yes, sir. I'm sure you're welcome, sir. We'll fetch the overcaptain, sir. Just ride in."

Alucius nodded and continued into the dusty courtyard where he reined up. "Hold position!"

They didn't have to wait long.

The overcaptain who appeared shortly was thin, graying, and a good fifteen years older than Alucius. And nervous. He looked up at Alucius.

316   L. E. MODESITT, JR.

"Overcaptain? I received word that you would be returning Twenty-third Company." He glanced past Alucius, clearly looking for more blue-and-cream uniforms.

"Overcaptain. Sarapyr and Aelyn are the sole survivors of Twenty-third Company." Alucius turned Wildebeast slightly so that the Southern Guard officer could see the two.

"Two men . . . just two?" The Southern Guard overcaptain's voice wavered between disbelief, concern, and horror.

"You may not have heard," Alucius said quietly. "We faced over a hundred companies of nomads. We also had to fight off pteridons ridden by nomads with skylances. We broke them and killed close to seventy companies. We did take some casualties." He smiled coldly. "We left with six officers and over five hundred troopers. We came back with three officers and a hundred and sixty troopers. Oh, and the Deforyans lost over half their lancers as well."

The Southern Guard overcaptain shrank under Alucius's gaze. "We weren't told."

"Twenty-Third Company was the company that faced the pteridons first, and they took very heavy losses from the beginning, before we could find a way to destroy the beasts. Sarapyr and Aelyn can tell you all that happened. They showed great courage and unbelievable bravery," Alucius concluded. He decided against mentioning that all the troopers had done the same.

"Majer Draspyr? Captain Clifyr?"

"They were both killed leading their men. The Lord-Protector and Marshal Wyerl already know all this." Alucius smiled, professionally. "We still have to reach Dekhron. I'm not their commander, but I strongly suggest that Aelyn and Sarapyr deserve a healthy furlough." He turned, "Aelyn, Sarapyr?"

The two Southern Guards eased their mounts out of the column and to the side.

The overcaptain looked from the two troopers to Alucius, then back at the troopers.

"Furlough would be the least that they deserve," Alucius said mildly, projecting a sense of rightness and justice.

The overcaptain radiated confusion.

"I'm supposed to meet with the Lord-Protector," Alucius added. "I'm certain that he'll ask me about the Twenty-third Company." This time Alucius projected command and power.

The overcaptain stepped back. "Yes, they should have furlough. They should."

Alucius smiled. "I'm glad to know that. So will the Lord-Protector." After a moment, he added, "We'll be on our way." He glanced to Feran and Egyl, then ordered, "To the rear, ride."

As the column made its way back out through the open gates, Alucius could hear the whisper from Heslyn to Egyl. "Is he . . . I mean . . ."

"He leads from the front and stands behind his men. Always has," Egyl replied. "Saw him take a bullet in the shoulder and never wince. Finished the battle, too."

That was an exaggeration, but Alucius wasn't about to correct Egyl, not in front of anyone. He did look to Feran and give the slightest of helpless shrugs.

Feran grinned back, then murmured, "Good thing you're getting out. Be impossible to live up to your legends."

Alucius just hoped that neither the colonel nor the Lord-Protector— or Marshal Wyerl, for that matter—had any unpleasant surprises along those lines.

The hoofs of the mounts echoed on the bridge, without other traffic except for two wagons heading southward, empty, back to Salaan. Alucius glanced at the River Vedra. The cracking mud banks on each side told him that the river was flowing well below normal levels. So did the trade piers to the west, where temporary extensions had been built farther out into the water. Only a single barge was tied up, with a handful of loaders moving barrels about on the stern section. The guardhouse on the northern shore, once manned by the militia, was empty, but, unlike on the southern side, the gates had actually been removed.

The entrance of the high road into Dekhron reminded Alucius of Hieron, because the causeway clearly predated much of the trade section close to the river, and ramps and inclined roads had been built later to connect to the eternastone surface. The buildings were much more like those in Iron Stem, mostly of stone, and with either tile or slate roofs. A number of those nearest the river piers were two or even three stories in height. While not crowded, merchants, buyers, passersby, and occasional beggars were all visible on the streets and lanes of Dekhron. A number looked up at the passing troopers, but almost all looked away as quickly as they had lifted their heads.

Disinterest? Veiled anger? Alucius could sense both, as well as regret.

"Little more lively here," observed Feran. "Best if we turn at the street short of the square. Runs straight to headquarters."

Unlike in Salaan, the headquarters of the Northern Guard was not on the river, but slightly north and to the west. Alucius had no doubts that was because the space closer to the river and the high road were far more valuable to the traders who had controlled the council and the militia. "I thought that was it, but you've been here more than I have."

"More than I'd like," Feran admitted. "Would have liked to go back to Emal."

Alucius nodded. So would he, but they'd been ordered to Dekhron.

Dekhron felt tired. That was the only way Alucius could have described the town. Once he might have called it a city, but half its streets were dusty packed clay, and only the area around the river piers contained even halfway-imposing structures.

The column turned westward and rode on, passing smaller dwellings. Now and again, a child looked up at the dusty troopers, and once, a mother dragged a youngster away from the dusty avenue.

Headquarters was a much larger version of Emal Post, clearly visible from several hundred yards away, with a stone wall enclosing a space almost half a vingt on a side, and stables, barracks, and officers' quarters all of dressed limestone, with split-slate roofs on all the buildings, and stone pavement covering all the courtyard spaces. The two troopers at the front gate stiffened as they caught sight of the column riding down the avenue that paralleled the river.

Alucius rode forward, then slowed Wildebeast. "Overcaptain Alucius and four companies reporting as ordered."

"Yes, sir."

Alucius didn't wait for acknowledgment, but just kept riding, gesturing for the rest of the column to follow. He had barely reined up outside the stables on the south side of the outpost when Colonel Weslyn appeared, followed by a captain and several squad leaders. The colonel wore a well-tailored and immaculate black uniform with the blue silk shoulder wedges. Alucius was all too aware of his worn uniform and the hastily mended rent in his sleeve.

"Overcaptain Alucius! Welcome back! You and your troopers have done the impossible." Weslyn smiled broadly. "That's what the Lord-Protector claims, and who are we to argue with the Lord-Protector?"

"It all depends on what you mean by impossible, Colonel." Before Weslyn could answer, Alucius added, "We killed pteridons and their riders who used the ancient skylances, and we destroyed over seventy companies of nomads after the Deforyans were trapped and surrounded. The Landarch of Deforya awarded us the Star of Gallantry and reprovisioned us and sent us home. The Lord-Protector agreed, and here we are."

"Indeed you are." Weslyn offered another overbroad smile. "I imagine you are road-weary and would like to settle your men."

"And our mounts." Alucius looked back toward the end of the column at the supply wagons. "We do have some supplies left. Not many, but some that might be useful. They'll need to be unloaded. I'm sure you have some troopers who could do that."

"That we do."

Alucius would have distrusted the colonel's helpfulness, even had he not picked up the sense of anger and discomfort behind the pleasant words. He waited.

"Arms-Commander Wyerl has conveyed his appreciation of the tasks you accomplished and he has commended the Northern Guard. Once you have gotten your men quartered, and settled in the visiting officers' quarters . . . As an overcaptain in charge of multiple companies, you rate senior officers' quarters." Weslyn paused, then went on. "Majer Imealt and I would like to take you and your officers to dinner, not just at the mess. You deserve better than that."

"Thank you, sir. I think Captain Feran, Captain Koryt, and I would very much appreciate that."

"Until then, Overcaptain, Captains. Captain Dezyn will help you and answer any questions."

At the colonel's nod, the slender blond captain stepped forward. Weslyn smiled broadly before heading back into the headquarters building.

"Sir . . . how many troopers . . ."

"One hundred and sixty-one, plus three squad leaders, ten wagoners, and seven wagons. And three officers. Also, ten spare mounts." Except they hadn't been spare until after the fight with the nomads. "We've got troopers assigned to three companies, but they came from four."

"Yes, sir. The best barracks are the north ones, and they're empty and clean . . ."

Alucius nodded.

It took more than a glass to get the mounts stabled and the troopers settled, and Alucius found himself escorted up the steps to the top level of the officers' quarters by Captain Dezyn, carrying both rifles and saddlebags.

Dezyn looked at the pair of rifles, but said nothing until they reached the top of the steps. "You have your pick, sir, but the second quarters are the best."

"I'll take them." Alucius hoped they would be clean, and the bed decent.

"Ah . . . sir. The colonel will meet you below in just over half a glass."

"Thank you for reminding me." Alucius forced a smile. As tired as he was, he dreaded having dinner with the colonel, but his tiredness was probably why the colonel was insisting—and including Koryt and Feran. "Would you mind telling Captain Feran and Captain Koryt?"

"No, sir. I'd planned to." Dezyn opened the second door off the balcony. "The key is on the desk, and linens are already here."

"Thank you." Alucius stepped inside and closed the door.

The room was clean, and larger than any quarters Alucius had seen in the Iron Valleys—a good six yards by four, with a double-width bed, a large writing desk, twin wall lamps, an armoire, a weapons rack, boot trees, and an attached washroom. But then, he'd never been put in senior quarters before. That worried him—almost as much as having dinner with the colonel.

All he really wanted to do was get back to Wendra and the stead. He had been able to handle—if barely—nomads and raiders and battles. What he hadn't been able to best was golds and intrigue, and he worried that somehow getting back to the stead and his wife was going to be far harder than it seemed, even if he didn't know why.

Slowly, he hung up his gear and undressed, before walking to the washroom.

It took the full half glass just to wash up and clean off his uniform as well as he could.

After dressing, he rebelted his sabre and walked to the door. He took a deep breath and stepped out into the late afternoon. The colonel and a dapper majer with smooth black hair and deep blue eyes were waiting at the base of the stairs up to the senior officer's quarters. Feran and Koryt had already joined them.

Weslyn nodded to the majer. "Overcaptain Alucius, this is Majer Imealt."

Alucius inclined his head. "I'm pleased to meet you."

"The pleasure is mine, Overcaptain. Tales of your exploits are already legend."

"I fear that I could not live up to any such tales," Alucius demurred. "I'm just a herder who's tried to do his best."

"Would that we had more such."

"You don't mind walking a few yards, do you?" asked the colonel. "I had thought we would go to Elyset's. The board says it's the Red Ram, but everyone calls it by her name. I sent someone over to have her hold the large corner table for us."

"You know where it might be best," Alucius replied. "So long as it's not too far."

"It's close, and very friendly," Majer Imealt added.

"I take it that it was a long ride back," commented Weslyn, walking beside Alucius and leading the way toward the smaller south gate, an archway in the wall, guarded by but a single trooper, large enough only for those on foot.

"More than two weeks. We had to stop a few days at Fort Senelmyr. Both the men and the horses needed the rest." Alucius offered a head-shake. "I didn't realize how barren it is to the east. There's nothing there."

"It is a long road, I've been told," Weslyn said. "How did you find the Lanachronan majer?"

"He was a bit doubtful at first, but, in the end, we got along well. I'd say he was a good officer. He was just unlucky enough to be caught in the wrong place in the final battle."

Weslyn was right about one thing. The Red Ram was less than a hundred yards south of the post, an old redstone building set on the corner, with ancient and narrow windows. Elyset met them at the door. The graying proprietress smiled professionally at the colonel. "The corner table's ready for you, Colonel."

Alucius could sense that she didn't care much for Weslyn, smile or not, and that the colonel knew it and didn't care.

"Thank you, Elyset." Weslyn gestured to Alucius. "This is Overcaptain Alucius. He's the one who led the force that turned back the nomads."

Alucius smiled and inclined his head, projecting warmth and friendliness. "We did what needed to be done. I'm pleased to meet you." He grinned. "What's the tastiest thing you have tonight?"

Elyset laughed, as Alucius hoped she would. "He's a real trooper, Colonel!" She turned to Alucius, and said in a lower voice, "there's some quail. Girls won't tell you, but tell 'em I told you."

"I'll tell them."

Weslyn repressed a frown and forced a smile. "I told you he was."

Alucius nodded toward the two captains to the right of Majer Imealt. "So are they. Couldn't have done it without them."

"Let's get you seated." Elyset moved away from the officers, leading the way toward the corner beside a cold hearth covered with a wicker screen. "Here you go."

The majer and the colonel moved to seat themselves in the armless wooden chairs on each side of Alucius. While he might have avoided it, he decided to be oblivious to the maneuver.

Lagging slightly behind the others, Feran caught Alucius's eye and raised his eyebrows. Alucius returned the gesture with the slightest of nods at the moment when the colonel and majer were seating themselves. Feran grinned, then wiped the expression from his mouth.

"What'll you swells have?" asked the server, a woman neither young nor old.

"What do you have?" asked Imealt.

"You know the drinks. Tonight . . . there's stew. Always stew. Lamb cutlets, and the Vedra chicken with the heavy noodles. And lymbyl."

"Lymbyl with the good red wine," Imealt ordered.

Both captains chose the chicken with ale, and the colonel had the lymbyl with ale. The server looked at Alucius.

Some folk couldn't get enough of lymbyl, but Alucius had never liked the eel-like fish. "The ale . . . and . . . ah . . . Elyset mentioned something about quail . . ."

"Might be some. Let you know." With that, the server was gone.

Imealt turned to Koryt. "You're commanding the Third *and* Eleventh Companies?"

"What's left of them, sir. Fifty-seven troopers in all." Koryt waited.

"You said you had something like a hundred and sixty men left out of four hundred?" Weslyn inquired of Alucius, almost absently, as if he had to ask something.

"That's about right. About a third of our losses came in the Barrier Range, after the Deforyans withdrew and left us holding Black Ridge. The rest came after we fought clear and got back to Dereka and had to defend the city. Aellyan Edyss had somewhere over a hundred companies. And the pteridons."

"Pteridons?"

Alucius could sense the colonel's surprise, and that bothered him because he'd already mentioned the pteridons. Hadn't the man been listening? "We didn't find out about that until we met the Southern Guards at Senelmyr. We were all worried when Majer Draspyr told us." Alucius decided against mentioning that the pteridons had routed the forces of the Praetor of Lustrea. "That was one reason why they wanted the Northern Guard. We carry heavier rifles, and they thought that anything that was good against a sander might be better than what they had against a pteridon."

"I gather it was," Weslyn suggested.

"Not as good as we'd have liked, but we managed." Alucius picked up the beaker of ale the server had set before him and took a slow swallow.

"I understand that you and the Deforyans routed the nomads, and they returned to Illegea."

"Not exactly, sir," Feran replied before Alucius could. "The nomads tried to encircle everyone. The overcaptain used a tight formation, we broke free. Let us shoot down the pteridons and catch the blue bastards from behind."

"Blue . . ."

"Oh, the nomads wore blue breastplates," Feran replied. "We killed so many that the Landarch covered his courtyard wall with them. Deforyans aren't all that good."

"Ah . . ." Imealt glanced at Koryt. "You haven't said much, Captain."

"Not much to say, sir. Captain Feran had it right. Without the over-captain, we'd have been slaughtered. Instead, we did the slaughtering. Lost a lot of troopers, but they lost a lot more." Koryt took refuge behind his beaker of ale.

"The dispatch from Marshal Wyerl said that the nomads brought over a hundred companies against you." Weslyn's voice conveyed polite doubt.

"I don't know the exact number," Alucius admitted. "But the Landarch recovered something like six thousand breastplates. There could have been more, but that's how many he had attached to the walls."

"Quite an accomplishment," Weslyn replied. "No wonder the Lord-Protector wishes to see you . . ."

"Here you go!" The server slid platters in front of each of the men.

Alucius noted that he had gotten his quail. He waited only until the others had theirs before cutting and taking a bite. He was hungry, and the fowl was tasty—and tender.

For a brief time, no one talked, but it wasn't long before Weslyn finished a sip of his wine and looked once more at Alucius. "It's a very rare honor, even in Lanachrona, to be summoned to the Lord-Protector."

"I'd heard that."

"And you are representing the Northern Guard—all of us, so to speak. It's at a time when golds are short here in the north . . ."

"They've always been short," interjected Feran dryly.

"Ah, yes. That they have, but perhaps with the performance that you all have achieved the Lord-Protector might look upon us more favorably and more wisely than did the Council . . ."

Alucius wondered if it were possible to have looked less wisely than had the Council.

". . . future assignments . . . promotions . . . all those hang in the balance at present . . .

As Weslyn continued to talk, pressing Alucius to provide favorable information to the Lord-Protector, Alucius took in two traders, one round-faced and in a dark blue tunic, and the second, white-haired and in black, who sat at a wall table less than three yards away. Although they talked to each other, and ate, they also listened, often intently. Alucius made a point of not looking at them, even as he wondered why they were interested—and what exactly they wanted. More than once, he could feel their eyes on him.

". . . important that the Lord-Protector can believe that the Northern Guard is trustworthy as well as effective . . ."

For the rest of the meal, Alucius mainly listened—and ate—and tried to keep from yawning too often, tired as he was.

No one spoke much on the way back to the post.

Outside the visiting officers' quarters, Colonel Weslyn offered last words. "I'll see you all in the morning, after the regular muster, but you and your men are excused from that."

"Thank you," Alucius replied, waiting and watching until the colonel and the majer left.

After that, Alucius made sure that Egyl and the squad leaders knew that they and the troopers did not have to muster, although, if they wanted to eat, they'd still have to get up early. Then he climbed the steps to his room. Even before he had done more than loosen his sword belt, there was a knock on the door to Alucius's quarters. Alucius could sense Feran even before he opened the door and motioned for the other to enter.

"What do you think?" asked Feran, glancing back at the closed door.

"Weslyn's worried. The traders don't trust him; the Lord-Protector doesn't trust him. I'd be worried too."

"You think they'll still send Fifth Company to Eastice?"

"Not immediately, I'd guess. They'll have to consolidate companies. They might merge Twenty-first Company and Fifth Company—if they let me go back to being a herder. If they do that, I'd guess you'd get— we'll all get a month of furlough, then light duty for a month, and then they'll send you someplace like Wesrigg for a season . . ."

"And *then* to Eastice?"

"Or Soulend for an attack on Madrien," Alucius suggested.

"You're always so cheerful. You really think they'll let you go?"

"I worry about it," Alucius admitted. "I worry a lot."

"How could they hold you?"

"Threaten to raise tariffs on nightsilk, or on the stead lands. Or the Lord-Protector could just order me to stay." Alucius shook his head. "Just what could I do if they did any of that?"

"You couldn't."

"Exactly." Alucius paused. "But, if it comes up . . . and I can, I'll see what I can do for you and Fifth Company."

"You don't—"

"Who else? I'd rather have you with Fifth Company—and Twenty-first." Alucius stifled a yawn.

"You're tired."

"Aren't we all?"

"Get some sleep." Feran smiled. "I'll see you in the morning."

After Feran left, Alucius disrobed slowly. What could he do? What should he do? And he still didn't know why the spirit-woman had shown him the mural in Dereka, but he feared what might happen when he found out.

83

Alucius had spent most of the morning working with the clerks at Northern Guard headquarters to arrange for the back pay of troopers, since his stocks of golds—those sent to the companies before leaving Emal—had run out at about the time he had been recovering from his wounds in Dereka. Then, he'd had to argue over sending the two-gold payment to the families of the dead—the golds supplied by the Landarch—because he didn't have the records of families with him. Even Majer Imealt had sided with him on that, but that could have been because the golds weren't coming out of the Northern Guard's treasury.

After that, he'd had to arrange for replacement uniforms and gear, then write out the letters and appointments necessary to promote Egyl to senior squad leader and four other experienced troopers to squad leader. By that time, it was almost noon.

Immediately after the midday dinner, Alucius slipped back to his comparatively capacious quarters and wrote a letter to Wendra, knowing that at last he had a chance to get word to her.

My dearest Wendra—
This letter will tell you that I am alive and well, if only recently returned to full strength. I was wounded in the final battle at Dereka, but we prevailed, and the nomads retreated to Illegea. It did take several weeks for me to recover enough to be able to ride, and then two more weeks on the high road before we reached Dekhron yesterday.

328   L. E. MODESITT, JR.

I am still in Dekhron, but I will not be heading home soon. I am preparing for a journey to Tempre to meet the Lord-Protector, since he has requested my presence to congratulate me on behalf of all those in the Northern Guard. It is still hard at times to think that we are the Northern Guard of Lanachrona, rather than the militia of the Iron Valleys. How long the journey and return will last, I do not know, but it will take several days even before we can depart. I also have no idea how long I will be in Tempre. I will be accompanied by a full squad, but not by the entire company, or what remains of Twenty-first Company. We left the Iron Valleys with four companies at close to full strength, and returned with fewer than two. Twenty-first Company was more fortunate than the others, but we came back with little more than half those who left.

I was most surprised at how empty and how barren the eastern part of northern Lanachrona is, and how few live there. It is almost as dry as our quarasote lands, but dusty rather than sandy. I fear I would never be a southerner. I miss the cool and the open spaces of the stead, and you most of all, and I look forward to the time when I can lay aside the uniform and return.

With all my love

After signing the missive, Alucius folded and sealed it, then wrote Wendra's name and the address of her father's cooperage in Iron Stem on the outside before slipping it inside his tunic until he found a guard messenger headed north.

He slowly stood and stretched, then headed out of his quarters. He still had to arrange for the reshoeing of a number of mounts. He also had to write up a report on the losses of mounts and equipment in the battles in Deforya. The colonel had insisted on the report, explaining that while such reports were a formality, they were still required by the Arms-Commander of Lanachrona. Alucius wondered how many other letters and reports would be necessary over the next few days.

84

Tempre, Lanachrona

In the gray light of a cloudy morning, not long after dawn, the Recorder of Deeds stood in his undergarments before the mirror in his private quarters, an apartment consisting of a capacious but not luxurious sitting chamber, a bedchamber, and a combined washroom and dressing room. The quarters had always been those of the Recorder of Deeds and were located on the second level of the Lord-Protector's palace, a structure rebuilt—and greatly enlarged—several generations earlier upon the foundations of another structure. The Recorder's chambers were located above the ancient foundations and the underground chambers that had survived the Cataclysm and more.

After taking from the unmarked blue bottle the unguent he had formulated earlier, the Recorder slowly worked it into his dark black hair, then brushed his hair thoroughly. As he brushed, his hair lightened into silver. He studied his reflected visage for a long moment, then set the hairbrush aside. Next, he poured the contents of a second brownish bottle into his hands, and worked the lotionlike liquid into his skin, so that when he had finished, his face appeared lightly tanned, rather than shimmering white. Finally, he lifted a tiny brush and dipped it in a dark liquid. Carefully, most carefully, he applied the liquid along the faintest remnants of the lines that had once creased his face. When he finished, he nodded approvingly before replacing the containers in the plain wooden box. He returned the box to the hidden compartment in the false back of the commode.

Only then did he don his silver vestments as Recorder of Deeds and turn toward the door to begin his day.

85

Alucius struggled through yet another day filled with more administrative details, including having to get authorization from the overcaptain who handled the accounts for horses in order to pay the farrier for reshoeing some fifty mounts, then having to use his Talent to persuade the quartermaster to issue more uniforms without charging the troopers. The quartermaster captain had wanted to insist that the damaged and missing uniforms were the result of carelessness and not normal wear. The captain's new quartermaster's manual—sent from Tempre—did not mention battle damage. By using his orders from the Lord-Protector—and his Talent—Alucius managed to get the uniforms for all the returned troopers under the rubric of "at the request of the Lord-Protector."

He walked around the courtyard for a quarter of a glass after that, taking long and slow deep breaths, before returning to the headquarters building to meet, again, with Colonel Weslyn.

Weslyn had a study on the second level of the building, with a balcony overlooking the courtyard. The double doors were open when Alucius stepped into the room, but the colonel was seated behind an old walnut desk and did not rise.

Weslyn set down the papers he held and looked over the low stacks of papers neatly arranged across the front of the desk. "Good afternoon, Overcaptain. How are matters coming?"

Alucius glanced at the stacks of papers. "I'd thought I'd seen enough paper, but I'd not want to go through all those."

"The Northern Guard has more reports than the militia did, I fear. It has its advantages and disadvantages. The Council did not wish to see reports, and what they did not wish to see spelled the end of their power, and now I must report directly to the Arms-Commander of Lanachrona. The reports mean that we can explain our situations and our needs, but they take far too much time." The colonel shrugged. "You had asked to see me?"

"Yes, sir. The Council is no longer—"

"The Lord-Protector dissolved it. He threatened to execute any of the members who protested, then gave them amnesty. Now . . . what did you have in mind?"

Alucius decided against asking more about the Council. "I had hoped we could talk about the companies that returned from Deforya, if you would not mind." Alucius looked at the well-dressed colonel.

"Part of that will not be my decision at all," Weslyn replied smoothly. "I will be making my recommendations to Marshal Wyerl. He is the arms-commander over both the Northern and the Southern Guards, you know, and he will either accept or change my recommendations. It may be some time before we hear. I had thought, based on your recommendation, that we would give the men a month's furlough. With luck, by the time they return, we will know how to proceed." Weslyn smiled. "What would you suggest?"

Alucius returned the smile with one equally false, and probably as transparent. "Before we left Emal Outpost, you had mentioned that the Lord-Protector was more interested in adding and reinforcing Northern Guard posts to the north and west. Because we have been well away from the Iron Valleys, I have no knowledge of what has been recommended and accomplished. I would not wish to suggest something contrary to his and your desires. If you could enlighten me, briefly, on where matters stand, and what posts are short of companies?"

The colonel leaned back slightly in the old wooden armchair, smiling more broadly. "Yes . . . we must consider what is possible, and I wish more officers understood that."

Alucius ignored the implication that he didn't, continued smiling politely, and waited.

"The outpost at Soulend was moved to the former stead at the west end of the valley just short of the Westerhills—the same stead, I believe, where the Matrites encamped. It has been expanded to a staging base capable of holding as many as ten companies. There are five there at present. Matters have been slower farther north. This summer we completed a small post for two companies in Eastice, and work is proceeding on a temporary post in the Westerhills east of Klamat. The arms-commander had hoped to begin a northern campaign late this summer, but the logistics dissuaded him. The post in Wesrigg has also been expanded, and there are now five companies there, with space for another five."

"I see. You have twelve companies on the high roads leading to the northern part of Madrien. We had four companies, and I would assume that you have a company here. If I might ask, where are the other four stationed? Along the River Vedra to the west?"

"Exactly." The colonel smiled. "In fact, the arms-commander has been so impressed with the performance of the Northern Guard that he has indicated that we will receive enough golds to recruit enough troopers to replace those lost in Deforya and train and add three more companies before next spring."

Alucius could feel his stomach tighten. Clearly, the Lord-Protector intended to use the Northern Guard as the spearhead of the northern assault on Madrien. While Alucius had no great love of Madrien, he also did not see much good in having the troopers of the Iron Valleys die in such an assault, when the benefits would go almost entirely to the south, effectively weakening the Iron Valleys and further strengthening Lanachrona.

Yet, the traders would approve—or not oppose the strategy, Alucius was certain, because it would put more golds in their coffers. More mounts would be purchased, more saddles, more uniforms, and more supplies, and Dekhron would become even more tightly bound to Tempre and Lanachrona—and the herders of the north would become even more isolated.

"Where would you recommend that your companies go?" asked the colonel. "After their furlough?"

Alucius didn't want to answer the question. If he made a recommendation, it was effectively endorsing the strategy. "I've been away for a time, Colonel, and I might have missed something . . . but . . . there are a couple of matters. First, more than half of Twenty-first Company troopers finish their tours at year-end."

"Including their overcaptain, and I've been told that your releases will be honored. I had thought that those remaining in Twenty-first Company would be transferred to Fifth Company, except perhaps for any who might be good squad leader material in another company. What else?"

"Well . . . it seems to me that we'll be fighting the same war a second time, except that the Lord-Protector will be supplying the golds while we provide the men and blood."

Weslyn tilted his head to the side, then nodded thoughtfully. "That is a real possibility, Overcaptain. It's not a good bargain, but it's the best one we could strike. The Iron Valleys are poor, far poorer than anyone outside the former Council ever knew. We could not have raised the golds to fight off the Lanachronans. We were without the golds even to pay the militia we had, and that was without being in a fight. We had no golds even for ammunition. And a war would have destroyed us. The Southern Guard has been fighting Madrien in the south. They have taken Zalt, and hold Southgate. That was all that allowed us to push back the Matrites the last time. Fighting the Matrites again is not what any of us would wish, but it is far better than anything else that was going to happen."

Alucius could tell that the colonel honestly believed his own words. Worse, Alucius himself wasn't so sure that the colonel wasn't right. "I can't say that I like the situation . . ."

"Overcaptain, none of us likes it, and the former members of the Council will like it least of all in time. But you haven't addressed my question."

"If I had a choice for those companies," Alucius said quietly, "I'd request that they be assigned to Soulend."

"I would have thought Wesrigg."

"Wesrigg would be more pleasant, but the fighting will be worse, and they've fought a great deal with little support."

Colonel Weslyn frowned. "Why do you think the fighting will be worse out of Wesrigg?"

"Because the lower high road leads to Arwyn, and there are more Matrite companies there, and because Arwyn is far closer to Hieron and can be reinforced more directly and quickly."

"There won't be much fighting at all out of Eastice," Weslyn pointed out.

"No . . . but a number of troopers said they'd rather do some fighting than be that far north."

"You asked them?"

"No. They told me so in the spring, when you indicated that many companies would be reassigned. I just recalled what they said then."

"I see. Well . . . we'll see what we can do." Weslyn cleared his throat and squared his shoulders. "What squad do you intend to take to Tempre?"

"My orders from Marshal Wyerl stated that I was to bring a full squad of my choosing. I don't have a full squad anywhere. I thought I'd bring the third and fourth squads from Twenty-first Company. That works out to nineteen troopers. But I would still want them to get furlough when we return. A full month, the same as the others."

"That would be satisfactory. When do you plan to leave?"

"The day after tomorrow. That's as soon as everything will be ready."

"Good." With his professional smile, the colonel stood. "Let me know if there's anything else you need help with . . . although, from what I've seen, you do quite well without it, Overcaptain."

Alucius stood. "We do the best we can, sir." He bowed slightly, before leaving.

86

In the early evening, Feran and Alucius sat at one of the small wall tables at Elyset's Red Ram. Although the shutters were open to let in the cooler evening air, the main room was dim, the wall lamps not yet lit. Each officer had a beaker of amber ale before him.

"What did you find out from the colonel?" asked Feran, before taking a sip of the ale.

"Things are worse than we thought. The Council doesn't even control the Northern Guard any longer. The Lord-Protector just dissolved the Council. The colonel reports directly to the Arms-Commander of Lanachrona. The Lord-Protector is sending more golds, enough to raise and equip three more Northern Guard companies by next spring. That's for the attack on Madrien. The colonel didn't say that, but there's no other reason to build up the posts east of the Westerhills, and that will weaken us and strengthen Lanachrona by spending our troopers."

"And . . . Weslyn . . . the Council . . . they're accepting this?"

"What choice do they have? The Lord-Protector threatened to execute all the members of the Council. No one wanted to fight before. Do you think they would now? Even before that happened, before last spring, the Iron Valleys didn't have two golds to rub together. They didn't even have enough coin for ammunition to last the summer."

"So we go out and die so that they don't lose their golds. Is that it?"

"They will anyway, in time. No . . . we go out and fight on Madrien lands so that we don't fight on Iron Valley lands and so that blood doesn't flow inside our boundaries. We're the sacrifice for our families and friends." Except, Alucius refrained from saying, Feran would be the sacrifice if Alucius went back to being a herder.

"When you put it that way . . ." Feran sighed, then took a longer swallow of his ale.

"It doesn't make it much better," Alucius admitted. "It's still bad for anyone in the Northern Guard. It's better for most people, though."

"How . . . how did they ever let it get this bad?"

"You know as well as I do. The traders on the Council didn't want to spend the golds. Neither did the farmers and the crafters. Well . . . you pay one way or another, and now they'll all end up paying higher tariffs with less independence because they didn't want to pay higher tariffs before." Alucius took a sip of his own ale, then leaned back as the server eased the stew in front of him, and then set a basket of bread between the two men.

"Be a silver each, swells."

Alucius slipped out a silver and a copper, as did Feran.

Once the woman had left, Feran looked down at his cutlets. "Last year . . . got the same thing for three coppers."

"Prices will keep going up." Alucius broke off a chunk of the rye bread. He would have preferred the softer dark bread, but there wasn't any molasses, or so the server had said.

"So we pay more for food, too?"

His mouth full of the peppery stew, Alucius nodded.

"You get any chance to find out what they want to do with us?"

"The colonel asked for my recommendation. I tried to find out more, and that's when he told me about the extra companies. He wasn't happy about it, either."

"You have this habit of telling me things I'd rather not hear, Overcaptain."

"Might as well get all the bad things over. I suggested sending Fifth Company to Soulend."

"You volunteered us to go to Soulend?" asked Feran. "You know how I hate the cold."

"No . . . I was given choices. You could go to Eastice for the winter, or Soulend, or Wesrigg. At Wesrigg, you'd spearhead next spring's attack on Arwyn, where the Matrites will bring in every company and weapon they have. You told me you'd do anything to avoid Eastice. So I picked the next least bad choice."

"Sander-shit world where you win battles that should kill you and still have to settle for the least evil choice," Feran mumbled as he used his belt knife to cut off a section of cutlet.

"Would you rather have been in Eastice?"

"No. Soulend is better than that . . . think you're right about Wesrigg, too." Feran took another swallow of ale and held the empty beaker up. "What about you?"

"Leave the day after tomorrow for Tempre. The colonel let me consolidate third and fourth squads to take with me. I'll take Faisyn and leave Egyl in charge of the company—except they'll be on furlough. So will you. Everyone gets a month. We get a month when we get back."

"Nothing's happening this harvest or fall, then." Feran handed the beaker to the server.

"Except building up the posts in the Westerhills and training more troopers."

"Why do you think the Lord-Protector wants you to go to Tempre?"

"I don't know. It worries me. I'm just a lowly overcaptain, and a very junior one. He rules an entire land. If it's just a gesture, it's a strange one."

"Maybe . . . maybe he knows . . ."

"Knows?" Alucius replied disingenuously.

Feran snorted. "You're a herder. Everyone knows that." He lowered his voice and leaned forward. "More than a few troopers and Egyl and Koryt and I know that you're a lot more than that. We don't say anything because it works better that way, and you've saved our asses more than once. But there are tales about Talent-wielders in Tempre . . . and about a Table with a mirror that can see things that belongs to the Lord-Protector."

"You've said that before. When we were headed to Deforya."

"I did. Was I wrong? Could anyone else have stopped those pteridons?"

"I don't know."

"Alucius . . ." Feran's voice was low, but firm. "We both know the answer to that, and it's a good wager that the Lord-Protector does, too. You'd better be ready for that. He's going to want something. I can't guess what, but I'd not want to be in your boots for all the gold in Tempre."

Alucius laughed. The sound was hollow. "I'm not sure I'd like to be in them, either, but I am." He took a long swallow and finished the ale.

Feran shook his head, then took a deep draught of his second ale.

87

By late afternoon on Sexdi, two days after leaving Dekhron, Alucius and his reconstituted third squad—composed of those left from third and fourth squads—had reached the point on the high road where it rejoined the River Vedra. The dry grasslands of eastern Lanachrona had been replaced by tilled fields on both sides of the road, fields watered by mule-powered irrigation pumps that spewed river water into long narrow ditches. Rows of healthy maize alternated with rows of a shorter plant that Alucius did not recognize.

Although it was harvest, it was warm enough to have been full summer. Alucius took another swallow from his second water bottle before replacing it in its holder. He'd had plenty of time to think, and, for all that thought, there were still too many questions unanswered. Earlier, on the brief ride through Dekhron, the troopers had not only been ignored, but Alucius had felt the hostility. Was the militia, now the Northern Guard, being blamed for the annexation of the Iron Valleys into Lanachrona? And if that happened to be the case, he wondered who was spreading those sorts of tales. The two traders who had been watching him at the Red Ram? Former members of the Council, disgruntled and upset by the Lord-Protector's dissolution of the Council?

He kept the frown he felt to himself.

"Less than a glass to Borlan Post, sir," Heslyn called forward. "It's on this side of the river. The Vyana, I mean."

"Thank you." Alucius saw little ahead except steads and fields and two rivers, the Vyana to his left, running westward through the lower fields to the south, and the Vedra to his right.

A quarter glass passed, and Alucius could make out the walls of Borlan Post, set on the right side of the high road ahead, and situated on the higher triangle of land formed by the junction of the River Vedra and the River Vyana. While there were some dwellings around the post, the town was on the lower western side of the River Vyana, over the bridge that carried the high road.

At first, Alucius thought it strange that the high road crossed the Vyana, but not the Vedra, then turned south from Borlan to Krost, when it would have been far quicker to run the road straight from Borlan to Tempre. Then, as the image of the fast-moving ship from the mural in Dereka crossed his thoughts, he understood. The Vedra was wide and deep from Borlan westward, and the ancients would have used the river had they needed to travel directly to Tempre, while the high road opened up all of the south of Lanachrona.

The post itself had yellow brick walls close to three yards in height, with rows of two-story buildings within the walls.

"Sir . . . if you would allow me to announce you," suggested Heslyn.

"If you would . . ." It was a good idea, and one that Alucius should have thought of himself.

Heslyn pulled out of the column and galloped toward the post, then reined up at the gates, three hundred yards from where Alucius and the others rode. While Alucius watched, one of the two guards at the open gates scurried away, then returned within moments. Heslyn reined up and waited outside the gates.

When Alucius and third squad reached the stone road leading to the post, a road about fifty yards in length and cracked and repaired many times, they turned and rode toward the post gates. A trumpet sounded—off-key—a series of triplets.

"Never gotten a fanfare before," Faisyn murmured.

The trumpet sounded again as Alucius reached the sentries. Through the gates he could see a half squad of Southern Guards lined up in an honor guard of sorts. Just what had Heslyn told the sentries? That he and third squad were some sort of legendary heroes?

A blond Southern Guard majer stood beside ranked troopers who waited.

Alucius signaled for the squad to halt as he drew up Wildebeast inside the gates and opposite the honor guard.

"Squad halt!" Faisyn ordered.

"Overcaptain Alucius, Northern Guard, welcome to Borlan Post! You do us honor, and we offer all that we can to ease your journey." The majer smiled broadly.

Behind the smile, Alucius sensed both concern and curiosity, but he replied immediately. "Your courtesy and your friendliness do you honor, and we deeply appreciate the welcome."

The majer gestured, and a senior squad leader stepped forward. "Lethyn will see that your men are shown the stables and their quarters, and, of course, the mess. He can also make sure that any mounts that need attention can be attended by our farrier. He'll also help with resupplying you for the next part of your journey."

In turn, Alucius singled out his own squad leader. "This is Faisyn, third squad leader."

The two squad leaders conferred briefly, then third squad headed toward the stables in the northwest corner of the post.

"I'm Ebuin, temporarily in charge of Borlan Post," offered the majer. "Let's get you to the officers' stable, then I'll show you to the visiting officers' quarters." His voice was friendly.

"You're most kind." While Alucius did not sense the arrogance and falsity he had with some officers, such as Colonel Weslyn and the marshals of Deforya, Ebuin radiated a coolness.

"I'm most curious," Ebuin admitted. "But . . . if you don't mind, I'll defer that until later. I would hope that you would join me in the officers' mess after you're settled." The majer walked swiftly across the packed clay of the inner courtyard, halting outside an open archway at one end of the stables. "Take any open stall that suits you. I'll just wait out here."

True to his word, Ebuin was waiting after Alucius had groomed Wildebeast.

Alucius carried his saddlebags over his shoulder and a rifle in each hand.

"Two rifles?" Ebuin raised his eyebrows.

"At times, it has helped not to have to reload," Alucius admitted.

"I can see that." Ebuin turned and walked back toward the smaller two-story structure behind the headquarters building. "The visiting officers' quarters are the same as ours. They're just the last three rooms on the upper level. We all share the same washroom. Not many overcaptains or other senior officers come through here. Most of the fighting's been in the west. Except for your expedition."

"I thought you held Southgate."

"Marshal's been moving up the southwest coast road toward Fola. He wants to flank Dimor. They've got some weapon there."

"It's a crystal spear-thrower," Alucius volunteered. "Fires half-yard-long crystal spikes. Scores at a time."

"You've seen it?"

"They used it against us at Soulend. There's only one, and I'd heard it went south after they gave up in the north."

"I see." Ebuin stopped by the steps on the north side of the quarters' building. "Up these stairs. The officers' mess is at the front of the main mess building. I'll finish up the reports I was working on and meet you there in a glass. If that's suitable."

"That would be fine. I can get off some of the road dust," Alucius said with a smile. He also intended to check with Faisyn on how matters were with third squad. After the majer turned, Alucius climbed the steps.

The quarters consisted of a single modest room with a moderately wide bed for one, a writing desk, boot and weapons racks, and a narrow armoire. The water in the washroom was cool, but there was plenty, and Alucius used it to wash out one uniform and one set of nightsilk undergarments before washing himself. After dressing, he went down the back steps and made his way to the barracks.

Faisyn was dressing, and Alucius waited until the squad leader finished before slipping into the barracks. The floor was slightly dusty, but the sturdy bunks were well separated, and there were wall pegs for uniforms and weapons.

"How are things?"

"Better than most places, sir. Had to lean on a couple of them to wash up."

"Sylat?"

Faisyn laughed. "Him and Vercal."

"Anything we need that I don't know about?"

The squad leader frowned. "No, sir. One of the bottles of leather oil broke, but Lethyn already got us another."

"Good. I wanted to check before I met with the majer. I'll see you later, then."

"Yes, sir."

Ebuin was waiting in the small mess, with but three tables, and only one set for two people. The majer rose from the table as Alucius stepped inside. "Supper should be here in a moment." He gestured to the other place.

Alucius seated himself. A pitcher of amber ale sat on the table, with two empty beakers.

"It's good ale, the best part of the meals around here," offered the older blond officer. "Go ahead and pour."

Alucius filled both beakers and took the one on the left.

"The captain-colonel is in Tempre. Otherwise, I'm certain he would have joined us." Ebuin raised the ancient beaker. "To your health . . ."

"To yours." Alucius returned the toast, lifting his own beaker.

"We'd received instructions several weeks ago that you'd be coming through. They didn't say much except that you'd taken over command of the joint force after Majer Draspyr's death and that you'd routed the nomads attacking Dereka. You were heavily outnumbered, weren't you?"

"Could have been three to one, or four to one." Alucius took a small swallow of the ale. Ebuin had been right. The ale was cool, with just enough bite to cut through the dust in his throat.

"Did that include the Deforyans?"

"The Deforyan Lancers numbered twenty-five companies. We were down to four by then."

"The nomads had more than a hundred and twenty companies?"

"That's what one of the Deforyan marshals told me later. They collected more than six thousand nomad breastplates."

The number clearly surprised Ebuin, although he nodded and took a swallow of his ale before going on. "Someone mentioned that they had some sort of Talent-creatures . . ."

"Pteridons. Blue-skinned flying beasts with riders that had ancient skylances. The lances shot blue flames." Alucius paused as a serving boy carried in two large platters and set them in the middle of the table.

One contained strips of meat covered with a brownish sauce and lightly browned almonds, garnished with lime slices. The second held a glazed and fried rice.

"Whistlepig," Ebuin explained. "They're like scrats, except much larger and tamer. They taste like fowl."

Alucius had his doubts, but took several strips and a goodly amount of rice.

Ebuin sliced off several morsels and began to eat. Alucius followed, more carefully, deciding that the whistlepigs were edible, better than prickle, but not so good as fowl, and certainly not so good as the quail he'd had at Elyset's.

"About those pteridon things," Ebuin said, after a time. "I thought rifles weren't much good against Talent-beasts."

"It's harder. But we use larger cartridges than you do. Trade-off." Alucius had to take a quick swallow of the rice, because some sort of seasoning or pepper burned his mouth. "Larger cartridges means fewer in a magazine."

"That's why you carry two rifles?"

"One reason."

"How effective were your cartridges against the beasts?"

"Not nearly as effective as against the nomads," Alucius said with a rueful laugh. "We did kill them, but they only had something like eleven pteridons, and they wiped out about half the Deforyans."

"And they didn't get you?"

"They got enough of us. I could see what was coming . . ." Alucius gave a short description of his tight formation charge and what happened afterward, except for the details of darkening the bullets used against the pteridons. ". . . and when I could see again, I was being tended by some very elderly women. Then, after I was better, the Landarch pinned a decoration on me, overloaded us with supplies, and sent us packing."

"It is a rather amazing story, I must say," Ebuin observed. "I have the feeling that you have understated what you did. Otherwise, the Lord-Protector would not wish to see you."

"He seems to know a great deal," Alucius said blandly. "And often before he could have received messengers."

Ebuin did not reply.

"That's obvious," Alucius pressed. "He sent messengers to meet us, and they caught us just out of the Upper Spine Mountains. There was no way that a messenger could have ridden to him with the details and all the way back in that time. He must have some devices of his own."

"There are rumors," Ebuin said vaguely, "but that's not something I'd know. They don't tell majers that much."

Alucius could detect the lie, but only said, "And they tell overcaptains even less."

"Isn't it always so?"

"You've been here for a time, haven't you? At Borlan?"

"Two years. I'm supposed to be rotated west at year-end."

"When I was at Emal, we had several raider attacks. The raiders wore red, like Deforyans, but they weren't. You didn't know anything about that, did you?"

"I'd heard that there were raiders out east, but we never saw any," Ebuin said smoothly.

"You were fortunate." Alucius took another swallow of the ale, then refilled his beaker. He looked to the other officer.

"Yes, thank you." Ebuin raised the beaker slightly, then drank. "It's said that Dereka is a very old city."

"It's very old. The Landarch's palace was built before the Cataclysm, and the city is served by an aqueduct equally old."

"You won't find anything in Tempre that ancient," Ebuin offered. "The Lord-Protector and his sire have rebuilt almost everything, except for his palace, but that was totally reconstructed by his grand-sire . . ."

From that point onward, the conversation remained centered on cities, travel times, and other innocuous subjects.

It was well past dark when Alucius returned to his quarters.

As he disrobed, he reflected on what he had learned. The majer had made an effort to appear uninformed, but he had known a great deal more about the raiders than he had said. For Alucius to pursue that would have revealed more than he would have gained. The majer had also known more about the pteridons, and about the mysterious mirror or Table that the Lord-Protector possessed. And why was the captain-colonel absent? Because that officer knew too much, and the Lord-Protector didn't want Alucius to find out too much?

From Ebuin's questions, it was clear that he suspected that Alucius was far more than a good officer—and it was also clear he had known about Alucius for more than a season. The majer had been far too calm, far too accepting.

And all of that worried Alucius even more.

88

Tempre, Lanachrona

Although the Lord-Protector's steps were light and he attempted to reach the Table of the Recorders without alerting anyone, the Recorder of Deeds stood at the entrance to his underground chamber, waiting. "Lord-Protector."

"Greetings, Recorder."

"You wished something?"

"I did not see you this morning, nor as often in recent weeks."

"I have been working on ways in which I might improve what the Table displays," replied the Recorder.

"What sort of success have you had?" inquired the Lord-Protector, easing toward the black cube of the Table.

"There are several . . . possibilities, but it is too early to tell. You will be the first to know. That I can assure you."

"Have you discovered what has happened with the nomads of Illegea?" asked the Lord-Protector.

"Without Aellyan Edyss, they are returning to independent and wandering tribes, Lord-Protector. They could not agree on a single leader, and they will not threaten Lanachrona or Deforya for years to come, if ever in your lifetime."

"And the Landarch?"

"Little has changed in Deforya. Little will, it appears." An ironic laugh followed the Recorder's words. "Then, little has changed there in generations."

"You think someone will supplant the Landarch?"

"It is possible, but it will change nothing. Whoever is Landarch will remain a captive of the landowners."

"You are far more cynical these days, Recorder."

"I would term it . . . realistic, Lord-Protector."

"I suppose one could call it that." The younger man paused, looked at the blank Table of the Recorders, then asked, "What have you determined about Overcaptain Alucius?"

"He has left Dekhron and passed through Borlan on his way to Krost on his journey here, Lord-Protector. It would appear that he has enemies within the Northern Guard and among the traders of Dekhron, but they have not yet acted."

"Whatever happens, it cannot but benefit us," replied the Lord-Protector. "If they fear him, they will be more temperate in their actions. If they decide to act, and somehow kill him, we will have less of a problem from the herders. If he kills or weakens the traders, we will be able to exert more control over Dekhron sooner than we had planned."

"That is true."

"You no longer seem that concerned about the overcaptain. Are you still opposed to his coming here?"

"I have reconsidered, Lord-Protector. As you had said much earlier, it may be for the very best that he comes here. The very best."

The Lord-Protector nodded. "I'm glad to hear that."

"That way, you can judge for yourself whether he represents a danger or an opportunity for Lanachrona."

"And what if he is both?"

"You are the Lord-Protector." The Recorder laughed once more. "You must decide, as always."

89

After six more days of solid travel, and sleeping out on hard ground, by Londi afternoon Alucius and his squad were just north of Krost. Once they had gotten well south of Borlan the land had become hillier and far more lush, and Alucius and third squad passed meadows still green even in early harvest, tilled fields filled with crops ranging from beans to oilseeds, and vingt upon vingt of almond orchards. The stead houses and outbuildings were wooden, but well kept and numerous. The high road had far more traffic, with wagons headed in both directions. The air was also damper, and Alucius was perspiring and drinking more and more water.

Ahead, Alucius could see the crossroads where the two high roads intersected, and where he and his troopers would turn westward to reach Krost Post. To the southeast of the city, larger than Borlan, but perhaps half the size of Hieron, were hills covered in rows of staked green vines. Alucius recalled that Krost was near the wine-making area of Vyan Hills. Heslyn was once more riding directly behind Faisyn and Alucius.

"Tell us something about Krost, Heslyn," Alucius suggested, turning in the saddle.

"People say that it is where the best wines in all of Corus are produced, but that is not true. Vyan is where the best grapes are grown and where the very best wines are produced. Some of the vintners come from families that produced wine well before the Cataclysm. Even today, the wines are sent all over the world. Krost is a city of merchants, wine merchants, and traders, and Krost is where more bottles are produced than anywhere else in the world. Thousands upon thousands of bottles. You see those three tall chimneys to the left of the crossroads? That is the glassworks. They also produce goblets there, for no true Lanachronan would drink good wine in other than glass. If you look to the east, on the south side of the other high road, you can see a large hill that looks like half of it has been cut away."

Alucius looked for—and found—the odd-shaped hill.

"That is where the finest sand is found. From there, they take it to the glassworks . . . the lead for the crystal, it must be brought all the way from Soupat, and they say that is why the high road runs there . . ."

Before that long, as Heslyn offered his knowledge, the squad had reached the crossroads in the center of Krost and turned westward. The high roads ran amid a welter of buildings, some of them four stories tall, and many of them ancient—but not of eternastone. There had to have been equally ancient buildings in the past, Alucius noted, because the high road was on the same level as the streets. Either that, or over time, the streets and buildings of the city had been built up on ruins until they were level with the high road.

Once more, Alucius let Heslyn ride ahead, but sent Makyr with him, to announce their arrival at Krost. Once they rode through the gates, a half squad was lined up to welcome them, with a senior squad leader in the front. Alucius and third squad had just reined up inside the gates of the post when three officers hurried out into the paved courtyard. All wore spotless blue-and-cream uniforms. Alucius recognized the collar insignia of the captain and the majer, but did not know that of the gray-haired and presumably senior officer who stepped forward.

"Overcaptain Alucius, Northern Guard, en route to Tempre."

"We're most pleased to see you, Overcaptain. I'm Captain-Colonel Jesopyr." He inclined his head to the others. "Majer Fedosyr and Captain Quelyn. And Senior Squad Leader Desar."

"We're pleased to be here, sir."

"We're pleased to have you. No formalities. Let's just get you and your men settled."

Jesopyr's manner and the feelings behind it were so open, so friendly, and so at odds with what Alucius had experienced with Majer Ebuin that Alucius just nodded, momentarily finding himself without words.

"Captain Quelyn will escort you, and Desar will make sure your troopers and squad leaders lack for nothing. We've plenty of space here . . ."

In moments, Alucius was walking Wildebeast toward the stables, listening to Quelyn.

". . . received word you'd be here, must have been several weeks ago . . . Now, we're just using number one stable these days . . . visiting officers here through the first archway . . ."

The stable held spaces for close to four hundred mounts, from what Alucius could count, and fewer than a quarter of the stalls were in use. The other stable appeared unused. From the stable, Alucius carried his gear back across the courtyard to a two-story gray stone structure that was a good hundred yards in length. The officers' quarters had rooms— or doorways—for close to fifty, but the wing through which Captain Quelyn led Alucius appeared empty.

Quelyn opened the door. "Really are a colonel's quarters, but anyone who led five companies rates as a colonel. If there's anything you need, let me or one of the senior squad leaders know."

Alucius glanced across the spacious room—a good ten yards by four—with an antique desk, a double-width bed of equally ancient vintage, a double armoire, a carved weapons and boot rack, wide shuttered windows, and an attached washroom. "This looks more than adequate."

"The captain-colonel planned a formal supper in about two glasses," Quelyn went on.

"I just have my uniform," Alucius pointed out.

"Oh, formal means uniform here, except he'll be serving wine instead of ale, and he can tap into the good supplies." Quelyn grinned. "We all enjoy having visiting dignitaries."

Alucius scarcely felt like a dignitary, whatever that was, only like a tired Northern Guard officer.

"He wanted to make sure you had time to check on your troopers and supplies so that we'd know anything your men would need before you leave tomorrow." Quelyn smiled. "The officers' mess is on the lower level here in the front. In two glasses, then?"

"I'll be there," Alucius promised.

Quelyn shut the door, leaving Alucius to puzzle over the clear friendliness and lack of deception behind the captain's and the captain-colonel's words. Finally, he racked his weapons and hung up his clothes and gear before checking the washroom. It even had a tub, and a spigot that filled it with lukewarm water. Alucius did enjoy the bath.

He had more than enough time to wash out dirty uniforms and garments, and to walk to the barracks and confer with Faisyn, but there was little to discuss, because the Lanachronans had been so helpful.

"It's like we were heroes, sir."

"You all were, even if most people don't know it. Let them enjoy it for now, but remind them—gently—that we are guests. And if they don't behave like guests . . . I'll have more than a few things to say."

"Yes, sir." Faisyn grinned.

So did Alucius.

He took a little more time to walk around the post, but everything he saw confirmed his first impressions. The post had been constructed to house between ten and fifteen full companies and there was only a company or a company and a half in residence. But the facilities were not abandoned or obviously disused, and could have been utilized almost immediately.

Quelyn was standing outside the building that held both officers' quarters and the mess when Alucius returned.

"The colonel thought you'd be checking on your men. He said he could tell you were the type." Quelyn coughed. "Ah . . . he said something about . . . you're having been there."

Alucius smiled. "It's no secret, not in the Iron Valleys anyway, that I started out a trooper. I've been a squad leader and senior squad leader. Only thing I never was an undercaptain."

"You must have entered service very young."

"I did. Very young." Alucius didn't see much point in explaining further.

"Excuse me. We'd better get inside. The captain-colonel wouldn't be happy if I kept you out here."

Alucius followed the young captain in through the double oak doors and down a short hallway floored in blue-and-white marble tiles shaped like diamonds. The mess itself held more tables than Alucius could quickly count, but only one was set, with white linen and cutlery. Five officers, including the captain-colonel, were waiting, standing around the table talking quietly. The talk stopped as Alucius and Quelyn entered.

"Right on the moment. I said he would be," Captain-Colonel Jesopyr announced. "Overcaptain, I'd like to present to you those officers you have not already met. Captain Bersyr, Captain Zenoryn, and Overcaptain Klynosyr. You recall Majer Fedosyr."

"I'm pleased to meet you all."

The captain-colonel steered Alucius to one end of the table. "All of you take your seats."

Alucius sat, as did the others.

Then Jesopyr turned to the table behind him, where he picked up one of the amber-colored bottles. He screwed a device with a twisted metal prong into the cork of the bottle, then pulled out the cork. "This is one of the best reds. That is," he added apologetically, "one of the best reds that a Southern Guard officer can reasonably afford, and I have been saving this for just such an occasion."

"Since the last occasion a month ago?" asked the fresh-faced overcaptain—Klynosyr—with the square-cut beard.

"No, this is a two-month . . . no, a two-season occasion. How often have we had a chance to dine with an overcaptain who has fought pteridons and nomads and been decorated by the Landarch of Deforya?" Jesopyr bent forward and half filled the crystal goblet before Alucius, then filled the other six goblets, emptying the bottle in the process.

Jesopyr raised his goblet. "To our guest. May he travel to Tempre in health and return in both health and wisdom."

"Thank you." Alucius lifted his own goblet. "And to your hospitality."

The deep amber wine was far better than anything Alucius had ever

tasted, not that he had drunk that much wine, he reflected. It was also
stronger than ale.

Two troopers in white jackets appeared, quickly setting plates before
each officer. On each plate were thin strips of something covered with a
glaze.

Alucius tried the first course, discovering it was some sort of tangy
fish, covered with a lemon-almond glaze that went down easily.

"Have you had lemon-smoked oarfish before?" asked the majer.

"I'd had oarfish, but not prepared this way," Alucius admitted.
"What I've had wasn't nearly this good."

"I'm glad to hear that." The colonel smiled, as if he had won a wager
of some sort. "I imagine you didn't see much fish on your travels to
Deforya."

"None at all, but the Landarch served a very tasty antelope dish."

"What about pteridons?" murmured someone.

The colonel looked sharply toward the junior captains.

Alucius smiled. "I don't imagine they'd taste very good. They seemed
rather . . . oily."

"Did you . . ." One of the two captains whose names Alucius hadn't
remembered, sitting at the end of the table, broke off his words.

"Fight real pteridons?" Alucius allowed an amused tone to creep into
his voice. "Some of the nomads flew big blue-winged beasts and bore
blue metal skylances that fired blue flame. They looked like the old pic-
tures and the pieces in a leschec set. Maybe they were something else,
but if a pteridon is worse than what we fought . . . well, I'd rather not see
a pteridon."

There was a low laugh around the table.

"They had the ancient skylances?" pursued Majer Fedosyr.

"The kind that fires waves of blue flame? They did. We didn't know
about the lances, and that's how they killed Captain Clifyr and a good
bunch of the Twenty-third Company."

Quelyn looked at one of the other junior captains, but neither spoke
as the trooper servers reappeared with a second course, soup in low
bowls. Alucius thought it was bland, but not objectionable, and similar
to his grandmother's gourd soup.

"We heard that, under your command, the Lanachronan forces

destroyed more than half of the nomads. How, if I might ask, did you manage that when you were so badly outnumbered?" asked Fedosyr.

Once more, Alucius went through his selectively abbreviated description of the battle for Dereka. ". . . and, while I didn't see the last part of the battle, I was assured by my officers and by the Deforyan marshals that was what happened."

"They burned your uniform right off you?" asked Quelyn wonderingly.

"I was most fortunate. Most who were struck by skylance fires died. It took several weeks for me to recover fully."

"Over a hundred companies?"

"Something like that."

Once more the servers reappeared, this time presenting some sort of meat pounded almost paper-thin, then rolled into tubes filled with a whitish green substance. The meat turned out to be a tender beef and the filling of parsley-cream and cheese. Alucius ate it all. At some time, the amber wine he had not finished had been replaced with a deep red vintage.

"I had heard that the Landarch awarded you the Star of Gallantry." The colonel looked to the majer. "There have only been twenty ever given before, and that's since the Cataclysm."

Yet again, Alucius was bothered, both by what the captain-colonel knew, and his obvious cheer in telling of Alucius's exploits.

"You know," Jesopyr added, with a laugh, "you'll have to watch yourself in Tempre. They're not used to real heroes there."

The absolute chill behind the warm words nearly stiffened Alucius right at the table. The warning was as direct and honest as a dagger, and felt nearly as deadly.

"The officers there," Jesopyr continued, "except for Marshal Wyerl, of course, haven't seen a real battle in years, and they think more in terms of golds and trade, and how to defeat other lands without having to fight."

". . . didn't do so well, either, until they sent Wyerl and Alyniat west . . ."

". . . some of the Matrites could fight . . . heard about one squad that nearly wiped out a whole company . . ."

"What was your experience with the Matrites, Overcaptain?" asked the other overcaptain at the table.

"Some fought very well. Their real leaders were usually the senior squad leaders." Alucius took a sip of the red wine, also good—and strong.

"They inflicted heavy casualties on the . . . militia. We heard that, anyway."

"That was at the beginning, when they had the crystal spearthrower . . ." Alucius went on to explain that, ending as the servers brought in small slices of honey-cake.

As the officers finished the dessert, Captain-Colonel Jesopyr smiled at Alucius. "You have been most forthcoming, Overcaptain. I hope some of our younger officers have listened intently. But . . . do you have any questions . . . anything where we might be of service to you?"

"This is a rather . . . impressive post," Alucius said.

"And you wonder why we're all rattling around in it?" asked the captain-colonel.

"It had occurred to me."

"We had ten companies here less than a year ago. Marshal Wyerl pulled out nine and dispatched them to Zalt and Southgate. We'll be getting a company of recruits to train next month, and another the month after that. You caught us at our lowest."

Truth rang through the colonel's words, and that sense of truth disturbed Alucius in a fashion more than deception might have.

"It's taking more troopers than you'd thought in the west, then?"

"Exactly, and that is one reason why, I would judge, the Lord-Protector wishes to honor you. We do not have that many companies to spare, and you removed a great potential threat from the east."

"It could have been a great threat to the Iron Valleys as well," Alucius pointed out, stifling a yawn.

"That may be, but we are all grateful—or should be, since there are but a few handfuls of companies remaining in the east." The captain-colonel smiled professionally. "You are tired. That, even I can see."

"It has been a long day."

"We will see you in the morning." The captain-colonel stood.

And with that, Alucius found himself standing and being escorted from the mess, the other officers following as well. For all the courtesy, and all the supposed honor involved in the long trip to Tempre, Alucius still would have preferred to be back on the stead, getting up before dawn and riding all day—and coming home to Wendra.

90

Tempre, Lanachrona

The Lord-Protector stepped through the door into the private study, closing it behind him, and smiling at Alerya, who looked up from the desk and the sheet on which she had been writing.

"How are you feeling?" he asked.

"As I have, dear consort." Alerya sipped from the goblet and replaced it on the desk. "You have that thoughtful look."

"I would like you to read this." The Lord-Protector handed two sheets of paper to his consort.

She took them and read, frowning well before she had finished. "He is making himself look older than he is? Has someone taken his place? Someone younger? How has it taken so long to have discovered such?"

"There were subterfuges . . . and we had not watched his bathchamber."

"I like this not. Are you certain it is Enyll?"

"Of that I am certain. I have known Enyll since I was a child. His features have not changed. Nor has his voice. Nor has the way he speaks."

"Then he has discovered a way to become younger?" Alerya's laugh was sharp, almost bitter. "Fortunate man."

"Are you sure you are all right, dearest?"

"I am not so well suited to being a mother as we had hoped. Or my body is not. Perhaps you did not pick so well."

The Lord-Protector slipped behind her chair, then bent and slipped his arms around her, gently. "I prefer the lady I picked, and nothing will change that."

"I am glad." For a moment, she leaned her head back against him. "There is more, I fear."

"There is. He has changed his view of the herder overcaptain. Now he is pleased that Overcaptain Alucius is on his way to Tempre. He is almost excited that it is so, and before he was most fretful."

"Fretful? As I recall, he was angry and spoke most sharply to you." Alerya tried to conceal a burp. "Would that food would rest more easily in me."

"That will pass, they say."

Alerya shook her head. "A most terrible word play, Talryn. Most terrible." She took the smallest of sips from the goblet. "Do you think it a mistake that you ordered this Alucius here?"

"I think not, but men do not change long-held views without reason."

"Men seldom change views, long-held or otherwise. That is why I asked if the Recorder were truly Enyll."

"I would swear that it is Enyll."

"Could it be the Table?"

"There is no record of any such, and I have searched the private archives."

"Have any spent the time at the Table that he does?"

"He is the first true Recorder in generations." The Lord-Protector sighed. "And now I must watch every action and every word with him."

"As you must with everyone."

"Except for you, for which I am most grateful." The Lord-Protector squeezed her shoulders. His eyes went to the goblet on the desk, the level of the liquid scarcely diminished, and his eyes darkened.

91

Slightly before noon on Septi, Alucius and third squad turned off the lower east–west high road and onto the shorter stretch that ran northwest to Tempre and the River Vedra. With each vingt that they rode, the land became ever so slightly more hilly, with fewer tilled fields and more orchards. The orchards were of apples and pears, not almonds. Alucius also saw more flocks of what he would have called town sheep, the white-and-gray fleeced animals that bore the rougher and weaker wool, and whose flesh was edible, unlike that of nightsheep.

A quarter glass after passing an oblong stone set beside the high road indicating five vingts to Tempre, Alucius saw Makyr riding back down from a long and low incline in the high road.

"There's something ahead," Alucius told Faisyn.

"Another honor guard, sir."

"You think so?"

"Yes, sir. Seems to me that the Lord-Protector has ways of knowing things before the rest of us. Might be why we're now part of Lanachrona."

"That could be."

Before long, Makyr was less than twenty yards away.

"Sir!" the scout called. "There's a squad of Southern Guards headed this way, sir. Captain, he's leading 'em. Says they're to escort us to the Southern Guard headquarters."

"That's where we're supposed to go. We'll keep riding until we meet them. Just fall in behind Faisyn and me."

"Yes, sir."

Alucius and Wildebeast had almost reached the top of the incline in the high road, so gentle that it had taken several vingts to climb less than fifty yards. Given what he had seen in the Upper Spine Mountains, Alucius wondered why the ancient builders had not just cut through the large and gradual ridge, but he supposed there were all too many matters like that, and a man could spend his whole life puzzling over such without ever learning the reasons.

Drawn up in the turnout at the top of the incline were Waris, the Southern Guard captain, and a squad of Southern Guard in very crisp blue-and-cream uniforms. The captain rode forward.

"Squad, halt!" Alucius ordered.

"Overcaptain Alucius, sir?"

"Yes, Captain. With the third squad of Twenty-first Company. Reporting as ordered by Marshal Wyerl."

"Sir." The officer stiffened. "Welcome to Tempre. Captain Gueryl and the honor squad at your service."

"Thank you, Captain. I imagine you'll take us where we're supposed to go."

"Yes, sir."

"Would you join me?"

"Yes, sir." The captain nodded to a squad leader. "Lead the way, Byryn."

The honor squad swung out of the ancient enternastone turnout and headed down the almost imperceptible slope toward the city. Faisyn held his place as Alucius eased Wildebeast forward, and the captain eased in on Alucius's right side. Unlike the other Southern Guards Alucius had seen, both the captain and the troopers wore blue shoulder braid.

"You got here sooner than we had thought, sir," Gueryl offered. "We had intended to meet you where the high roads split."

"You found us early enough," Alucius said. "How long to headquarters . . . or wherever we're being quartered?"

"Headquarters, sir. Less than a glass."

From the rise in the road, Alucius could see Tempre spread out in all directions. The upper part of the wide low ridge that they had just crossed on the high road contained no steads and no dwellings, as if for a vingt or so on each side of the flat crest any building had been forbidden. The unsettled space included open meadows and stands of hardwood and softwood, but neither walls nor fences, nor any evergreens. Alucius wondered about the lack of evergreens.

The first steads below the open space contained neat dwellings on small patches of ground, some of them as little as two hundred yards on a side, although most were larger, and all had at least some fruit trees, even some small orchards. The grass everywhere was still green, as were the leaves on all the fruit-laden trees. The high road descended ever so gently toward the river and a pair of twin green towers.

"Is that the Lord-Protector's palace?" Alucius asked Captain Gueryl. "Where the towers are?"

"No, sir." Gueryl laughed. "Most who see Tempre for the first time think so, but the towers date to before the Cataclysm, and they flank the Grand Piers on the river."

"The piers are eternastone, then."

"Yes, sir. How did you know?" Gueryl asked.

"The towers. We have one of those in Iron Stem. There is a pair in Dereka. Tempre was a trading center in the days of the Duarachy. The Grand Piers were probably the reason why Tempre was important then. I'd wager that most trade went by the river down to Faitel and Elcien." Alucius offered a laugh. "I don't know, though. Do you?"

Gueryl was silent for a moment. "I hadn't thought about it. Most long-distance trade these days goes by the high road to Southgate or east to Lustrea."

"Is there more trade now that Lanachrona holds Southgate?"

"Quite a bit, they say."

Looking down the high road through the space between the towers, Alucius could see that, across the River Vedra, beyond the smooth dark waters, rose the southernmost part of the Westerhills, but unlike the northern Westerhills, where the trees were junipers and pines spread widely on rocky and sandy ground, the trees north of Tempre were mixed pine and softwoods, and formed a near-continuous canopy of foliage.

On the river itself were barges headed downriver, and sailing craft headed upriver, the sails augmented on at least one craft by a bank of oarsmen. Alucius couldn't help but think of the ancient ship in the mural, speeding across vast oceans without sails or rowers.

Before long, the steads flanking the road were replaced by more of the yellow brick dwellings on smaller plots of land, and by occasional groupings of shops. All appeared neat, well maintained, and cleaned.

"The dwellings here are well kept," Alucius said.

"Yes, sir. The Lord-Protector places a tariff on any dwelling not kept in good repair."

Ahead, on the right side of the high road, was a far larger dwelling, more like an ancient mansion of greenish white marble, except that the stonework was crisp and new. Long and low stables were set on each side of the three-story structure, which boasted arches and large windows above a circular portico where two retainers in green livery waited. A low wall surrounded the property, and two guards, also in green, flanked the open gate.

Alucius looked again at the structure—one that looked more like a small palace—and out of place amid the more modest shops and dwellings. "Who owns that?"

The young captain did not respond, and Alucius could sense his reluctance.

"Captain?"

"That's the dust palace. Drimeer owns it."

"And those who are wealthy pay golds for the slightest sniff of the dreamdust? And this Drimeer gets more and more golds?"

Gueryl nodded, curtly. "What do you know about dreamdust?"

"That it ruins people." Alucius wasn't about to mention that Iron Stem was one of its sources.

"More than that."

"How did this Drimeer . . . ?"

"He bought up ten or twelve dwellings and built this . . ." Gueryl gestured to the mansion as they rode past the gates. "He obeys all the laws and keeps it in good repair. If the Lord-Protector did anything against him . . . all the merchants would fear that the laws would mean nothing."

Alucius nodded. He also suspected that the dreamdust mansion was a good way to show that the Lord-Protector respected those laws.

"We'll be turning shortly, onto the Avenue of the Guard. It's east of the Avenue of the Palace, but both avenues run north from the high road." Gueryl pointed to his right. "You can see the square towers of the palace there."

Alucius followed his gesture and took in the yellow-cream stone structure.

"To the right—the long lower structure behind the park? That's the main building of Guard headquarters. The senior officers' quarters and the meeting rooms and spaces for the senior officers are there. That's where you'll be quartered, sir. Then the regular officers' quarters, and the stables and barracks are behind across the rear courtyard."

Immediately after the column turned onto the first avenue, a Southern Guard rider pulled away from the honor squad preceding Alucius and first squad and hastened down the avenue.

Before Alucius could say anything, Captain Gueryl spoke quickly. "Marshal Alyniat had indicated that he wanted to greet you when you arrived, sir. That is quite an honor. He is second only to the arms-commander."

The honors he was supposedly receiving were making Alucius more than a little nervous, and he shifted his weight in the saddle as they neared the gray granite walls of the headquarters, modest in size against the low hills directly behind the buildings. Once more, he noted that the low hill behind the headquarters, more like a ridge that ran westward toward the river and toward the palace of the Lord-Protector, held no structures or walls or fences within a half vingt or so of the crest.

Alucius half expected trumpets as they rode through the gates to the Southern Guard headquarters, but the four guards flanking the gateposts, for there were no actual gates, barely gave the column of riders a glance. That was more what Alucius would have expected for a mere overcaptain in a land where even colonels were common.

The main building was a good four stories in height, and its clean gray marble walls loomed over the smooth granite paving stones that covered most of the space inside the walls—except for the small walled garden set forward of the squared-off portico that was the main entrance. There were two handsome carriages drawn up short of the mounting blocks at the portico, clearly waiting for someone of importance, and the first carriages of such workmanship that Alucius had ever seen. Only wagons were used in Iron Stem.

The honor squad led the way around the east side of the main headquarters building and into the expansive paved rear courtyard. The rear courtyard had been cut out of the hillside, with the stables to the right, and barracks and quarters behind, but forward of a stone wall that rose almost fifteen yards. The effect was to conceal—or minimize—the extent of the buildings as seen from outside the walls.

The Southern Guard squad turned to the left again, heading toward a smaller rear entrance, smaller only in comparison to the impressive nature of the one in front, but almost as large as that of the Landarch's palace in Dereka. Alucius could see several figures in Southern Guard uniforms standing on the steps above the mounting blocks.

"Is that Marshal Alyniat?" Alucius asked quietly.

"I think so, sir. I've never seen him close, but it looks like him. I know it's not Marshal Wyerl, and there aren't any other marshals in Tempre now."

The honor squad rode past the steps, leaving space for Alucius to rein up opposite the marshal and a small set of personal guards—and a majer and a colonel of some sort. Alucius reined up, and inclined his head. "Marshal."

"Overcaptain Alucius. Welcome to Tempre and to headquarters. I wanted to greet you personally. It is not often that one has a chance to meet an officer who has triumphed against such overwhelming forces."

"Our success came from the sacrifices of troopers and officers who fought valiantly, knowing that they faced both Talent-creatures and vast numbers. We would not be here without their efforts."

"That is certainly so." Alyniat smiled. "But never in any history that I have read has a junior overcaptain commanded so brilliantly and fearlessly. I must ask, tactless as it may be, if it is true that your uniform was burned off you, and that every span of your body was so bruised that your skin was purple from head to toe?"

Alucius smiled in return, understanding full well the reason for the question. "So I was told, sir, but since it was sometime after the last battle before I was able to look at myself, I could not personally confirm that. I can attest to the fact that all my hair was burned off. It is still rather short."

Alyniat laughed. "Marshal Wyerl sends his best as well, and we look forward to dining with you this evening. Again . . . on behalf of the Lord-Protector, I welcome you all to Tempre." He nodded, clearly ending the unofficial ceremony.

Alucius bowed from the saddle. "We thank you, and the Lord-Protector, and are pleased that we have been of service." Then he waited to see what would happen.

"Forward."

The honor squad moved from the portico, and Alucius and third squad followed.

"You must have truly impressed the arms-commander," Gueryl said.

"It may just have been that we're the first unit of the Northern Guard to visit Tempre and headquarters," Alucius suggested.

"That could be," Gueryl said amiably.

Although Alucius sensed the other's doubt, he was glad that Gueryl did not say more.

Outside the stables, once both squads had halted, Gueryl gestured, and the senior squad leader from the honor squad joined them. Alucius turned Wildebeast so that Faisyn was included.

"Byryn here will work with your squad leader . . ."

"Faisyn," Alucius supplied, nodding to the third squad leader.

"To make sure that your troopers and mounts are quartered and well taken care of," Gueryl concluded.

When Alucius had finished with Wildebeast, the two officers left the stables. The walk back to the main building was almost half a vingt—or so Alucius felt. He still carried both rifles, but the captain made no comment.

Once inside the main building, Gueryl led the way up a wide stone staircase. "Your quarters are on the third level on the west end. The sitting room has a direct view of the Lord-Protector's palace and of the towers."

364   L. E. MODESITT, JR.

The mention of quarters with a sitting room didn't ease Alucius's concerns in the slightest, not when he recalled Feran's warning about the Lord-Protector wanting something.

At the third level, they turned left, past a pair of Southern Guards, with blue braid on their shoulders, similar to that worn by Gueryl. As the two officers continued down the marble-floored corridor, Alucius picked up the faint murmurs from the two guards.

"Overcaptain . . . on this level?"

". . . more than that, they say . . . big hero . . . saved the whole eastern expedition . . . routed the nomads . . ."

". . . some honor . . ."

". . . nomads broken through . . . would have had to send scores of companies east . . . maybe you . . ."

There was only a grunt in return.

Was the Lord-Protector overcommitted? With too many forces in the west? Alucius's lips quirked into a smile. Was that just human nature? To reach for more than you had the ability to hold against adversity?

Gueryl stopped at the very last set of doors—golden oak double doors that shimmered with polish and care. After producing a shining brass key, he opened the lock and door, then presented the key to Alucius.

Inside was a small foyer, the floor tiled in blue and gold. Beyond the foyer, through a square archway, was a sitting room a good ten yards in width and fifteen in length, the long side containing three side-by-side wide windows, offering a view of the Lord-Protector's golden cream palace. In the sitting room were a dark blue upholstered settee, two matching armchairs, an imposing carved fruitwood desk set against the north wall, with an equally imposing and matching carved desk chair. Five wall lamps were spaced around the chamber, and in the center was a dark blue carpet bearing a design of intertwined eight-pointed green stars, outlined in gold.

"The bedchamber is this way . . ."

Roughly five yards by ten, the bedroom was only small by comparison to the sitting room. It also had a view of the palace, and a high triple-width bed and two matching armoires. Alucius set down his saddlebags and laid the rifles on the weapons rack, then followed Gueryl to the next doorway. Beyond the bedchamber was a bathchamber with a tub carved out of an oblong marble block, and with two spigots, both of shimmering bronze.

After showing the bathchamber to Alucius, the captain returned to the sitting room. Alucius followed.

"You'll need your uniforms cleaned, of course. To summon the orderly, just use the bellpull here. If you let them know tonight, they can have them cleaned and pressed before noon tomorrow."

"That would be helpful," Alucius said politely.

"Now . . . I doubt I will see you again, sir, but it has been a pleasure. Majer Keiryn will be here in about two glasses to escort you to dinner. I had not realized that it was to be with the marshals. If there is any change, either I or the majer will let you know."

"Thank you. You have been most helpful."

"My pleasure, sir." Gueryl bowed, then departed.

Once the door was closed, Alucius walked back into the sitting room and to the windows. The two on each end were open, and a faint cool breeze rustled through the chamber. For a time he stood there, not really seeing the palace, considering.

The captain had been truthful in all that he had said. So, from what Alucius could determine, had the marshal. While the captain certainly had not been told what his superiors did not wish revealed, the apparent truthfulness of the marshal, and his casual mention of what had happened in Dereka were a powerful message. That message had been delivered with understated and great impact.

Amid the luxury of his guest quarters, Alucius still wondered what the Lord-Protector wanted.

92

Prosp, Lustrea

Vestor studied the waist-high black lorken cube that bore a shimmering mirror surface, bordered in lorken as well. The smooth-finished wooden sides continued downward another third of a yard beneath the stone floor and rested directly on the granite bedrock. The floor of the small chamber, less than ten yards square, had been completed around the cube in green marble tiles scavenged from the ruins beyond the center of Prosp. The wall columns and facings had come from other ruins, although the color of the marble matched. The roof over the chamber had been completed just the day before, and little else of the structure that surrounded the chamber had been finished, save for that roof and the outer walls.

Vestor glanced at the polished surface of the Table once more, one of the components that had been fabricated far earlier than the Praetor had known. He took a look toward the unfinished marble archway before extracting the sheet of parchment that had come from the Praetorian archives, then the newer matching sheet that he had created before he had left Alustre many weeks before.

Laying a sheet on each side of the mirror surface, he bent down and extracted a small assembly of crystals from the case at his feet and set the assembly in the middle of the Table. He studied the sheets, and readjusted one of the crystals, then another. Finally, he took the ancient device that resembled a light-torch from his tunic, readjusting the focus on the discharge end.

After a moment of studying the ancient manuscript, then the newer one, he took a deep breath and flicked on the modified light-torch, focusing it on the prismlike receptor crystal.

A web of ruby light flashed from the assembly—which vanished. Then a series of patterned interlocking lights flared across the mirror surface, burning into the flat crystal before disappearing. The lorken cube shivered ever so slightly, as if minutely aligning itself and settling into the granite below.

For a long moment, there was silence.

Then, from the mirror surface rose a thin tendril of silver mist, followed by a second tendril, of ruby. Both thickened into cablelike—or serpentlike—tentacles.

With a frown, Vestor stepped back from the roiling silver and the ruby mist tentacles that reached upward, but the twin coils of roiling silver and ruby mist swirled out of the Table and into the chamber, entwining themselves around the Praetorian engineer before he could take another step backward.

"No . . . no!" Then, seemingly against his will, Vestor's mouth closed abruptly, and he stood two yards back from the Table, swaying, as if in a struggle against an unseen enemy.

The twin mists suffused his body, slowly vanishing.

Vestor stood stock-still for a time.

One of the Praetorian Guards stepped through the uncompleted marble archway. "Sir . . . I heard something. Are you all right?"

Vestor straightened, brushing his tunic, and offering a smile. "I was just surprised. I'm fine. I haven't felt this good in years. Many years."

"That's good, sir." The guard stepped back quickly.

Vestor smiled sardonically and looked down at the new and fully functioning Table of the Recorders, murmuring to himself. "He created it well, indeed he did. With three, now we can begin."

He stepped forward to the Table.

93

Majer Keiryn—tall and redheaded—had indeed arrived almost precisely two glasses after the departure of Captain Gueryl. He had escorted Alucius down two levels and to the eastern end of the headquarters building to a private dining room, empty when they stepped into it. The single circular table was covered in a shimmering white linen, with blue linen napkins. Each of the four places was set with silver cutlery, platters and plates of cream porcelain rimmed in gold and blue, and with two goblets set before each of the four diners. On a side table were several bottles of wine in the amber bottles.

"The marshals should be joining us shortly, I'm certain." Keiryn paused. "Your exploits have created quite a stir, you know. It's not often that an overcaptain takes command and wins a massed battle with hundreds of companies. And even less often that Talent-creatures like pteridons are involved."

"It was as much a matter of luck as anything," Alucius lied.

"I doubt that luck had much to do with it. According to Marshal Wyerl, you have seldom if ever lost a fight, and you have more combat experience than almost any officer in Corus today."

"I have fought more than I would have wished, but I am certain there are other officers equally experienced—" Alucius stopped as the door to the dining room opened, and two men in Southern Guard uniforms stepped inside.

The majer stepped forward. "Marshals . . ."

"Good evening, Majer," said Alyniat, easing forward and inclining his head to Alucius, "Overcaptain." He half turned to the older and slightly shorter marshal. "Marshal Wyerl, I'd like to present Overcaptain Alucius of the Northern Guard."

Alyniat's blond hair, Alucius could see now that he was closer, was as much silver as blond, and there was a web of fine wrinkles radiating from his eyes. Wyerl's short-cut hair was irregularly mixed silver and brown, and despite the dark circles under his eyes, the man radiated a youthful charm.

"I have wanted to meet you for quite some time, Overcaptain Alucius." Wyerl offered a truly boyish smile. "You have a fearsome reputation."

"I can do little about what others say, Marshal." Alucius inclined his head. "I fear that they have made me into something that I am not."

"That is true of all who fight for a living and survive." Wyerl laughed softly, then motioned to the table. "We might as well be seated."

The two marshals sat across from each other, with Alucius facing Majer Keiryn. No sooner were all seated than two orderlies appeared and immediately poured a pale amber wine from one of the bottles into the smaller goblet in front of each officer.

Wyerl lifted his goblet. "To our guest."

"With my gratitude for your hospitality," Alucius replied, lifting his own goblet.

The wine seemed excellent to Alucius, although he was well aware that his experience in judging such was most limited.

The orderlies vanished and reappeared to set a small plate atop the one before each diner. On the small plate was a pastry no more than the width of three fingers. Alucius watched, and then used his fork to take a small and flaky section. Whatever was inside was warm, and both sweet and spicy at the same time, with an overtaste of butter and something else that he did not recognize.

"Do you like the charysa?" asked Alyniat.

"It's good. I've never had it before," Alucius admitted.

"Like most officers, I'll wager he'll eat almost anything first and judge afterward," suggested Wyerl. "I'd also wager there's little he doesn't like."

"Only honeyed prickle slices," Alucius admitted.

"I cannot say I've heard of that," Alyniat ventured.

"It's a cactus that grows in the quarasote lands. To me, it tastes like oil and sawdust, but it was a family favorite. After eating that growing up . . ." Alucius shrugged expressively.

The marshals laughed. After the slightest of hesitations, so did Keiryn.

"How was the fare in Dereka?" asked Wyerl.

"Mostly troopers' fare, except for the one banquet for officers hosted by the Landarch. That was plains antelope with a plumapple sauce. It was good."

"Never had that," mused Alyniat.

The plates that had held the charysa were whisked away, and replaced by greenery lightly covered with oil and grated cheese and nuts. The dressing tasted like an almond oil.

"You should enjoy the next dish," suggested Wyerl.

Alucius even recognized it—feral hog—lightly seasoned with peppers and accompanied by apple slices quick-fried and cut like lace potatoes.

"The guard offers a bounty on the wild hogs," Alyniat said. "Too many of them, and they rip up the bottomland crops. So we offer a silver for each one that's fresh. The stead holders get paid for doing what benefits them, and we get some good meat."

"How does it compare to the plains antelope?" asked Wyerl.

"It's good. They're different. They're both too rich to eat all the time," Alucius said.

"Not for the Landarch, I'd wager. Doesn't his palace date back?"

"It's built of gold eternastone. I'd guess that means it was built before the Cataclysm," Alucius acknowledged.

"You had said that the Landarch actually decorated the courtyard walls of his palace with nomad breastplates?" asked Marshal Wyerl.

Alucius had indeed, but to no one in Tempre. "He had that done, sir. I counted—estimated, really—that there were more than three thousand on the walls in the front courtyard. His submarshal said that there were as many in the rear courtyard, but those I did not actually see."

"Six thousand dead. Really quite an achievement, don't you think?" Wyerl looked to Alyniat. "And killing pteridons, as well."

"Without all that much help from the Deforyans, I'd imagine." Alyniat looked squarely at Alucius.

"They did their best," Alucius temporized.

"Most of their officers above captain are the sons of the large landowners, aren't they?"

"From what I saw. Their captains are really more like senior squad leaders," Alucius admitted. "They seemed better at handling the lancers."

"What sort of marksmen are they . . . ?"

"Did they say anything about where they normally stationed the lancers . . . ?"

As Wyerl pressed his questions, in between answering, Alucius finished the main course, and saw his platter noiselessly removed. Next came dessert, orange-cream in color and molded in an oval with a raised seal upon it—that of the Southern Guard.

Alucius took a small bite, and found it sweet, creamy as it looked, and tasting of almond and orange.

"You're a herder by birth, and you're the heir to your stead, I understand," said Alyniat. "Yet you entered the militia as a trooper. Was that not unusual?"

"I didn't have a great deal of choice. The Council entered a conscription order, and I was the only son on the stead. They set the buyout so high that it would have destroyed the stead." Alucius understood that the two already knew what he was telling them, and he had a good idea where the discussion was headed.

"Yet herder families are reputed to be . . . shall we say, wealthy," suggested Wyerl.

Majer Keiryn exuded quiet bewilderment, and that bothered Alucius more than the leading questions.

"With the land and the equipment, many would reckon us well-off," Alucius admitted, "but compared to the value of all that it takes to operate a stead and produce nightsilk, the golds we take in are few indeed. And we must purchase the solvents from Lanachrona. That requires extra golds for the distance they must be carried."

"There are not many herders, these days, are there?"

"I don't know the numbers of people, but I would judge that there are less than a hundred steads that produce nightsilk, and fewer every year. Most of the steads in the north and west have been abandoned in the last ten or twenty years."

"Why might that be?" asked Wyerl.

Alucius could tell that question was a divergence, and that the marshal was truly interested in the answer—beyond the other agenda.

"There has been less rain over the past generation, according to my grandsire. Quarasote cannot live where it is too wet, but without some rain, the bushes will not produce enough new growth for the nightsheep to eat."

"New growth?"

"Even a nightram cannot eat the spines once they are more than a year old. They harden into spikes that can scratch steel and run right through a man or mount."

"Quarasote is that strong?"

"That was one reason why the Matrites had trouble, even though they outnumbered us. They thought that by attacking from the north, where we have few people, they could sweep down the high road from Soulend." Alucius smiled. "But the midroad runs through the quarasote hills and flats. You can't run a horse through them, especially an untrained mount. We knew the back trails. I don't know the exact numbers, but they lost something like ten companies for every one we lost."

Wyerl nodded. "That's good to know. Still . . . those lands must be pretty barren . . . some of them."

"Toward the Westerhills west of Soulend, there aren't many steads left. It's been drier there."

"There's not much room for more expenses, then?"

"No," Alucius admitted, waiting.

"So any higher tariffs on herders could force more of them off their land?"

"Higher tariffs might well do that," Alucius admitted.

"Even to your stead?"

"I have not seen the accounts in some time." Alucius shrugged. "My grandsire has been keeping those."

"And your wife is a herder as well?"

"She comes from a herder family."

"It would be a shame to have to give up that heritage." Wyerl looked to Alyniat. "Don't you think so?"

"It certainly would be." Alyniat laughed. "We might not get any more officers like the overcaptain."

Alucius relaxed slightly, sensing that the message—or one message—had been delivered.

"I see that you didn't like the almorange," observed Marshal Wyerl, glancing at Alucius's empty dessert plate.

"Not at all, sir. Not at all."

"It's one of my favorites, as well . . ."

With those words, and the feeling behind them, Alucius knew that the marshals had delivered the first message, even if he had no idea exactly what the Lord-Protector wanted. Did he want Alucius to head an expedition somewhere else? Attack the Matrites in Dimor? Or lead an effort to take over Deforya?

Or was it something else altogether?

94

On Octdi morning, Alucius woke early, his stomach growling. Not wanting to wait for someone to tell him how and where to eat, he washed up and dressed quickly, then set out to see if he could find someone who could tell him where the officers' mess might be—or where he could get something to eat.

He decided to ask the formal guards stationed by the staircase, walking right up to the pair and looking directly at the older one. "Where is the officers' mess—or where I could get some breakfast?"

"Ah . . . that's on the first level, sir, halfway down the west end. They'll serve for another glass."

"Thank you."

"Yes, sir."

374 L. E. MODESITT, JR.

There was a brief conversation behind him, but so low that Alucius could not pick it up without obviously stopping and eavesdropping. Finding the officers' mess was easy. Alucius just followed two young captains, if discreetly, and stepped up to the long table behind which stood several orderlies. He listened, then, when the others had taken their ale and platters, stepped up and ordered, "I'd like egg toast, with the ham and biscuits. And the ale."

The nearest orderly looked at Alucius's uniform. "Ah . . . Over-captain?"

"That's right, Northern Guard. Here on orders."

"Just a moment, sir." As he had with the captains, the trooper filled the platter and handed it to Alucius with a beaker of ale.

"Thank you." As Alucius stepped away with the platter of egg toast, ham strips, and some sort of biscuits and gravy, he could hear the conversation behind him.

"Don't know if he . . ."

"What does it matter? 'Sides, if he's the one, you want to tell him no?"

With a faint smile, Alucius looked over the officers, then picked a graying overcaptain sitting by himself.

"Would you mind if I joined you?"

The overcaptain appeared startled, then grinned. "No, I'd be most pleased. I didn't think any of us would get to talk with you. You are the one who took on the nomads in Deforya?"

"Alucius—that's me." He slipped into the chair across from the older officer.

"Paerkl, that's me. I'm here temporarily to provide information to the mapping engineers."

"Mapping engineers?"

"They rotate companies to do recon in places where we don't have good maps. See if we can find anything left from the Cataclysm—roads, artifacts—and then we bring back information. So I've got a week to go over all my drawings and maps, and then it's back to Hyalt."

Alucius nodded, his mouth full of egg toast.

"Is all that true about the nomads having more than a hundred companies and pteridons?"

"Don't know about everything people are saying. They had over a hundred companies and pteridons. There were maybe twenty-five companies of Deforyan Lancers, and we had five companies. One Southern Guard, four Northern Guard, and Majer Draspyr—Southern Guard— was in command."

"Draspyr? Was he the one who disobeyed Submarshal Frynkel and broke the mercs at Southgate?"

"I'd never met the majer before, and he didn't talk about what he'd done before." Alucius tried to recall Draspyr's appearance. "Fairly tall, blond, scar across one cheek."

"That's Draspyr. Or was. He didn't make it, did he?"

"We lost more than half the troopers, half the officers. He was one of those they got. We came back with less than two companies out of five." Alucius took a swallow of ale.

"And you were the senior officer left?"

Alucius nodded again.

Paerkl shook his head. "Pteridons, you said? You have any idea where they got those?"

"If anyone knew, they never told me. The Deforyans didn't believe that the nomads had them—not until they flamed a couple of squads."

"That must have been something."

"Not something I'd like to do again." Alucius paused, then said, "We rode here from Dekhron, through Borlan and Krost. Seemed like all the posts were understrength. Is that because of the Southgate campaign?"

"Mostly. It's over three hundred vingts from our old border with Madrien to Southgate. Built up the fort at Zalt, but to hold the high road takes fifteen companies. Minimum. Doesn't count the push they're making toward Fola." Paerkl frowned, momentarily. "You stopped at Krost, at the post there?"

"We did."

"Was Captain-Colonel Jesopyr there?"

"He was. He's the post commander, is he not?"

"For the moment. He's got enough time for a stipend. Imagine he'll be honored at the arms-commander's next awards dinner in Tempre. Good man. Liked serving with him. Old style. Appreciates a talented enemy more than an inept friend. He's also not one who tells you what you want to hear, then slips a knife into your gut while hugging you."

"There are always those kinds. We had some in the militia before we became the Northern Guard. More worried about a half-silver than a trooper's life."

Paerkl shook his head, then took a last sip from his beaker of ale. "The fewer the better."

"Did you ever run across a Majer Ebuin?"

Paerkl's slight stiffening told Alucius more than the overcaptain's words. "He's the number two at Borlan. Under Captain-Colonel Yermyn. They think alike, I'm told. Don't know either personally."

"Even after he said something," Alucius offered, "I couldn't be sure what he meant. But he was most courteous."

"Courteous. Good word." Paerkl eased back his chair. "Glad to see you, and hope everything goes well. Lord-Protector ought to give you some sort of reward. Good to see that a fighting officer gets recognized. Doesn't happen enough." Then, with a smile, Overcaptain Paerkl was gone.

No one joined Alucius as he finished his breakfast. Nor did anyone approach him as he walked back up to his quarters. He debated going exploring, but he had no idea where to look for what—or even what he might need to find. He also suspected that, before long, someone would be looking for him.

About that, he was right. A young captain Alucius did not recognize was pacing back and forth in the corridor outside Alucius's quarters.

"Overcaptain Alucius?"

"Yes?"

"I'm Captain Deen. Majer Keiryn detailed me to be your aide while you're here in Tempre." The captain offered an embarrassed smile, and the expression matched his inner chagrin. "But I didn't get the orders until this morning."

"It's not a problem. I was hungry and went and found the officers' mess."

"Ah . . . which one?"

"The one on the first level. I followed some captains."

"Ah . . . we'll need to show you the one for senior officers. That's where they expect you. It's on the other side of the first level. When you weren't here . . . I checked with them, but they hadn't seen you."

"I had a solid breakfast," Alucius said.

"That's good. You'll likely have a busy few days here in Tempre."

Alucius raised his eyebrows.

"Captain-Colonel Omaryk—he's the head of the planning staff—he has requested that you brief him on the nomads, and on the abilities of the Landarch's forces, as well as on the high road through the Upper Spine Mountains. Then, Captain-Colonel Dytryl—he's mapping—has you scheduled for two glasses this afternoon. And, of course, you're the guest at the senior officers' dinner at midday . . ."

"My orders mentioned the Lord-Protector . . ." Alucius ventured.

"Oh, yes. That's on Londi. He doesn't have audiences on the end days, and he couldn't possibly meet with you until you've briefed everyone, and on Decdi the arms-commander is having you to his residence. Submarshal Frynkel wanted to meet you privately, and having you two to supper was the easiest way to handle that over the end days. He said that you had valuable knowledge about the southwest highway and the Matrites . . ."

One thing that the Lord-Protector was getting was information. But was that all?

Alucius would just have to see.

95

Prosp, Lustrea

The man in the uniform of a Praetorian engineer worked quickly on the device laid out on the makeshift workbench. He stood in the harvest warmth of the workroom outside the chamber that held the first newly built Table of the Recorders in more than a millennium.

The device resembled an antique gunpowder pistol in general shape, but the design was far more ancient, with the barrel a crystal discharge formulator, and the butt holding the crystal light-charges. The engineer's fingers moved deftly, and he silently finished his work, screwing the plates that doubled as handgrips and light collectors into place. Then he straightened and slipped the weapon into the holster on his left side.

He walked toward the archway into the chamber that held the Table, nodding at the Praetorian Guard who stood at the outer doorway.

As Vestor shut the door to the Table chamber, the sound of masons and carpenters working on finishing the rooms in the outer circle died away. He walked to the single table desk set against the wall and lifted several sheets of parchment from it. Then he turned. His eyes ranged over the the waist-high black lorken cube as he stepped from the desk and up to the Table. There he looked down at the mirror surface and concentrated.

The ruby mists swirled, then dropped away, revealing the face of an alabaster-skinned and violet-eyed man, who smiled.

Vestor nodded, then set the first sheet of parchment on the surface of the table. It vanished. He repeated the process with the second and third sheets. After the third sheet vanished, he stepped back and took a deep breath, then blotted his sweating forehead. His entire body shivered, and his chest was heaving as though he had run a vingt at full speed. A moment passed, and he walked slowly to the stool beside the table desk, where he seated himself.

All the images that had appeared in the Table had also vanished, leaving a clear mirror that reflected the heavy beams overhead.

96

Alucius walked quickly toward his quarters, half-listening to Captain Deen.

". . . and when the logistics staff was reorganized—that was because Majer-colonel Hurgenyr took his stipend right before the Lord-Protector's father died—his successor there thought I might be of more use on the mapping staff. But Captain-Colonel Dytryl doesn't want any junior officers on the staff, just cartographers and older junior officers who came up through the ranks and who have been stationed all over Lanachrona . . . Luckily, Marshal Wyerl thought I'd be useful to Majer Keiryn . . ."

"I'm sure you're quite valuable in making sure that officers like me and others get where they're supposed to be—"

"That's what Keiryn said just the other day, even gave thanks to the One Who Is, but you know that it's really a privilege to be on staff here at headquarters. My father's pleased. You know he was a majer-colonel in charge of river logistics, and my cousin, well, really, my father's cousin's daughter, she's the Lord-Protector's wife and consort. We all keep hoping it won't be too long before she has a son. Anyway, the majer even said it would be a shame to send me out to a company . . ."

Alucius opened the door and stepped into the foyer of his quarters. "If you'd just wait here in the foyer. I'll only be a moment. I need to gather some notes." Escaping to the bedchamber, Alucius closed the door behind him and took a deep breath. Then he checked his saddle-bags for the few notes on his travels that had survived and might be of interest and use when he was briefed—or debriefed by Captain-Colonel Omaryk.

As he straightened up, he glanced out the twin bedchamber windows, catching sight of the Lord-Protector's palace.

He paused, sensing something he had not sensed in a while, and really looked at the palace. The feel of the purple-tinged blackness flowing upward from somewhere in the Lord-Protector's palace was so clear that he wondered why he hadn't felt it before. Because he hadn't been look-ing? Because he'd been preoccupied and hurried from place to place?

He took a long look, concentrating. The blackness had the same evil overtones as had the pinkish purpleness that had come from the crystal in the Matrial's residence. Was that why he had been warned in Dereka? Was the Lord-Protector like the Matrial?

Even as Alucius watched, the blackness faded. So, he reflected, what-ever caused that sense of evil was not continuous the way the purple crystal had been. But that made it even harder to determine what to do. He couldn't very well watch the palace every moment, especially not when he was meeting with so many officers, then gallop over there, even with his concealment abilities, and try to find who or what was creating the purplish black.

With a deep breath, he slipped the few sheets he had inside his tunic and turned to rejoin Captain Deen.

The captain was waiting, smiling, in the foyer. "That didn't take long, Overcaptain. Now, we're headed down to the planning staff. That's Captain-Colonel Omaryk . . . was one of the first appointments that the new Lord-Protector made, that is after Marshal Slayern's unfortunate death and after stipending off Marshal Retyln, when he chose Marshal Wyerl as arms-commander . . . then brought Omaryk from Borlan . . ."

Alucius tried to listen intently as he accompanied the young captain down to the second level and eastward along the main corridor.

Within moments, Alucius was stepping into a small conference room.

Captain-Colonel Omaryk was rail-thin, with freckles, and a long face. He nodded to the empty chair across from him. "Please have a seat, Overcaptain. This is Majer Kurelyn. He heads one of the analytical sections. He also writes well and quickly." A faint smile crossed Omaryk's face.

Alucius seated himself and waited.

"Let's dispense with unnecessary formalities. As I understand your background, you have traveled the midroad from Soulend through the Westerhills, and the innercoast road all the way south to Zalt. You are also familiar with the southwest high road from the former Lanachronan border to Zalt. Your latest duties carried you from Senelmyr to Dereka, then south to the end of the Barrier Range, and then back to Salaan and thence to here. You are well familiarized with Matrite training and tactics, and you are possibly more familiar with the tactics and capabilities of both the Illegean nomads and the Deforyan Lancers than any other officer in Lanachrona. Are those reasonably correct suppositions?"

"With some qualifications, sir."

"What are those qualifications?"

"There may have been other officers who have been to Dereka, sir. I'm not familiar with them, but I just don't know."

"What about the Matrites?"

"I'm more familiar with their tactics and training than anyone in the Northern Guard. I don't know about the Southern Guard."

"That's better . . ." Omaryk paused. "Were you ever debriefed on the Matrites by your superiors in the Northern Guard?"

"Only by Colonel Clyon. I don't know what he did with the information."

"Neither do we. Let's begin with the Deforyan Lancers. First, I'd like your overall impressions of the Lancers and your understanding of their command structure."

382   L. E. MODESITT, JR.

"According to what I was told by various officers, the Deforyan Lancers consisted of twenty-five companies . . ." Alucius went on to report everything that he had learned or overheard, but not necessarily all that he had surmised.

"You're suggesting that the Deforyan Lancers are overofficered, and that the abilities of those officers are marginal at best."

"Yes, sir. That might be charitable."

"Do you have any examples of why you think this is so?"

"When we were at Black Ridge . . ." Alucius explained the retreat of the Deforyans and their abandonment of the cooks.

"You don't think that was a wise decision?"

"No, sir. We would have had to retreat in time, but we had a superior physical position, from which we could inflict greater casualties. Had the Deforyans done what they had stated, they could have inflicted even heavier losses on the nomads when they tried to reach the main road. The Lancers made no effort, but hurried back to Deforya. Then they let themselves be encircled in the main battle."

"You were not encircled?"

"No, sir. Their attack was massive, but not tight. I ordered my troopers into a tight wedge, and we fought through their forces, then regrouped and cut hundreds of them down from behind. They also disregarded even the reports from their own officers about the pteridons."

"And what happened?"

"The nomads encircled them, and then the pteridons flamed the center of the Deforyans, and cut down the outside until we could bring down the pteridons and break through the encirclement." That was generally true, if simplistic, Alucius felt.

"You've simplified that some, I believe, Overcaptain." The faint smile crossed Omaryk's face. "Since you're not the question, however, we'll go on. What orders did you or the Deforyan companies receive prior to the attack outside Dereka?"

"We were lined up on the ring road, but there were never any direct orders given once the attack began. So I took the initiative."

"None?"

"No, sir."

From there the questions became more and more detailed, dealing with everything from Deforyan marksmanship to the numbers of captains and overcaptains, and their backgrounds, even with the officers' café and the roads and aqueducts serving Dereka, and the placement of orchards and fountains along the high road.

97

Alucius did not sleep well either Octdi or Novdi night. His dreams—those that he remembered—combined alabaster-skinned figures with pteridons and wild sandoxes as he scrambled through endless tunnels trying to discover . . . something. That, he reflected, was his problem. Everyone around him seemed to have something they wanted from him. Some, like Captain-Colonel Omaryk, had been very clear on what they wanted. Others, like Majer Ebuin, had been far less obvious.

On Decdi, the headquarters was largely empty, as Alucius would have expected on end day, but he spent the morning, after eating, checking on third squad, then returned to his quarters to try to consider what might lie before him.

Except for the one time, he had not sensed the purpleness coming from the Lord-Protector's palace—or anywhere else; nor had he received any messages, veiled or otherwise, since the one delivered by the marshals on his arrival. He had not seen anyone with a pale white face or alabaster skin. Nor had he seen or sensed any soarers, sanders, or Talent-creatures.

The only message he had been given was that, unless he did what the Lord-Protector wanted, his way of life, his family, his stead, could all be wiped out. But he still had no idea what the Lord-Protector wanted—

except that the Lord-Protector definitely wanted Alucius to be aware of that fact.

Finally, on Decdi afternoon, Captain Deen appeared to escort Alucius out to the personal dwelling of Arms-Commander Wyerl. The afternoon was cooler than those of the previous days, and while they rode past some other riders and several carriages, the streets and roads of Tempre were less than crowded, far less than on the Septi when Alucius had ridden into the capital city.

"... beautiful afternoon ... harvesttime is especially beautiful in Tempre. It's too bad you haven't had a chance to see the river ..."

"Does your family live near here?" Alucius interrupted Captain Deen's monologue.

"No, they live on the west side, out beyond the market section. You have to have coins to live here in the Golden Hills. That's why they call it the Golden Hills, you know. You have to have golds to live in these hills. Or be a marshal. One of my cousins lives just north of here. He calls where he lives part of the silver slopes because it's just downhill of the gold. He might make enough golds someday. He's already got fifteen wagons running the roads, most of them on the square, but a couple on the Southgate run—"

"On the square?"

"Oh, the high roads make close to a square between Tempre, Krost, Syan, and Hyalt—Vyan's in there, too, but it's really part of the Krost to Syan leg, and by running a regular schedule, he gets more goods from the traders. He's done well, and he's only a few years older than I am. Asked me if I wanted to head up the wagon guards, train them, that sort of thing. That's not what I'm good at, but I had to think. He offered more than a few golds ..."

Alucius kept listening as they crossed the ridge and rode along the stone-paved way over two more low hills. Marshal Wyerl's residence was a long and low structure set amid gardens, with a low stone wall a yard and a half high surrounding it. Two Southern Guards stood as Alucius and Deen rode through the opening in the wall and along the circular lane to the main entry.

"The marshal said he'd send an escort back with you, sir. I'll see you in the morning. Remember, you're to meet the Lord-Protector a glass before noon."

"I'll be ready. Until then." Alucius reined up and dismounted.

One of the Southern Guards took the reins from Alucius. "He'll be stabled in back, sir."

"Thank you."

Even before Alucius reached the golden oak door, it opened. A round-faced woman with golden hair in tight-curled ringlets stood there. "You must be Overcaptain Alucius. I'm Queyela. Wyerl said you'd be here any moment. Do come in."

Alucius bowed. "Thank you." He stepped though the doorway into a golden-tiled foyer three yards on a side.

A girl who looked to be ten or twelve stood in the archway on the left side of the foyer.

"Elizien . . ."

Before the girl's mother could finish, Alucius moved forward several steps, stopping well short of the girl, who might have reached midchest on him. "Elizien, that's a beautiful name. Do you like it?" Alucius grinned.

"It *is* my name," the girl replied.

"Mine is Alucius."

"I know. You're an officer who was a herder in the north."

"I'd still like to think I am," Alucius replied.

"Did you really kill a pteridon?"

"Several, actually."

"Why? They're awfully rare. Father says that there haven't been any in Corus since before the Cataclysm."

"I didn't have much choice. The pteridons' riders were trying to kill my troopers."

"Couldn't you have stopped them some other way?"

"Elizien . . . if I had known any other way . . ." Alucius shrugged helplessly. "If they hadn't been trying to kill us, I wouldn't have wanted to do anything to them."

"That's sad."

"Elizien . . ." offered the girl's mother gently, "your father is expecting the overcaptain."

"I know." Elizien bowed, then slipped back down the corridor and out of sight.

"Do you have children, Overcaptain?" asked Queyela.

"No. I expect we will . . . at least I hope we will."

"No matter what you think, you'll be surprised," the woman said with a laugh. "They're expecting you out back. If you come this way . . ."

Alucius followed her to a door open to the rear terrace where the two marshals stood, looking at the garden beyond.

Alucius did his best with his Talent-senses to pick up what they might be saying.

". . . here he comes . . . Recorder claims he's the most dangerous man in Corus . . ."

". . . that was last month . . . good officer . . . Recorder doesn't like them . . ."

". . . don't interrogate him long, Frynkel . . . want a pleasant meal . . ."

". . . just a few moments . . ."

Alucius kept a pleasant smile on his face as he stepped out onto the terrace.

"Alucius!" Wyerl smiled broadly.

Alucius could detect neither malice nor caution behind the words. "Marshal . . . you're most kind to have me here."

"Kind, perhaps, but we always have motives. Submarshal Frynkel wanted a few words with you. I've told him to be brief, but he wished to speak with you before your audience with the Lord-Protector tomorrow."

"It may indeed be brief. I doubt that there is much I have not already told someone."

"I will bring you something to drink. What might you have?"

"Ale or white wine."

"We do have some rather fine ale." Wyerl turned away, leaving Alucius with the other officer.

Submarshal Frynkel stood a span or so less than did Marshal Wyerl, and had already lost most of the hair on his head. What remained was fine and black. His face was dominated by a sharp nose and deep and intent black eyes.

"Overcaptain Alucius. The hero of Dereka." The words were gently spoken, not quite mockingly, but not totally seriously.

"Others may have said such." Alucius laughed. "I only claim to have survived."

"Surviving is often all any of us can claim. Yet your men say little. Did you know that?"

"I cannot say I am surprised. Few would wish to talk about a campaign where they lost so many comrades. Nor one so far from home."

"They would lose more to protect you, Overcaptain," Frynkel added. "That loyalty is most rare."

"They're good troopers, sir, and we've been through much together."

"You lead your men from the front, Overcaptain. Do you know how many officers last through a year of battle in that position?"

"No, sir."

"I've had my staff look into it. There are many things we keep track of. I'm sure you've come to notice that."

"Yes, sir."

"That is not something that we keep track of. So I have sent letters to every commander that I can trust. Do you know what the responses I have received indicate?"

Alucius had a very good idea, but merely answered, "I would not wish to guess against your diligence, sir."

"I wish I had captain-colonels who could tell me 'no' that gracefully." Frynkel laughed, then added, "Not one could recall any officer who consistently led from the front and survived. I'd be most interested in your explanation as to how you have survived something like three years of combat in leadership."

"What else could it be, but luck, or fortune, sir? I've been wounded a number of times, and some of those wounds could have been deadly had they been a span in one direction or another."

"That would have been my first thought. That is, until Captain-Colonel Omaryk and I had supper together. You led at least four charges through vastly superior forces, as the point rider, just at the battle of Dereka. Even nightsilk shouldn't have saved you."

"Sir, I can't explain that. Herders are a shade tougher, because of our training, but I've been cut, bruised, wounded, and burned enough to know that I'm as mortal as any other man." That was absolutely true, so far as Alucius knew.

"You won't get more than that, Frynkel," suggested Wyerl, handing Alucius a tall beaker of pale amber ale and a second one to the submarshal.

"I was hoping. I did have one more question."

Alucius nodded as he took a small swallow of the ale.

"Would it be better for Lanachrona to honor your obligation and release you, or request your service for another year?"

Alucius tilted his head slightly. "That is another question I can't answer. I'm a good officer. There are doubtless others as good. Most of the Northern Guard officers know my situation. If the arms-commander or the Lord-Protector extended my service against my wishes, or created conditions where I had no choice but to agree, I would judge that the effect on other officers in the Northern Guard would be less than desirable. Whether what I might accomplish would be worth that is not something I have the knowledge to weigh."

Wyerl smiled broadly, shaking his head. "What the man is saying, Frynkel, is that he's accomplished miracles and survived, just in hopes of going home. If we extend him, half the officers in the Northern Guard will lose all desire to act as officers should. I wouldn't be surprised if that didn't spill over to our Southern Guard."

With Wyerl's comments, and the heartfelt emotions behind them, Alucius was totally confused. Why had he been ordered to Tempre? Just for information and to be thanked? He doubted that, yet . . .

"You're probably right," Frynkel admitted, "but I was requested to explore that possibility."

"Enough. We have a wonderful meal planned, and we *are* going to enjoy it." Wyerl gestured toward the garden. "This is Queyela's herb garden, or rather the right section is. I don't imagine the ground and climate in the Iron Valleys allow this sort of thing, do they?"

"South of Iron Stem, I've seen a few, but on the quarasote flats, and below the Plateau, where we live, the ground is too dry and sandy for that."

"Is the Plateau truly as tall as they claim?"

"It's higher than the Upper Spine Mountains. My grandsire told me once that the edges rose close to seven thousand yards straight up above the Valleys . . ."

Wyerl nodded.

Alucius understood that the marshal had meant what he had said, that the meal would be just that, and he hoped that he would enjoy it.

"Here's Elizien." Wyerl turned and watched as the brown-haired girl smiled, then beckoned to her father. "I told her she could join us for supper. You don't mind, do you?"

"I'd like that." Alucius smiled. Perhaps he could enjoy the meal.

98

Tempre, Lanachrona

"You are kind, Talryn." Alerya, her countenance ashen, looked up from the pillows of the high bed at her consort. "I am so sorry. I had hoped this time . . . It would have made your tasks easier. Now . . . everyone will know, and matters will be more difficult . . ."

"Having an heir has little impact on who can attack and whom I can trust. The trustworthy remain so, as the untrustworthy remain untrustworthy." The Lord-Protector shook his head slowly. "There are always too few of the former, and too many of the latter."

"You are meeting with the herder overcaptain later this morning, are you not?" Alerya's voice was low, yet forced.

"I am."

"What will you do? Have you decided?"

"Reward him, of course. You knew that. What else can I do? Should I allow his service to be shortened as well?"

"He is a Talent-wielder, is he not?"

"He was successful against the pteridons, and they were most certainly Talent-creatures. At the least he must have a way with them. Enyll claims he is, but I trust Enyll's motives not at all." The Lord-Protector looked at his weak and exhausted consort. "What would you have me do?"

"Tell Enyll that you wish him in the audience chamber for just a moment, to observe the overcaptain and to slip out before you speak. Then ask Enyll afterward what he observed. That will tell you much of what you wish to know."

"And then what?" The Lord-Protector smiled down on his consort, reaching out and caressing her pale cheek. "I should not tire you."

"You have someone give the overcaptain a tour of the palace, of *all* the palace."

"And you think that will—"

"There are . . ." she winced, then continued, "the overcaptain could be like Enyll, or he could be as we believe, a man compelled to do what he believes best, even if he wishes otherwise. Whatever happens or does not will tell you much. If the overcaptain is merely a good man, he will accept your graces and be thankful and return to the Iron Valleys. If he is more, he may act, or not. Or, if he is more, Enyll may act. Ask the overcaptain to wait for you to ready a missive to his colonel. Then . . . you must watch, and be prepared to do what is necessary." Her smile faded. "I . . . am tired . . . so tired."

The Lord-Protector lifted the bell on the table by the bed, then bent down beside Alerya's ear. "I am so sorry. I did not mean to tire you . . ."

"You . . . did not . . ."

He held her hand, and they waited.

99

True to his word, Captain Deen arrived early on Londi, pacing outside the senior officers' mess when Alucius came out after eating breakfast.

"Good morning, sir." Deen bowed as he hurried toward Alucius.

"Good morning." Alucius waited for Deen to join him before he turned down the wide corridor toward the stairs up to his quarters, knowing that he had at least a glass before he had to get ready to leave for the palace.

"I just wanted to brief you on the formalities of an audience with the Lord-Protector," the captain began. "There are a few aspects . . ."

"Go ahead. You might as well start now."

"You must be there, and present yourself to Captain-Colonel Ratyf at least half a glass early. Captain-Colonel Ratyf is the director of appointments. You may wear your working uniform, since there is no fully formal Northern Guard uniform, and your sabre; it's considered a ceremonial weapon, but no other weapons, belt knives excepted, are permitted in the presence of the Lord-Protector. I'm not allowed to accompany you into the audience. This is a private audience, not a public one. There will still be guards behind the screens, and the Lord-Protector's secretary will write down what is said, but you won't even see him . . . really quite an honor, a private audience . . . only a few granted every year . . ."

Alucius continued to listen as they climbed the stairs to the third floor and turned back westward toward his quarters, passing the duty guards.

". . . the Lord-Protector is always addressed as 'Lord-Protector.'

Sometimes he allows his senior ministers and marshals to call him 'sir,' but that is a privilege he must grant . . . and he seldom does . . ."

As they entered the senior officers' quarters, Alucius turned to the captain. "If you would just take a seat here somewhere, while I wash up and get ready?"

"Oh . . . yes, sir."

Alucius closed the door to the sleeping chamber firmly but quietly. Alone there, he debated, then slipped off his tunic. After washing up, he returned and slid the nightsilk vest into place, and then the tunic. He already wore the nightsilk undergarments. In fact, he never went anywhere in public without them, not after all the wounds they had saved him.

The Lord-Protector wanted something, and he didn't want it made too public. Or was the private audience because he didn't want to make too much of a furor over what could have been a disaster in the east while he was overcommitted in the west? Or was it something else entirely? He wouldn't find out until he met the Lord-Protector, and, in some ways, he wasn't certain he wanted to discover what the Lord-Protector had in mind.

Alucius glanced out the window toward the palace. There was also no sign of the purpleness he had felt earlier, nor had there been anytime he had looked.

Finally, he rejoined Captain Deen in the sitting room. "Shall we go?"

"Perhaps we should. We might be early, but better that than to be late. Especially today." Deen stood quickly and turned.

Although he wondered what Deen meant by "especially today," Alucius let that pass for the moment and followed the captain out and down to the courtyard. When Alucius reached Wildebeast's stall, he discovered that his saddle and other tack had been thoroughly cleaned and oiled and rubbed dry and polished.

The stallion tossed his head slightly when Alucius led him out into the courtyard—as if he happened to be pleased to be out of the stall and into the open air.

"There . . . you'll get a ride. Not a long one, but a ride." Alucius mounted and waited for the captain to join him.

Then the two officers rode around the east side of the building. Outside the gates of the headquarters buildings, they turned right, westward toward the river and the Grand Piers that lay beyond the Lord-Protector's palace.

"Why wouldn't it be a good idea to be late, especially today?" Alucius finally asked.

"His consort has been . . . ill."

"Ill?"

"Well . . . she was hoping for an heir . . . and . . ." Deen shrugged helplessly. "They're young, though."

Alucius nodded, not in agreement, but in understanding, while hoping that the Lord-Protector wouldn't take any emotion he might have out on Alucius.

On both sides of the boulevard were what appeared to be gardens. A number of guards in cream-shaded uniforms were posted at intervals along the low stone walls bordering the boulevard, and others walked along the stone paths, many bordered with rows of brilliant blooms and greenery, some of it trimmed into the shape of animals. Alucius saw one tall bush that depicted a rearing horse. Fountains spaced irregularly sprayed into the air. Several women with small children, and at least one older man also walked the paths.

"These are the Lord-Protectors' gardens. They were begun by the Lord-Protector's grandsire. Anyone may come here," Captain Deen said.

"They look well kept," Alucius said.

"They are. The Lord-Protector tariffs anyone who harms them or despoils the flowers or trees."

"If they cannot pay?"

"Then they must work in the gardens at the rate of a laborer until the tariff is paid."

"I imagine few despoil the gardens," Alucius suggested.

"Very few. Many enjoy them. There are flowers from all across Corus, and some even from the western isles. Others come from places one could never imagine, while others . . ."

Beyond both the gardens and the palace, the green towers flanking the Grand Piers were clearly visible, spires identical to the one in Iron Stem and those in Dereka.

"What is inside the towers?" asked Alucius.

"Nothing, sir. The insides are empty, and so far as any know, they have been so since the Cataclysm. There are not even steps or signs of supports for them, only a single entrance at the base. And there are no windows."

"There is one in Iron Stem, and it is exactly the same." Alucius wondered, briefly, what function the towers had served for the Duarchy. In his travels, all that the Duarchy had created to last, such as the eterna-stone high roads, had been built for a purpose. "Does anyone know why it was built?"

"No, sir, unless it was to mark the piers."

The gardens ended at a wall on the right side of the boulevard, a stone wall a good four yards high, which marked the beginning of the palace grounds. On the left side, the gardens—although divided by the Avenue of the Palace running northward from the high road—continued all the way to the Grand Piers.

"We enter here, sir." Captain Dean gestured to the first entrance.

The entryway to the palace was a covered portico little larger or more impressive than that of the entry to Southern Guard headquarters, except that there was a half squad of guards in dark blue uniforms, trimmed with silver, rather than with the cream of the Southern Guard. There were also several stableboys, waiting as the two officers reined up.

Another captain waited at the top of the steps above the mounting blocks. Like Captain Gueryl, he wore blue braid across his shoulders.

Captain Deen did not dismount. "I leave you here, sir."

"Thank you, Captain. I'll find my way back somehow."

"Yes, sir."

Alucius dismounted.

The graying captain stepped down to meet Alucius. "Captain Alfaryl, Overcaptain. Captain-Colonel Ratyf asked me to escort you."

"Thank you." Alucius glanced up. While not quite so large as the Landarch's palace, the structure was still imposing, at least five floors, and stretching a good two hundred yards from east to west. "Has anyone ever gotten lost?"

"We try not to let that happen, sir."

"I can imagine." Alucius followed the older captain through the double stone arches and inside into a square, vaulted entry hall that rose a good ten yards overhead and measured fifteen yards on a side. Light poured through the high clerestory windows on the south side. The floor was polished granite, inlaid with long strips of what appeared to be blue marble, creating a blue-edged diamond pattern.

Captain Alfaryl crossed the entry hall, leading Alucius through the middle of three square arches into a corridor that stretched a good forty yards, but after about twenty yards they turned left into a short corridor, not more than ten yards long. At the end was a set of high double doors. In front of the doors were four more of the guards in blue and silver. Without a word, the guard in the center opened one of the doors, holding it as Alucius and the captain stepped through and closing it behind them.

Alucius found himself in a large chamber, with a number of settees and upholstered armchairs, and with blue-and-cream hangings, and heavy carpets, in blue and cream, laid over the granite floor. On the light-wood-paneled walls hung several portraits, all of men, and presumably of past Lord-Protectors. Except for Alucius, Captain Alfaryl, and the captain-colonel who walked toward them, the chamber was empty.

"Captain-Colonel Ratyf," said Alfaryl, "Overcaptain Alucius."

"Ah . . . yes, sir. The Lord-Protector was wondering . . . Since you're here early, I'll check. The Lord-Protector might wish to see you sooner . . ." The captain-colonel vanished through a small doorway.

Captain Alfaryl looked at Alucius, then around the chamber. "Most unusual . . ."

"The Lord-Protector seeing someone early?"

"He has many demands on his time, sir."

"Usually there are many people here?"

"Yes, sir."

That didn't help put Alucius any more at ease, not when the captain-colonel returned and beckoned. "He'd like to see you now, sir, since you're here."

Alucius turned to Alfaryl. "Thank you."

"My pleasure, sir."

Alucius followed the captain-colonel's gesture, stepping through the larger door in the rear of the waiting chamber.

Ratyf held the door and announced in a deep voice, "Overcaptain Alucius of the Northern Guard."

Alucius stepped into the audience hall, hearing the door click shut behind him.

The hall itself was not that much larger than the corridor leading to the waiting chamber, but the goldenstone walls were draped with rich blue hangings, and light-torches were everywhere, giving the chamber an impression of airiness. The floor was polished white marble, patterned with the blue stone Alucius had seen in the outer entry hall, but the pattern was that of smaller oblongs, not diamonds. He could sense neither apprehension, nor fear—but there was a vague sense of purpleness that he had not felt before.

The Lord-Protector stood before a white onyx throne, a slender dark-haired man in a blue-violet tunic without decorations or ornamentation. The throne's high stone back rose into a spire, a good three yards high, and at the tip of the spire was a shimmering blue crystal star. For a moment, Alucius caught his breath, but let it out as he sensed that the jewel was merely a jewel and not a focus of power the way the crystal of the Matrial had been.

"Overcaptain."

"Lord-Protector." Alucius bowed. As he straightened, he caught sight of a figure to the right and to the rear of the Lord-Protector—an older-looking man in silver vestments. But the silver-garbed man did not *feel* old to Alucius, and his lifethread was black and purple . . . with the tinge of evil that Alucius had only felt with the pteridons and the Matrial.

Before Alucius could more than perceive that, silently and quickly the man in silver vanished through a side door half-hidden on the right side of the dais. Alucius knew that he had missed something beyond the evil, but not what.

"Please join me." The Lord-Protector gestured to a simple chair set on the wide step below the throne-chair, then seated himself on the cushion—the sole softness within the onyx.

Alucius took the chair, noting that he was a perfect target for the marksman who was concealed in the left gallery, and whom he could sense but not see. His eyes did flicker upward. He also worried about the man who had left so quickly.

"Yes," the Lord-Protector said with a smile, "there are guards there. It's a pity, but they have proved necessary in the past. I'd expected you would find them immediately. From what I've heard and seen reported, you miss very little, Overcaptain Alucius."

"I try not to, Lord-Protector." Alucius grinned, hoping it was self-conscious. "There was a minister or someone in silver, who was leaving as I entered . . ."

"Oh . . . the Recorder of Deeds, one of my oldest advisors."

What the Lord-Protector said was true, but far from all that he might have said, Alucius knew, from the combination of both acceptance and surprise felt by the Lord-Protector.

"Is he your secretary . . . I had heard . . ."

"No." The Lord-Protector laughed. "Majer Suntyl is acting as secretary today. That is a position, not an individual." Before Alucius could ask another question, he continued. "You are younger than I had thought, and yet somehow much older. I suppose that follows from all that you have been through. Tell me . . . what was it like to wear a Matrite collar?"

"It made me extremely cautious, Lord-Protector. When someone can kill you without touching you and without an obvious weapon, you try to be very careful."

"Cautious?" The older man smiled. "That is scarcely a word most would apply to you. Yet it fits. What may seem foolhardy to some may be in fact most cautious to a man prepared for the worst. I had heard that when you discovered that you would be facing pteridons, you immediately devised a moving target on which your men could practice. Was that true?"

"Yes, Lord-Protector. I fear it did not help so much as we had hoped."

"I also understand you were a Matrite squad leader in Zalt. I assume that required you to kill Southern Guards."

Alucius didn't hesitate. "Quite a number, sir."

The faintest smile appeared. "Yet you risked your life to save Southern Guards and Lanachrona?"

"When I wore a Matrite collar, my actions were not totally free. Without a collar, I could choose, Lord-Protector." Alucius had to wonder exactly where the audience was headed.

"How did you feel about the union of the Iron Valleys and Lanachrona?"

"I cannot say I was pleased. I felt the Council had acted so unwisely in the past that there were few choices left. From what I have seen, I would rather have the Iron Valleys ruled from Tempre than from Hieron or Dereka or Lyterna."

"That is not the most enthusiastic of replies, Overcaptain," replied the Lord-Protector, a tone of amusement in his voice.

"I am usually better at honesty than deception, Lord-Protector."

"Usually . . . an interesting word, there." The Lord-Protector laughed before continuing. "You are a herder, and you would like to return to being one, I assume?"

"I had hoped to, Lord Protector. I had never planned to remain in the militia, and then the Northern Guard, as long as I have. When I was captured . . . the term was two years, but when I returned, it was four."

"And that term ends at the turn of winter, as I recall."

"It does," Alucius agreed. Unless something else happened.

The Lord-Protector leaned back, as if musing, but Alucius sensed only calculation, not speculation. "Some of the best officers have come from the herders, few as you are. Herding is a very special way of life." He leaned forward. "Everyone has told me that. How would you say that it is special?"

Alucius did not reply immediately, sensing the need for care in responding. Finally, he said, "That is hard to describe, Lord-Protector. A herder needs to understand the nightsheep, the quarasote, and the land. He needs to be comfortable by himself. There are so few herders that I could not say whether we make better officers."

"It would be a shame if the Iron Valleys lost the herders, and yet it could happen so easily."

"It could," Alucius admitted. "The Council came close to destroying us. They only saw the price of finished nightsilk and not the costs of producing it."

"They tried to set the tariffs too high?"

"And they conscripted too many herders. My grandsire is well over twelve quints, and my father is dead. I am the only child, yet they judged that I should be conscripted."

"They did not allow a buyout of some sort?"

Alucius laughed, if gently. "It was set at half the golds received from the sale of nightsilk each year. A herder is fortunate if he retains a tenth part after expenses. Some are fortunate to break even, especially in the dry years."

"Stupidity . . ." murmured the Lord-Protector. "Truly unwise."

Alucius felt the honesty of that judgment.

The Lord-Protector straightened in the onyx throne. "I have read all of the reports of all of the senior officers who have questioned you since you arrived in Tempre. No one disputes that you accomplished what you and others reported. There is too much evidence about the number of nomads and about the destructiveness of the pteridons. Yet . . . no one has been able to explain to my satisfaction how you accomplished this remarkable feat. I would hear it from you."

"I will tell you as best I can. Once we arrived in Dereka . . ." Alucius went on to relate everything he had told everyone else, without adding or subtracting anything that he had stated before, and concluding with his awakening in the officers' quarters in Dereka. ". . . and that was how it came about."

"Truly remarkable," mused the Lord-Protector. "You make it seem as though any thoughtful officer should have been able to do what you did." He laughed once more. "*We* know that for an officer to do what needs to be done in the heat of battle—and when he is not in command—that is most rare. I have perused many reports over the past few years, and many have had good ideas and been unable to carry them out. Yet you, Overcaptain, have always carried out your tactics. Why are you different?" The Lord-Protector focused his entire being on Alucius.

Alucius met his glance and did not look away. "Because, Lord-Protector, I am a herder, and because my grandsire trained me as well as he possibly could. Because I was a trooper and a scout, then a captive, then a Matrite squad leader, and because my men have always trusted me and followed me."

The Lord-Protector nodded slowly. "And because there are no other officers who have been through what you have been." He straightened and smiled. "You are indeed unique, Overcaptain Alucius. More unique than either of us can possibly *say*." The emphasis on the last word was barely there, but it was certainly there in the feelings of the Lord-Protector.

"I have been fortunate, Lord-Protector, and for that I am thankful."

"I notice that you are not wearing the Star of Gallantry."

"No, sir. I didn't feel it was right to wear it. Every trooper there at the battles in Deforya deserved it."

"I see." The Lord-Protector fingered his chin for a moment. "I had requested your presence for several reasons, Overcaptain. First, I had to meet you. It is seldom that one gets to meet a true hero. And second, I wished to reward you myself, because your accomplishments saved Lanachrona from what eventually could have been a most difficult situation, and I wished that you understand that personally." The Lord-Protector lifted a medal—a star, blue enamel over gold, with the gold showing at the edges. "This is the Star of Honor. The last one was bestowed over a generation ago. It may be a generation more before another is bestowed." He smiled. "This is your honor, and if I must, I order you to wear it on all formal and ceremonial occasions."

"Yes, Lord-Protector—"

" 'Sir' will suffice." The Lord-Protector pinned it on Alucius, smiling, and whispering, "Nightsilk vest?"

Alucius nodded.

The Lord-Protector laughed. "I see why you have survived. For such a comparatively young officer, you leave little to chance. My Recorder of Deeds worried that you would not serve Lanachrona well, but you have served far beyond what anyone could expect of any officer. Would that he understood."

Alucius caught *something,* but could not read the message.

"I have tried to do my best in all situations, sir."

"And I trust that you will continue to do so, both here and when you return to the Iron Valleys." Once more there was the slightest emphasis on a word—"here"—but so slight that anyone not as close as Alucius could have caught it. "As part of our appreciation for your efforts, I will be sending back orders to the Northern Guard, ordering your release and return to being a herder, within two weeks of your arrival back in Dekhron."

Alucius managed not to drop his jaw. That—that he had not expected.

"You will have to remain here for a few days, while the marshals and the clerks write up those orders, but it will not be that long."

"Thank you, sir. I deeply appreciate that. *Very* deeply."

"You have the ability to put things to rights, Overcaptain, even when not directly ordered to do so. I hope and trust that you will continue to do so, both here and in the Iron Valleys. It would be a shame to lose herders and their ability to see the right and accomplish it when it is so needed." The Lord-Protector stood.

Alucius stood as quickly as he could. "I will do my best, sir."

"That is all any could ask." The Lord-Protector smiled, then asked, almost as if it were an afterthought, "Would you like a tour of the palace, Overcaptain?"

Alucius understood all too well that it was anything but an afterthought.

"I would, indeed, Lord-Protector, if it would not be a problem. It is most unlikely that I will be returning here, and I would like to be able to relate to others what I have seen."

The Lord-Protector gestured, and a majer appeared to the left of the onyx throne. "Overcaptain, this is Majer Suntyl."

Alucius inclined his head.

"Majer, it would please me if you were to provide the overcaptain with a complete tour of the palace, excepting only my private chambers and the actual chamber of the Table."

Chamber of the Table? Another phrase . . . where had he heard it?

"As you command, Lord-Protector."

"My thanks a last time, Overcaptain," said the Lord-Protector.

Alucius bowed, then retreated down the steps, backward, to avoid turning his back on the Lord-Protector. Majer Suntyl followed.

Once the two men were outside in the corridor off the audience chamber, Alucius turned. "You're weren't required for other appointments?"

"Most times, I would be." The majer shifted his weight, as if uncomfortable.

Alucius tried to project both friendship and openness. "But this morning, he's going somewhere?"

"He canceled all his other appointments this morning, and so . . ." Suntyl shrugged.

Alucius smiled, pressing with his Talent the idea that he needed to know and that the Lord-Protector wanted Alucius to know.

"His consort, you know . . ."

402   L. E. MODESITT, JR.

"How badly is the Lord-Protector's consort ailing?" Alucius said in a low voice. "I had heard . . ."

The majer paused. "Ah . . . I do not know . . . but . . . words . . . rumors . . . there had been no heir, and then everyone was smiling . . . and then, on the end days . . . they were not . . . I fear . . . she did not hold the child . . ."

"That is most unfortunate. I know I would be most distraught if that happened to my wife." Even as he pressed reassurance at the majer, Alucius tried to think of a way that he might be able to use the information, but then tucked that thought away. He needed to concentrate on the tour and the palace, because Feran had been right. The Lord-Protector wanted something. Even without saying anything directly, effectively, the Lord-Protector had requested that Alucius put something to rights in Tempre—and the only thing that seemed not right was the Recorder of Deeds. Did the Lord-Protector suspect the evilness of the Recorder? If he did, and Alucius believed he did, the man was incredibly percep-tive, because the Lord-Protector had no Talent. Of that, Alucius was absolutely certain. So he had brought Alucius to Tempre in a way that the Recorder could not find terribly suspicious.

Alucius smiled faintly.

"I suppose we should start with the Hall of Portraits," Suntyl began. "You've never been here before, have you?"

"No. I haven't. I could be wrong, but I think I'm the first Northern Guard officer ever to visit Tempre. I think the Lord-Protector wanted me to, shall we say, carry back a strong impression of Tempre."

Suntyl smiled. "That sounds very much like him. Very well—the Hall of Portraits. It's the other large hall here on the main level. Most of the chambers here are work spaces. Each of us who serves as his secretary has a space where we write out the records. It's very important that they be accurate . . ."

Alucius nodded, listening as they turned back into the main corridor and continued to the left they reached another short corridor, again with double doors.

"All of the portraits in here are relatives . . . the first on the left, that is the great-grandsire of the present Lord-Protector . . ."

From the Hall of Portraits, they retraced their steps, and saw working spaces, several other receiving halls, a small enclosed garden, and a library holding all the laws of Lanachrona. Then came the lower level, with the kitchens, storerooms, wine cellars, even a small cooperage and carpentry shop. From there, they proceeded down a long and much older corridor toward another set of steps.

They moved past an archway, beyond which Alucius could sense . . . something . . . that purpleness, he thought, although it was so faint that he could not be certain. Alucius had no doubts that he needed to seek out the Recorder of Deeds. Even his momentary sight of the man had made it clear that the Recorder was a danger to both Alucius and even possibly the Lord-Protector, who appeared a more honorable ruler than either the Landarch or the Council, and certainly than the Matrial.

"Where does that go?" Alucius asked.

"Ah . . ." The majer paused. "Those are the working chambers of the Recorder."

"And the chamber of the Table?"

"It is before his chambers. But . . ." The majer radiated worry.

Alucius smiled. "I know. The Lord-Protector said that I was to see everything except it. I certainly wouldn't ask you to go against his wishes, nor to intrude upon the Recorder." Not at the moment. "Is there anything farther down this corridor?"

"Only the root cellars . . ."

Alucius laughed. "Would the Lord-Protector mind if we skipped the root cellars?"

Suntyl smiled. "I think not."

From the lower level, Suntyl led Alucius up two flights to the second level, and through the music room, and the attached concert hall—Alucius had never seen one, nor the clavichord with its polished bone keys. The chambers stretched on and on, and Alucius nodded and listened, trying to keep in mind the location of the chamber of the Table.

Close to two glasses later, the two officers had returned to the main entry hall just off the entry to the palace.

"Thank you very much. The palace is beautiful, and I greatly appreciate your taking the time." As he spoke, Alucius used his Talent to touch the lifeweb thread of the majer, ever so gently.

"Oh . . . feel dizzy . . ." The older man's legs buckled.

One of the guards hurried toward Alucius.

"He said he felt dizzy. Is there someone . . . ?" Alucius looked around. "Could we take him to the receiving room. Would you help me?"

Between the two of them, they carried Suntyl to the receiving room and laid him on one of the settees.

As Alucius straightened, the captain-colonel scurried forward through the smaller door. The guard stepped back, dismissed by a gesture from the senior officer, and quietly left.

"He had given me a tour of the palace, and we were standing in the outer hall," Alucius explained. "He said he felt dizzy, then he collapsed. I didn't know where . . ."

"Oh . . ." Suntyl half moaned.

"It looks like he'll be all right." Alucius looked relieved, as he was, because touching lifeweb threads was a delicate business. "I can find my way back to the entry."

"Are you—"

"I'm most certain, and I thank you both greatly." Alucius bowed, then slipped away, out through the double doors, walking rapidly down the corridor toward the main entry hall.

100

Once away from the Lord-Protector's receiving room, Alucius employed his Talent to create the impression that he was a captain-colonel. It was far easier to twist the impression of something already existing than to create an illusion in the eyes of others of something that did not exist, even if that were an illusion of an empty corridor—and there were more than a few Southern Guard officers in the palace. He paused for a moment, considering. Did he really want to seek out the Recorder?

Did he have any choice? The Lord-Protector would not have set matters up so were there any other option, and if the Lord-Protector happened to be that cautious, the Recorder was indeed dangerous. Alucius disliked the intermittent evil feel that flowed from the man, and he worried how the Recorder would affect the herders and the Iron Valleys if he were not stopped. Yet . . . if Alucius did stop him . . . how might that affect Alucius? Then too, there was the possibility that the Recorder was far stronger than he appeared.

For a time, Alucius just stood in the corridor. Then he turned and made his way down the steps, past the kitchens, using the walk of an officer in a hurry and not wishing to be bothered. So far as he could sense, not a single person gave him even a second glance. Before long, he was walking along the back corridor toward the archway leading into the chambers of the Recorder. As he walked, he realized something else. The Recorder's chambers were well to the north side of the palace, perhaps even under the rear courtyard of the palace.

No one was near him as he stopped before the archway. Somewhere beyond the archway was the distant sense of purpleness. While the stones and structure of the archway resembled the square arches on the upper level, Alucius could feel that they were older, far older, than the remainder of the palace, as if the palace had been built around them. And for a palace to have been built around ancient chambers argued that those chambers contained something of value—or power—like a Table that could see events anywhere?

He took a step toward the doorway, then another. Finally, he eased open the door and slipped inside, into a narrower stone-walled corridor, one that not only felt older, but far more damp, and darker, with but a single light-torch on the wall. Alucius moved forward. He came to a closed door on the left, but he could sense that no one was in the chamber, nor was there any hint of the purpleness.

He walked forward toward the door at the end of the short hallway, a door that was just slightly ajar, then stopped short of it. The sense of evil beyond was strong—and almost palpable. Alucius eased forward and let his senses examine the chamber. The chamber was empty except for one person and the Table. The Table itself appeared rooted into the ground, with a trunk of purple darkness reaching downward and to the north. The Recorder was facing the Table, sideways, so that he would not see the door unless he turned.

Alucius took a slow deep breath and created his illusion of nothingness before he eased the door slightly wider and stepped into the chamber.

The light within the chamber was both golden and pinkish purple. The golden light came from the four light-torches mounted on the wall, set in sconces that had been old generations before, while the pinkish purple light was that seen only through Talent, and radiating from both the Table and the Recorder.

The lifethread of the Recorder was monstrous. Alucius froze for a moment, in spite of himself. The thread was not the normal brown or tan or yellow, black or black shot with green, or even black shot with purple or pink, or the dual pink and black threads he had seen with the torques of the Matrial. Instead, there was the thinnest of amber threads, and braided around that thin amber thread was a pulsing purple rope, and the purpled rope rose from the Table in the middle of the chamber. The Table itself was a dark lorken wood cube with a shimmering upper surface that resembled a mirror.

The Recorder turned, looking straight at Alucius. His smile was chill. "Your illusions mean nothing here, lamaial. You were warned."

"Warned?" Alucius dropped the illusion, and studied the figure beside the Table, who appeared to present two separate images—an older white-haired man and a taller alabaster-skinned and black-haired figure so much like those in the mural—or his dreams.

"Warned," the Recorder reiterated. "You were told that to act against me would set you as the lamaial, and that all lamaials fail."

"I have done nothing, except explore."

"You came here to confront me. Do not deny it. You may not know it, but you were sent. Those who sent you failed before, and they will fail now." The Recorder laughed, a deep and melodic sound that was more chilling than if he had cackled. "In many ways, that will make my task easier, for you are one of the three."

One of the three? That made little sense to Alucius, but then, in dealing with Talent-matters, very little had until after the fact. He couldn't deny that the spirit-woman had warned him, as well, but she certainly hadn't sent him. "No one sent me."

"Then you are doubly a fool, here without allies."

Rather than wait, Alucius reached out with his Talent-sense to strike the lifeweb thread of the Recorder—only to find that the purple-black thread felt armored.

The Recorder laughed. "I am not one of your weakling Coreans, a town sheep to be slaughtered."

Corean? Alucius had never even heard the word.

He could sense a purple mist rising from both the Table and the Recorder himself, shedding a darkness over the chamber, even though golden light flooded from the light-torches.

"I think it best you become someone else . . . and the poor Lord-Protector can say little. You will walk out of the palace . . . and will return to your stead, and no one will be the wiser." The Recorder remained with both his hands on the surface of the Table.

While the Recorder's words continued to make little sense, the danger behind them was more than clear. A wave of purpleness swept toward Alucius, and instinctively, his sabre was in his hand, coated with the darkness of life. He cut through the clinging purpleness and stepped toward the Recorder, although each step was like climbing a yard-high step—slow and deliberate.

"You do have a little Talent, and we can put that to good use, in the right time and place," observed the Recorder.

Ruby mists—unseen except through Alucius's Talent—began to rise out of the Table, swirling around the Recorder and beginning to extend like sinuous arms toward Alucius.

Alucius focused more darkness into the sabre, darkness that flowed outward. The purpleness fell back before the darkness, but the ruby mist-arms did not, boring through the darkness with a sinister glow, twisting toward Alucius.

Alucius stepped sideways, sabre still before him, moving to the side of the Table opposite the Recorder, whose hands remained fixed upon the Table. The man who was older and yet who was not kept his eyes on Alucius, and the ruby mist-arms turned yet again, but undulated through the air around the Table, rather than over it.

Alucius felt coated in sweat, yet he had only been in the Table chamber for the smallest fraction of a glass. Breathing heavily, he willed darkness—pure darkness—toward those dangerous ruby appendages.

For a moment, the arms fell back, and Alucius tried to move around the Table, to reach the Recorder with his sabre. But the red mist-arms swept wider, as if to encircle Alucius. While the darkness-coated sabre stopped the purpleness, the undulating and approaching arms simply twisted away from the blade.

From somewhere came an idea, faint, but clear. *The Table . . . enter the Table.*

Enter the Table? How? It was solid. And why?

Enter the Table.

Alucius struggled to raise more darkness, but both the purpleness and the ruby mists circled around the Table, moving ever closer to Alucius.

How could the Recorder—or the creature that he was—be so strong?

And what could Alucius do? Enter the Table? Just how was he supposed to do that?

Perhaps he could get on it. The mists and the purpleness were avoiding it. And then . . . with the sabre, he could strike directly at the Recorder.

Alucius leapt onto the Table, hoping it would hold him. Landing on the Table with his boots was like landing on stone from several yards, but Alucius still managed to strike at the Recorder with his sabre.

The Recorder jumped back, and a wide smile crossed the man-creature's face. "Even better!"

The solid surface of the Table disappeared, and Alucius felt himself dropping into purplish blackness.

Purplish blackness swirled around Alucius, as if in a stream, an underground and lightless stream, and one in which he was trapped—but there was no current, and the chill was worse than winter at Soulend in a blizzard. He could not see, not with his eyes, and he could not move his body, much as he tried.

His Talent senses revealed the blackness, and through it, he could feel threads, or arrows. One was darkish purple, overlaid with blue, and it was the brightest. Another was the same darkish purple and nearby, but overlaid with silver. A third was golden green, thin, and almost not there, as if hidden, or walled away behind a purplish barrier, or even outside the blackness. Then, there was a long and deep purple-black arrow, so deep, so evil that even considering nearing it with his Talent-senses raised nausea within Alucius.

What could he do?

He concentrated on the blue overlaid arrow, but as he did, he could almost sense the Recorder and the ruby arms searching.

His attention went to the silver arrow, still purple, but without the greedy sense of searching and seeking. Alucius tried to use his Talent to carry him toward the silver arrow—bring the arrow toward him, before the darkness of the Table chilled him so much that he could not even think or use his Talent.

Nothing happened—not that he could sense.

What could he do? Somewhere in the darkness "behind" him, he could sense the ruby mist-arms reaching toward him, and he knew, if they touched him, that he would become . . . either something horrible like the Recorder . . . or cease to exist at all.

He tried to visualize a long thin line of purple, a lifeline of energy, linking him to the silver arrow, pulsing, guiding him toward that silveriness.

Abruptly, silver and light flashed around him.

101

Tempre, Lanachrona

The Recorder of Deeds stood at the doorway to the chamber of the Table, holding it wide for the younger man, similar in appearance to the Lord-Protector, with dark hair, but shorter and with a broader frame.

"Lord Waleryn . . . have you ever seen the Table?" asked the Recorder.

"Only one or twice, with my sire, as you may well recall," replied Waleryn, his voice smooth and polished. "Since then, my invitations have been few. Nonexistent in point of fact."

"I thought perhaps you should see it," suggested Enyll. "I found some references . . . and have improved it."

"I'm not the Lord-Protector, Recorder. There is little I can do."

"That may be for now, but the Lord-Protector has no heirs but you, and you should know what the Table can do. The Lord-Protector has not so informed you, has he?"

"He has been somewhat . . . occupied of late with his consort. Alerya has been less than well . . ."

"I do understand. He is most deeply concerned about her." The sympathy in the Recorder's voice was less than deep.

"What exactly do you have in mind, Enyll? You did not invite me here to discuss either the Table or my elder brother's domestic difficulties."

"Domestic? If there is no heir, the difficulties go far beyond domestic. But . . . that is not our matter at present. I did in fact invite you here to show you the Table. And there is the matter of heirs, in a differing fashion."

"A differing fashion? That is a decidedly odd phrase."

"Not at all. I am not so young as I once was," the Recorder said flatly. "I have seen none with Talent who can use the Table. What is not known is that someone with an agile mind can use some of the Table's functions. Not all, but enough, and I would propose that you, having the interest of your family at heart, would be someone to whom I could entrust such knowledge."

The faintest smile crossed Waleryn's lips, then vanished.

"There must be someone," the Recorder added. "You would not wish that such knowledge be lost to your family, would you?"

"No, indeed. That I would not."

Both men smiled.

102

Alucius found himself standing on the Table—alone in the chamber—still holding his sabre. His entire body was shaking, shivering, and his legs felt weak, but his uniform was dry, although frost appeared upon it, then melted away almost instantly without wetting the fabric.

He looked around, bewildered as he realized that he was in another chamber, windowless, and similar to the Recorder's chamber, and standing on another Table, similar, but not identical. He quickly sheathed the sabre and eased his way off the Table, studying both the chamber and the Table. Unlike the Recorder's Table, the one before him was far newer, as if it had been recently created. And the chamber in which it was contained was clearly newly built. In fact, Alucius realized, it had not even been completed. There were no wall hangings, and only a pair of light-torches on the wall, of a design he had never seen, and those torches were hung on simple wooden pegs inserted between the stones of the wall. While the stones were far older, they had doubtless come from another structure.

On one side of the chamber was a table desk, with a stool before it.

His eyes flicking to the closed door, Alucius moved quickly toward the desk and the single short stack of paper upon it.

He glanced at the top sheet, a diagram of some sort, but squinted at the writing. Some words looked familiar, but others were not, much in the way written Madrien had first appeared to him immediately after he had been captured by the Matrial's forces.

Where was he? And how had the Table brought him? Or how exactly had his Talent allowed him to use the Table to escape the Recorder? And how could the Recorder have been so strong? Alucius had never felt that kind of Talent-strength before.

Then, Alucius realized, he had never confronted the Matrial directly. He had destroyed the crystal, and that had destroyed the Matrial. He glanced at the Table, looking at it with both eyes and Talent, seeing it deeply rooted into the earth—and far, far more deeply—linked through the dark conduit to something . . . somewhere far, far distant.

Leaving the Table and the incomprehensible diagram, he eased to the door, letting his senses range beyond it.

A sentry was posted outside, and with his ear against the oak of the door, Alucius could hear the sounds of chisels and hammers, as if the structure without were still being built.

Where was he? And what was he going to do about it? What could he do? He glanced around the chamber again, taking in the lack of windows and a certain earthy smell. Did the Tables have to be built so that they were in contact with the earth or rock? There were other thoughts, impressions, but he could not remember them, that he knew fitted with that idea.

Someone was coming—another person exuding the pinkish purpleness that felt so evil.

Alucius surveyed the chamber yet again. Except behind the Table, there was no place to hide. With nowhere to conceal himself, he unsheathed the sabre and stood against the wall, behind where the door would open.

The door swung open, creaking as if it had not been well fitted, and a thin man not that much older than Alucius stepped through. He closed the door firmly, with a solid click. Then he slammed a bolt in place and whirled, reaching for what looked to be a holstered pistol.

Alucius slashed across the other's right shoulder, and the sabre felt as though it had struck mail—or nightsilk. Alucius could barely hang on to the blade, so severe was the impact, but he managed to bring the blade back up, aiming for the other's uncovered wrist.

Instead of striking the wrist, Alucius hit his forearm, with another impact like hitting nightsilk.

For a moment, the two staggered. Alucius switched the sabre to his right hand, because his left was so numb that he doubted he could hold on to the blade for another slash or thrust.

The other man sprang sideways and wrestled out the pistol, moving away from Alucius.

A beam of blue light flashed by Alucius's shoulder. A pattering of solid stone droplets hit the stone floor, and the stones on the wall steamed around a triangular gap where the light beam had eaten them away as if they were snow dropped onto a hot stove.

Blue light that destroyed stone? With but a sabre, Alucius felt very much at a disadvantage. Very much. He lunged forward, grabbing the stool by one leg and throwing it at the man—or Recorder.

As the other dodged, moving to block the door, Alucius dashed to the Table, putting it between him and the other.

"Who are you?" asked the thin man, who, like the Recorder, seemed to be two individuals, one of them alabaster-skinned and violet-eyed, although that image appeared only to Alucius's Talent-senses.

"Alucius." He kept his body low. "Who are you? Another Recorder?"

"Vestor is the current name. You could call me an engineer."

"Where are we?"

"Here. In Prosp. Where else would we be?" Vestor raised the black handgun.

Alucius dropped below the top of the Table, knowing that Vestor would not destroy it. Still the line of blue light flashed just above his head. Behind him, more stone vaporized, then condensed into solid droplets, falling like hail. Alucius did not look back or up, but rather used his Talent-senses to watch the other.

The other man kept the weapon leveled, waiting. But he did not call for the sentry outside, and that was in itself chilling to Alucius.

Alucius reached out toward the other's purple-twined lifethread, serpentlike, and struck. It was like using the sabre all over again, with his Talent rebounding against him. But, unlike the Recorder, Vestor staggered as well as Alucius.

Then, as before with the Recorder, Vestor, still holding the light-knife, looked toward the Table, and ruby mists began to rise from the silvered surface. For a few moments, they were but gossamer fog, but they quickly began to thicken into the same kind of arms that the Recorder had created and with which he had attacked Alucius.

Alucius could find no way out of the room, except by the barred door. Or the Table. And trying to attack a man whose weapon sliced through solid stone, and who appeared invulnerable to both a sabre and a Talent-attack—that was doomed to failure.

Alucius swallowed, trying to compose himself, then bounded up and threw himself flat onto the Table, willing himself to be anywhere else. Anywhere else. For a long moment, he just lay there, exposed, wondering if he'd made another huge mistake.

Vestor lowered the black weapon, as if trying to line it up to strike Alucius and not the Table itself.

The blue beam slashed toward Alucius, and, despite the nightsilk, he could feel the heat and the incredible pain—before he again fell through the once-solid surface of the Table.

Even as Alucius hurtled downward into the chill purple-blackness, he had to wonder how he could do something, anything. He hadn't planned on running into the actual figures in the Derekan mural—or their descendants—who had Tables that saw everything and functioned as doors to other places. Who wore the equivalent of nightsilk and whose Talent-powers were far greater than his. And who regarded him as little more than an annoyance.

For a moment, the chill was welcome, damping out the agony of fire in his shoulder, but within instants, he felt both the fire and the chill, and he would have convulsed into feverish shivers—except his body was immobile in the stream of blackened purple.

What could he do? The blue arrow led back to the Recorder, the silver to the Recorder, and the dark purple conduits to something far worse, he feared.

With his Talent, and a mind becoming increasingly sluggish, he groped toward the golden yellow arrow thread, frail, hidden, and walled away. The nearer he seemed to come, the more distant it seemed to be.

Instead of trying to approach the golden green, he tried something else—just to be with and like it, to find peace in the cool green, to escape the fire in his shoulder, and the ice that chilled the rest of him.

Once more, he burst through a barrier, two barriers, in fact, one of purple-blackness, and the second one of gold and silver that sprayed away from him as light flared around him.

Then, red agony and blackness smashed into him.

103

Northeast of Iron Stem, Iron Valleys

The afternoon harvest sun flooded the quarasote flats under the Aerial Plateau with both light and heat, and sandy dust rose with each step of the two mounts—and the lighter steps of the nightsheep.

From where she had been riding, to the east of the nightsheep, Wendra reined up abruptly, wincing.

"What is it?" Royalt called out even as he eased his gray toward her.

Wendra pulled off her heavy herders' gloves and looked down at the black crystal of her ring, then at the reddened skin that bordered it. She waited until Royalt neared and reined up almost beside her.

"There's something wrong," she said. "Alucius is hurt. It's not the same as last time."

"What do you mean?" asked Royalt.

"The ring. It turned cold, like ice. That was perhaps a glass back, but then it warmed up. I wondered, but I could feel that he was all right. This time, there was fire, enough to redden my skin, and then . . . then there was more of the chill."

"Is he . . . ?"

"He's alive, but he's badly hurt." Wendra swallowed. "This feels different from the last time. I don't know how, but it does."

"He should be in Tempre. Sanders . . . I hope that the Lord-Protector . . ." Royalt shook his head. "But it doesn't make sense. Why would the Lord-Protector make such an announcement, inviting him there, and then . . . ?"

"Do you suppose he was on his way home? Or back to Dekhron?" asked Wendra, still looking down at the black crystal.

"That could be. That could be. Some of those on the Council—or that sandsnake Weslyn . . . They've tried before."

"He stopped them, then, didn't he?"

"He did," the older man admitted, "but even sandsnakes learn from their mistakes, and when you're successful, you don't learn much."

"You worry that he's been too successful, don't you?" asked the woman.

"Alucius has seen evil, Wendra, but what he hasn't seen, not yet, is how easily it can spread, and how effective it can be. He has not seen or felt truly powerful evil. That is something an old herder can sense—even if I know not the cause." He paused. "Should we head back to the stead?"

She shook her head. "I can't do anything, and I'd just fret." A bitter laugh followed her words. "I'll worry anyway, but here I'll have something to do."

Royalt nodded.

104

Once more, Alucius found himself standing in a strange room, an empty chamber with a single wide window before him. The walls were of an amberlike stone, holding depths of light. He glanced down. Beneath his feet was a simple silver square, looking like a mirror, except that it showed absolutely no reflection. His shoulder felt as though it were on fire, and when he glanced down, he could see that the engineer's weapon had sliced away a section of his tunic and shirt, but not the nightsilk beneath.

Even as he looked up and took in the room, he could feel the room begin to spin around him. He staggered several steps toward the wall, putting out his left hand to steady himself as his legs began to tremble and give way.

He sagged to the floor, wondering where—once more—he might be, even as the pain from his right shoulder continued to mount. Redness blurred over his eyes, and the room began to spin around him, faster . . . and even faster.

Was there some sort of greenness?

Or was it wistful thinking?

He tried to raise his head, to focus on a shimmering golden green-ness . . . and failed.

Darkness—deep darkness—swept across him.

The darkness lightened, and he could sense figures who appeared around him, blocky figures, followed by green and shimmering figures. But another wave of darkness, hot and feverish darkness washed over him, dragging him into depths that were cooler.

How long he lingered in the darkness, Alucius had no idea, save that once more the deep green darkness lifted, so that he felt himself in more of a fog, silent, with no sounds, no echoes, and, once more red agony seared through his shoulder. Yet after that ravaging blast of red pain, the heat and the pain in his shoulder began to subside.

Before he could appreciate that, he drifted—or was pushed—back into the dark depths.

He struggled through more darkness, darkness interspersed with dreams of alabaster-skinned men and women with snakelike unseen appendages, and with pistols that fired blue light-knives that always seemed to find his shoulder, no matter how he ducked or tried to raise the lifeweb darkness against them.

Once more, Alucius woke slowly, lying on the narrow bed, feeling the heat pour off his forehead, and from his shoulder. He could barely turn his head, just enough to see that a shimmering dressing was fastened across his right shoulder, a dressing that provided both heat and chill simultaneously. His eyes lifted, but he could only see the amber walls, those and a solid doorway, smaller than he would have thought.

A small feminine figure appeared beside his bed.

You must eat. Then you must rest. You were badly injured. You will be better. But you must eat.

"How . . . ?" Alucius couldn't even lift his arms, they felt so heavy.

You will recover . . . eat to strengthen your body . . .

She spooned something from a platter into his mouth, a mushy substance tasting vaguely of prickle, but far better, or so it seemed. Alucius swallowed slowly, then accepted some more. The third spoonful was something else, fruitlike, cooler.

As he ate, he could feel himself getting more and more tired, and his eyelids heavier and heavier . . . and he slid slowly into the comforting green darkness, and slept, this time without dreams.

105

Alucius yawned and started to stretch. A twinge of pain ran down his right arm, and he stopped. It was only a twinge, not the searing agony it had been. Suddenly, he realized that he was awake, truly awake. He had no idea how long he had drifted between sleeping and waking, with shadowy figures amid the green-washed darkness. He remembered talking to someone, but not whom, nor what he had said.

He glanced around the room. Whether it was the same room in which he had found himself after struggling to escape from the strange engineer he had no idea, only that it had the same amber walls, walls containing a depth beneath their surface—and a shade similar to the yellow golden thread he had followed through the darkness between the Tables. He did not recall seeing a bed in the first room, but he had not seen much before he collapsed.

Slowly, he turned his head to the right. There was a single window in the room, and through it he could see the silver-green sky of Corus. He studied the window and its casement more closely, realizing that the glass was so clear, so transparent. He had never seen glass so fine. Likewise, the glass was set not in wood, but in a shimmering silvery metal that was not silver. On the wall there was a row of amber pegs, pegs that were seamlessly attached to the walls. From the pegs hung his uniform, his nightsilk undergarments, and his sabre. There was no sign of the burns and damage to his tunic. His boots were neatly set against the wall under his uniform.

Only then did he fully realize that he was wearing a dark green, loose-fitting gown of some sort, of a fabric even smoother than nightsilk. He fingered the fabric with his left hand, trying to determine what it might be.

Finally, he eased his legs over the side of the narrow bed and stood. His legs and knees felt unsteady, but he took three steps until he stood before the door, a solid sheet of golden wood without windows, or peep-holes, and a single lever handle of the same metal as the window case-ments. He touched the door, which felt far smoother than wood but showed no grain. The door lever did not turn, no matter how hard he pressed down or lifted. He pushed at the door itself, but it did not even vibrate. He tried to probe the door with his Talent, but something in both door and walls stopped him.

He stepped back. He was definitely confined. He looked toward the window, its casements of the same polished and shining amberlike stone as the walls. As he did, he realized something else. The room was wedge-shaped, far narrower at the end with the door, and wider at the window. The wall in which the window was set also curved.

He walked slowly to the window, and the glass that was so clear. For a moment, he stood there studying it, until he saw the flat bracket on one side. He pressed it and tugged. The window slid to the left so easily that he almost lost his balance, and a chill wind rushed into the room, a wind that was winterlike.

He shut the window, quickly. The gown was scarcely proof against winter cold. Then he frowned, realizing that the silvery frame had slipped right into the stone of the casement. He opened the window again, just slightly. The frame did not move, but the glass slipped through the silvery metal without even the faintest of cracks showing between glass and metal.

He tried to use his Talent, but while he could sense beyond the window, something about the amber stone prevented him from perceiving anything inside the structure.

After closing the window once more, he studied the view. He was in a round tower of some sort. Below were other structures of circular and arcing designs that extended a vingt or so from the tower to a circular wall of the same amber stone that comprised the tower and the buildings below. Out beyond the walls, the ground was white, white sand that shimmered and glittered in the morning sun. Farther out, the whiteness ended in a rampart of dark rock, rising at least half a vingt straight up. All along the top of that rampart ran green-tinted crystal oblongs, but those crystals did not so much reflect as draw in and catch the sun's rays.

The crystals looked familiar . . .

Alucius sensed a greenish radiance behind him. He turned back as the door opened, and a soarer appeared.

You are much better. The soarer looked young, and very feminine, her shape shrouded by the golden-tinged green mist that acted as a garment. Her lips did not move, although Alucius understood the words clearly.

He looked into her eyes, brilliant green eyes that were clear, and deep—and very old, Alucius felt, so old that he felt like a ten-year-old on the stead again. "Where am I?"

The hidden city. It is not for you. Not once you are well and prepared to do what must be done.

"The hidden city? How . . . ?"

You know how you reached us. You could not have come here without knowing how.

"But I don't know where."

That does not matter. What matters is that you must finish healing and learn more about how to master yourself and your Talent.

"Were you the one who showed me the mural?"

That matters little. You saw the mural and were warned, but you did not understand fully its meaning. Or the power of those shown.

Alucius considered her words for a moment, stifling a yawn. Perhaps he was not so strong as he had thought. He moved toward the bed and sat down, his eyes still on the soarer. "I saw that the Duarchy was actually ruled by a different people, the alabaster-skinned people, who were like the Matrial."

The Matrial and even the engineer and the Recorder of Deeds are but pale weaklings compared to those who once ruled Corus and who will return if you do not undertake to learn and master yourself.

"Why can't you?" Alucius didn't like being rushed into things he didn't understand, recalling all too clearly his grandsire's advice about that, and about how superiors used people. And he was feeling that he had been used—or had let himself be used, again and again. He thought about the mural and the Cataclysm. "You did it before, didn't you?"

The soarer remained standing before him. Standing, not soaring—and silent.

"Why me? You've been protecting and watching me for years, haven't you? What do you want from me?"

If you do not learn, and return and kill the engineer and his sibling, Corus will once again become as it once was, before it dies.

"As it was? In the time before the Cataclysm? How could that happen?"

The soarer shrugged. *One of the dark . . . ifrits . . . has taken possession of the engineer.*

"Ifrits?"

Creatures . . . beings with great and evil powers. With but one fully working portal, possession is all that is possible for higher intelligence. These ifrits can transport Talent-creatures, but those creatures cannot last long in your world. If the ifrit in Prosp remains there and can construct another portal while his sibling repairs the one in Tempre, then they can transport other dark ifrits into your world where they will possess anyone they wish. They prefer those with Talent, like you or your Wendra.

"But why?"

Their world is slowly dying. It is dying because they seize and drink in the lifeforces of all around them, because they use the lifeforces of a world for everything. Once they have sucked a world dry, they look for others. Through dreams, visions, they entice beings throughout the endless worlds circling endless stars to build the Tables, promising great knowledge and power.

"And the Cataclysm?"

It was a Cataclysm . . . we managed to break all the lines of force that held the portals together . . . and they sought another world . . . less intractable . . . but it too is now dying, and they are trying to return here.

"Why can't you—"

We are an old race, and there are few of us left . . . fewer every generation . . . we no longer possess the power to wrench whole world-threads the way we once did.

Alucius could sense the quiet desperation. "What do I do? How can I best them? The Recorder almost destroyed me."

You have been through the Table portals with all your being, not just your mind. You can draw upon the power of the portals and the world, more strongly than they can now. The portals are tools, nothing more. When you are stronger, we can help you master yourself.

"Why me?" Alucius asked once more, feeling the heaviness in his eyes.

Who else? Your race is young, and there are few with Talent. Except among your herders. Talent is not valued. Among others, it is despised. In many lands, those with Talent are killed at birth if they are recognized, later if they are not.

Just like everyone else, the soarers wanted to use him.

No! The soarer's response was like a hot and cold shock, indignant and with a truth Alucius had trouble ignoring. *You have promise, much promise, and you could do far better than did we.*

"You . . . you have this city, and you can soar and—"

There is much you do not know. We have counted more failures than any would wish. We cannot compel you. We cannot force you. We can only show you and hope you will see the need. The soarer's unspoken words felt softer at the end, softer, almost pleading, and despairing.

Alucius had no words, and his eyelids were heavy, so heavy.

Whatever may come, you must rest.

The green radiant darkness was a welcome relief from all the thoughts that swirled in and around and through his mind.

106

Tempre, Lanachrona

In the cool of the early evening, the Lord-Protector eased his way into the bedchamber, peering toward the bed.

"I am awake, Talryn."

The Lord-Protector closed the chamber door behind him and crossed the room, settling himself into the chair beside the high bed. "How are you feeling, dearest?"

"I am better," replied Alerya.

"But not so much as I would prefer."

"You should have gotten a stronger consort, my dear." Alerya's voice betrayed the effort to speak.

"I wanted you. I love you for your depth and your thoughts."

"Would that . . . my body were as strong as my thoughts."

Talryn leaned forward, reaching out and touching her cheek. "You will get stronger. It will take time, but you will."

"You are tired . . . and fret much. The war in the west . . . or the over-captain . . . or both?"

"The war is going as we had thought. The Northern Guard took Klamat and advances steadily southward. They also are a good hundred vingts to the west of the Westerhills on the midroad. If all goes not too badly, we should hold Harmony by the end of fall. It could be earlier."

"Be careful."

"I have cautioned both Alyniat and Wyerl that we wish to hold the lands, not ravage them, and to advance only when we can control what we take." Talryn moistened his lips. "I am still worried about the over-captain. He left Suntyl and Ratyf, and everyone saw him walk out. But he never reached the palace entry." Talryn frowned. "That was near-on a week ago. There have been no reports of unknown officers. No one has found a body. I cannot tell anyone that one of my officers vanished from the palace. Can you imagine that? Yet sooner or later, we will have to send some dispatch north to Dekhron. No matter how I handle it, it will cause trouble. I summon the man to Tempre and commend him—and he vanishes? Everyone will think the worst."

"That is not all bad. They will at least not think you weak. Tell his squad that he is undertaking some commission for you. Give them furlough. If he does not return, commend him further and send golds to his widow, then send the squad back."

"That may be what I must do, but he is a good officer, and he saved me from great difficulty."

"Have you asked Enyll to use the Table?"

"No. I can see no good in that. The overcaptain has enough Talent that the Table will not show him. If Enyll is somehow behind this, as I fear he is, then it will reveal clearly that I suspect him. Yet . . . how could he have caused the man to vanish, without anyone seeing, without any trace? Every hall is watched, every door guarded. Does this mean I can trust none of it?"

"You never could, dearest." The faintest laugh colored Alerya's words.

The Lord-Protector laughed, too loudly. "You are good to remind me of that. But there are some I can trust, and they would have heard. Eventually, word does pass."

Alerya nodded, waiting for her husband to continue.

"Then, there's Waleryn. He has less than good on his mind. He's wearing that smile that means nothing except that he's plotting something."

"Do you think it has to do with the overcaptain?" Alerya coughed.

The Lord-Protector immediately stood and offered her a sip from the goblet on the bedside table. "You should not talk. I should not talk to you. I would not weary you."

"I can listen . . ."

"Then . . . listen only . . . I cannot deny that it helps to clear my mind, for me to talk to you, and to see how you hear what I say." He leaned forward, half-standing, and kissed her forehead. "You are still too warm."

"Your healer says that I am better . . . Go on . . ."

Talryn opened his mouth, as if to protest, then smiled faintly before speaking. "Waleryn . . . I do not think he had anything to do with the overcaptain. He could not best the man, not by himself, and where there are more than one or two gathered together, then in time I do hear. I have heard nothing. That does not mean that Enyll has not hatched something with my dear brother." He looked at Alerya. "Rulers should not feel guilty, but I do. I hinted that Enyll might be a difficulty to be set right. To the overcaptain. He caught my meaning. I *know* he did. Now he has vanished."

"Then . . . best . . . you be most careful with Enyll . . . and send Waleryn someplace far from Tempre for the harvest . . . and fall . . ." Alerya paled.

The Lord-Protector bolted upright and reached for the bell.

"No . . . be better . . . moment . . . hold my hand . . ."

Talryn continued to hold the bell in one hand, holding his consort's in the other. But he did not set the bell down as he watched Alerya closely.

107

Alucius opened his eyes. For a time, he did not move at all. The room remained as it had been. His uniform and boots were still hung from the pegs on the wall. Through the clear glass of the window, he could see a clear silver-green sky that darkened as he watched. He eased himself into a sitting position, favoring his right side and arm, but there was barely a hint of discomfort in the once-injured arm and shoulder. He had clearly slept most of the day.

The chamber remained silent, and he turned and swung his feet over the side of the narrow bed, letting them rest on the cool green tiles of the floor. There was no sign of the square mirror, a good indication that he had been moved from the room in which he had originally appeared. He hadn't even thought of the mirror when he had wakened before, a sure sign that he had not been as alert as he had thought he had been.

Why didn't the alabaster-skinned people or creatures sense the yellow thread? If they were so powerful, why hadn't they attacked the soarers? And if the soarers were strong enough to keep them from entering the hidden city, why couldn't they stop the invasion through the Tables—or portals? They certainly built well enough to keep his Talent confined within the room.

The eaters of lifeforces cannot sense what you call the yellow thread. It is not within their dark conduit. You sensed it beyond the conduit, and you had to reach outside the conduit. That shows how strong you are.

Alucius turned his head. He had not heard or seen the soarer—or sensed her.

We can watch without being sensed. That takes little energy. A sense of ruefulness accompanied the words.

"You say that I am strong. I didn't feel that way against them. How can I overcome . . . such strength?" In fighting both the Recorder and the engineer, Alucius had not felt so helpless since he had been seventeen and had been manhandled in the training given by his grandsire.

A small man with one of your rifles can kill a far larger and stronger man who is unarmed. Compared to the ifrits, you were unarmed. You must first learn what strength is.

"What is it?"

You have seen the lifethreads, and the way that they hold and embrace the world. Each world that holds life holds threads. All life is one, and the threads link all that lives. You see but the larger threads.

Alucius considered her words for a moment, before replying. "*All* life creates threads, even the shellbeetles and the bugs and—?"

Life does not create the threads. Where there is life, there are threads. The two are inseparable. A touch of dark humor radiated from the soarer. *You should know. You have seen what happens when you break the thread.*

Alucius nodded, aware that even that movement left him with the slightest sense of dizziness.

You still are weak.

"I can feel that." He tried to gather scattered thoughts. "Just knowing that there are more threads isn't going to help me much."

Each thread is composed of smaller threads. Those, in turn, have yet smaller threads.

Alucius could sense the condescension, and, had he not been so weak, might have said something, but just sitting on the edge of the bed and listening took an effort.

Whoever . . . whatever controls the smallest of threads . . . controls what will be. To control such threads takes both knowledge and strength. We have the knowledge, but no longer have the strength. You have the strength, but not the understanding. If you are willing, we will teach you.

Willing? It wasn't as though he had a choice. Would the soarers even let him leave if he didn't agree?

We could guide you back to the portal in Tempre.

Alucius laughed. That would leave him little better off. Even if he could find a way to kill the Recorder—and he wondered if even a rifle would work—he'd *know* that the other creature was still at work. Sometimes, what appeared to be choices weren't.

It is still a choice. What limits your choice is understanding. A wise spirit always has fewer choices than a foolish one.

"I'm not exactly wise. A wise man wouldn't have gotten himself in this situation."

Even the wisest of spirits can find themselves in the greatest of difficulties.

Alucius could sense the sadness behind those words, a sadness he did not wish to look into. He had enough problems as it was, and he had a definite feeling that, if the soarer felt that Alucius's problems were not that difficult, whatever might be the "greatest of difficulties" for soarers was doubtless well beyond his poor abilities.

"What do I do?" he finally asked.

The soarer extended a tray on which were a platter and a tall beaker of the amber beverage that was similar to ale, but was not. *For now . . . you must eat and rest. In the morning, we will begin. What lies before you is far more difficult than anything you have yet attempted.*

More difficult than anything he had attempted? Those were words Alucius could have done without.

108

Alucius stood. Still wearing the greenish gown that came but to his knees, he walked to the window, that sheet of glass so clear that it appeared not to be there, set in its shimmering silvery frame. He pressed the bracket and slid the window open, leaning out into the chill, and trying to see more of the tower. There was little to see, except that he could tell it was circular and perhaps thirty yards across, although that was a guess. Below, he saw no movement, just the same buildings of amber stone.

He eased his upper torso back into the room and tugged the window shut. He was shivering.

Alucius sensed the soarer and turned.

She stood inside the door, again with a tray that contained the alelike drink and his breakfast, something similar to egg toast, with honey, and thin slices of ham. A plumapple was set at one side as well.

While you eat, I will tell you more.

Alucius walked back to the bed, where he seated himself, the beaker on the floor, the tray in his lap, because there was no other furniture in the room except for the bed and a chest-high and narrow washstand— and what passed for a chamber pot.

Once there was a world with a deep green sky . . .

"This world?" mumbled Alucius.

The soarer ignored the question. *The winds were fierce, and the summers were as cold as the winters are now in Corus. In the winter, all the rivers froze, even to the depths of the river beds. There were small animals, the size of your hand, if not smaller, who learned to link themselves to the lifethreads of the world itself and travel those threads as if they could fly. They were so small and light that the world did not notice. That was good, because the life of the world was young, and the threads were yet delicate. The ages passed, and more animals appeared, and many were large. Some were fierce, and their lifethreads were far stronger. They preyed upon others, including those who had learned to travel above the ground. Those who soared had become larger, and some came to use the lifethreads of the very predators to escape them. Others used the lifethreads to prey upon the predators. Yet they were one, although some were soarers and others were not. The ages passed. Like your ancestors, they became aware of themselves and their world. They began to change the world, to better suit their needs, and the days became warmer—*

"Change the world? How?"

Listen to the story, first.

At the tartness of the soarer's response, Alucius tightened his lips, then took a deep breath, and a swallow of the amber alelike drink, better than any ale he had tasted before.

The days became warmer, and the winds gentler, and there was more rain, and the rivers did not freeze solid in winter, and plants like quarasote spread northward and across the lands. Those who could soar grew in size and knowledge in this youth of the world. And then, the world changed. Webs of darkness slashed across that early world, and when they lifted, there were other, strange creatures now living in the warmer and lower lands. These creatures were different, for they had not arisen from the crystal, but from the coal.

"Coal?" Alucius couldn't help the inadvertent question.

The elementary substance which is at the heart of coal. In time, you will understand. Please do not interrupt. So there were two kinds of life in the world, and yet both were linked with their lifethreads, to each other and to the world itself. There were those creatures who had arisen first, out of the

very crystal and fury of the world, and those that had come from else-
where. At first, the new creatures lived only in a few southern valleys, but
the plants and the trees that came with them also began to change the
world, making the air warmer and damper, and the soils moist and thick.
Most of those who soared felt uncomfortable in the dampness and heat,
and they retreated to the north and the heights of the world, where they
built new and glorious cities. Some few remained in the warmer lands, but
even they preferred drier or higher lands. As time passed, some creatures
arose that partook of both heritages. The soarer stopped, as if waiting for
Alucius to ask a question.

Alucius finished the last of the egg toast, then took a long swallow
of the drink before speaking. "You're saying that, sometime long, long
ago, the lifeforce-eaters—the . . . ifrits . . . put people like us on . . . this
world . . . on our world?"

Yes.

"But . . . why? Why did they do that, then leave it . . . us alone?"

Farmers plant crops and make sure that they grow. It is not from kind-
ness.

Alucius disliked thinking of himself as a crop, ready to be harvested.
"Then . . . they're older than you are. And you think I can best them?"

They are not what they once were. Neither are we. You are more than
you once were. We have seen to that.

"You?"

Enough. You have little enough time to learn what you must. You
needed to know from where you came, and how all this came to be. You do
not act well in ignorance. A sense of laughter followed.

Who did, Alucius asked himself. "But the Cataclysm?"

At first, when the lifeforce-eaters appeared among the primitive farmers
in the south, we did not even notice, and that was our great mistake. None
of us cared for the heavy damp lands to the south. Unless we looked
closely, there was little difference between the poor farmers and those who
came to rule them. In the beginning, there was no difference, for those of
your ancestors were guided by dreams and visions, not directly. Even the
building of the first cities was guided from afar. Then came the building of
the portals—what you call Tables—and the first of the actual ifrits

appeared in body upon the lands of Corus. Then, when we saw what had happened, we tried, as you did, to attack. Thousands of us died under the light-knives and the firelances. Thousands of them died as well, but there were more of them.

The soarer's story was making Alucius more and more uneasy.

They increased the crops and the numbers of your people, so that they could feast. We returned to the north and our hidden cities and turned our thoughts to the very basis of being. When we had learned what we could, we wrenched the very world threads, in a way that severed the lifethreads of all those of the purple, and slashed the conduits to their worlds. When we wrenched the world threads, we also made other changes, those that we could . . .

"The nightsheep and the sanders and sandwolves?"

The nightsheep and sandwolves . . . yes. The sanders are kin to us. Those efforts exhausted us, and many died. We have never had many children.

"How many of there are you? Now?"

Once more, the soarer did not reply, and Alucius sat on the bed, numb. His people, his ancestors, sent from elsewhere, almost as . . . town sheep or cattle, less than footwarriors in a leschec game between the soarers and the ifrits. And not a hint of it in anything he had learned. Truly, the Legacy of the Duarches was to be feared and shunned, and yet no one he knew had ever known why, except as a feeling.

Why would you question? The soarer was gentle. *They were gone, and we never made known what we had done.*

Alucius continued to sit on the bed. How could he believe what the soarer had told him? Yet, after having seen what he had, and after having experienced the power of the Recorder and the engineer, how could he not believe the soarer?

The soarer waited, silently.

Finally, Alucius looked up. "What about you?"

What you do cannot change what will be for us. We hope it will change matters for you and for the world.

"But we're not even from this world, you said."

You and yours, especially those who are herders and the like, are of this world, and must sustain it.

"Why?" asked Alucius flatly.

You have seen the lifethreads and how they bind and strengthen the world, have you not?

"Yes."

Whatever may have happened . . . that is past. You are what will sustain the world, and all that we have done will be for naught if you cannot stop the ifrits.

"You didn't answer my question—about you."

The soarer remained silent, and the silence dragged out.

Finally, Alucius asked, tiredly, "What do I do? Where do we start?"

Look at yourself, at your own lifethread. Do not touch it. Just look.

Alucius tried to focus his Talent upon his own thread.

He swallowed. His thread was not the black shot with green that he recalled, or that he had sensed with other herders. Instead, it was a brilliant green, with but a few thin lines of black within that green.

Study one of the black threads. See if you can discern the smaller threads within.

His eyes felt like they were blurring, even though his Talent was "looking," not his eyes. But all he could sense was a fuzziness around the black thread.

Think of it as spun and then woven together.

Alucius concentrated harder, creating a mental picture, then trying to make the picture fit the sense of the thread, but the thread remained solid.

The soarer said nothing.

Would it work the other way? He tried to see the thread, as if it were being spun from tinier threads and being woven into a unitary piece. For a moment, he thought he had something, but the sense he received was—again—of a solid thread.

The soarer remained still, neither suggesting nor criticizing.

Could he visualize the thread in another way?

Do not make it what it is not. It is a thread composed of smaller threads. It is. That is what it is. You must learn to see it as it is.

"How?" snapped Alucius. "It's easy enough for you."

Try again. Just think of the thread.

Alucius tried to clear his thoughts, just thinking about that one thin black strand. Not conceiving of it as anything but a thread. Sweat poured from his forehead, and his whole body shivered.

For an instant—just an instant—he caught the most fleeting sense of threads twined into each other, threads twined from smaller and smaller threads. Then the feeling was gone, and he was shivering almost uncontrollably.

You can do no more now. You should rest.

No praise. No acknowledgment. The soarer lifted the empty platter and ale beaker and turned toward the door.

As the soarer left, Alucius cast his Talent-senses at her. Her lifethread was the same brilliant green as his—except without any traces of black.

He swallowed once more. According to his Talent, in the ways of Talent, he was closer to the soarers than to the herders. He knew the old song about the soarer's child. The lines came to mind easily, although it had been years since he had heard them.

> . . . But the soarer's child praise the most,
> for he will rout the sanders' host,
> and raise the lost banners high
> under the green-and-silver sky.

But . . . the sanders' host? The soarer had said that the sanders were kin to the soarers, and even as tired as he was, Alucius had sensed the truth of her words. Also, the soarer and the sander were paired in the leschec game—the soarer queen and the sander king. But then, the game also had pteridons and alectors.

His head was splitting, and he still lacked so many answers. He didn't even know if he had been asking the right questions, either, and that made it even harder.

With a sigh, he turned and stretched out on the bed. His eyes felt so heavy.

109

Alucius stood in front of the window, a place where he had often found himself standing over the past days, looking out into the late afternoon, squinting to see against the white disc of the sun. At least a week had gone by, perhaps longer, with sessions two and three times a day with the soarer. He had gone back to wearing his uniform, except for the outer tunic. Although it was an illusion, he knew, he felt less helpless in the uniform than he had in the gown—which the soarers had left for him to sleep in.

It had taken three days before he had really been able to see the next lower level of threads, and five before he could do so with any degree of ease—and that was just for his own lifethread. Then he had been forced to try to discern the threads woven into the lifethread of the soarer. That alone would have convinced him of the earnestness of the soarers, because it implied a certain degree of trust. Even so, he had to wonder.

No matter how he had questioned the soarer, he had gotten no answers about her. He had no idea how many soarers remained or what the relationship between sanders and soarers might be, whether the sanders were another people or more like nightsheep to the soarers. He had not seen or sensed another soarer—even from a distance, but he had no idea if that might be because of the amber walls of the tower. When he had opened the window and used his Talent-senses, he had felt nothing but emptiness.

The soarer kept telling him that he had greater strength than did either the soarers or the ifrits. Yet both had been more than able to handle him. Still . . . what choice did he have?

You always have choices. The soarer appeared in the late-afternoon sunlight that angled through the window.

"Not good ones," Alucius turned as he spoke. "And poor choices are only good for creating the illusion of choice."

Not all choices are as poor as they first appear. Some choices look good, but in time prove far less wise.

"That's if you are a soarer and have lived many years and seen far more than a poor herder and officer of the Northern Guard."

You are not poor as either. The soarer lifted her hands slightly. She held a scrat, loosely. The reddish brown rodent looked up at Alucius, its black eyes wide, but other than twitching its whiskers, and looking quickly from side to side, it did not move.

Alucius had never been able to get within yards of one of the skittish little creatures, yet it sat in the palm of the soarer's hand, quiet, unafraid, and looking curiously at Alucius.

Do not move closer. Use your Talent to study its lifethread. Do not touch the thread with your Talent. It is frail compared to you.

Alucius accepted the unnecessary warning and set to study the small animal. The scrat's threads were thinner—and finer—than the threads composing Alucius's lifethread, or those of the soarer.

Observe the nodes, those points where the threads twist together.

Nodes? Even as he questioned, Alucius tried to find the nodes in the threads of the scrat, which remained calmly observing him.

Wherever there are threads, of any sort, there are nodes. Where there are nodes, there is weakness.

"Weakness. But they are stronger there."

That is only a seeming.

Alucius concentrated on the nodes, seeking one of the largest. Still, it looked stronger than any of the woven threads.

Before he could speak, the soarer did. *Watch closely.*

Alucius observed as a thin line of golden green extended from the soarer to the scrat, as that golden green probe slipped around one of the largest nodes, just where the lifethread left the body of the rodent itself. Then the probe branched into multiple fingers, and each finger *twisted.*

The threads separated into a spray of loosely connected lines, fading even as Alucius watched.

The scrat collapsed.

Alucius gaped. The soarer had just killed the scrat.

No! Watch!

He continued to watch. This time, the golden green probe gathered the individual threads that Alucius could barely perceive and twisted them back together, in what Alucius could only have called a tighter weave.

After a moment, the scrat shivered and looked up, its eyes bright.

"You . . . killed it, and then brought it back to life."

No. It only seemed so. A body does not die in the instant a lifethread is severed or changed. Shortly, and swiftly, but not instantaneously. If the damage is repaired quickly, no lasting harm is done. You will learn to do this.

Alucius almost protested, then thought, "You cannot kill, but you wish me to learn how to do both?"

It is the beginning of what you need to know to defeat the ifrits.

The beginning? Just the beginning?

Yes.

The room dropped into dusk as the sun slipped beneath the dark stone ramparts to the west of the tower.

You have much to learn, yet, and little time. Do not worry about the scrat. I will guide you, and it will not be harmed so long as you are deft and gentle.

"But it would be dangerous to practice this on people or larger animals?"

It is dangerous for the scrat, but there is no other way, not in time.

Alucius looked at the bright-eyed rodent, looking at him, almost trustingly. He looked away, not wanting to meet the rodent's eyes, even knowing that his reluctance was irrational. He'd killed hundreds, and he was worried about a scrat?

It is good that you are, but you must try.

After a moment, Alucius asked, "How do I start?"

You saw. Try to do the same.

Slowly, Alucius attempted to fashion the same sort of green golden probe, then have it enfold the major node before trying to split it into separate fingers.

He killed the scrat four times, and each time the soarer revived it.

Enough. You are too tired to continue. Still, you think in terms of force.

"This wouldn't do anything to one of those ifrits," Alucius protested, trying to keep anger and frustration out of his voice and being.

It would. Consider what would happen if all your Talent were focused on one small point in a node. Or, if you used your Talent to deflect another's thrust. With the hint of a nod, the soarer turned and departed with the scrat.

Alucius stood at the window of the darkened tower room for a long time. Then he turned and studied the door. The door was bolted from the outside. Within a few days of regaining his strength, he had discovered that, but he had not found a way to unbolt it.

Perhaps what the soarer had showed him might work.

He visualized a long thin golden probe, sliding under the thinnest of openings between the bottom of the door and the green floor tiles.

Alucius smiled as he could sense the thin probe slipping up to the silver metal bolt, where he wrapped it around the protrusion at one end. Then, he tried to tug on the bolt, to slide it back out. Nothing happened. It felt as though the metal were greased and his Talent-probe kept slipping off the bolt.

He tried to make his probe with rougher edges, and greater strength. That didn't work either. Then he tried to make it sticky, like drying honey, as he pulled.

That worked.

He pushed the door open and stepped out into a circular room—a landing of sorts, except he saw no stairs. Directly before him on the far side of the landing was a square opening in the green floor tiles. Alucius stepped forward, carefully, looking down the long shaft. In the darkness he could see little, but with his Talent he felt that the shaft descended at least fifty yards, and rose another ten or fifteen yards. He turned, carefully, and surveyed the landing.

Besides the door to his room—or cell—there were two other doors, both closed. Only his door had a bolt on it, and that bolt felt much newer. Had it been added just for him? He pressed the lever on the door to the left and opened it. The room was empty. Although there was no furniture and no dust, it felt as though it had not been used in years, perhaps longer.

Alucius closed the door and opened the other door, wondering if it might be the top of a staircase, but it was also an empty room. Unlike the other two rooms, it had the square mirror built into the floor—but no furniture. Leaving the door open, Alucius walked to the mirror, studying it.

He could definitely feel the golden thread beneath it—that and the darkness beyond. He could certainly leave.

And then what? The only places he knew he could reach were where the two ifrits waited.

Alucius took a deep breath, recalling once more his grandsire's advice about not acting until he knew what to do. After a long moment, he walked around the mirror to the window, identical to the one in his room. The view was the same.

He turned and walked out of the room, stopping on the landing outside and looking at the space that was at the top of the access shaft, smiling ruefully. There was no way to climb down the shaft. The tower had certainly been built for soarers, because there weren't any stairs. Except for the mirror, he was still trapped, and given where the mirror led, it was better to wait than strike out blindly. The last times he'd done that, he'd paid dearly.

With a deep breath, he went back into his room.

He did leave the door ajar.

110

Another week passed, and the soarer never said a word about the open or unlocked door. During that time, in his efforts to learn to handle threads, Alucius managed to kill several scrats, a grayjay, and a sandsnake. The soarer patiently revived them. In the end, Alucius finally grasped the techniques and actually managed to unlock the thread nodes and revive the sandsnake and the last scrat on his own. And without a word of comment, the soarer departed.

The following morning, she appeared with his breakfast.

As Alucius ate, she offered nothing until he was almost finished.

The ifrits are working on building another portal. You are fortunate that such work takes much time.

"I'm fortunate. What about you?"

There are not many of us. A burst of dry humor infused the thought. *You have already discovered that the tower is mostly empty, have you not?*

Alucius took a last swallow of the ale. "You know that."

Most of the city is as well. That is why you see little from the window.

"But you keep me here."

It will not be that long, if you will learn. Follow me.

Alucius followed the soarer out of his room, onto the landing, and into the empty room with the silver mirror set into the floor.

Now . . . you must learn to use your knowledge.

Alucius thought he had been. He paused. "Wait a moment. The Tables are set into the ground. But this mirror—it's in a tower, and it's not connected to the ground."

It is linked to the nodes of the world. Use your Talent.

Alucius concentrated. As he did, he became aware that the entire tower, indeed, the entire city, was linked deep into the world, in a fashion that was similar to that of the Tables, yet without the pinkish purpleness.

Now . . . you must face what defeated you.

A line of purplish Talent flared toward him, and Alucius raised a line of darkness. While the darkness held, the force pushed him backward.

Deflect when you can.

A second line of force struck, but Alucius countered, using his own Talent, more like a sabre, and parried the attack.

For a short while, less than a quarter of a glass, he practiced against the lines and darts of purpleness thrown by the soarer.

Enough. The greatest danger comes not from a single ifrit.

Alucius tightened his lips as the all-too-familiar crimson mist rose from the mirror and formed into a pair of sinuous crimson arms that reached toward him. Instinctively, he raised the darkness of lifeforce, around which the arms undulated.

The nodes! Where were the nodes? As he dodged the probing arms, one of them brushed his elbow.

"Oh!" The pain was a line of excruciating fire. He jumped back, aware that he was trapped almost against the wall.

You will not die, but you may wish you had if you cannot halt them.

"Thank you," mumbled Alucius, throwing up darkness as a momentary barrier, his Talent-senses trying to find where the crimson mist-arms had the nodes—or if they did.

There were thick places that might be nodes. Alucius probed with his Talent, circling and ducking, but the thickened nodes felt like armor. He had to jump sideways, but, again one of the arms brushed his knee. The slash of fire numbed his lower right leg, and he stumbled and fell. To avoid the probing tentacles, he had to roll across the corner of the mirror, and another wave of pain—this one cold chill—stabbed through his shoulder.

Focus your probe! Tightly!

That was easy enough for the soarer to say.

Still, Alucius tried to concentrate his Talent-force into a narrow tip that lanced at a node.

Abruptly, the arm below the node disintegrated into a spray of threads that vanished.

So did Alucius's smile as the other arm slashed into his left hand, leaving it numb.

Alucius tried to stand, but he was moving slowly, with his right leg, left shoulder, and hand all numb. Desperately, he focused another line of golden green Talent at the larger node on the longer remaining arm.

It, too, vanished in a spray of threads. Then both arms, and the ruby mists began to dissipate.

Alucius stood back, unsteadily. He was panting heavily. His undergarments were soaked, and sweat was pouring down his forehead. The numbness remained in his leg, hand, and shoulder.

That is enough for this day. The soarer turned, as if to depart.

Alucius could sense a weariness in the soarer, and he had to wonder if the exercise were a drain on her.

How long . . .

Until you can stop the arms before they near you. In facing the ifrits, if an arm even touches you, they will possess you—or kill you. Pain is the most I can do, but I use it because your body is still part animal, and you will not understand, deep within yourself, the dangers without pain. We wish it were otherwise.

Alucius couldn't help but feel partly insulted. Yet he had the feeling she was right. He hadn't really learned from his grandsire until he had been hurt. Before the soarer left, he asked the other question he had been pondering, especially after seeing the access shaft, "When this is all over . . . will I be able to soar . . . like you do?"

In some places, but those places are not where you might wish to be seen. Humor—impish humor—overlaid the words.

"Why?"

The soarer did not answer, but a sense of impatience issued forth.

Alucius considered. He still had too much of a tendency to blurt out questions with the soarer. He hadn't done that in years. Why was he doing it with the soarer? Because she reminded him of his grandsire? And because he was again acting like a child?

"Is it because it would require using the energy of lifeforces, and because I'm larger and heavier than you are, and the only places where lifeforces are concentrated enough is in towns and cities?"

That is part of the difficulty. The impatience had vanished. *The other part is that using Talent to soar takes your own lifeforce and energy if there are not enough other lifethreads near. Unless you are in a place such as here or unless you act like the dark ifrits.*

Alucius frowned. "You soar here, and yet there is little—"

You could soar here as well. The hidden city was built to tap the lifeforce of the world itself. You already sensed that.

"I could?" He paused. "Wait a moment. You told me that—"

Worlds are also alive—if they have life within and upon them. It takes great strength to reach deeply enough into the heart of a world to tap those threads. We could not do that now. In the end, after the ifrits have feasted on all the life-forms, they will tap the world itself and use its strength to drive a conduit to other worlds. But they must have many ifrits in their own bodies upon the next world before they can do such.

"They would leave the entire world . . . dead?"

We have told you that. More than once.

"I'm sorry. It takes some getting used to."

The soarer glided out of the room and toward the shaft.

Alucius limped after her.

You can practice soaring here . . . but do not try the shaft yet.

Alucius watched as she soared to the shaft and descended, a glimpse of golden green that vanished below.

He could soar? How?

She had said that it required linking to lifethreads, but there were none in the tower but his own. For a time, he studied the very tower itself, until he could make out the web of golden green threads that infused the walls and floors—indeed everything.

He glanced down. His boots were a good third of a yard off the tiles.

So surprised was he that he lost his linkage and dropped to the tiles. His boots hit with a heavy thud, and he staggered on his still-numb leg, trying to keep from tottering toward the darkness of the shaft. He straightened with relief.

He could see why she'd suggested not trying the access shaft. Still, he could practice that as well. Any new skill might help.

He slowly limped back to his room. Later, after the numbness and the tiredness passed, he would try again.

111

Tempre, Lanachrona

The Lord-Protector stood at the edge of the table desk in the small private study off the audience hall, looking at his brother. "I have seen more of you in the past month than in a year."

"That is true," admitted Waleryn. "Should not I care about my brother's struggles and troubles?"

"That is kind of you," replied the Lord-Protector, brushing back dark hair that was longer than usual. "It has been a difficult year, if successful in most aspects."

"In most, that is true." Waleryn nodded. "How fares Alerya?"

"She is better, but her recovery will take time."

"Some have said that she can have no children now," suggested the younger man.

The Lord-Protector half turned. "Often what is said has little truth, but reflects what others may wish. There is no reason she cannot bear a child, once she is strong again."

"Brother . . . it is unlikely she will be that strong." Waleryn looked hard at his older brother. "Do you not think you should consider . . . another consort?"

"Why?"

"The future of Lanachrona, perhaps?" Waleryn shrugged. "If you love her too much to put her aside, you might consider . . . other arrangements. There are many willing women—even from good families."

"Waleryn . . . I cannot believe you are suggesting . . ."

"My dear Talryn . . . I am not suggesting anything. Not yet. I do think you should consider what alternatives are open to you." Waleryn bowed. "I had merely stopped to see how you are faring, and it is clear that you are as always, doing well, and I will not trouble you further."

"I thank you for your kindness," replied the Lord-Protector, not leaving his table desk as his brother bowed again and departed.

The Lord-Protector waited until the study door closed, then checked the ancient time-glass set on the bookshelf. He nodded and opened the doorway to the circular stairs leading up to his private apartments. When he reached the door at the top, he took the brass key from his belt and unlocked the first door, then stepped out into the main foyer, past the guards, and into the private foyer.

Beyond, in the sitting room, Alerya was at her writing desk, if in her dressing gown.

"Dearest . . . I had not expected you until later." She smiled warmly at her husband.

"I have a little time before my next appointment." He paused. "Are you certain you should be up?"

"I write for a time, then I rest. I cannot get stronger by remaining always in bed."

"You must not do too much," he cautioned.

"I do not. I am most careful." Her eyes took in his face. "You look troubled."

"I am, dearest. Waleryn came to see me. He suggested . . . that I should either seek another consort—or as he put it, make other arrangements. I refused."

"If I do not heal fully . . . you may have little choice."

"We are both young," the Lord-Protector replied. "Such talk is foolish now."

"It is not foolish for others. That is not why you are upset."

"No. I worry because Waleryn did not mean what he said. He did not try to persuade me, or handle the matter gently. He was far too direct—as if he wished me to reject his words."

"Ah . . . he does not wish you to have an heir," Alerya said.

"That is my thought. Someone else has put him up to this."

"Enyll?"

"I would judge so." The Lord-Protector frowned. "I do so wish that the overcaptain had been successful in dealing with him."

"Enyll is not difficult with you."

"No. He is more polite and solicitous than ever, and I trust him not at all. In fact, less than ever."

"Do you think he killed the overcaptain somehow? Or Waleryn did?"

"Waleryn could not have done so. He had not returned from Vanyr. As for Enyll . . ." The Lord-Protector shrugged. "He certainly would not have hesitated to do so. Yet . . . I cannot say. My mind says that he did. My feelings say that he did not. I feel that he would be acting . . . differently."

"Trust the feelings."

"In matters of state, that is sometimes hard." The Lord-Protector slipped behind his consort, bending slightly and slipping his arms around her, kissing her cheek. "Where you are, that is far easier."

He held her, silently, for a time, before straightening, and saying, "I fear I must return for my next audience. And you must rest."

"After this letter." She watched, smiling sadly, as he hurried to the foyer and out of the private apartments.

112

Another three days of parrying and countering ever-stronger Talent-force blows and eluding and disintegrating the crimson arms went by, each session clearly exhausting both Alucius and the soarer. In between sessions, Alucius tried to learn better how to soar, but he was so tired that his efforts were limited.

On the following day, he woke earlier than usual and washed up and dressed, fingering the short dark gray beard that he had grown over the time of his lessons and captivity. Did it take captivity and pain for him to learn something? That thought bothered him as he walked to the window and looked out at the city below, or what he could see of it, a city largely deserted and empty. That he could sense, now.

Beyond the amber stone of the tower and the buildings below, the morning sun cast long shadows out across the white sand. The shadows fell far short of the dark rock rampart that marked the edge of the valley in which the hidden city rested. The crystal oblongs arranged at the top of that rampart glinted green-tinted silver in the morning sunlight, although most of the sun's rays were drawn into the crystals rather than reflected.

The sky was darker than it was in Tempre or Dekhron, not by much, but by a fraction of a shade of green.

When he sensed the soarer nearing, Alucius turned and waited.

The soarer appeared just inside the door, once more with his breakfast. *You must eat.*

Alucius took the tray and ale from her and settled himself on the bed.

It is time now. You must return and finish the battle.

"I don't know exactly how to use my Talent against the ifrits." That worried Alucius. Greatly. He could still recall the power of the two creatures.

You must do the same against them as you have against the arms. The method is the same against all life-forms.

"You think I have learned enough?"

The sense of a smile conveyed itself to Alucius. *No one ever learns enough, for each learning opens one to further learning. Those who do not keep learning die, inside at first, then all over. You have much yet to learn, but you cannot learn more here.*

"Right now, you mean?" Alucius finished the last bite of the egg toast and took a long swallow of the ale.

Ever. You have learned what we can teach. We must all hope it is enough.

"Thank you for your confidence," Alucius said dryly.

You have the skills and knowledge to prevail. That does not mean you will.

Alucius scarcely needed that reminder. "What do I do?"

You will use the mirror in the adjoining chamber. Bring your sabre.

Alucius set aside the tray and stood, then walked to the wall, where he took down the sabre and clipped the scabbard to his belt. The soarer had already left the room, and Alucius followed her out and into the chamber with the mirror.

She stood beside the mirror.

Alucius glanced to her.

Stand on the mirror. Seek the depths. Repeat what you did to reach the hidden city. Think about the engineer, about Prosp, about anything that will draw you to that portal Table.

"Prosp—because that Table is the more dangerous?"

Both the Table there and the ifrit who has possessed the engineer are more dangerous than the Table in Tempre.

Alucius walked into the middle of the square mirror, sensing its golden green depths beneath him, and the ties to the earth—and beyond. Then he paused and looked at the soarer. "Thank you." After a moment, he asked, "Will I ever see you, any of you, again?"

You are welcome. If you succeed . . . then the future will be what it will be, and that will thank us more than words.

The soarer's words both reassured and troubled Alucius, but he could not say why.

You must go, before it is too late.

He nodded, squared his shoulders, and took a deep breath. Then he concentrated on the depths beneath, on the ties that led deep into the earth.

He felt himself falling . . .

The chill surrounded him, a deep coldness infusing the dark golden green, but a cold less edged and bitter than the chill of the purple-blackness of the ifrits' conduit. He could sense the difference, because this time, he was within the golden green, and beyond, parallel to the golden green conduit, was the dark conduit.

Reluctantly, Alucius reached for the ugly purple-blackness, this time using a narrow Talent pulse of golden green, rather than the purple line he had used to reach the hidden city.

Abruptly, he was within the black conduit, where he cast forth his Talent-senses to search for the silver arrow that he recalled. He scarcely had to seek it, so bright did it appear, beckoning coldly to him.

After steeling himself for the possibility that the engineer might be waiting, he focused his concentration on the portal Table.

Silver light flared around him.

113

Alucius blinked. He was standing on the newer Table—in an unlit dimness. Was it evening in Prosp? Before, when he had traveled the ifrits' conduit, the time of day had been the same as in the hidden city, or so he had thought. Then he smiled. How would he know the time of day? The chamber was underground.

Even as he slipped off the table, he could sense that the Table was more "alive." He wondered exactly what the engineer who was an ifrit had done to create that effect—and what it meant. In the dimness, he quickly surveyed the chamber with eyes and Talent, but it was indeed empty. He walked quietly toward the door, where he stopped and listened, using his Talent as well to probe into adjoining larger chamber.

As before, there was a guard outside, but Alucius sensed no one else nearby. With the gentlest of touches, he extended a golden green probe, pressing the guard's lifethread firmly, but gently. He could sense—and hear—the guard fall. Only then did he ease the door open.

The brightness of the light coming down the stairwell from above into the lower room confirmed to Alucius that it was morning—or day—in Prosp, and that, besides the unconscious guard in silver and black, the lower part of the building was empty.

Had the engineer gone elsewhere? To set up another Table somewhere? Or was it just earlier than the engineer arrived?

Alucius surveyed the outer chamber quickly. He could still hear the sounds of building, but they were muffled—outside, or on an upper level.

Then, he heard steps, hurried steps, and he slipped back into an alcove in the outer chamber a good ten yards from the door, which he had left ajar. As he stood there, he did his best to mask the brilliance of his lifethread, trying to let it show as the brown and black of an average workman.

That effort must have sufficed. The engineer halted at the fallen guard, but only momentarily, before entering the Table chamber, and he did not even look in Alucius's direction.

Alucius followed, easing along the edge of the wall. Before he even reached the still-open door to the Table chamber, his first effort was to use his Talent to focus on the weapon held by the engineer, who stood inside the door, probing the Table with jabs of purpled Talent-force.

Alucius eased into the Table chamber behind the engineer, forcing himself to use his Talent-probe to go further and unravel the linkages inside the weapon.

Vestor turned and lifted the light-knife, pointing it at Alucius. Nothing happened. He set it on the writing desk with a smile. "So . . . you have learned some tricks."

Alucius sent out a Talent-probe, the slimmest and strongest he could manage.

The engineer staggered, then jabbed back with his own burst of intense purple Talent-force, a force that came as much from the Table as from Vestor himself.

Rather than trying to block the Talent-thrust, Alucius slipped it past him, as he might have handled a sabre slash, then thrust again.

While the engineer did not block the second thrust, and even halted momentarily, he stepped to the Table, the way the Recorder had, and pressed his hands against the mirror surface. Immediately, the ruby mists swirled upward, and a greater swelling of purpleness enfolded the engineer.

Alucius dropped a darkening mist over the Table, momentarily forcing the mists back. He was the one to ease to the door and slip the bolt in place. He hoped he was not being foolish, but he didn't want to worry about being attacked from behind as he tried to fight the engineer. And he knew, instinctively, that, if he did not win, he would not be captured, not in any way he could accept, but that, one way or another, he would be dead.

"Rather confident for a poor Corean Talent-steer." The engineer sneered, marshaling yet more of the ruby mists, which re-formed into the sinuous arms Alucius recalled all too well.

Alucius concentrated on seeking the nodes, before probing, and driving a golden green line of fire into the larger node of the leftmost arm, the one nearest to him, at the point closest to where it left the Table.

His hands still upon the surface of the Table, Vestor grunted, his pale forehead damp, and another layer of bright pinkish purple reinforced the ruby arms.

After Alucius slid his probe under the purple shield, he tried to twist and unravel the smaller threads within the node. As he did, he could feel heat rising all around him and sweat popping out of his forehead. He felt

452   L. E. MODESITT, JR.

as though he were fumbling, and that time all around him had slowed to a creep as the tiny point of his Talent-probe knifed into the node of the ruby mist-arm, then twisted, and cut the links of the smaller threads.

Suddenly, the arm vanished in a spray of tiny purple threads that were sucked back into the Table itself.

"You are no Talent-steer," said the engineer tightly. "You're one of the dying ones. You cannot prevail. You cannot stop us. Not this time. Not a mere handful of ancient dodderers who will die within a handful of years."

Alucius couldn't help the momentary surprise, then had to catch himself and concentrate on the other ruby arm, now thicker and more armored in a sheen of purple.

Neither Alucius nor the engineer spoke, as golden green Talent-force battled pink-purple Talent-force.

Alucius hammered his Talent-probe into the main node of the ruby mist-arm, but the engineer, veins standing out across his temples, forced layer after layer of purpleness around that probe, so that Alucius could barely move it.

With great effort, Alucius twisted the probe, but not enough to break the linkages.

The engineer threw a line of purple farther back around Alucius's probe.

Alucius expanded his probe just slightly, and the purpleness shattered away.

Vestor fired another gout of purple force at Alucius, and Alucius deflected it, then twisted the probe, just about ready to break the node, when the arm vanished.

Alucius felt himself stagger.

A second arm appeared, larger and more massively defended than the first and second ones had been, arrowing toward Alucius.

Alucius jabbed a probe into a smaller node, less defended, but more toward the attacking end of the tentacle-like arm. The last two yards of the arm vanished in a spray of purple threads.

Another bolt of purple flared toward Alucius, one that he barely managed to parry before throwing a quick blast of golden green at the engineer.

Vestor grunted, but the ruby mist-arm began to thicken and grow again, undulating through the air of the Table chamber toward Alucius.

Alucius could see the purple Talent-armor of the engineer thinning. Hurriedly, he drove a second probe at Vestor's main lifethread node, where the two threads—the one from the Table and the one of the engineer himself—intertwined. After a moment of resistance, Alucius's probe was through, and into the node, where he twisted deftly, but savagely.

The purpled lifethread exploded into thousands of smaller threads, unraveling and fraying into ever-smaller pieces.

The engineer gaped at Alucius, as if he were seeing the overcaptain for the very first time.

Alucius did not hesitate, but struck a second time, severing the remaining lifethread.

As Vestor's knees buckled, the engineer's pale face crumpled and darkened. Then he pitched forward onto the stone floor.

Alucius swallowed as the Table sucked in the few remaining smaller threads of what had been the monstrous purple-black lifethread. As the last thread vanished into the Table, the building shivered. A flash of purple light—visible only with Alucius's Talent—flared from the Table through the chamber, and Alucius could feel that at least part of the Table had died, or had ceased to work, with the death of the engineer.

For several moments, despite the shaking of the building, Alucius just stood there, breathing deeply and trying to catch his breath. He felt as though he had run a vingt or more at full speed, and yet he had barely moved twenty yards since he had come through the Table.

The vibrations continued, and the building began to sway more violently. A large stone wall tile, weighing as much as Alucius, vibrated out of the inner walls of the chamber, crashing down onto the floor stones with an impact that shook Alucius and sent cracks radiating through the stone floor. Before the vibration from that impact died away, a second stone followed the first, and an ominous creaking and groaning filled the building.

Alucius could hear men yelling, their voices muffled by the grinding of stones and continued shaking of the structure and the earth.

More stones fell.

Alucius glanced from the door to the Table. As a wide crack appeared in the wall beside him, he jumped onto the Table, and concentrated on seeking the purple-black conduit.

This time, he dropped through—or into the Table—quickly.

Once more, chill surrounded him, and the shock was greater because of how hot Alucius had become in battling the engineer. Within the black-ness and chill, he paused for a moment, although he doubted time passed quickly—or at all—in the dark conduit. Now what? He hadn't expected to have to flee from a collapsing building through the Table. Could he return to the hidden city and regroup?

He began to search for the golden thread lying beyond the black con-duit . . . but it was impossibly distant—as though it had been moved. He pressed toward it, and it vanished. He tried keeping it in mind and moving away, but that had no effect either. Neither did trying to move himself to the golden thread, which wavered—just out of his Talent-reach.

He could feel the chill seeping into his very being. Why was it so hard to find the nodes back to the hidden city—or to use them?

Because the soarers didn't want him returning? Because, now that he knew how to do it, they had taken steps so that he and others could not?

With near desperation, Alucius began to search for the blue arrow, the one that would return him to Tempre—and the Recorder of Deeds. As he did, he could see that the silver arrow had faded—but it had not vanished, although it continued to fade. He drove himself—or his being—toward the blue arrow . . . willing himself beyond it.

At that moment, a brilliant blue light coruscated around him.

114

Two figures lurched back from the Table of the Recorders as Alucius appeared upon it, steamlike mist evaporating from his face and figure. His skin was chill, as if the sweat had turned to ice, then sublimated away.

Alucius glanced from the Recorder to the second man, who resembled the Lord-Protector, but who was shorter, stockier, and younger. Then, his eyes focused on the Recorder, who lifted a pistol-like weapon.

"Get him, Waleryn, if you value your life. He is an evil spirit who will steal your very being!" snapped the Recorder.

Alucius barely managed to drop behind the Table as the light-knife flared over his head. Stone droplets pattered down onto the floor, and the odor of hot stone or metal filled the ancient chamber. From behind the Table, he quickly reached out with his Talent-probe and touched Waleryn's lifethread, enough to stun the man, who sagged to the floor, his fingers momentarily grasping at the edge of the Table, before he slumped forward.

The Recorder said nothing, but another blast of bluish light flared into the wall behind Alucius, more stone droplets sprayed across the stones, and an acrid scent filled the room.

Alucius extended his Talent-probe to the light-knife, unraveling the connections between the crystals.

"Waleryn!" snapped the Recorder. "Weakling . . ."

Alucius eased up from behind the Table, facing the ifrit, checking the monstrous lifethread, and probing for the most vulnerable of nodes.

The Recorder leveled the light-knife at Alucius, but no light beam flared from the weapon, and he set it on the Table. "That will not help you long."

The all-too-familiar ruby mists began to rise from the Table, and as they did, a wall of purplish power slammed toward Alucius.

Alucius formed a golden green wedge and let the force flare around him, then struck back, aiming at the node where the Recorder's lifethreads intertwined, the one from the Table and the one linked to somewhere in Lanachrona.

A purplish shield blocked the thrust, but for a moment, the Recorder's hands left the Table, and the ruby mists subsided. Alucius dropped a line of darkness over the Table, further smothering the mists.

"That won't last," the Recorder said quietly, replacing his hands upon the Table.

"Long enough." Alucius probed for the main lifethread node, keeping his line of golden green tight and focused.

"You cannot stand against all of us," the Recorder said. "But you could join us." He hurled another blast of purple at Alucius.

Alucius slipped the purple force aside and jabbed at the Recorder's face with golden light designed to dazzle.

The other blinked, then retaliated with another wave of purple as the ruby mist-arms rose once more from the Table.

Understanding the arms better the second time—or fourth, he realized absently—Alucius attacked their nodes just beyond the Table, and both sprayed apart in instants, with threads flying into the air, then retreating into the Table and the unseen conduit beneath.

"You can't be . . ." murmured the Recorder, leveling another blast at Alucius.

As the force sheeted past his golden green shield, Alucius struck, hard, and tight, against the main lifethread nodes.

Purple flared all around the Recorder. He pitched forward against the Table, then crumpled to the stone floor.

A wave of dizziness assaulted Alucius, and for a time, he just leaned on the edge of the Table, panting and trying to catch his breath. His arms and legs both felt heavy, as if it would be a chore to lift either.

He hoped that the death of the Recorder and the entity that had possessed him did not trigger another building collapse, but there were no rumblings in the earth, no shivers of the palace, for which he was glad, because he had no place to retreat through the Table.

Finally, he straightened.

Now what? What could he do to the Table? If it remained in the palace, sooner or later someone else would be snared, then . . .

Alucius shook his head and began to probe, seeking out nodes, linkages, and connections. Without worrying about the Recorder, he could follow the lessons of the soarers more deliberately and closely. He just hoped that he could use more finesse and skill than strength in dealing with the Table, since he was running close to his Talent-limits. That, he could tell.

He continued to probe the Table until he found what he was seeking, a multiple node that wove together different threads—two that were deep greenish black and thick, the purplish black of the ifrit conduit, and a lighter purple thread that left him squeamish even to consider. Still, he could sense the power, and he had the definite feeling that if he unraveled the nodes and the threads, there would be a reaction, and it would not be wise to be anywhere close.

He looked at the still-unconscious Waleryn, then bent and grabbed the man's tunic, dragging the Lord-Protector's brother out of the Table chamber and down the narrow corridor into the room of those nearby farthest from the Table. By then, Alucius was breathing deeply once more, but he eased his way back to the doorway of the Table chamber.

From the doorway, his hand upon the heavy door, Alucius extended a thin golden-green probe to the nexus of the threads, and, tiny thread by tiny thread, began to unlink them.

When he was little more than halfway done, the purplish thread bucked and flared fire, a line of force that Alucius blocked, although the effort set him back on his heels for a moment. With that kind of reaction, Alucius closed the door and backed away as he continued to unravel the joints.

He did not finish, because when he was close to three-quarters finished—or so he judged—all four threads flew apart.

Alucius sprinted down the corridor. He made it to the outer archway when a dull rumbling explosion shook the walls and floors, bursting the door to the Table chamber from its hinges and flinging it against the opposite stone wall of the outer corridor. Great gouts of gray dust, carrying a purple Talent-sheen billowed from the chamber.

The entire palace shook—once, twice—and then subsided.

Alucius watched, panting, sweating profusely, as the dust began to settle. He did not have to return to the chamber to know that the Table no longer functioned. A half smile crossed his lips. That was good, because he doubted he had the Talent-strength left to do anything at all, beyond perhaps a minor illusion, at least for a while.

He slipped along the corridor toward the kitchen, casting an illusion of a captain-colonel, being ignored as cooks and their helpers scurried about . . . passing him and generally ignoring him, except for one woman, who demanded, "What happened?"

"There was an explosion in the Recorder's chambers. Nowhere else," Alucius replied.

". . . knew he'd come to no good."

Alucius kept moving. Before he dealt with the Lord-Protector, he had one other chore to handle. He hoped he was up to it.

He smiled to himself. He had one advantage. No one knew he was back except Waleryn, and the Lord-Protector's brother wasn't likely to wake for several glasses.

The first order of action was to get something to eat. Amid the scurrying and the guards in the outer corridor, he used a deeper illusion to slip into the kitchen and help himself to a meat pie and a beaker of ale. Then he found a dark alcove off the game larder and relaxed his illusions.

His vision was blurring and his hands were trembling as he began to eat and drink. After he finished, he remained there, listening, watching, but no one came his way, although he could hear guards and officers questioning people.

Then, a good half glass later, some of his strength restored, with a concealment shield in place, he made his way upward and through the back corridors, wending his way toward the topmost floor and the Lord-Protector's private apartments.

After more than a few wrong turns, he found them. He had to stun both guards in the corridor outside the Lord-Protector's apartments, then use his Talent-probe to unlock the door to the private foyer.

The Lord-Protector's consort sat at her writing desk, not facing the foyer, for which Alucius was grateful. Ever so gently, Alucius touched her lifethread, and the woman slumped over the desk.

Carefully, as he moved toward the unconscious woman, he probed her figure with the tiniest of golden Talent-probes, noting the reddish ugliness in places within her body. He stretched her out on the lounge, then concentrated, melding what he had already known about healing with what the soarers had taught him.

When he left, she was breathing more easily.

Alucius was sweating again, even after drinking some of the dark ale in the crystal flagon on the desk.

His next effort was to see if he could find the Lord-Protector, preferably in a private setting.

After finding the concealed stairs across the main foyer from the private apartments, he descended the circular staircase. He found no one in what had to be the private study of the Lord-Protector, but he could hear voices from the adjoining hall. He seated himself in one of the straight-backed chairs and listened. As he waited and rested in the private study, hoping the audience would not be too long, he took the Star of Honor from his belt wallet and pinned it back on his tunic.

". . . the Table is destroyed? How could that happen?"

". . . do not know, Lord-Protector . . . the Recorder is dead. The Lord Waleryn remains unconscious. The walls are cracked, but we can find no signs of any explosives, and there is no smell of gunpowder."

"My own palace, and you cannot tell me . . ."

The conversation went on for some time, then died away.

Alucius stood, waiting.

". . . surrounded by idiots . . ." The Lord-Protector was so engrossed that he did not look up as he stepped into the study, followed by Majer Suntyl.

"Sir!" blurted Suntyl.

The Lord-Protector looked up. He stopped, then turned to Suntyl. "You may leave us, Majer. I'm certain that the overcaptain has much to report. Please close the door. Firmly."

"Yes, Lord-Protector." Suntyl backed away.

Once the door closed, the Lord-Protector laughed. "I should have guessed. I had hoped, but not after so long. Not when you vanished without a trace." The Lord-Protector studied Alucius. "You look as though someone had confined you."

"They did. I've spent much more time than I would have liked in Prosp. The Recorder sent me there." Alucius knew he couldn't keep everything from the Lord-Protector, not and have his story make sense, but he saw no point in bringing in the soarers.

"Sent you there?"

"Through the Table. It was a way of transport in the time of the Duarchy. There was another Table there."

"Was?"

"A building was falling on it when I departed. In great haste."

"So there is no way to use the Table in that fashion any longer?"

"No. You would not wish that anyway. Not for the price you would pay." Alucius asked quickly, "Is Waleryn your brother?"

"Why?" asked the Lord-Protector.

"He was with the Recorder. I left him unconscious in one of the Recorder's chambers."

"You just left him?"

"You already knew that. He'll be fine when he wakes." Alucius looked calmly at the Lord-Protector, who stepped back.

After a long moment, Alucius spoke. "You asked me to take care of your problem with the Recorder of Deeds, and you were right. Sooner or later, he would have killed you, or had your spirit possessed by another of his kind. Or he might have just had you die in some unfortunate accident and had your brother become Lord-Protector. Of course, your brother would already have been possessed."

"That . . . you are mad."

"No." Alucius projected absolute certainly. Cold and brutal assurance. "Unlike some. I want nothing from you—except for what you already promised. You can believe me or not. There is a . . . presence . . . that can use the Tables to take over those who summon images in them. That is why the Tables would not have been a . . . reliable form of transport. The Matrial was one of those."

"How could she have been? She did not have a Table."

"She had a purple crystal that performed similar functions. That was how she controlled the torques."

"How do you know . . . Should I ask?"

"You can ask." Alucius smiled. "It's better that I don't answer that one, except to say that I know, and that I didn't destroy her." He hadn't. He'd destroyed the crystal, which had killed her. "How is your consort?"

The Lord-Protector looked sharply at Alucius. "What do you know of that?"

"Before I . . . left, the majer who was acting as your secretary was kind enough to tell me that she was ailing."

"What . . . ?"

"Now that the Recorder is dead—and your brother is no longer working with him—you may find that your consort will recover."

"Are you suggesting that the Recorder—and my brother—had something to do with her illness?"

"It was in both their interests that you not have an heir," Alucius pointed out. "That way he could groom Waleryn . . ."

The Lord-Protector's shoulders sagged. "I should have seen . . . I knew . . . I knew Waleryn was up to something."

"You can ask him, when he wakes. He will wake shortly, if he has not done so already."

"What did you do to the Table? It could have been a great tool."

"The Table failed after the Recorder died," Alucius replied. That was true, in a sense. "He—or the creature that possessed him—had done something to it." That was also true. "The Table, even when it worked, could not have transported more than a handful of people, and all those would have become creatures like the Recorder—deathless and evil." Alucius was exaggerating, although it was clear that the Matrial had certainly been.

"I find this tale of possession difficult."

"You do not have to believe me." Alucius shrugged. "You can believe whatever and however you like, sir. If you find it more to your liking, you can simply state that the Recorder was plotting to replace you. You can name your brother or not. That is your choice."

The Lord-Protector nodded, reluctant, and clearly not totally pleased. "And you?"

"As I said before . . . all I wish is to go home, in the way you promised before."

"And you will—"

"I will do as I promised. The Iron Valleys can no longer stand alone, but the herders need to remain."

"You're a most unusual officer, Overcaptain."

"That could be because I never sought to be one, sir."

The Lord-Protector lifted the bell from the desk. "We could talk more, but I do not think either of us would add much."

"I think not."

The older man rang the bell.

Majer Suntyl appeared, as if he had been standing beside the door, which he had, Alucius knew.

"Majer . . . Overcaptain Alucius has returned from a mission on which I had sent him, somewhat earlier than I had thought. Would you have his mount saddled and readied for him—and summon an escort for him back to the Southern Guard headquarters . . ."

As he let the Lord-Protector talk, Alucius still wondered about the wisdom of leaving Waleryn alive.

Still, Alucius and his family had to live in the Iron Valleys, and the Iron Valleys were ruled by Lanachrona—and while Alucius had been asked to deal with the Recorder, he doubted that the Lord-Protector would have been that pleased to find his brother dead, unless the Lord-Protector knew more than Alucius thought the ruler did.

The majer departed, and the Lord-Protector looked to Alucius. "Majer Suntyl will return when your mount and escort are ready."

"Thank you." Alucius bowed slightly.

"I am sure we will both be pleased to see you return to the Iron Valleys." The Lord-Protector laughed softly, but not harshly. "I had not realized the disadvantages of so effective and devoted an officer."

"Like weapons that never fail?"

"Something like that," the Lord-Protector admitted.

"I am not that infallible, sir, nor do I wish to be considered as such."

"I may find it difficult to change my views," the Lord-Protector replied, "but I will honor, most willingly, my promises."

Alucius could sense that the man wished to—he just hoped that circumstances did not change those wishes.

115

Tempre, Lanachrona

The Lord-Protector hurried through the foyer of his private apartments and into the main sitting room.

Alerya was not at her desk but standing before the open door to the balcony. She turned with a wide smile.

"Dearest . . . are you . . . ?"

"I'm fine. I'm better than fine." She paused, then spoke more slowly, reflectively. "Talryn . . . the strangest thing happened today."

"Not so strange as what happened to me, I'd wager. Did you feel when the palace shook?"

"Yes. It felt like the earth moved."

"The Table exploded, and the overcaptain returned. He said he had been in Prosp." Talryn frowned. "He was not lying. Yet no horse could have gotten him there and back in little more than a month. He said Enyll had used the Table to send him to Prosp. Then he returned and fought with Enyll and killed him. He said that some sort of evil creature had possessed Enyll. He did not say much more, no matter that I pressed him, and since he would not, I did not."

"I knew it! Enyll didn't feel right. I told you that."

"I am glad that you and the overcaptain agree," Talryn said dryly. "It may be difficult to explain."

"Not at all. Enyll tried to move the Table—unwisely. It exploded. He died. You have told me often that the other Tables exploded when they were moved. Those who know the Tables know that is so, and no one else need know."

Talryn nodded, then looked closely at his consort. "I have not seen such strength in you since . . ."

"Not ever, dearest. Not ever. That was what was so strange. This afternoon . . . I was sitting at my desk . . . I was trying to write a note to Mother. She is still at the summer house in Lesyna, you recall."

"Yes, go on."

"Suddenly, I felt very weak, and I fainted, right at the desk."

"That was good?"

"Yes, dearest. When I woke, it was almost two glasses later, and I was as I am now. It is as if I had never been ill." Alerya smiled. "I know . . . I know . . . that . . . you . . . we . . ."

"Let us wait and see," Talryn offered, cautiously.

"I will wait, but you will see." Alerya threw her arms around him—forcefully. "You will."

"How . . . ?" murmured the Lord-Protector, more to himself than to Alerya.

"Does it matter, dear one?"

A slow smile crossed Talryn's face. "No . . . for once . . . it does not. It most certainly does not." His arms tightened around her gently, protectively.

"You will not have to treat me as fine porcelain, now."

"For a time, yet."

"Only for a time."

They both smiled, but the Lord-Protector's eyes drifted eastward, toward the headquarters of the Southern Guard.

116

Not to Alucius's surprise, his discharge orders arrived early the next morning—a Sexdi, he discovered. He was somewhat more surprised to discover that Faisyn and third squad had remained in Tempre. He would have written Wendra, but it was more likely that he would arrive long before any letter would . . . but he did write a page or so . . . just in case.

Much as Alucius had enjoyed the luxury of a hot bath and shaving, and of completely clean uniforms, he was more than ready to leave Tempre when he and third squad formed up in the rear courtyard of the Southern Guard headquarters compound at midmorning.

"Third squad, present and ready, sir!" Faisyn snapped out, a broad smile following the crisp words.

"Let's head home, Faisyn."

"Yes, sir! Third squad, forward!"

No formal escort preceded them as they rode around the eastern end of the headquarters building, out through the gates, and southward onto the Avenue of the Guard. The air was so warm that Alucius found it hard to believe that harvest season was almost over, and it was but a few weeks until the turn of fall.

The small force rode past the eastern end of the formal gardens of the Lord-Protector, and Alucius turned in the saddle, glancing back at the palace and at the hills beyond it—the hills without dwellings, fences, walls—or anything near them. What looked to be two lines of ridges joined, just behind the palace.

Abruptly, he laughed, seeing for the first time, with eyes and Talent-senses, the world lifethreads that ran there. Clearly, the ancient ifrits had built the Tables where those threads intersected near the surface of the land.

In time, could he or others build Tables for transport? Now, that was a poor idea, because it would open Corus to another attack from the ifrits. But . . . in the future? Or would there always be too great a threat and a danger?

Alucius couldn't have said that he knew the answer.

"Sir?" asked Faisyn.

"It's hard to explain . . ." Alucius shook his head.

"Can you tell us, sir," Faisyn asked, "about the commission that the Lord-Protector had for you. No one said anything about what it was. Not at all. Just that he had tasked you with it."

"I wish I could, Faisyn," Alucius replied. "But that wouldn't be good for either of us. Let's just say that it was dangerous, that I was wounded and captured, and lucky to escape and finish the mission, and that I'd never want to do anything at all like that again." And that was certainly true.

"We be getting furlough when we get back?"

"Colonel Weslyn said you would," Alucius replied. "As far as I'm concerned, you were all on duty in Tempre."

"Yes, sir. Thank you, sir."

As they rode south on the Avenue of the Guard and past the dust palace, Alucius glanced over at the imposing structure, seeing no one except for a single guard in green livery, the greenish white marble walls bright in the harvest morning sunlight. When he had first seen Drimeer's marble mansion, Alucius had found it hard to believe that the dustcat warrens outside of Iron Stem spawned such corrupt luxury. Upon reflection, it didn't seen so unbelievable, especially not compared to what he'd learned about the Duarchy in the past few months.

He shifted his weight in the saddle, glad to be riding out of Tempre, glad to be heading homeward.

117

The ride back from Tempre to Dekhron was long, still hot, late as it was in harvest, and, thankfully, totally uneventful. All the Southern Guard officers were courteous along the way, but not terribly curious, as if the surprise of a Northern Guard officer being summoned to Tempre had passed and been accepted.

Alucius and third squad reached Salaan in midafternoon of the second day of fall. A faint drizzle had begun to drift down from the low clouds as the small force rode over the River Vedra bridge from Salaan into Dekhron. In the drizzle, only a single cart, its pony led by a graying woman, headed southward. She did not even look at the riders of third squad. Despite the clouds and moisture, the river remained low, with the same cracking mud banks that Alucius recalled from early in harvest. Below the bridge, the barge piers were empty, the warehouses shuttered.

Even with the misty drizzle, the air in Dekhron smelled dusty. While most of the shops on the main street that was the high road were open, Alucius saw few buyers and but a handful of people on either the streets or the porches.

Alucius and Faisyn turned westward on the street short of the main square—also nearly deserted from what Alucius could see—and third squad followed. The mist thickened as they neared the headquarters post, but the drizzle lessened.

The two troopers on guard merely nodded when they caught sight of Alucius's insignia, but by the time Alucius and third squad had reined up outside the stables, Colonel Weslyn appeared, followed by Majer Imealt.

"Welcome back, Overcaptain!" Weslyn's voice was warm and hearty.

Alucius sensed the concern and worry behind the façade. "It's good to be back, Colonel. Before I forget, I have some dispatches for you from the Lord-Protector himself. Once we're settled, I'll bring them to you." Alucius wasn't about to hand them over without watching the colonel open them.

"That would be good. We have much to discuss, Overcaptain. I will see you shortly." With another smile and a nod, the colonel stepped back, then turned. Majer Imealt followed.

Alucius made certain that all mounts were stabled, and all the troopers quartered, before he carried his gear to the senior officers' quarters, again following Dezyn, the same blond captain who had assisted him a season before. Alucius spent but a few moments washing up and brushing off road detritus before gathering himself together and heading down to meet the colonel.

Weslyn was waiting, seated behind his desk, but only gestured for Alucius to enter, and said nothing until Alucius closed the door.

Alucius did not wait for an invitation, but extended the two sealed dispatches and seated himself in the chair across the desk from the colonel.

Weslyn set them before him, but made no movement to open either. "The last dispatches we had," he began smoothly, "indicated that you had been commended, and had been requested to remain as an aide to the Lord-Protector for several weeks."

"That's true. He wanted to know more about the Northern Guard, and about the Matrites. They haven't had that much knowledge about Hieron in recent years," offered Alucius.

"The commendation?"

"Oh . . ." Alucius eased the medal from his belt wallet. "The Star of Honor. The Lord-Protector said it had been a generation since it had been awarded."

"And he presented it personally?"

"In his audience hall, yes, sir. He sent those to me later, by messenger." Alucius gestured to the two folded and sealed dispatches. "They're for you."

"You act as if I'm supposed to open these while you're here."

"It might be best," Alucius suggested.

Weslyn frowned. "You know what is in these?"

"I didn't unseal either, sir. I was told that I have a copy of one, the one that orders my release upon my return to Dekhron."

Weslyn said nothing as he lifted the first, broke the seal, and read the single sheet with the embossed seals at the bottom. Finally, he looked up. "The Lord-Protector must think highly of you, Overcaptain. You are released to return to your stead, with full pay to the end of the year." A half-rueful smile followed. "And you cannot be recalled to any duty without the express written authorization of the Lord-Protector."

That surprised Alucius.

Weslyn opened the second and read it before speaking again. "The Northern Guard has also been ordered not to conscript any more herders, again without the permission of the Lord-Protector. Do you know why?"

"No, sir. I never said anything to the Lord-Protector about conscription. He only asked what herders did and what our lives were like."

"You must have been rather persuasive."

"I asked for nothing except my timely release."

"Can you tell me what duties you performed for the Lord-Protector?"

"He requested that I not speak of such, sir, but I can say that it had nothing to do with anything that affected the Northern Guard, the Iron Valleys, or you directly."

"Directly?" Weslyn raised his fine blond and silver eyebrows.

"Anything the Lord-Protector does may affect us all indirectly."

"That is most true. Most true." Weslyn offered a forced chuckle.

"Sir?"

"Yes?"

"Have you had any word on Fifth Company and Captain Feran?"

Weslyn nodded. "Fifth Company is holding the outpost at Soulend. In the spring, if necessary, they may join the attack on Arwyn, if the Lord Protector so requires."

"Thank you."

"Both Captain Feran and the Northern Guard will miss you, Over-captain. You could be a majer in another five years, and with the support of the Lord-Protector, commandant some day."

Alucius smiled. "I'll miss both, Colonel, but I'm a better herder than an officer, and it's time to get back to that. You're more comfortable being commandant than I ever would be."

"There are many who would dispute that, Overcaptain; but the Lord-Protector has made his wishes known, and that is what will be. You can leave in the morning, if you would like." Weslyn stood.

"I would, and I do appreciate that, Colonel." Alucius stood and bowed. He could sense both worry and relief—warring within the commandant of the Northern Guard.

As he walked back to his temporary quarters, he could not help but wonder at the colonel's easy acquiescence. Had Weslyn feared that Alucius had been seeking the position of commandant? Was that why the colonel had suggested that Alucius could be commandant? Or was that an obligatory pleasantry?

Weslyn was so adept at masking his feelings that Alucius could not tell, not for certain. What Alucius could tell was that he was ready to leave the Northern Guard and ride home. More than ready.

118

Dekhron, Iron Valleys

The round-faced trader in a severe gray tunic walked through the mist toward the large dwelling on the side street. When he stepped onto the porch, out of the light night rain, the door opened.

A taller white-haired man, sharp-featured even in dim light coming from the hallway behind him, stood aside to let the younger man enter, then closed the door. "Erhelya is at Halyne's for the evening, and the servants were pleased to get the night off." He turned and walked through the front sitting room and into the study behind it, lit by a single oil lamp on the corner of the desk. There he seated himself and waited for the other to take the wooden armchair across from him.

"I had to rearrange the evening to meet you, Tarolt," pointed out the younger man.

"I understand." The pale-faced older man nodded. "It was necessary. You know what happened earlier? It may be that the one who had something to do with it might be within our reach. But there is little time. I received a message just a while ago." His fingers tapped on the polished wood of the desk. "We will need golds, tonight."

"For what, Halanat?"

"The overcaptain. Before he reaches the range of the Aerlal Plateau."

"You had said—"

"Matters have changed. Greatly. This had to be arranged quickly, because the colonel is at times an idiot, most carefully—and most indirectly. No one who comes in contact with the overcaptain, however distantly, will know anything. Also, those employed for . . . direct . . . action needed to be most proficient with rifles. That is why we need more than the usual for this."

"Oh?"

"The overcaptain is clearly a herder. They will have to use Lanachronan rifles. They carry farther. Much farther—beyond the ability of a herder, in fact." Tarolt smiled cruelly. "Nightsilk has its limits, you know."

"The last time . . . he killed all four. How many have you been able to find in an afternoon?"

"Enough. They will succeed, or they will not. Either way, something will be accomplished. At the very least, the colonel will be reminded of where his allegiances must lie. And it is possible that, if they do not succeed, the overcaptain will wish even more strongly to remain a herder. If he does so long enough, his abilities will not matter. It would be best, however, if that were not left to fate. I will need four hundred golds within the glass. Here."

"Four . . . hundred?" stammered Halanat. "Four hundred?"

"For him, and for what is at stake, it is cheap at the price. Once he reaches the quarasote lands, even twenty bravos and four hundred golds will not suffice." Tarolt stood. "Best you hasten."

Slowly, as if stunned, Halanat also rose.

119

Alucius woke early on Tridi, then, even after saying his good-byes to third squad, had to wait for the clerks to arrive so that he could make sure that Faisyn and the third squad rankers got their furlough and pay. He also had to wait for his own release orders and pay.

Alucius would have liked to have said a formal good-bye to the rest of Twenty-first Company, but, as he had suspected, those who opted to remain as troopers had already been transferred to Fifth Company and were in Soulend under Feran—where those of third squad who wished to stay in service would eventually join them. The others had been released early, doubtless as a gold-saving practice, as would be those of third squad who were due for release in the next month.

So Alucius saddled and packed Wildebeast—then waited for clerks who were late, later than normal, and who apologized profusely. Two were most apprehensive, but Alucius could not determine why, even with his Talent. Also, all that morning Alucius had not seen Colonel Weslyn, and so had to tender his farewells to Majer Imealt. Still, by the third glass of the morning, he and Wildebeast had left Northern Guard headquarters.

The dwellings on the northern side of Dekhron, once more, seemed dilapidated, both in comparison to those in Tempre and those he recalled in Madrien. Shutters were unpainted, or splitting, or the paint was peeling. Most of the dwellings had been built of salvaged stones from even more ancient dwellings, and most mixed stones of differing sizes and colors. The roads reflected the same lack of care. Except for the high road itself, the side roads and lanes were dirt and clay, somewhat muddy from the rain of the night before.

None of this was new to Alucius, but whenever he had returned home from a prolonged absence, it was as though he saw the Iron Valleys as a stranger might.

As he rode through the north side of Dekhron away from Northern Guard headquarters for the last time, Alucius guided Wildebeast around a produce wagon, headed north to Iron Stem, he suspected. Just beyond the wagon Alucius passed the last dwellings that could have been said to have been part of Dekhron, although there were isolated huts and holdings and small farms all along the high road, except in one swampy area north of the road to Sudon and in a few rockier hill areas where little grew.

Ahead the high road was empty—for the moment. Alucius stood in the stirrups and stretched, then settled into the saddle. He wished he'd been able to get away earlier, since it would be late in the evening, possibly close to midnight, before he reached the stead. If Wildebeast got too tired, Alucius could stop in Iron Stem, much as he disliked prolonging the journey home—and back to Wendra.

The clouds had lifted somewhat, but the sky remained gray, and the wind was no longer warm but carried a definite touch of fall. For the first time in months, Alucius was not perspiring under his nightsilk undergarments, and it was also the first time that he wasn't riding into either battle or unfamiliar lands.

He smiled slightly at the irony.

With the road clear, by early in the afternoon he was nearing the crossroads where the side road west led to Sudon, the location of the Northern Guard training post. He also realized that something was nagging at him.

He had looked back over his shoulder several times, but so far as he could see, and that was at least three vingts back, there was no one on the road. Ahead, the road rose gradually as it passed through the low rolling hills that extended from before him over three vingts until about a vingt before the crossroads. He could still see a vingt ahead, and that part of the road was clear.

Alucius reined up and listened. Outside of a few birds, calling from a low hedge beside a lane that led to the east, he could hear nothing.

Nearby, he could sense nothing of any size with his Talent. He thought he could sense a number of men farther ahead, but that was probably some squad or company riding to or from Sudon Post—or possibly a training group on maneuvers.

After a time, he urged Wildebeast forward once more, but he kept scanning the road ahead, as well as the areas to each side of the road.

He rode another vingt northward until he reached the gentle incline that was the only real slope on the high road between Dekhron and Soulend. The clouds remained low, but without offering more rain. The sense of men ahead was stronger, yet he could sense none that close to the road. There were two groups, one in the low hills on each side of the road—somewhere more than a vingt ahead. From what he could determine, each had the lifethread of a normal man, and not the purple double-thread of an ifrit-possessed puppet, nor the green-shot blackness of a herder.

He checked the rifles at his knees, making sure each was fully loaded, then uncorked a water bottle and took a long swallow. Rather than hurry Wildebeast, he stopped, dismounted, and used one of the water bottles to water his mount before he resumed riding, at a slightly slower pace. The road behind him remained empty.

After another half vingt, Alucius was certain. There were two groups in the hills ahead, each at least several hundred yards back from the high road, one group on the east, and the other on the west.

He took a long deep breath. Now what?

He had no proof that the men were waiting for him. Yet he could not imagine any good reason for them to be waiting on both sides of the road except to attack travelers. Was he becoming so fretful and self-centered that he thought that ordinary brigands were out after him personally—or were they? He shook his head. All he wanted was to get home, but, whatever the men were, continuing on the high road would have been foolhardy.

With a sigh, he turned Wildebeast westward, because the hills were slightly higher there, and because the men who waited would have more trouble seeing his approach from the southwest. When his Talent-sense indicated that he was within a hill line of the group of men on the west side of the high road, Alucius rode Wildebeast up the hillside, red sandy

476   L. E. MODESITT, JR.

soil and rocks, with scattered pines and junipers, until he reached a cluster of junipers less than thirty yards from the top. There he dismounted and tied Wildebeast to the center juniper, where his mount would not be seen unless someone ventured within less than fifty yards.

Taking both rifles and the one ammunition belt he had retained, Alucius edged up the back side of the hill to the top, and an area with more pines, enough that, while his Talent could sense the waiting men, his eyes could not. Step by step, he slipped downhill and northward until he had a clear view, from behind a pine with low, spreading branches, of those he sought.

The men in the westernmost group were not soldiers, but bravos in dark gray, and Alucius just watched for a time. What exactly should he do? There were ten of them, all waiting, some sitting, some stretched out in firing positions, but a good two hundred yards from the road. The distance alone convinced Alucius that they had been dispatched to kill him.

Despite his efforts to remain calm, he could feel a slow rage building. He wasn't trying to hurt anyone. He had done his best to do his duty and protect his land and his family—and yet people kept trying to kill him— and he still didn't know who or why, although he had his suspicions that Colonel Weslyn wasn't exactly innocent—and that some traders who had been members of the disbanded Council might be involved. But his suspicions were only that.

For a time, he just watched the men who watched the road.

He could ride around them, and they would never know. And he didn't know that they were out to kill him—not absolutely. From their weapons, and the carefully chosen position with a clear line of fire across the high road, there was no doubt that they intended to kill someone. Their clothing, their "Talent-feel" indicated to Alucius that they were not troopers, but hired bravos.

Finally, he began to ease downhill, as quietly as possible, until he was less than a hundred yards away, just a few yards higher than they were, but on the adjoining hill. He studied the bravos again, noting the one on the end, who appeared to be in charge. Then, he lifted his rifle.

Crack!

The head bravo dropped.

Alucius continued to fire, deliberately, until he emptied the magazine of the first rifle. Then he picked up the second and continued.

When it was empty, there were three bravos alive and scrambling toward cover.

Alucius reloaded both rifles, then cast out his Talent-senses. One of the bravos had edged northward and was running to his mount. The other two would have had to circle or to cross open ground to reach their mounts.

Ignoring the departing rider, about whom he could do nothing, since the man was not in clear rifle-shot range and beyond the reach of Alucius's Talent, Alucius waited for a moment, then another. He could sense that the bravo who had escaped was riding due east, straight toward the other group of bravos, and that meant Alucius couldn't afford to stay where he was very long at all.

As he was debating whether he should withdraw immediately, one of the bravos tried a dash for his mount.

Alucius dropped him in two shots.

The other began to circle eastward. Alucius immediately retreated back up the hill, then down toward the cluster of junipers where he had tied Wildebeast.

Once there, he reloaded both rifles and scanned the area with his Talent.

Someone with the bravos was a good tracker, because Alucius could tell that they were following the general path he had, and that certainly meant that they were following him. He glanced around the hillside, but the cluster of junipers where he stood provided the best cover. Wildebeast had already carried him nearly twenty vingts, and Alucius doubted that his mount, strong as he was, could give him that much of a lead over more than ten men on fresher mounts chasing him.

Alucius dropped behind the junipers, settling behind the one that gave him the best view of the approach from below, and waited. Farther to the north, Wildebeast remained, tethered and quiet.

Good sense would have dictated that he should have just avoided the bravos and ridden on, but his feelings had told him that so-called good sense wouldn't work. Good sense had told him, back in training years

478   L. E. MODESITT, JR.

before, to avoid Dolesy. That hadn't worked, either, and in the end, he'd had to fight. His feelings had told him that it was better to fight when he had an edge than when he was caught unaware.

Before long, in less than a tenth of a glass, below him, Alucius could hear mounts—and voices—if barely.

". . . why we doing this . . . killed eight . . ."

". . . ten golds a man . . . that's why . . . and because, we don't get him . . . who hires us?"

Ten golds a man? That was more than a trooper made in two years. Alucius swallowed and continued to wait, lying behind the thick trunk of the ancient juniper.

". . . quiet . . . can't be too much farther . . . Sylor . . . ease out to the left . . ."

While Alucius could have shot the bravo who had been ordered out ahead, he did not, but waited, and before long, he could see—as well as sense—the first four men in the rough column that followed his tracks uphill.

He waited a bit longer, then lifted the rifle.

Crack! Crack! Crack!

"Frig!"

The riders retreated back into cover behind the scattered pines and junipers, and Alucius quickly reloaded. He had killed two of the attackers, and wounded the third, gravely. But he had less than twenty cartridges left for something like ten bravos.

He could sense conversations from below, and feel as the attackers split into three groups.

Three separate groups burst from behind copses of pines, spurring their mounts up the gentle slope.

Crack! Crack! Crack!

Alucius fired at the center group, the one slightly ahead of the others, then when he'd emptied his first rifle, turned to the one on the right—to the west.

He'd fired four more shots when splinters cascaded across his face, momentarily blocking his vision.

Then his whole body was yanked sideways, and pain flared up his left leg.

Somehow, he managed to roll to the right enough to avoid being hit again, but for several moments, he could not see, both from the wood splinters and the intense watering of his eyes. Lying flat, he fumbled more cartridges into the rifle he held, trying to blink away the involuntary tears.

Thunk! Another bullet plowed into the juniper above him.

Eeeiiee!

Alucius winced at the scream from Wildebeast, sensing his mount dying under a flurry of bullets. He moistened his dry mouth and finally was able to clear his eyes.

From what he could see and sense, beyond the throbbing agony in his leg and left side, there were still five bravos—three behind a pine to the east, slightly above him, and two others, below and to his right.

". . . keep firing . . . can't have many cartridges left . . ."

". . . earn those golds today . . ."

Alucius forced his concentration onto the those behind the pine, easing his rifle around and waiting.

It felt like he had waited a quarter glass or more when one looked up.

Crack! Crack!

The red-washed dark void that passed Alucius confirmed that death, and that left four.

Thunk! More splinters cascaded down, but not into Alucius's eyes.

He turned back to the two behind the pine, almost willing one to move.

Time passed, and then a bravo lurched sideways—enough. Still it took two shots Alucius reloaded . . . too slowly.

"Circle uphill . . ." someone called. "Keep low. You can fire down on him."

The remaining bravo from the two at the pine began to move, keeping very low, especially his head. Alucius couldn't get a clear shot, but he kept watching, moving his rifle, and waiting for an opening.

Another shot shook the tree, and scraps of juniper rained down on Alucius.

With the shot, the uphill bravo scrambled across an open space.

Alucius fired, once, twice, before his third shot caught the man in the leg. As the bravo twisted, involuntarily, Alucius's fourth shot caught him in the chest.

Alucius reloaded—as much as he could—and that left him with three cartridges and two bravos.

"Now!" came a voice.

From somewhere another bravo appeared, mounted, and using the horse as a shield, moved toward Alucius.

Much as he hated to, Alucius brought down the horse with a single shot, but it took two more to get the rider.

So far as Alucius could tell, there was but a single bravo remaining. Unfortunately, Alucius had no ammunition left, and his left side was a mass of pain. His head throbbed.

Thunk! Thunk! As the bullets hit the tree above him—barely above his head—more juniper greenery and splinters cascaded around Alucius.

The remaining bravo had ammunition, and sooner, or later, he couldn't help but get Alucius, unless . . .

Another bullet flew within a span of Alucius's head.

With a last desperate effort, Alucius extended a thin Talent-probe, snaking it across the fifty yards or more between him and the man, trying to hold it, trying to use skill, rather than force. Everything wavered before his eyes, and he could barely sense the other. He struggled to reach the man's main lifethread node, trying to find and unlock that node.

Alucius felt the sickening twist, and then a snap of Talent-energy—followed by a wave of blackness that swept over him. Just blackness, without a hint of green.

Caawww . . . caawww . . .

Something jabbed at Alucius's outstretched hand. He tried to move it, and another wave of pain swept over him. Slowly, he opened his eyes. A yard beyond his hand, a crow looked at him, then took a hop and flew away.

"Not . . . ready . . . for you . . . yet . . ." Alucius dragged himself out from under the juniper and toward Wildebeast. Flies were already settling onto his dead mount. He swallowed. Wildebeast had carried him from Madrien to Deforya to Lanachrona and back, and through the bloodiest of battles—and he'd died from bravos' bullets in an ambush. Because Alucius had been a proud fool, thinking he was invulnerable.

After a moment, Alucius glanced from the dead—and faithful—stallion to the sun, now but a span above the western horizon. He doubted he could walk, and he didn't have a mount.

Despite the headache he had, he cast out his Talent-sense . . . hoping to find one of the bravo's horses. He could sense two.

He tried to Talent-project the sense of feed, of grain and water.

After a time, both horses began to move.

The sun was almost touching the horizon by the time he managed to entice one close enough to grab the stirrup and lever himself up, then climb and crawl into the saddle, all the time using Talent to reassure the mare. His left leg was still totally numb.

Then he urged the mount northward.

He just hoped he could last until he could make Sudon Post—or the road to it.

He didn't remember much of the ride, just the growing darkness.

At some point, he heard someone talking, and he forced himself to concentrate.

"Sir . . . sir?"

A young face in a Northern Guard uniform looked out of a circle of darkness at him.

"Brigands . . ." Alucius managed. "In the hills . . . off high road . . . south of the Sudon crossroad . . ."

The sentry looked up at the overcaptain.

Alucius tried to hang on, but, once more, blackness swept over him.

120

For glasses—or days—Alucius could not tell which—he wandered through a darkness of pain. He thought he had been fed and talked to people, but he could not recall what he had eaten or to whom he had talked.

Then, almost suddenly, he found himself aware of lying in a bed.

A senior squad leader looked down at Alucius. "How do you feel, sir?"

Alucius looked up. "Like my left side's on fire." He should have recognized the squad leader, but his eyes blurred, and his head throbbed.

"We found the brigands—Dekhron bravos—and your mount, Overcaptain." There was a pause. "Was there anyone with you, sir?"

"No . . . was heading home."

"You'll be here for a bit."

"How . . . my leg?"

"You've been here almost three days. You were hit in the thigh, twice, and in the ribs. The nightsilk stopped the bullets, but the healer says that you've got a cracked rib, maybe two, and there's not a place below your shoulder on the left that's without bruising."

Alucius finally recognized the squad leader, the man who had trained him years before. "You're still here, Estepp?"

"I went out for a tour, and they sent me back here. Got here a month ago." The older man laughed. "It had to be you, Overcaptain. You know that you killed twenty-one of them? One of 'em, we can't figure out. Not a mark on him. Could be you scared him to death."

"I don't know." Alucius didn't try to shake his head. He knew any movement would hurt.

"Hope you don't mind, but I did tell some of the trainees about you. Too good a story to waste. Officer's been released, but he can't let go of duty and takes on more than twenty bravos to keep some innocent from being killed. We had to report it to headquarters. Got a message back this afternoon from the commandant. They added the Commandant's Star to your other awards, sir."

"I'm so pleased," Alucius said dryly. "I just wanted to get home."

Estepp smiled. "For a man who never wanted to be a trooper, sir, you've done more than any officer in generations."

"Maybe . . . because I didn't want to . . ."

"You may not want to be one, sir, but you're a trooper officer at heart, just like your grandsire." Estepp paused. "Need to check on the trainees, sir."

"Go ahead. I need the rest."

Estepp eased back, and the door closed.

As Alucius lay there in the darkness in what he realized were senior officers' quarters, thoughts circled through his mind.

The would-be assassins still bothered him. He'd seen deeply enough into the Lord-Protector, and the man would not have acted so. Nor was it likely that Waleryn could have organized such an attack and gotten word to Dekhron quickly enough.

The colonel? Weslyn was a possibility . . . but the man didn't operate that way. He might order—and had ordered—Alucius into situations where he might be killed, but Weslyn lacked the courage to act directly.

But someone had. Alucius just didn't know who it could be—or why.

He could feel his eyelids closing.

121

A week later, in late afternoon, Alucius rode through the square in Iron Stem at the head of a column of replacement troopers, roughly a squad's worth, headed northward to Soulend. He rode upon the best mount gleaned from those of the bravos captured by the Northern Guard, a gray stallion, not quite so spirited as Wildebeast, but solid. Alucius did not stop at the cooperage, since his Talent told him that Wendra was not there. He had not expected she would be at her father's, but he had checked as he neared the square.

Both Estepp and Overcaptain Culyn—the head of the training post at Sudon—had insisted that he accompany the detachment. Since his left side was yellow and purple and sore all over, Alucius did not stand on pride but accepted the offer. Parts of Alucius's left thigh and chest remained numb. He could barely move his left arm, and his fingers tingled on occasion. His Talent told him that it would be some time before the injuries healed completely.

"Your place is north of town, sir?" asked Zearyt, the squad leader who would be taking over the fourth squad of Twelfth Company.

"Almost ten vingts north," Alucius confirmed. "You don't need to escort me—"

"Sir . . . if I didn't see you to your door, both Estepp and Overcaptain Culyn would have my head, and there wouldn't be enough left of me for a banner to fly against the Matrites." Zearyt grinned, an expression between rue and pleasure at being able to insist. "Besides . . . most of us would like to see your stead, if you don't mind."

"It's really not mine, yet. My grandsire and mother are still there. And my wife."

"She a herder, too?"

Alucius knew what Zearyt meant. "Yes. She takes the flock often."

The squad leader shook his head. "Only seen nightsheep up close a few times. Wouldn't want to get that close. True that they can gut a sandwolf?"

"One-on-one, a nightram can. But the sandwolves try for ewes or lambs that are stragglers."

As he rode past the green tower just north of the pleasure palace, Alucius was reminded of the towers in Dereka and Tempre—and of the alabaster-skinned ifrits. He shifted his weight in the saddle, hoping he had seen the last of them—either with his eyes or his Talent. He couldn't say he'd been pleased with what he'd learned, but some of the hints had always been there—like the leschec board and game pieces—green and black, the twinned colors of life. And that the pteridons had left no remains when they burned—that had been another hint. Yet who could have guessed what they had really meant?

The other thing that both bothered and pleased him was that, after the last attack, he had not sensed the green radiance of soarers. Had the soarers done all they could? Had they abandoned him? Or were they merely seeing if he could survive without their aid? He had done that, but it had been a close thing—closer than Alucius would have liked.

Alucius smiled faintly, to himself, then frowned as the voices rose behind him as they neared the dustcat works. All through the trip, there had been murmurs from the raw troopers in the column, but, for the most part, Alucius had ignored them. Sometimes, it was hard.

"Still . . . looks so young for an overcaptain . . ."

". . . hear what he's been through . . . rather be a ranker . . ."

". . . where he started . . . years back . . ."

"Estepp said he'd been left for dead something like four times . . . Star of Gallantry from Deforya, Star of Honor from the Lord-Protector, and Commandant's Star . . ."

". . . don't give those unless you die . . . or come so close you might as well have . . ."

Unhappily, Alucius reflected, the young ranker was right. Alucius had come close enough to dying even more times than anyone knew—or would—except for his family.

"... killed twenty brigands by himself ... still hard to believe ..."

"... twenty-one ... was on the detail that brought in the bodies ... killed his mount ..."

At the thought of Wildebeast, Alucius winced. The stallion had deserved better, but Alucius wasn't certain what else he could have done—not after he'd made the initial stupid decision to take on the bravos.

Yet ... had it been stupid? Or had his tactics just been stupid, relying once more on what amounted to brute force? The soarer had tried to teach him, but he still hadn't learned to apply the lesson on a wider scale.

The sun was low in the west when they neared the turnoff to the stead, and Alucius was all too aware of the aches in his ribs and leg.

"The lane on the right, half vingt ahead," he said quietly.

"You're far out here, sir. Nothing much in sight," observed Zearyt.

"That's the way with most steads," replied Alucius.

When they neared the stead, Alucius could see two figures, waiting on the porch—his mother and Wendra. That Royalt was not there indicated that he was still out with the nightsheep.

As he neared the dwelling, Alucius reached out to Wendra with his Talent, then paused. She was no longer black, shot with green, but her lifethread and being was green, with but a handful of black threads. Alucius smiled.

Her smile was like brilliant sun after a cold winter.

Followed by the troopers, Alucius rode to the porch, where he dismounted stiffly, then turned. "I thank you all."

Wendra stepped down from the porch and put her hand over his. Even without turning, Alucius could feel the meldinglike feel as their lifethreads brushed.

"We thank you, as well," Wendra said from where she stood a step above Alucius, offering a warm smile.

"We thought he deserved an escort, madame." Zearyt bowed in the saddle. "Not that often that the Iron Valleys have an officer wins the stars of three lands." He turned to Alucius. "A pleasure, sir, and we'll be departing."

"You can't stay here this evening?" asked Wendra.

"That we'd wish, but orders are orders, and we need to make the way station tonight."

Wendra surveyed the column. "Let us at least send a full cooked shoulder with you, for when you do stop."

Zearyt smiled. "Now . . . I can't say that'd be against orders."

Alucius smothered a grin and let Wendra work, his right hand on the railing of the steps to the porch.

In the end, half a glass later, his escorts left with enough fresh-cooked food to feed the entire squad, and with smiles upon more than a few faces.

Wendra stepped up to him. Her fingers touched his cheeks. "I've been so worried." She leaned forward, ever so gently, and kissed him.

For that moment, the warmth and the welcome drove away all the numbness and pain.

Wendra stepped back. "We need to get you off your feet."

"I'll unsaddle your mount," Lucenda said.

"I can—"

"You'll do no such thing," Wendra said. "I saw you dismount, and I can feel how much it hurts, and how you can barely stand. We're getting you up and into a comfortable chair—if not bed."

"Just the chair," Alucius conceded. He surrendered the gray's reins to his mother.

"He is hurt," Lucenda said dryly. She looked to her son, inquiringly.

"Two cracked ribs, and more than a few bruises."

"You'll tell us once your grandsire arrives?"

"Everything." Alucius knew he had little choice, not between Wendra and his grandsire.

"Do you need—"

"I can manage."

"He's still as stubborn as ever," Lucenda said.

"Not quite," Alucius retorted.

Once Alucius was inside, Wendra hurried ahead and dragged the armchair from the main room to the archway into the kitchen. "Sit."

Alucius eased himself into the chair and found her bending down and kissing him, gently, but warmly.

"I would have hugged you, but that would have hurt more than it helped," she said softly. "I'm so glad you're home."

"So am I. So am I."

She gave him another kiss before straightening. "I'll get you some ale, and you can just sit there and sip it while I finish supper. I'll tell you what's happened here. Your mother and grandsire know that, and whatever you tell me you'd just have to tell them again."

Alucius laughed and waited for the ale. After Wendra set the beaker in his right hand, he smiled and asked, "What happened? You met a soarer, didn't you?"

"So did you, didn't you?"

"Takes one to know one." Alucius grinned, enjoying the warmth and affection radiating from her. "Did you tell Grandsire . . . or Mother?"

"Your grandsire knows, I think. I didn't say anything. It . . . she taught me how to wrap the darkness around cartridges."

"She taught you more than that—or you've learned more than that."

"It frightened me. So I tried to make sense of it." Wendra glanced toward the door.

Lucenda entered the kitchen, glanced at Alucius, and nodded. "Left your saddlebags in the foyer. You lost Wildebeast?"

"He was killed in the attack on the way home," Alucius replied. "I'll tell you all about it, once Grandsire gets here."

"It won't be long. He's on the lower slope of Westridge now." Lucenda surveyed her son. "You look better already. Not all that good, but better."

"You've always had a way with compliments, Mother."

Wendra laughed.

After a moment, so did Lucenda, before she turned to Wendra. "What can I do?"

"If you'd do the potatoes . . ."

Alucius set the ale on the table and stood.

Both women looked at him.

"I'd just like to wash up . . . and take care of a few things. It was a long ride."

He headed for the washroom, knowing he'd have little peace once his grandfather arrived—not until he'd told everything.

122

All through supper, in between bites, Alucius talked, recounting everything from his initial departure from Emal through the attack of the bravos—and even the role of the soarer, and her observations about the ifrits and the Duarchy.

"You think she was telling you the truth?" asked Royalt. "Seems . . . well . . . strange . . ."

"She was telling the truth," Wendra said.

Both Lucenda and Royalt looked at the younger woman.

Wendra smiled politely and asked her husband, "Where do you think this hidden city is?"

"I don't know. But if I had to guess . . ." Alucius glanced eastward.

"That'd make sense," Royalt said slowly. "Few enough would risk a climb of more than six thousand yards straight up. A few fellows tried, years back. Three died, one never walked straight again. Only got up about two thousand yards."

"Also . . . the oblong crystals . . . I wonder if they're what we sometimes see at sunrise and sunset," Alucius said.

"That could be," mused Lucenda. "but do you think that they're telling you everything?"

"I doubt they are. From what I've seen, though, I'd trust them further than I'd trust any of the ifrits."

"That's probably so," agreed Royalt. "Soarers don't cause trouble Haven't for years. What about the Lord-Protector? You think he can be trusted to keep his word? You sure he didn't have anything to do with that last attack?"

"I'd stake just about anything on that." Alucius took another sip of the ale. "I wouldn't put it past his brother. Waleryn makes sandsnakes look harmless—but it takes time to organize something like that attack, and we traveled fast back from Tempre." He shook his head. "Someone in Dekhron . . . it had to be."

"That cowardly cur Weslyn?" asked Royalt.

"No. Weslyn's a coward, and he had something to do with it—maybe provided the information and had me delayed in leaving Dekhron—but he didn't set it up. It has to be one of the traders in Dekhron . . . but who? I wouldn't even know where to start."

"Kustyl might," suggested Royalt.

"Have him be very careful," Alucius said.

Royalt laughed. "He can be very indirect when it suits him."

"Have him be more indirect than that," suggested Alucius, finishing the last of his ale. He shrugged, as if to ask if they had any more questions.

"Are you ready for some rest?" asked Lucenda.

"No. I'm tired, and I'm still sore. But I'm not sleepy. I'd just like to sit in the main room and spend some time with Wendra."

Both Lucenda and Royalt laughed.

Alucius found himself flushing and, glancing at Wendra, saw that she was as well.

Royalt stood. "I'm going down to check on the nightsheep."

Lucenda stood as well. "I'll take care of the dishes. Wendra—take him into the main room." She paused and looked at Alucius. "Would it be better to stretch out?"

"Right now . . . sitting actually is easier." Alucius stood, carefully. He felt better, and he wondered if some of that had come from Wendra when their lifethreads had touched and melded for that long moment. "I feel much better, already."

"Good," replied Wendra with a smile.

Alucius walked into the main room, where he settled onto the settee and glanced at his wife, then at the space beside him.

"Are you sure?" she asked.

"I'm very sure."

Wendra eased beside him, on his right side.

Alucius turned his head and murmured into her ear, "You did something . . . with your Talent."

"How could I not?" she murmured back. "You hurt so much. I could feel it when you were almost a vingt away. I don't see how you rode so far that way."

"I wanted to see you. I wanted to come home."

She reached out and squeezed his hand gently. "I'm glad, but you could have waited."

"No . . . I couldn't."

She smiled, and for a time, they sat quietly, Alucius leaning his head against Wendra's, just enjoying the quiet and her warmth and welcome.

Then, Wendra turned and looked at him. "You don't think this is over, do you?"

"No. Nothing is over, not until we're dead, and after what I saw with the Tables, I'm not sure about that. In some ways, though, there's little we can do now. There's no certainty of anything, at present. One of the few things I am sure of, from what I've seen, is that the greatest evils come when someone willfully creates misery and pain and forces other people to do evil in order to survive and avoid pain. What I *am* certain about is that we only have each moment once, and that nothing can bring back a moment once it has passed."

"That's all true. You didn't answer my question. Not really."

"It's not over," Alucius admitted. "Whatever lies behind the Tables is still there. But there's nothing I can do about that. Not with the Tables destroyed. It's been at least a millennium since that evil ruled Corus, and it might be another before it surfaces again."

"And it might surface again tomorrow. Or next season."

"It might." Alucius nodded.

"And it might have already surfaced."

"Because of the last attack on me?"

"Who else would spend two hundred golds to try to kill a man who doesn't even want to . . . who only wants to be a herder?"

"I don't know that there's anything else I can do, now." Alucius paused, then added in a low voice, "After this last attack . . . I didn't feel or sense the soarers."

"And . . . you think they're gone?"

"No. I don't know what to think. It could be that they don't know that something is happening. Or that it's up to us now. Or that there's nothing to be done now." His lips quirked. "I don't know."

The silence drew out before he spoke again. "I do know that I've needed to be here with you. It almost seems as though the whole world wanted to keep me from you, that every time I thought I could head home, something else happened." He looked into her deep, golden green eyes, eyes that mirrored her very being.

"Perhaps it did . . . but you're here."

Once more, their lips met, gently, as did lifethreads and spirits.

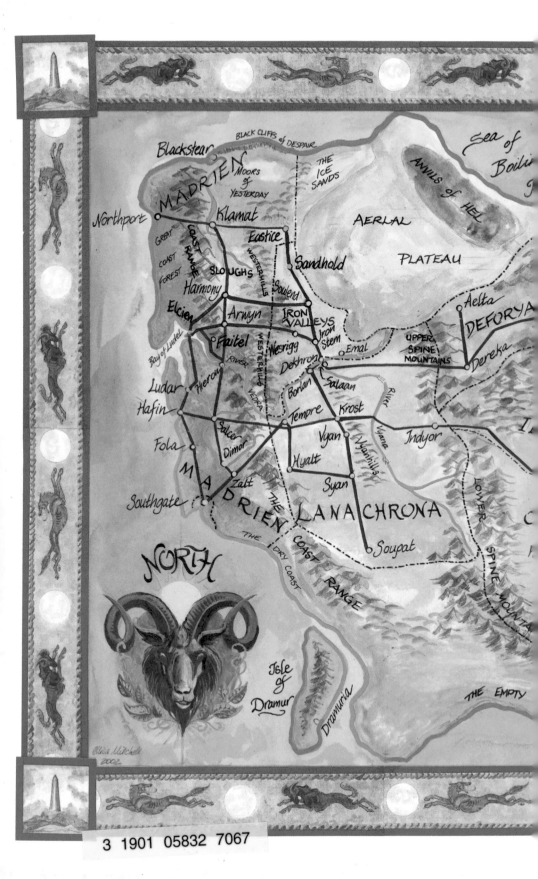